Jua

The Complete Works of Saint John of The Cross, of the Order of our Lady of Mount Carmel

Vol. 1

SALZWASSER
VERLAG

Juan De Yepes Alvarez

The Complete Works of Saint John of The Cross, of the Order of our Lady of Mount Carmel

Vol. 1

Reprint of the original, first published in 1864.

1st Edition 2022 | ISBN: 978-3-75259-284-9

Verlag (Publisher): Salzwasser Verlag GmbH, Zeilweg 44, 60439 Frankfurt, Deutschland
Vertretungsberechtigt (Authorized to represent): E. Roepke, Zeilweg 44, 60439 Frankfurt, Deutschland
Druck (Print): Books on Demand GmbH, In de Tarpen 42, 22848 Norderstedt, Deutschland

THE
COMPLETE WORKS
OF
SAINT JOHN OF THE CROSS,
OF THE
ORDER OF OUR LADY OF MOUNT CARMEL.

TRANSLATED FROM THE ORIGINAL SPANISH
BY
DAVID LEWIS, Esq. M.A.

EDITED BY THE OBLATE FATHERS OF SAINT CHARLES.

WITH A PREFACE
BY
HIS EMINENCE CARDINAL WISEMAN.

VOL. I.

LONDON:

1864.

PREFACE.

IT is now many years ago, long before the episcopal burthen pressed upon his shoulders, that the author enjoyed the pleasure of knowing, and frequently conversing with, the estimable Görres, at Munich. One day, the conversation turned on a remark in that deep writer's 'Philosophy of Mysticism,' to the effect, that saints most remarkable for their mystical learning and piety were far from exhibiting, in their features and expression, the characteristics usually attributed to them. They are popularly considered, and by artists represented, as soft, fainting, and perhaps hysterical persons; whereas their portraits present to us countenances of men, or women, of a practical, business-like, working character.

The author asked Görres if he had ever seen an original likeness of S. Teresa, in whom he thought these remarks were particularly exemplified. He replied that he never had; and the writer, on returning to Rome, fulfilled the promise which he had made the philosopher, by procuring a sketch of an authentic portrait of that saint, preserved with great care in the Monastery of S. Sylvester, near Tusculum.

It was painted for Philip II. by a concealed artist, while he was conversing with her.

This portrait confirms most strongly the theory of Görres, as the author wrote to him with the drawing; for while no mystical saint has ever been more idealised by artists, or represented as living in a continual swoon, than S. Teresa, her true portraits all represent her with strong, firmly set, and almost masculine features, with forms and lines that denoted vigour, resolution, and strong sense. Her handwriting perfectly suggests the same conclusion.

Still more does the successful activity of her life, in her many painful struggles, under every possible disadvantage, and her final and complete triumph, strengthen this idea of her. And then, her almost superhuman prudence, by which she guided so many minds, and prosperously conducted so many complicated interests and affairs, and her wonderful influence over men of high education and position, and of great powers, are further evidences of her strong, commanding nature; such as, in the world, might have claimed an almost unexampled preeminence.

It is not improbable that some who take up these volumes, or dip into them here and there, may conceive that they were written by a dreamy ascetic, who passed his life in hazy contemplation of things unreal and unpractical. Yet it was quite the contrary. Twin-saint, it may be said, to S. Teresa — sharer in her labours and in her sufferings, S. John of the Cross, actively and unflinchingly pursued their joint object, that of reforming and restoring to its primitive purity and observance the religious Order of Carmelites, and founding, throughout Spain, a severer branch, known as discalced, or barefooted Carmelites, or more briefly as Teresians.

We do not possess any autobiography of S. John, as we do of S. Teresa, or the more active portion and character of his life would be at once apparent. Moreover, only very few of his letters have been preserved; not twenty, in fact, or we should undoubtedly have had sufficient evidence of his busy and active life. But, even as it is, proofs glance out from his epistles of this important element in his composition.

In his second letter (vol. ii. p. 318), he thus writes to the religious of Veas, a highly favoured foundation: 'What is wanting in you, if, indeed, anything be wanting, is . . . silence, and work. For, whereas speaking distracts, silence and action collect the thoughts, and strengthen the spirit.' And again, 'To arrest this evil, and to preserve our spirit, as I have said, there is no surer remedy than to suffer, to work, to be silent.'

It was not, therefore, a life of visionary or speculative meditation that S. John taught even the nuns to pursue, but one of activity and operative occupation. But we may judge of his own practice by a passage in another of his letters. Thus he writes:

'I have been waiting to finish these visitations and foundations, which our Lord has hastened forward in such wise that there has been no time to spare. The

Friars have been received at Cordova with the greatest joy and solemnity on the part of the whole city . . . . I am now busied at Seville with the removal of the nuns, who have bought one of the principal houses at a cost of about 14,000 ducats, being worth more than 20,000. They are now established there. Before my departure, I intend to establish another house of Friars here, so that there will be two of our Order in Seville. Before the Feast of S. John, I shall set forth to Ecija, where, with the Divine blessing, we shall found another; thence to Malaga . . . . I wish I had authority to make this foundation, as I had for the other. I do not expect much difficulty'* (p. 322).

This is only a few months' work, or rather some weeks'; for the interval described in the letter is from the Ascension to the 24th of June. We must allow some portion of this time for the slow travelling of those days and those regions, over *sierras*, on mule-back. And then S. John's travels were not triumphal progresses, but often were painful pilgrimages, crossed by arrests, and even long imprisonments, embittered by personal unkindness.

Yet, with calm firmness he persevered and travelled and worked at the establishment of his new houses in many parts of Spain, till the Order was fully and permanently planted. In fact, if we looked only at his life, we should naturally conclude that he was a man

* The writer has had the pleasure of visiting these early foundations at Seville, Ecija, Malaga, and Granada. The first fervour of the Order yet remains in them.

of an operative mind, always at work, ever in movement, who could not afford much time for inward concentration on abstract subjects.

But when we read his writings, another high quality, for which we are not prepared, must strike us forcibly as entering into the composition of his character. He must have given much time to reading and study. He is learned in all those pursuits which we desire and expect to find in an ecclesiastical scholar of his age. Every page in his book gives proof of thorough acquaintance with that mental discipline which trained and formed the mind in the schools, and gave a mould into which thought ran and settled itself in fixed principles; or, where this possessed extraordinary power, opened a channel through which it passed to further spheres of activity. Even the mind of a Bacon was conducted through the dialectics of those schools, to all the developments of his intellectual vigour.

In S. John we discover, at every turn, a mind so educated by reading and by study. His writings are far from being a string of loose disjointed thoughts, scattered apophthegms, or aimless rhapsodies. Quite on the contrary, there is ever a sequence and strict logical continuity in every division of his discourse, and all the several parts are coherent and consistent. However detailed his treatment of his subject, he never becomes entangled or confused; he never drops a thread of what may appear a fine-spun web of expansion in a difficult topic, and loses it; but he returns to what he has interrupted or intercalated with undisturbed fidelity, and repursues his reasoning with a distinctness and discrimination which shows that in truth there had been no interruption, but that unity of thought had pervaded all the design, and nothing had been left to chance or the idea of the moment.

Indeed, one feels in reading him that he has to deal with the master of a science. There is no wandering from the first purpose, no straying aside from the predetermined road, after even flowers that grow on its sides. Every division and subdivision of the way has been charted from the beginning by one who saw it all before him. And the secret lies in this, and nothing more: S. John invents nothing, borrows nothing from others, but gives us clearly the results of his own experience in himself and in others. He presents you with a portrait, not with a fancy picture. He represents the ideal of one who has passed, as he had done, through the career of the spiritual life, through its struggles and its victories.

Not only does he at all times exhibit proof of his mental cultivation by those processes which formed every great mind in those days, and the gradual decline of which, in later times, has led proportionably to looseness of reasoning and diminution of thinking power, but S. John throughout exhibits tokens of a personal culture of his own mental powers and many graceful gifts.

His mind is eminently poetical, imaginative, tender, and gentle. Whatever mystical theology may appear to the mind of the uninitiated, to S. John it was clearly a bright and well-loved pursuit; it was a work of the heart more than of the head; its place was rather in the affections than among the intellectual powers. Hence, with every rigour of logical precision, and an unbending exactness in his reasonings, there is blended a buoyancy of feeling, a richness of varied illustration, and often a sweet and elegant fancy playing with grave subjects, so as to render them attractive, which show a mind unfettered by mere formal methods, but easy in its movements and free in its flights. Indeed, often a point which is obscure and abstruse when barely treated, receives, from a lively illustration, a clearness and almost brilliancy quite unexpected.

But the prominent learning of the saint and the source of his most numerous and happiest elucidations, are to be found in the inspired Word of God. That is his treasure-house, that the inspirer of his wisdom, and subject of his meditation. The sacred volume must have been in his hands all day, and can hardly have dropped out of them at night. Even by merely glancing at the index of texts quoted by him, placed at the end of the second volume, anyone may convince himself of his rare familiarity with the inspired writings, and one very different from what we may find among readers of Scripture in our days.

For, first, it is an impartial familiarity, not confined to some favourite portions, as is often the case, where the reader thinks he finds passages or subjects that confirm his own views or encourage his tastes. But in S. John we discover nothing of this sort. Of course, such a book as the Canticle, the special food of mystics, is familiar to his pen as it was to the mouths of Jewish maidens, made sweeter and sweeter by frequent reiterations. But every other book is almost equally ready to his hand, to prove more formally, occasionally illustrate, every one of his positions. For the first purpose he must have deeply studied the sacred text; for the second, its expressions must have been his very household words.

Then, secondly, the beauty and elegance of his applications prove not mere familiarity, but a refined study, and a loving meditation on what he considers most holy and divine. Some of his quotations are richly set in his own graceful explanations and commentaries; and, though the adaptations which he makes may sometimes appear startling and original to an ordinary peruser of Scripture, they seem so apt and so profound in their spiritual wisdom that they often win approbation and even admiration.

So far, it may appear that this Preface has dealt with S. John of the Cross outside of the sphere in which the volume to which it is prefixed represents him as moving. It has not treated him as a mystical theologian. Why is this? it may be justly asked.

The answer must be honest and straightforward. It is too common for overlooking or disguising, to pronounce a contemplative life to be only a cloak for idleness, a pretext for abandoning or neglecting the active duties of domestic or social existence, and shrinking from their responsibilities. Those who profess to lead it are considered as the drones of the human hive, who leave its work to others, and yet exact a share of its sweets. And if, from time to time, one emerges from the passive, or, as it is deemed, indolent, condition of mere dreamers, and gives form and precision to the rules and laws which guide them, he is probably held merely to have more method and skill in his disordered ideas, and to be only more pernicious than his companions or followers.

This prejudice, firmly rooted in many English minds, it has been thought well to remove, as a preliminary to presenting S. John to his readers in his highest and distinctive character. He has been shown to possess other eminent qualities. He was a man of active life and practical abilities, industrious, conversant with business, where prudence, shrewdness, and calculation, as well as boldness, were required. He was a man of well-trained mind, cultivated by the exercise of intellectual faculties, and matured by solid, especially religious knowledge.

He has now to come before us as a diver into the very depths of thought, as a contemplative of the highest order.

A man with such a character as we have claimed for him cannot have dozed away his years of life in unpractical dreams, or in crude speculations. These would be incompatible with the rest of his character. His contemplativeness, and his mode of explaining it, may be anticipated to be methodical and practical, and at the same time feeling and attractive. And such both are; his own practice, and his communication of it to us.

But now, perhaps, many readers may ask for some introductory information on the very nature of the subjects treated in the volumes before him, and it cannot be reasonably refused. This may be conveyed in various ways; perhaps the most simple and appreciable will be found in an analogy, though imperfect, with other spheres of thought.

It is well known that a mind naturally adapted to a pursuit, and thus led ardently to follow it, after having become thoroughly conversant and familiar with all its resources, becomes almost, or altogether, independent of its methods, and attains conclusions by compendious processes, or by intuitive foresight, which require in others long and often complicated deductions. Familiar illustrations may be found in our habitual speaking without thinking of our grammar, which a foreigner has constantly to do while learning our language; or the almost inexplicable accuracy of calculation in even children, gifted with the power of instantaneous arithmetical solutions.

A mathematician acquires by study this faculty; and it is said that Laplace, in the decline of life, could not any longer fill up the gaps in the processes by which, at the age of greater mental vigour, he had reached, without effort, the most wonderful yet accurate conclusions.

What is to be found in these abstruser pursuits, exists no less in those of a lighter character. The literary mind, whether in thinking, writing, or speaking, when well disposed by abilities, and well tutored by application, takes in without effort the entire theme presented to it, even with its parts and its details. Sometimes it is like a landscape revealed, in a dark night, by one flash of lightning; oftener it resembles the calmer contemplation of it, in bright day, by an artist's eye, which is so filled with its various beauties, that it enables him to transfer it, at home, to the enduring canvas, on which many may enjoy it.

The historian may see, in one glance, the exact plan of a work, with its specific aims and views; its sources, too, and its auxiliary elucidations. The finished orator, no less, when suddenly called upon, will hold from end to end the drift and purpose of his entire discourse, and deliver, without effort, what to others appears an elaborate composition. But, still more, the poet indulges in noblest flights up to the regions of sublime, or over the surface of beautiful, thoughts, while he appears to be engaged in ordinary occupation, or momentarily musing in vague abstraction.

Indeed, even where manual action is required to give utterance to thought, the result is the same. The consummate musician sits down to a complicated instrument, silent and dumb, till his fingers communicate to it his improvised imaginings; bearing to its innermost organisation, by a sort of reflex action of the nerves of sensation on those of motion, the ready and inexhaustible workings of his brain, sweet melodies and rich harmonies, with tangled knots and delicious resolutions; effortless, as if the soul were in the hand, or the mechanical action in the head.

In the few examples which are here given, and which might easily be multiplied, the point illustrated is this; that where, with previous natural dispositions and persevering cultivation, perfection in any intellectual pursuit has been attained or approached, the faculty exercised in it becomes, in a manner, passive, dispenses with intermediate processes, and receives their ultimate conclusions like impressions stamped upon it. Labour almost ceases, and *spontaneity* of thought becomes its substitute.

In this condition of mind, familiar to any one possessing genius in any form, perceptions, ideas, reasonings, imagery, have not to be sought; they either dart at once complete into the thought, inborn, and perfect to their very arms, as Pallas was symbolically fabled to express this process; or they grow up, expanding from a small seed to a noble plant, but as if by an innate sap and vigour. There is a flow into the mind of unsought images, or reflections, or truths; whence they come, one hardly knows. They were not there before; they have not been forged, or cast, or distilled within.

And when this spontaneous productiveness has been gained, the occupation of mind is not interrupted. S. Thomas is said to have concluded an argument against the Manichees alone at the royal table; Bishop Walmesley renounced his mathematical studies on finding them painfully distract him at the altar.

Neither recreation, nor serious employment, nor noise, nor any condition of time or place, will suffice to dissipate or even to disturb the continuous, unlaborious, and unfatiguing absorption of thought in the mental region which has become its natural dwelling.

Let us now ask, why may not a soul, that is the mind accompanied by the best feelings, be placed in a similar position with relation to the noblest and sublimest object which it can pursue—GOD? He and His attributes present more perfect claims, motives, and allurements, and more full gratification, repletion, and reward to earnest and affectionate contemplation, than any other object or subject. How much soever the mathematician may strain his intellect in pursuit of the true; however the poet may luxuriate in the enjoyment of the beautiful; to whatsoever extent the moralist may delight in the apprehension of the good in its recondite quintessence, none of these can reach, in his special aim and longing, that elevation and consummation which can be attained in those of all the three, by one whose contemplation is directed to the Infinite in Truth, in Beauty, and in Goodness.*

Why, then, should not this, so comprehensive and so grand a source of every mental enjoyment, become a supreme, all-exhausting, and sole object of contempla-

* It is recorded of the celebrated, though perhaps eccentric scholar, Raymund Lully, that once he entered the school of Duns Scotus, to whom he was unknown. The lecturer addressed to him the question, *Quotuplex pars scientiæ est Deus?*—'What part of knowledge includes God?' His reply overmastered the interrogator: *Deus non est pars, qui est Totum*: 'God is in no part—He is the WHOLE.'

tive fruition? Why should not some, or rather many, minds be found which have selected this as their occupation, their solace, their delight; and found it to be what none other can of its nature be, inexhaustible? Everything else is measureable and fathomable; this alone unlimited.

Then, if there be no repugnance to such a choice being made in the aim of contemplation, it is natural for us to expect conditions and laws in its attainment analogous to what we find where the mental powers have selected for their exercise some inferior and more restricted object. There will be the same gradual and often slow course of assiduous training, the same difficulty of fixing and concentrating the thoughts; till by degrees forms and intermediate steps are dispensed with; when the mind becomes passive, and its trains of thought seem spontaneous and in-coming, rather than worked out by elaborating processes.

This state, when God is the sole occupier of thought, represents the highest condition of contemplation, the reaching of which Mystical Theology professes to direct.

There are, however, two essential differences between the natural and the spiritual exercises of the contemplative faculties. In treating of the first, a natural aptitude was named throughout as a condition for attaining that highest sphere of spontaneous suggestion in the mind. In the second, this condition is not included. Its place is taken by the supernatural power of GRACE.

Every believer in Christianity acknowledges the existence of an inward gift, which belongs of right to all; though many may not choose to claim it. It takes the place of mere natural advantages so completely, that its name has become a rooted word in our language, even apart from religion. We say that a man 'has had, or has not had, the grace' to do a good thing; 'a graceless act' is, in some way, evil; 'a graceless youth' is one walking, somehow, on the path leading to perdition. And we feel, and say, that it is grace which makes a poor man often more virtuous, and virtuously wise, though ignorant and in other ways not wise-minded, than clever, better-educated, and more intellectual rich ones.

Whoever thus believes in a superhuman gift, which supplies, in the higher life of man, the ordinary powers of nature, or elevates these to the attainment of what requires more than ordinary qualities, will hardly be able to deny that this supernatural aid will be copiously granted, where the whole energy of a soul is directed exclusively to the most holy and sublime of purposes, the knowledge and contemplation of God. If it be easily accepted that any one reading, with pure and simple docility, His written records is helped by this grace to understand them, it surely is not much to ask, that one may expect no less assistance when, instead of the eye running over a written page, the entire soul is centred in Him, and every power, and every affection, is absorbed in deep and silent meditation on His own Divine essence.

A further distinction between this application of man's noblest faculties combined to their simplest but sublimest possible object, and their separate exercise on any inferior speculation, consists in this. God, towards whom the mystical contemplative directs himself, is a living active Power, at once without and within the soul. Every Christian believes that He deals as such with the individual man; that in his natural life each one has received his destiny, his time, and place, and measure of both, by a special allotment; that in his outward being, whatever befalls him, he is the ward of a personal Providence; while in his inward and unseen existence, he receives visitations of light, of remorse, of strength, and of guidance, which can apply and belong to him alone.

If so, how can he doubt that one of his own kind and class, who, more than tens of thousands, singles out that Giver of every good gift as supereminent, or rather sole claimant of his soul's best tributes; the throne on which all his ideal conceptions of the great and the good are concentrated in a single unclouded vision of majesty and glory; the altar on which are laid, in willing oblation, all his tenderest affections, and, in ready immolation, every inferior appetite and desire—who can doubt that such a one establishes a right to a larger share than others of the active interposition of Divine kindness, and of personal favour in seconding his disinterested love?

These two differences, great and essential, show that we have been only illustrating, rather than vindicating, the spiritual science of S. John, by comparing it with other classes of knowledge. We have endeavoured to prove that, even prescinding from the spiritual quality, which is its characteristic, there is nothing singular, unnatural, or reprehensible in what would only add one more, and a most worthy, mental pursuit, to those which generally receive not mere approbation but praise.

And hence the religious and ascetic contemplative may be allowed not only to deserve equal admiration with the poet or philosopher, but to be as fit as either for the ordinary duties of life, and in as full possession of practical and social virtues.

Having thus, by this analogy, disposed the uninitiated reader to judge unprejudicedly of this spiritual occupation of so many persons of singularly virtuous life in the Catholic Church, we may invite him to consider if it have not strong presumptions in its favour.

But, first, it may be well to give a brief explanation of this religious mysticism, of which the works of S. John are considered to treat so admirably. What we have already said will greatly assist us.

In the Catholic Church, besides public or private vocal prayer, everyone is directed and urged to the practice of mental prayer, or meditation. For this duty the Church furnishes simple rules and methods, varying somewhat, but all with one practical end. She has at hand almost countless models, forms, and even fully-developed draughts, scarcely requiring to be filled in.

In carrying out this familiar practice, it will be obvious that very different degrees of success will be attained. To some it continues, almost to the end, irksome and trying, full of distraction and imperfection. This may easily arise from natural deficiencies in the mind, or from habitual negligence. But to a willing and persevering mind, these difficulties will diminish, and the power of concentrating the thoughts and affections upon a given subject will increase and strengthen.

Thus far, anyone may aspire, with every chance of success. Then comes a higher stage; when this power of fixing the mind is not only easy, but most pleasing; when, without formal guidance, the soul rests, like the bird poised upon its wings, motionless above the earth, plunged, as it were, in the calm atmosphere which surrounds and sustains it on every side. This is the state of contemplation, when the placid action of a deeply inward thoughtfulness, undisturbed by other objects, is intent on gazing upon images and scenes fixed or passing as on a mirror before it, without exertion or fatigue, almost without note of time.

This condition, with its requisite power, is also attainable by those who regularly and seriously apply to meditation.* Yet, when we have reached it, we are still standing on the ground, and have not set foot on

* Anyone familiar with the Exercises of S. Ignatius will understand the difference between meditation and contemplation, in the sense here used; and how from one he is led to the other. This is very different from the 'prayer of contemplation,' which belongs to mystical theology.

the first step of the 'mystical ladder,' which S. John teaches how to mount.

Far above this earthly exercise of contemplation, is one which belongs to a much higher and purer sphere, above the clouds and mists of the one in which we move. To reach it, is given to few; and of those few, fewer still have left us records of their experience. Yet—and this is sufficient for our present purpose—that the consummation of their desires, and attainment of their scope, was a closer union with God, is acknowledged by all. The soul, thoroughly purified of all other affections, reaches a sublime and supernatural power of settling all its faculties in the contemplation of the Supreme Being with such clearness and intensity, that its very existence seems lost in Him; the most perfect conformity and uniformity with all the emanations of His Will are established as its guiding laws; and, as far as is yet compatible, union the most complete is obtained between the imperfect spirit of man and the infinite Spirit that created it to its own image and likeness.

Now, this aim of infirm humanity, and the possibility of reaching it, may appear, at first sight, extravagant and presumptuous. Yet there has hardly ever, if ever, existed a religious system which has not supposed such an aspiration as its highest, but still possible, flight to be within the reach of some more favoured votaries.

It is too well known to require proof that there existed, beyond a gross visible idolatry, a hidden, esoteric, and mysterious system in the mythologies of the East, handed down in the succession of their priesthoods. The mystic teachings of India, the best known to us, because we possess their works, reveal this doctrine to us, that contemplation is the means by which a man may attain to unification of himself with the Deity, rising by steps gradually to this almost blissful enjoyment of His presence. In China the sect or school of Lao-tseu, with which the learned Abel-Remusat made Europe acquainted by a special memoir, taught and practised the same mystical system.

Chaldea and Egypt no doubt held it also; for it was from them that Pythagoras borrowed, and infused into the philosophy of Greece and Italy precisely the same doctrine; for, while his foolish theory, also Oriental, of transmigration put off to an indefinite period the fruition of the Divine essence, he taught that the soul, thoroughly purified and detached from every inferior affection, could, through contemplation, attain a union with God.

Although this sublime philosophy became obscured in the ages which succeeded him, it shone forth again in the Neo-platonic school—in Plotinus, Porphyrius, and their followers. Whether they merely revived a faded, or published an occult, tradition of their heathen philosophy, or whether they drew disfigured doctrines and practices from the still young and fresh Christianity of their times, it matters but little. In the one case we conclude how instinctive it is to man, even amidst absurd wanderings of his intellect, to expect, nay to crave for, not merely an approach to God, but unification with Him;* and such a noble and holy desire and longing of humanity may naturally expect to find satisfaction in the true revelation of man's Creator.

In the second hypothesis, we must admit that already Christianity had sufficiently developed the germs of its mystical system to be known to aliens, and even enemies.

Indeed, we cannot doubt that the religion of Christ, following the early manifestations of God in the Old Testament, laid deep those seeds of highest contemplation which were at once matured in His apostles. S. Paul, who was taken to the third heaven, to hear words unutterable to man, and to require a severe counterpoise to the greatness of his revelations (2 Cor. xii.), came so to be united with his Lord as to hold but one life with and in Him (Gal. ii. 20; Phil. i. 21).

As to the existence, in the seers and holy sages of the Old Law, of a state of unitive contemplation, as in Abraham, Job, Moses, and Elias, we are not called aside to speak or consider. This point may be safely left in the hands of S. John of the Cross; for, though he does not anywhere expressly treat of this point, he has so filled his pages with quotations from every part of Scripture in illustration of his teaching, and the texts alleged by him are so apt and naturally applied, as to force conviction upon us that the mystical and spiritual

* In races of both continents a ruder yet deeply symbolical feeling prevailed at all times, that incorporation with the Deity was obtained by partaking of the victims offered to Him.—See Gerbet's beautiful treatise, *Sur le Dogme générateur de la Piété Catholique.*

communion with God was carried to the highest degree. Nay, does not a state of close intercommunion between God and man, through revelations, manifestations, angelic messages, and the prophetic spirit, on the one hand, and visions and ecstasies on the other, necessarily suppose it? And does the frequent boldness of the Psalmist's familiarity with God, still more the domestic intimacy with Him so tenderly shadowed forth in the Canticle of Canticles, allow of any alternative except the highest and purest admission of a perishable and frail creature into the very sanctuary of the Divine glory? Surely on Sinai and in the cave of Horeb such loving intercourse of almost friendship was held.

But the history of the Church soon unfolds to us a bright page, on which is emblazoned, as its title, CONTEMPLATION. At the very time when martyrs are shedding their blood and receiving the highest homage and praise, the Church, which so loves and honours them, reveres scarcely less the hundreds who fled from the very persecutions which the martyrs encountered and overcame. And the reason was, that the anchorets and cenobites, who retired to the desert, and did not again return to the world after peace was restored to the Church, but swelled their numbers to thousands, were considered by her no less conquerors of the world and triumphers over the weakness of nature. Their lives of solitude and silence were not idle, for they laboured with their hands for their slender sustenance; but this was expressly the rule of their lives, that, even while their hands were at work, their minds should be fixed on God. And hours of the dark night had no other occupation.

It was this power of fixed and unflagging contemplation which sustained them through eighty, often, and a hundred years of this seclusion. Many were men of refined minds and high education, who, in their thoughtful meditative lives, must be supposed to have attained the highest refinement of devout application to spiritual things which can be enjoyed on earth. And what pious solitaries thus gained in the desert of the Thebais, our own hermits, like Guthlake, and monks, like Cuthbert, as surely possessed. Without the peaceful enjoyment of such a sweet interior reward, their lives would have been intolerable.

So necessary does the power of communing with God alone, and 'face to face,' appear to every class of Christians, that not only the ascetics of the Eastern Church, or the mystics of the Western, profess to possess it, but even the least enthusiastic forms of religion claim, or admit it. Jacob Böhme and Swedenborg have found plenty of admirers; the latter is still leader of a sect. It would be invidious to enter into a comparison between the writings of these men and the volumes before us. We refer to them only as evidence that every form of Christianity feels the want of some transcendental piety, which bears the soul beyond the dominion and almost out of the prison of the 'body of death,' and allows it a free and familiar intercourse with God, as of spirit with spirit.

When, however, perusing the writings of S. John,

the reader will find no symptom of fanaticism, no arrogation of superior privileges, of inspirations, Divine guidance, or angelic ministrations, as are to be found in pretended mystics. There is scarcely an allusion to himself, except occasionally to apologise for being so unequal to the sublime doctrines which he is unfolding, or for the rudeness of his style. Never, for a moment, does he let us know, that he is communicating to us the treasures of his own experience, or describing his own sensations. One sees and knows it. A man who writes a handbook of travel need not tell us, whether or no, he has passed over the route himself. We feel if he has, by the minuteness of his details, by the freshness of his descriptions, by the exactness of his acquaintance with men and things.

Then, no one who had not tasted, and relished, the sweetness of the spiritual food prepared by him, could possibly treat of it with such zest; its delicious flavour is on the lips that speak about it. Nor need the reader imagine that he will hear from this humble and holy man accounts of visions, or ecstasies, or marvellous occurrences to himself, or others; or rules, or means for attaining supernatural illuminations, or miraculous gifts. No; he proposes to guide any pupil, who feels drawn by God, to supreme love of Him, and towards those regions of contemplative prayer in which He often communicates Himself most intimately to the human soul; but only through a dark and painful road, from which all joy and almost consolation is excluded.

It is now time to lay before the reader an outline, though imperfect, of what he will find in the volumes before him. The first contains two treatises, embodying what may be called the portion of mystical instruction, most fully and excellently imparted by S. John.

It may be considered a rule in this highest spiritual life, that, before it is attained, there must be a period of severe probation, lasting often many years, and separating it from the previous state, which may have been one of most exalted virtue. Probably, many whom the Catholic Church honours as saints have never received this singular gift. But, in reading the biography of such as have been favoured with it, we shall invariably find that the possession of it has been preceded, not only by a voluntary course of mortification of sense, fervent devotion, constant meditation, and separation from the world, but also by a trying course of dryness, weariness of spirit, insipidity of devotional duties, and, what is infinitely worse, dejection, despondency, temptation to give all up in disgust, and almost despair. During this tremendous probation, the soul is dark, parched, and wayless, as 'earth without water,' as one staggering across a desert; or, to rise to a nobler illustration, like Him, remotely, who lay on the ground on Olivet, loathing the cup which he had longed for, beyond the sweet chalice which He had drunk with His Apostles just before.

Assuming, as we do, that this trial comes upon the soul from God, its purpose is clear. That sublime condition to which it aspires, and is called, of spiritual union with infinite holiness, and of the nearest approach allowable to the closer gazing of blessed spirits into the unfathomable glory, requires a purity like gold in the crucible, and a spiritualising unclothing of whatever can be cast off, of our earthly and almost of our corporeal existence. The soul is to be winged, strongly as the eagle, gently as the dove,* to leave all this world behind it, and seek a sweet repose.

Detachment and purity are the reasons for this intermediate state of desolation; detachment not merely from outward objects and from visible bonds, but from our own wills and desires, however virtuous; detachment from our own ways of even seeking God, and still more from our sensible enjoyment of devotion, and the very sweetness of His service. There must be no trust in one's own intellect, where faith alone can guide through the deep darkness; no reliance upon the ordinary aids to contemplation, for the very impulses and first thrilling touches of love must come from God's delicate hand; no impatience for release, no desire to return back. It is an earthly purgatory, in which all dross is painfully drained out, all straw and stubble burnt up.

And what is the result? The soul has indeed been brought into a state little below that of angels; but it has given proof of a love than which theirs cannot be higher. That dark period of hard probation

* 'They shall take wings as eagles, they shall run and not be weary' (Isa. xl. 31); 'Who will give me wings like a dove, and I will fly and be at rest?' Psalm liv. 7).

has completely inured her to fidelity to God, not for the sake of His rewards, not for the happiness of His service even here below, but for His own dear and good sake, because He *is* her God. And this persevering and persisting love of Him, without a ray or even a glimmering of the brightness of His countenance to light and cheer the dreary path, has surely, by gentle patience, won a returning love beyond the claims of ordinarily virtuous souls.

It is after this often long, but always severe, trial of faithful love, that what one may call the mystical espousals of God with the soul take place; when its spiritual existence may be said to have been raised into a heavenly sphere; when the exercise of that sublime privilege of contemplation has become so habitual, that scarce do the knees touch the ground in prayer, than the affections flash upwards from the heart, and are embosomed and absorbed at once in almost blissful fruition in God's mighty love; and when the body is busy with the affairs of life, these no more hinder the familiar colloquies and the burning glances of affection directed to the one exclusive Ruler of the soul, than did the slim and light palm-leaves woven by the desert anchoret distract his thoughts.

This happy consummation of both trials and desires forms the subject of mystical treatises by many who have enjoyed it. S. John does not, except incidentally, dwell upon it. He does not systematically deal with those who bask on the summit of that spiritual Thabor; he only guides the pilgrim to it. The ascent to the mystical mountain is rugged and steep; the journey can only be made in the darkness of probationary privations of inward light and joy. Hence the titles of his two great treatises—'The Ascent of Mount Carmel;' 'The Obscure Night of the Soul.'

Each of these works may be said to go over the same ground, though without repetitions, or even tiresome similarities. To each is prefixed a poem of eight stanzas, which forms not merely an introduction, but an argument rather, to a full dissertation on mystical science. But our author does not go beyond the two or three first strophes in his commentary, which often extends to many chapters; copious, most methodical, and rich upon one only line.

Mount Carmel is his natural type of the spiritual mount: for there dwelt his 'Father Elias' (vol. i. p. 143), whom the Carmelites revere as their model and founder; and there in a dark cavern he spake with God, and even caught a glimpse of His glorious being, in His might, and in His gentleness (3 Kings xix. 8). Up, up, slowly but warily, he guides his scholar along the steep and perilous ascent. He may be compared to the Alpine guide who, himself familiar with the craggy path, and sure of his steps, is all solicitude for his inexperienced charge, and watches and directs every movement. He makes him keep his eyes intent on the rude path before his feet, or on the slippery stair which he has cut out for them. He does not allow him to look down into the valley below, beautiful though it be, lest his head turn giddy, and he topple over the bluff precipice; nor to gaze upwards, in immature hope, towards the bright pinnacles, which reflect and refract the sun's rays, lest he become weary at their distance, and blinded by their brilliancy, and unable to pick his steps. Now the faithful guide takes his hand and leads him; now he bids him rely on his trusty pole, throwing his weight upon it; now he encourages him to gather all his strength, and bound over the yawning crevasse. And so in the end he lands his charge safe upon the high and dizzy summit, whence he may look around, and above, and downwards in safety, and enjoy a sweet repose and a refreshing banquet. So careful, so minute, so tender, and so resolute is the guidance of S. John in the 'Ascent of Mount Carmel.'

And through 'The Obscure Night,' no less safe by its prudence, and encouraging by its firmness, is his leadership to the soul. The twofold night, that of sense and that of the spirit, may be securely traversed under his direction, and the soul return to a daylight sevenfold brighter than that of the ordinary sun.

After thus attempting, however imperfectly, to give an outline of S. John's principal treatises on the spiritual life, no space remains to say anything about the beautiful writings which fill the second volume. We are mistaken if many readers, who have not courage or disposition to master the abstruser and sublimer doctrines and precepts of the first, will not peruse with delight the more practical and cheerful maxims of the second part, and even find exquisite satisfaction in those lessons of Divine love, and in those aphorisms of a holy life, which are adapted for every devout soul.

Before closing this preface, it is a mere act of justice to say, that the translation of these difficult works has been made with a care seldom bestowed upon such books when rendered from a foreign language. So simple, so clear, and so thoroughly idiomatic is this version, that the reader will never have to read a sentence twice from any obscurity of language; however abstruse the subject may be. Indeed, he will almost find a difficulty in believing that the work is a translation, and has not been written originally as he reads it, in his own tongue.

London: *February* 23, 1864.

CONTENTS

OF

THE FIRST VOLUME.

THE ASCENT OF MOUNT CARMEL.

CHAPTER VI.

CHAPTER VII.

CHAPTER VIII.

CHAPTER IX.

CHAPTER X.

CHAPTER XI.

CHAPTER XII.

CHAPTER XIII.

CHAPTER XIV.

CHAPTER XV.

BOOK II.

PROXIMATE MEANS OF UNION, FAITH. THE SECOND NIGHT OF THE SPIRIT.

CHAPTER I.

CHAPTER II.

CHAPTER III.

CHAPTER IV.

CHAPTER V.

CHAPTER VI.

CHAPTER VII.

CHAPTER VIII.

CHAPTER IX.

CHAPTER X.

CHAPTER XI.

CHAPTER XII.

CHAPTER XIII.

CHAPTER XIV.

CHAPTER XV.

CHAPTER XVI.

CHAPTER XVII.

CHAPTER XVIII.

CHAPTER XIX.

CHAPTER XX.

CHAPTER XXI.

CHAPTER XXII.

CHAPTER XXIII.

CHAPTER XXIV.

CHAPTER XXV.

CHAPTER XXVI.

CHAPTER XXVII.

CHAPTER XXVIII.

CHAPTER XXIX.

CHAPTER XXX.

CHAPTER XXXI.

CHAPTER XXXII.

BOOK III.

THE PURGATION AND ACTIVE NIGHT OF THE MEMORY AND THE WILL.

CHAPTER X.

CHAPTER XI.

CHAPTER XII.

CHAPTER XIII.

CHAPTER XIV.

CHAPTER XV.

CHAPTER XVI.

CHAPTER XVII.

CHAPTER XVIII.

CHAPTER XIX.

CHAPTER XX.

CHAPTER XXI.

CHAPTER XXII.

CHAPTER XXIII.

CHAPTER XXIV.

CHAPTER XXV.

CHAPTER XXVI.

CHAPTER XXVII.

CHAPTER XXVIII.

CHAPTER XXIX.

CHAPTER XXX.

CHAPTER XXXI.

CHAPTER XXXII.

CHAPTER XXXIII.

CHAPTER XXXIV.

CHAPTER XXXV.

CHAPTER XXXVI.

CHAPTER XXXVII.

CHAPTER XXXVIII.

CHAPTER XXXIX.

CHAPTER XL.

CHAPTER XLI.

CHAPTER XLII.

THE OBSCURE NIGHT OF THE SOUL.

BOOK I.

OF THE NIGHT OF SENSE.

CHAPTER V.

CHAPTER VI.

CHAPTER VII.

CHAPTER VIII.

CHAPTER IX.

CHAPTER X.

CHAPTER XI.

CHAPTER XII.

CHAPTER XIII.

CHAPTER XIV.

CHAPTER XV.

CHAPTER XVI.

CHAPTER XVII.

CHAPTER XVIII.

CHAPTER XIX.

CHAPTER XX.

CHAPTER XXI.

CHAPTER XXII.

CHAPTER XXIII.

CHAPTER XXIV.

CHAPTER XXV.

THE

ASCENT OF MOUNT CARMEL.

THE

ASCENT OF MOUNT CARMEL.

ARGUMENT.

The following stanzas are a summary of the doctrine contained in this book of the Ascent of Mount Carmel. They also describe how we are to ascend to the summit of it, that is, to the high estate of perfection, called here union of the soul with God. I place all the stanzas together, because what I have to say is founded upon them. Thus the whole substance of my book may be comprehended at once. I shall also transcribe each stanza again, and each line separately, as the nature of my work requires. Perfection,—its definition.

STANZAS

I

In an obscure night,
With anxious love inflamed,
O, happy lot!
Forth unobserved I went,
My house being now at rest.

II

In darkness and obscurity,
By the secret ladder, disguised,
O, happy lot!
In darkness and concealment,
My house being now at rest.

STANZAS.

III

In that happy night,
In secret, seen of none,
Seeing nought myself,
Without other light or guide
Save that which in my heart was burning,

IV

That light guided me
More surely than the noonday sun
To the place where He was waiting for me,
Whom I knew well,
And where none but He appeared.

V

O, guiding night;
O, night more lovely than the dawn;
O, night that hast united
The Lover with His beloved,
And changed her into her Love.

VI

On my flowery bosom,
Kept whole for Him alone,
He reposed and slept;
I kept Him, and the waving
Of the cedars fanned Him.

VII

Then His hair floated in the breeze
That blew from the turret;
He struck me on the neck
With His gentle hand,
And all sensation left me.

VIII

I continued in oblivion lost,
My head was resting on my Love;
I fainted away, abandoned,
And, amid the lilies forgotten,
Threw all my cares away.

PROLOGUE.

PROLOGUE

THE dark night, through which the soul passes, on its way to the Divine light of the perfect union of the love of God — so far as it is in this life possible — requires for its explanation greater experience and light of knowledge than I possess. For so great are the trials, and so profound the darkness, spiritual as well as corporal, which souls must endure, if they will attain to perfection, that no human knowledge can comprehend them, nor experience describe them. He only who has passed through them can know them, but even he cannot explain them. Therefore, while touching but slightly on the subject of this dark night, I trust neither to experience nor to knowledge, for both may mislead me; but solely to the Holy Scriptures, under the teaching of which I cannot err, because he who speaks therein is the Holy Ghost. Nevertheless, I accept the aid of experience and knowledge, and if through ignorance I should err, it is not my intention to depart from the sound doctrine of our holy mother the Catholic Church. I resign myself absolutely to her light, and bow down before her decisions, and moreover to the better judgment herein of private men, be they who they may.

The Author's submission to the Church.

It is not any personal fitness which I recognise in myself that has led me to undertake this work, so high and so difficult, but solely my trust in our Lord, Who, I hope, will enable me to speak on account of the great necessities of many souls. Many persons begin to walk in the way of virtue — our Lord longing to lead them into the obscure night that they may travel onwards into the Divine union — but make no progress; sometimes because they will not enter upon this night, or suffer Him to lead them into it; and sometimes also because they do not understand their

PROLOGUE. Hindrances. own state, and are destitute of fit and wise directors who may guide them to the summit of the mount. How miserable it is to see many souls, to whom God has given grace to advance — and who, had they taken courage, would have reached perfection — remain satisfied with narrow-minded views of God's dealings, through want of will or through ignorance, or because there is not one to direct their steps, and to teach them how to go onwards from the beginning. And in the end, when our Lord has compassion on them, and leads them on in spite of these hindrances, they arrive late, with much difficulty, and less merit, because they have not submitted themselves to His ways, nor suffered Him to plant their feet on the pure and certain road of union. Though it is true that God, Who conducts them, can do so without these helps, still, because they do not yield themselves up to Him, they make less progress on the road, resisting their Guide; and they merit less because they do not submit their will, whereby their sufferings are increased.

1. Cowardice.

2. Self-will.

There are souls who, instead of abandoning themselves to the care and protection of God, hinder Him rather by their indiscreet behaviour, or resist Him like little children who, when their mothers would carry them in their arms, struggle and cry that they may be allowed to walk. These souls make no progress, or if they do, it is comparable only to the walking of an infant child.

So, then — that men may know, beginners as well as those who have made some progress, how to resign themselves into the hands of God when it is His pleasure to lead them — I purpose, by His help, to furnish some directions, so that they may understand the matter for themselves, or at least submit to the guidance of God. Some confessors and spiritual directors, because they have no perception or experience of these ways, are a hindrance and an evil, rather than a help to such souls: they are like the builders of Babel; who, when required to furnish certain materials, furnished others of a very different sort, because they knew not the language of those around them, and thus the building was stopped. 'Come ye therefore,' saith God, 'let us go down and there confound their tongue, that they may not understand one another's speech. And so the Lord scattered them.' * PROLOGUE.

It is a hard and miserable thing for souls when they cannot comprehend their own state, nor meet with any one who can. For when God leads any one along the highest road of obscure contemplation and aridity, such an one will think himself lost; and in this darkness and affliction, temptation and distress, some will be sure to tell him, like the comforters of Job,† that his sufferings are the effects of melancholy, or disordered health, or of natural temperament, or, it may be, of some secret sin for which God has abandoned him. Yea, they will decide that he is, or that he has been, exceedingly wicked, seeing that he is thus afflicted. Some also will say that he is going backwards, because he finds no consolation or pleasure, as before, in the things of God. Thus they multiply the sorrows of this poor soul, for his greatest trial is the knowledge of his own misery, when it seems to him clearer than light that he is full of evil and sin, because God enables him, as I shall hereafter explain, to see this in the obscure night of contemplation. And so, when he meets with those who tell him, in accordance with his own impressions, that his troubles arise out of his own sins, his grief and misery are infinitely increased and rendered more bitter than death. 3. Self-ignorance.

Such confessors as these, not satisfied with considering all his sorrows to flow from past sins, compel him to retrace his whole life, and to make frequent general confessions, putting him on the rack anew. They do not understand that this is not the time for such acts, but that it is now the day of 4. Want of a guide.

* Gen. xi. 7, 8. † Job iv.

PROLOGUE. God's purgation; and when they ought to leave him alone, comforting him, indeed, and encouraging him to bear his trials patiently until God shall be pleased to deliver him; for until then, notwithstanding all they may say or do, there can be no relief.

I have to treat this matter hereafter, and how the soul is to be guided, and how the confessor is to conduct himself with regard to his penitent, and what are the signs whereby we may ascertain whether this be a state of purgation, and if it be, whether of sense or of spirit—this is the obscure night—and whether or not it be the effect of melancholy or any other imperfection of body or soul. For there are persons who will think, or their confessors for them, that God is leading them along the road of the obscure night of spiritual purgation, and yet, perhaps, all is nothing but imperfection of sense and spirit; and others also who will think they do not pray when they pray much, and, on the other hand, there are others who think they pray much when they do not in reality pray scarcely at all.

5. Abuse of grace. There are some—and it is sad to see them—who toil and labour, wearying themselves, and yet go backwards, because they make the fruit which is profitable to consist in that which profits not, but which is rather a hindrance; and others who, in rest and quietness, make great advancement. Others also there are who turn the graces and the gifts of God, given them for their advancement, into embarrassments and stumbling-blocks on this road.

Those who travel on this road will meet with many occasions of joy and sorrow, hope and pain, some of which are the result of the spirit of perfection, others of imperfections. I shall endeavour, by God's help, to speak of all, so that everyone who shall read my book may, in some degree, see the road he takes, and that which he ought to take, if he wishes to ascend to the summit of this mount.

As my book treats of the obscure night in which the soul journeys on to God, let no one be surprised if he finds it also somewhat obscure. It will be so, certainly, at first, but as the reader advances he will understand it better, for one part of it will throw light on another. If it be read a second time it will become more intelligible, and the doctrine it contains will appear the more certain. But if still there should be any to whom it shall seem hard, let them ascribe it to my ignorance and poor style, for the matter of it is in itself good and most necessary. 6. Obscurity. How remedied.

But after all I believe that, if I had written it in a more perfect manner, many would not appreciate it, because its contents are not those moralities and soothing matters which those spiritual persons run after who desire to draw near to God in pleasant ways, but a solid and substantial doctrine suited to all, if they seek to advance to that detachment of spirit which is here described. My principal object, however, is not to address myself to all, but only to certain persons of our holy religion of Mount Carmel, who by the grace of God are on the pathway of this mount. It is at their request I have undertaken my task. They, indeed, already detached from the things of this life, will the better understand this doctrine of detachment of spirit.

BOOK I.

THE NATURE OF THE OBSCURE NIGHT, THE NECESSITY OF PASSING THROUGH IT IN ORDER TO ATTAIN TO THE DIVINE UNION: AND SPECIALLY THE OBSCURE NIGHT OF SENSE AND DESIRE, WITH THE EVILS WHICH THESE INFLICT ON THE SOUL.

CHAPTER I.

Two kinds of this night, corresponding with the division of the soul into higher and lower.

STANZA I.

In an obscure night,
With anxious love inflamed,
O, happy lot!
Forth unobserved I went,
My house being now at rest.

BOOK I.

THIS stanza describes the happy state of the soul at its departure from all things, from the appetites and imperfections of our sensual nature to which all are subject because of our disobedience to reason. I mean that, in order to reach perfection, the soul has to pass, ordinarily, through two kinds of night, which spiritual writers call purgations, or purifications of the soul, and which I have called night, because in the one as well as in the other the soul travels, as it were, by night, in darkness.

Perfection requires;

I. Purgation of the flesh.

II. Purgation of the spirit.

The first is the night, or purgation of the sensual part of the soul, treated of in this first stanza, and described in the first part of this work. The second is the night of the spiritual part, of which the second stanza speaks, and which I shall discuss in the second part of my work, so far as it relates to the soul's activity therein, and in the third and fourth part, so far as it relates to its passive condition in it.

Explanation of the first stanza.

The meaning of the stanza then is, that the soul went forth, led of God, through love of Him only, and with that love inflamed, into the obscure night, which is the privation of, and purgation from, all sensual desires, in all external things; all the pleasures of the flesh, and all the satisfactions of the will. This is wrought in this purgation of the will, and for this reason is it said that the soul departed, its house, that is the sensual part, being at rest—all the desires being at rest and asleep, and the soul asleep to them; for there is no departing from the pains and vexations of desire till it be mortified and put to sleep.

The happy lot of the soul, then, is this unobserved departure, when no carnal desire or aught else was able to detain it. And also in that this departure took place by night, which is the privation of all desire wrought by God, a condition which is as night to the soul. The happy lot of the soul, then, consists in being led by God into this night from which so great a blessing results, but into which it could not have entered of itself, because no one is able in his own strength to empty his heart of all desires, so as to draw near unto God. This is the meaning of the stanza. I now proceed to explain each line of it separately, and to discuss the subject of this book.

CHAPTER II.

The nature and cause of the obscure night.

Three parts of the obscure night. 1. Privation. 2. Faith. 3. God.

'IN an obscure night.'—The journey of the soul to the Divine union is called night for three reasons. The first is derived from the point from which the soul sets out, the privation of the desire of all pleasure in all the things

BOOK I.

of this world, by an entire detachment therefrom. This is as night for every desire and sense of man. The second, from the road by which it travels; that is faith, for faith is obscure, like night, to the intellect. The third, from the goal to which it tends, God, incomprehensible and infinite, Who in this life is as night to the soul. We must pass through these three nights if we are to attain to the Divine union with God.

Illustrated by the history of Tobias.

They are foreshadowed in Holy Scripture by the three nights which were to elapse, according to the command of the angel, between the betrothal and the marriage of the younger Tobias. 'When thou shalt take her,' said the angel, 'go into the chamber, and for three days keep thyself continent from her.'* On the first night he was to burn the liver of the fish in the fire, which is the heart whose affections are set on the things of this world, and which, if it will enter on the road that leadeth unto God, must be burned up, and purified of all created things in the fire of this love. This purgation drives away the evil spirit who has dominion over our soul, because of our attachment to those pleasures which flow from temporal and corporeal things.

'The second night,' said the angel, 'thou shalt be admitted into the society of the Holy Patriarchs,' the fathers of the faith. The soul having passed the first night, which is the privation of all sensible things, enters immediately into the second night, alone in pure faith, and by it alone directed: for faith is not subject to sense.

'The third night,' said the angel, 'thou shalt obtain a blessing'—that is, God, Who, in the second night of faith, communicates Himself so secretly and so intimately to the soul. This is another night, inasmuch as this communication is more obscure than the others, as I shall presently

* Tob. vi. 18.

explain. When this night is over, which is the accomplishment of the communication of God in spirit, ordinarily effected when the soul is in great darkness, the union with the bride, which is the Wisdom of God, immediately ensues. The angel adds also, saying to Tobias, 'When the third night is passed, thou shalt take the virgin with the fear of the Lord.' This fear is then perfect when it is also the love of God, and it is made perfect when the soul is by love transformed in God.

I shall speak of these three causes separately, that they may be the better understood, first reminding the reader that the three nights are but one divided into three parts. The first, which is that of the senses, may be likened to the commencement of night when material objects begin to be invisible. The second, of faith, may be compared to midnight, which is utter darkness. The third resembles the close of night, which is God, when the dawn of day is at hand.

CHAPTER III.

The first cause, the privation of the desire.

I. The night of privation.

THE privation of all pleasure to the desire in all things is here called night. For as night is nothing else but the absence of light, and, consequently, of visible objects, whereby the faculty of vision remains in darkness unemployed, so the mortification of the desires is as night to the soul. For when the soul denies itself those pleasures which outward things furnish to the desire, it is as it were in darkness, without occupation. As the faculty of vision is nourished by light and fed by visible objects, and ceases to be so fed when the light is withdrawn, so the soul by means of the desire feeds on those things which, corresponding with its powers, give it pleasure; but when the desire

BOOK I.

is mortified, it derives no more pleasure from them, and thus, so far as the desire is concerned, the soul abides in darkness, without occupation.

This may be illustrated in the case of all the faculties of the soul. When the soul denies itself the pleasure arising from all that gratifies the ear, it remains, so far as the faculty of hearing is concerned, in darkness, without occupation; and when it denies itself in all that is pleasing to the eye, it remains in darkness, so far as it relates to the faculty of sight. The same may be said of the other senses, so that he who shall deny himself all satisfaction derivable from external objects, mortifying the desire thereof, may be said to be in a state which is as night, and this is nothing else but an entire detachment from all things.

Philosophers say that the soul is a blank when first infused into the body, without knowledge of any kind whatever, and incapable of receiving knowledge, in the course of nature, in any other way than through the senses. Thus, while in the body, the soul is like a man imprisoned in darkness, who has no knowledge of what passes without beyond what he can learn by looking through the window of his cell, and who if he did not so look could in no other way learn anything at all. Thus, then, the soul cannot naturally know anything beyond what reaches it through the senses, which are the windows of its cell. If, then, the impressions and communications of sense be neglected and denied, we may well say that the soul is in darkness and empty, because according to this opinion there is no other natural way for knowledge or light to enter in. It is true, indeed, that we cannot help hearing, seeing, smelling, tasting, and touching, but this is of no moment, and does not trouble the soul, when the objects of sense are repelled, any more than if we neither heard nor saw; for he who shuts his eyes is as much in darkness as a blind man who cannot see. This is the meaning of the Psalmist when he said, 'I am poor and in labours from my youth.'* He says that he is poor, though it is certain he was rich; because he had not set his mind upon riches, he was really like a poor man. But if he had been really poor, yet not in spirit, he would not have been truly poor, for his soul would have been rich, full of desires.

Detachment may accompany possession.

I call this detachment the night of the soul, for I am not speaking here of the absence of things—for absence is not detachment, if the desire of them remain—but of that detachment which consists in suppressing desire, and avoiding pleasure; it is this that sets the soul free, even though possession may be still retained. The things of this world neither occupy nor injure the soul, because they do not enter within, but rather the will and desire of them which abide within it. This is the night of the sensual part of the soul. And now I proceed to explain how the soul is to depart from its house in the obscure night of sense, in order to be united with God.

CHAPTER IV.

The necessity of passing truly through the obscure night of sense, which is the mortification of the desire.

The soul cannot have two masters.

THE soul must of necessity—if we would attain to the Divine union of God—pass through the obscure night of mortification of the desires, and self-denial in all things. The reason is that all the love we bestow on creatures is in the eyes of God mere darkness, and that while we are involved therein, the soul is incapable of being enlightened and possessed by the pure and simple light of God, unless we first cast it away. Light hath no fellowship with dark-

* Psal. lxxxvii. 16.

ness, for as St. John saith, 'The light shineth in darkness, and the darkness did not comprehend it.'* Two contrary qualities, as the philosophers say, cannot co-exist in the same subject. Darkness, which is the love of creatures, and light, which is God, are contrary to one another, for 'What fellowship hath light with darkness?'† The light of the Divine union cannot, therefore, dwell in the soul if these affections are not cast away.

Love begets likeness.

The affection and attachment which the soul feels for the creature renders the soul its equal and its like, and the greater the affection the greater will be the likeness. Love begets a likeness between the lover and the object of his love, and so the Psalmist, speaking of those who set their heart upon idols, says, 'Let them that make them become like unto them, and all such as trust in them.'‡ Thus, he then who loves the creature becomes vile as that creature itself, and in one sense even viler, for love not only levels, but subjects also the lover to the object of his love.

The creature is nothing in comparison with the Creator.

He, therefore, who loveth anything beside God renders his soul incapable of the Divine union and transformation in God, for the vileness of the creature is much less capable of the dignity of the Creator than darkness is of light. All things in heaven and earth are nothing in comparison with God. 'I beheld the earth,' saith he, 'and lo, it was void and nothing, and the heavens, and there was no light in them.' § The earth 'void and nothing,' signifies that the earth and all it contains are nothing, and the heavens without light, that all the lights of heaven, in comparison with God, are perfect darkness. Thus all created things, with the affections bestowed upon them, are nothing, because they are a hindrance, and the privation of our transformation in God, just as darkness is nothing, and less than nothing, being the

* S. John i. 5.
† 2 Cor. vi. 14.
‡ Ps. cxiii. 8.
§ Jerem. iv. 23.

absence of light. And as he who is in darkness comprehends not the light, so the soul whose affections are given to the creature shall never comprehend God. Until our soul is purged of these affections we shall not possess God in this life in the pure transformation of love, nor in the life to come in the beatific vision. To make this more clear I shall enter into some particulars.

God alone is; 1. Being.

The whole creation, compared with the infinite Being of God, is nothing; and so the soul whose affections are set on created things is nothing, and even less than nothing before God, because love begets equality and likeness, and even inferiority to the object beloved. Such a soul, therefore, cannot by any possibility be united to the infinite Being of God, because that which is not can have no communion with that which is. All the beauty of the creation, in comparison with 2. Beauty. the infinite Beauty of God, is supreme deformity, for 'Favour is deceitful and beauty is vain,'* and so the soul whose affections are set on the beauty of any created thing whatever shows before God nothing but deformity, and can never be transformed in Beauty, which is God, because deformity cannot attain unto beauty. All the grace and comeliness of creation, compared with the Grace of God, is supreme disgrace and supreme disfavour, and that soul, therefore, which is captivated by the grace and comeliness of created things is in the eyes of God in disfavour and disgrace, incapable of the infinite grace and beauty, for that which is ill-favoured is far removed from that which is infinitely gracious.

All the goodness of the whole world together, in comparison with the infinite Goodness of God, is wickedness rather than goodness, for 'None is good but God alone,'† and that soul is, therefore, wicked before God, whose affections are set on the things of this world. And as wickedness can have no 3. Goodness.

* Prov. xxxi. 30.

† S. Luke xviii. 19.

BOOK I.

fellowship with goodness, so that soul cannot be united in perfect union with God, who is the supreme Goodness.

4. Wisdom.

All the wisdom of the world, and all human cunning, compared with the infinite Wisdom of God, is simple and supreme ignorance, 'for the wisdom of this world is foolishness with God.'* He, therefore, who shall labour to attain to union with the Wisdom of God, in reliance on his own wisdom and skill, is supremely ignorant, and infinitely distant therefrom: for ignorance knoweth not what wisdom is. They who consider themselves gifted with knowledge are in the eyes of God most ignorant, 'professing themselves to be wise, they become fools.'† They alone attain to the Divine Wisdom who, like children and ignorant ones, lay aside their own wisdom, and serve God in love. This is the wisdom to which the Apostle refers, saying, 'Let no man deceive himself; if any man among you seem to be wise in this world, let him become a fool that he may be wise. For the wisdom of this world is foolishness with God.'‡ Ignorance, therefore, and not knowledge, becomes that soul which strives after union with the Wisdom of God.

5. Liberty and Power.

All the liberty and power of the world, compared with the Power and Liberty of the Spirit of God, is but supreme slavery, wretchedness, and captivity; and so he who loves superiority and dignities, and the indulgence of his desires, stands before God, not as a son who is free, but as a person of mean condition, the slave of his passions, because he submits not to the holy teaching, which saith, 'He that is the greater among you, let him become as the younger."§ Such an one will never attain to the true liberty of spirit attainable in the Divine union, because slavery has no fellowship with liberty, liberty dwelleth not in a heart subject to desires, for that heart is in captivity, but in that which is free, the heart of a son. It

* 1 Cor. iii. 19. † Rom. i. 22.
‡ 1 Cor. iii. 18, 19. § S. Luke xxii. 26.

was for this reason that Sara said unto Abraham: 'Cast out this bond-woman and her son, for the son of the bond-woman shall not be heir with my son Isaac.' *

6. Happiness.

All the sweetness and all the pleasures which all the things of this world furnish to the will are, in comparison with the sweetness and pleasure which is God, supreme pain, torment, and bitterness. He, therefore, who shall set his heart upon them is, in the eyes of God, worthy of pain, torment, and bitterness, and can never attain to those delights with which the Divine union abounds.

7. Riches and honour.

All the riches and glory of the whole creation compared with the true riches, which is God, is supreme poverty and meanness, and he who sets his heart upon them is, in God's sight, supremely poor and mean, and can never attain to the blessed estate of riches and glory, which is the transformation of the soul in God; for that which is mean and poor is infinitely distant from that which is supremely rich and glorious.

For this cause, then, the Divine Wisdom bewails men; namely, because they make themselves loathsome, mean, wretched and poor, through their love for that which is beautiful, rich, and noble in the eyes of the world. 'O ye men, to you I call, and my voice is to the sons of men. O little ones, understand subtlety, and ye unwise take notice. Hear, for I will speak of great things. . . . With me are riches and glory, glorious riches and justice. For my fruit is better than gold and the precious stone, and my blossoms than choice silver. I walk in the way of justice, in the midst of the paths of judgment, that I may enrich them that love me, and may fill their treasures.' † Here God addresses Himself to those who set their affections on the things of this world; He calls them little ones, because they make themselves

* Gen. xxi. 10.

† Prov. viii. 4–6, 18–21.

BOOK I.

little, like the object of their love. He bids them 'understand subtlety,' and 'take notice,' because He is speaking of great things, and not of little things, such as they are. He tells them that great riches and glory, objects of their love, are with Him and in Him, and not where they think they shall find them. 'Glorious riches and justice' are with wisdom. For though the things of this world may seem to men to be something, yet let them take notice, the things of God are more. The fruit of wisdom is better than gold and precious stones, and that which wisdom produces in the soul is preferable to the choice silver which men covet. This is applicable to every kind of affection to which we are liable in this life.

CHAPTER V.

Continuation of the same subject. Proofs from Scripture.

I HAVE now explained how great is the distance between created things and God, and how souls which set their affections thereon are equally distant from Him, because — as I have said — love begets equality and likeness. This was well understood by S. Augustine when, considering his own inclination towards the creature, he thus spoke unto God: 'Miserable man that I am, what fellowship hath my perverseness with Thy uprightness? Thou art truly good, I wicked; Thou full of compassion, I impious; Thou holy, I miserable; Thou just, I unjust; Thou art light, I am blind; Thou art life, and I am dead; Thou art medicine, I am sick; Thou supreme truth, and I utter vanity.' *

S. Augustine.

It is, therefore, supreme ignorance for any one to think that he can ever attain to the high estate of union with

* Soliloq. c. ii. Opp. Ed. Ben. tom. vi. App. p. 86.

God before he casts away from him the desire of natural things, and of supernatural also, so far as it concerns self-love, because the distance between them and the state of perfection is the very greatest. For Christ our Lord hath said, 'Every one of you that doth not renounce all that he possesseth, cannot be My disciple.' * The doctrine of Christ which He came into the world to teach, is contempt of all things, that we may thereby have power to receive the reward of the Spirit of God. For he who does not withdraw himself from the things of the world, is not qualified to receive the Spirit of God in the pure transformation.

The manna a type of God.

This truth is foreshadowed in the book of Exodus,† where we read that God did not give the manna to the people of Israel till the corn they had brought from Egypt had failed them, for the bread of angels is not given to, neither is it meant for, that palate which is pleased with the bread of man. He who feeds on strange meats, and is delighted therewith, not only disqualifies himself for the reception of the Holy Ghost, but also provokes God to anger exceedingly, as all do who, while they seek spiritual food, are not content with God only, but intermingle therewith carnal and earthly satisfactions. This appears from the same history, where it is said that the people cried, 'Who will give us flesh to eat?'‡ They were not satisfied with food so pure, for they desired and demanded the flesh of beasts. God was grievously offended because they would mingle flesh, so vile and coarse, with the pure and heavenly bread which, though always the same, had in it 'the sweetness of every taste,'§ for while 'their meat was in their mouth the wrath of God came upon them, and He slew the fat ones amongst them, and brought down the chosen men of Israel.'‖ God regarded it as an evil wish to desire other food when He was giving them the bread of heaven.

* S. Luke, xiv. 33. † Ex. xvi. 4. ‡ Num. xi. 4.
§ Wisd. xvi. 20. ‖ Ps. lxxvii. 30, 31.

BOOK I.

Oh, would that spiritual persons knew how they are losing the good things of the Spirit, abundantly furnished, because they will not raise up their desires above trifles, and how they might have the sweetness of all things in the pure food of the Spirit if they would only forego them. But as they will not, so they shall not have such sweetness. The people of Israel perceived not the sweetness of every taste in the manna, though it was there, because they would not limit their desires to it alone. The sweetness and strength of the manna was not for them, not because it was not there, but because they longed for other meats beside it. He who loves any other thing with God makes light of Him, because he puts into the balance with Him that which is infinitely beneath Him. We know by experience that the will, when set on a particular object, magnifies it above all others, if it has no pleasure in them, though they may be of greater importance than what it desires. And if it should desire two things together, it does wrong to the chief of the two, because it establishes an unjust equality between them. There is nothing in the whole world to be compared with God; and, therefore, he who loves anything together with Him, wrongs Him. And if this be true, what does he do who loves anything more than God?

Mount Sinai a type of perfection.

This truth is set before us in the book of Exodus. When God commanded Moses to go up into Mount Sinai, He bade him go up alone; the children of Israel were to remain below, and even the cattle were not to feed in sight of the mountain. 'Thou shalt stand with Me on the top of the mount. Let no man go up with thee, and let not any man be seen throughout all the mount: neither let the oxen nor the sheep feed over against it.'* He, therefore, that will go up into the mount of perfection and hold communion with God,

* Ex. xxxiv. 2, 3.

must not only abandon everything, but restrain even his desires, the sheep and the cattle from feeding in sight of the mount—that is, upon anything which is not simply God, in Whom, in the estate of perfection, every desire must cease. This journey or ascent must therefore be a perpetual struggle with our desires to make them cease, and the more earnest we are the sooner shall we reach the summit. But until the desires cease we can never reach it, notwithstanding our many virtues, for virtue is not perfectly acquired before our souls are empty, detached, and purified from all desire.

Three commandments of Jacob: 1. Renunciation. 2. Purification. 3. Change of heart.

Of this truth we have a lively figure in the history of the patriarch Jacob. When he was on his way to Bethel to build an altar for sacrifice unto God, he commanded his household the observance of three things: the casting away of strange gods, self-purification, and the changing of their garments. 'Jacob having called together all his household, said, Cast away the strange gods that are among you, and be cleansed and change your garments.'* He, therefore, who will ascend to the mount of perfection, to build an altar there, whereon to offer unto God the sacrifice of pure love, praise, and adoration, must first of all perfectly fulfil the three commandments of Jacob. He must cast away the strange gods, the earthly affections and attachments. He must purify himself from the impressions which the desires have made on the soul, in the obscure night of sense, denying them and doing penance for their past indulgence, and, in the third place, he must change his garments. This God himself will do during the observance of the first two commandments; He will change them from old into new, by infusing into the soul a new understanding of God in God, the human understanding being set aside, and a new love of God in God, the will being detached from its old desires and human satisfactions, by

* Gen. xxxv. 2.

bringing the soul into a state of new knowledge nd of deep delight, all other knowledge and old imaginings being cast away; and, finally, by causing that which is of the old man to cease, which is our natural aptitudes, and investing us with a new supernatural aptitude corresponding with the powers of the soul, so that all that is human in the action of the soul may become divine. This is the object gained in the estate of union, in which the soul is nothing else but an altar of God whereon the sacrifice of praise and love is offered, and where He alone dwells.

The altar of God to be pure.

This is the reason why, under the old law, the altar of sacrifice was to be hollow within. 'Thou shalt not make it solid, but empty and hollow in the inside.'* It is the will of God that the soul should be empty of all created things, so that it may become a fitting altar of His Majesty. He would not endure strange fires on the altar, nor that His own should fail. 'Nadab and Abiu, the sons of Aaron, taking their censers, put fire therein, and incense on it, offering before the Lord strange fire: which was not commanded them, and fire coming out from the Lord destroyed them, and they died before the Lord.'† Because Nadab and Abiu, sons of Aaron the high priest, offered strange fire on the altar, God in His anger slew them before it. That soul, therefore, which would become a fitting altar, must not be without the love of God, nor mingle therewith any other and strange love. God will never dwell there where aught is present beside Himself. Thus, when the Philistines took the ark of God and brought it into the temple of Dagon, their idol was thrown to the ground, and at last broken to pieces.‡

The royal road of the Holy Cross.

One desire only doth God allow, and suffer, in His presence, that of perfectly observing His law, and of carrying the cross of Christ. We do not know that He commanded anything

* Ex. xxvii. 8. † Levit. x. 1, 2. ‡ 1 Kings v. 1-5.

except the book of the law, to be laid up with the ark where the manna was preserved.—'Take this book, and put it in the side of the ark of the covenant of the Lord your God'*—and the rod of Aaron, type of the cross. 'Take back the rod of Aaron into the tabernacle of the testimony.'† That soul which has no other aim than the perfect observance of the law of God, and the carrying of the cross of Christ, will be a true ark containing the true manna, which is God.

CHAPTER VI.

Two great evils of the desires: negative and positive. Proofs from Scripture.

I. Privation of God.

To make this matter clear, it is advisable here to explain how the desires inflict these two great evils on the soul. These evils are, the privation of the Spirit of God, and the fatigue, torture, darkness, defilement, and weakness of that soul which indulges them. 'My people have done two evils,' saith God, 'They have forsaken Me, the fountain of living water, and have digged to themselves cisterns, broken cisterns, that can hold no water.'‡ These two evils flow from one single act of desire; for it is clear that the instant we set our affections upon any one created thing, our capacity for union with God is diminished in proportion to the intensity of that act of affection. For, as I said before,§ two contrary qualities cannot coexist in the same subject; the love of God and the love of the creature are contrary, the one to the other, and so cannot dwell together in the same heart. What connection is there between the creature and the Creator? Between the sensual and the spiritual? The seen and the unseen? The temporal and the eternal?

* Deut. xxxi. 26; Ex. xvi. 33.
† Numb. xvii. 10.
‡ Jerem. ii. 13.
§ Ch. IV.

BOOK I.

Between the heavenly food, pure and spiritual, and the food of the flesh, simply sensual? Between the poverty of Christ and selfish attachments? As in natural generation, no new form results without the corruption of the one previously existing—for this obstructs the former by reason of the contrariety between them — so while our souls are under the dominion of the sensual and animal spirit, the pure and heavenly spirit can never enter within them.

God and not creatures, the end of man.

This explains those words of our Lord, 'It is not good to take the bread of children, and to cast it to the dogs;'* and 'Give not that which is holy to dogs.'† Our Lord compares those who, renouncing all earthly desires, prepare themselves in simplicity for the graces of the Holy Ghost, with children, and those who satisfy their desires in earthly things, with dogs: children are admitted to the Father's table, and nourished by the Spirit, but only the crumbs which fall from it are given to the dogs. All created things are but the crumbs which fall from the table of God. Thus they who go about feeding on the creature are rightly called dogs; the children's bread is withheld from such, because they will not rise from the crumbs of the creature to the table of the uncreated Spirit of their Father. These are always hungry like dogs, and justly so, because crumbs excite the appetite rather than appease hunger. These are they of whom it is written, 'They shall suffer hunger like dogs; and shall go round about the city—and shall murmur if they be not filled.'‡ They who gratify their desires are always morose and discontented, like hungry persons: for what is there in common between the hunger which the creature occasions, and the fulness which proceeds from the Spirit of God? The fulness of God cannot enter into the soul before we drive away the hunger of desire, for two contrary qualities, such as hunger and fulness, cannot dwell

* S. Matt. xv. 26. † Ib. vii. 6. ‡ Ps. lviii. 15, 16.

together in the same subject. We may see from this how much greater is the work of God in purifying the soul from these contrarieties, than it was when He first created it out of nothing. For these rebellious desires and opposing affections seem to resist God more than nothing: that which is not, cannot resist His Majesty, but not so the love of the creature. Let this suffice for the first great evil which desires inflict on the soul, namely, resistance to the Spirit of God.

II. Five wounds of the soul.

Let us now proceed to the second, which is manifold in its operations. The desires fatigue, torment, darken, defile and weaken the soul. Of these five forms of evil, I shall discuss each separately. As to the first, it is evident that the desires weary the soul, because they resemble little children, restless and dissatisfied, who always begging of their mother, now one thing, now another, are never content. As one given to covetousness fatigues himself digging for gold, so the soul wearies itself in the pursuit of those things which the desires demand, and though we may obtain them, yet the end is weariness, because we are never satisfied. We have recourse to broken cisterns, which can hold no water to quench our thirst, as it is written, 'Faint with thirst and his soul is empty.'* The soul which yields to its desires, is weary and faint, like one ill of a burning fever, never at rest, and whose thirst increases while the fever lasts. It is written in the book of Job, 'When he shall be filled, he shall be straitened, he shall burn, and every sorrow shall fall upon him.'† Thus is it with the soul, wearied and afflicted by the desires: they wound it, agitate and disturb it, as wind does water, harassing it, so that it can never repose on anything, or in any place.

1. Weariness.

Of such souls is it written, 'The wicked are like the

* Is. xxix. 8. † Job xx. 22.

BOOK I.

raging sea which cannot rest.'* The heart of the wicked is like the raging sea, and he is wicked who does not subdue his desires. That soul which seeks to satisfy them wearies and torments itself, and is like one who, in the pains of hunger, opens his mouth to be filled with the wind, and who, instead of being satisfied therewith, becomes still more hungry, for wind is not his meat and drink. Of such it is written, 'In the desire of his heart, he snuffed up the wind of his love,'† and again warning the soul against the increasing dryness towards which it tends: 'Keep thy foot,' that is thy thoughts, 'from being bare, and thy throat from thirst,'‡—that is, thy will from the gratification of the desire which is the occasion of greater dryness. As the ambitious man is wearied in the day of disappointed expectations, so the soul with its desires and their fulfilment, for they make it more empty and hungry than it was before. The desires are, as it is commonly said, like fire which burns when supplied with fuel, but which, when the fuel is consumed, immediately dies away. In truth, the desire is in a much worse condition: the fire is quenched when the fuel fails, but the desire ceases not with the matter on which it fed while it raged, even though that be utterly consumed; for instead of ceasing, like fire when the fuel is burnt out, the desire pines away in weariness, for hunger is increased, and food diminished.

A soul in this condition is thus described by the prophet, 'He shall turn to the right hand, and shall be hungry, and shall eat on the left hand, and shall not be filled.'§ They who mortify not their desires are justly punished with hunger when they 'turn to the right hand,' that is, when they swerve from the way of God; for they do not deserve the fulness of

* Is. lvii. 20.
† Jerem. ii. 24.
‡ Jerem. ii. 25.
§ Is. ix. 20.

His sweet Spirit, and justly also shall they 'not be filled,' when they 'eat on the left hand,' that is, when they satisfy their desire with created things; for then abandoning that which can alone satisfy them they feed on that which is the source of greater hunger. Thus, then, is it clear that the desires weary and fatigue the soul. CHAP. VI.

CHAPTER VII.

The desires torment the soul. Proofs and illustrations.

THE second positive evil which the desires inflict is a certain torment and affliction of soul, so that he who suffers therefrom is like one in torture, bound with chains, finding no rest until released. 'The cords of my sins,' that is, my desires, saith the Psalmist, 'have encompassed me.'* As a man who lies naked amid thorns and briars, so is the soul in the power of its desires; for they pierce, torture, and tear it painfully, as it is written, 'They surrounded me like bees, and they burned like fire among thorns.'† The desires, which are as thorns, increase the fire of affliction and trouble. As the husbandman, greedy of the harvest, goads the oxen at the plough, so concupiscence goads the soul harnessed to its desires, till it shall obtain its will. Such was the desire of Dalila to know the secret of the strength of Samson; she 'pressed him—giving him no time to rest,' so that 'his soul fainted away, and was wearied even unto death.'‡ 2. Torment.

The desire tortures the soul in proportion to its intensity, so that the pain equals the desires, and the more numerous the desires the greater the pain: for the words which the apostle heard are fulfilled even in this life.

* Ps. cxviii. 61. † Ib. cxvii. 12. ‡ Judg. xvi. 16.

BOOK I.

'As much as she hath glorified herself, and lived in delicacies, so much torment and sorrow give ye to her.'* As he is tormented who falls into the hands of his enemies, so is the soul carried away by its desires. This truth is foreshadowed in the history of Samson, who was once so strong and free, the judge of Israel. But when he had fallen into the hands of his enemies, they robbed him of his great strength, plucked out his eyes, imprisoned him in a mill, and 'made him grind,' torturing and afflicting him. So is it with the soul, whose enemies, its own desires, live and triumph: their first act is to weaken and blind the soul, then to torment it, imprisoning it in the mill of concupiscence, and the cords that bind it are its own desires themselves.

Example of Samson.

Invitation of God.

God, therefore, compassionating those who, with so much toil and cost, go about to satisfy the hunger and thirst of their desires in created things, thus speaks to them by the mouth of His prophet: 'All you that thirst' and desire 'come to the waters, and you that have no money,' self-will, 'make haste, buy and eat, come, buy wine and milk,' peace and spiritual sweetness, 'without money' of self-will, and 'without price,' without that labour which your desires demand. 'Why do you spend money' of self-will 'for that which is not bread,' that is, the Spirit of God, and the 'labour' of your desires 'for that which doth not satisfy you?' 'Hearken diligently unto Me and eat that which is good,' and which you desire, 'and your soul shall be delighted in fatness.'† We attain to this fatness when we abandon all created satisfactions, for pain and sorrow flow from the creature, and refreshment from the Spirit of God.

'Come to Me,' saith our Lord, 'all you that labour and

* Apoc. xviii. 7.

† Is. lv. 1, 2.

are burdened, and I will refresh you.'* All you who are tormented and afflicted, labouring beneath the burden of anxiety and desire, cast it aside, by coming unto Me, and I will refresh you; and your souls shall find that rest of which your desires rob you, for they 'as a heavy burden are become heavy upon Me.'†

CHAPTER VIII.

The desires darken the soul. Proofs and illustrations.

3. Darkness.

THE third evil which the desires inflict is darkness and blindness of soul. For as vapours darken the air, and hide the light of the sun, or as a stained mirror cannot clearly receive an image, or as muddy water cannot distinctly reflect his face who looks into it, so the soul, stained by its desires, is intellectually blind, so that neither the understanding itself nor the sun of natural reason, nor that of the supernatural wisdom of God, can inform and enlighten it. To this the Psalmist referred when he said, 'My iniquities have overtaken me, and I was not able to see.'‡ And thus, while the soul is intellectually blind, the will becomes torpid, the memory fails, and every lawful function is disordered. These faculties depend on the intellect, and it is therefore clear that, when the intellect is embarrassed, they must all be thrown into confusion and disorder. 'My soul,' saith the Psalmist, 'is troubled exceedingly,' § that is, all my faculties are in disorder; for, as I have said, the intellect in this state cannot receive the illumination of the Divine Wisdom, just as the obscured air cannot reflect the brightness of the sun. The will cannot embrace God in pure love, just as the stained mirror cannot represent an object

* S. Matt. xi. 28. † Ps. xxxvii. 5.
‡ Ps. xxxix. 13. § Ib. vi. 4.

BOOK I.

placed before it. The memory overclouded by desires cannot calmly dwell on the Image of God, just as muddy water cannot reflect the face of him who looks into it.

Reason and not desire the guide of man.

The desire also blinds and darkens the soul, for the desire, as such, is blind and unreasonable, and reason is that which ever guides the soul aright in its several acts. Hence it is that the soul becomes blind whenever the desires guide it, because it is as if one who saw were led by one who saw not: the result being the same as if both were blind. This is what our Lord referred to when He said, 'If the blind lead the blind, both fall into the pit.' * Eyes are of little service to the moth, whose desire for the beauty of the light leads it dazzled into the midst of the flame. He who gives the rein to his desires may be likened to the fish dazzled by the light which the fishermen throw over the water, that the nets may not be seen: in this case, light serves but to increase the obscurity.

This is the meaning of the Psalmist when he said, 'Fire hath fallen upon them, and they have not seen the sun,'† for the desire is like fire, warming with its heat, and dazzling with its light, and the effect of the desire in the soul is, that it enkindles concupiscence, and dazzles the intellect, so that it cannot see. The cause of this dazzling obscurity is, the interposition of another light between the object and the eye, whereon the eye rests, so as to see nothing beyond. Thus the desire comes so close to the soul, and within the range of its vision, that we are dazzled, and satisfied with the light it gives, and so it hides from us the clear light of the intellect, which we do not, and never shall see, until the glare of the desire shall have ceased.

This renders so deplorable their case who burden themselves with indiscreet penances, and other imprudent methods

* S. Matt. xv. 14. † Ps. lvii. 9.

of devotion—voluntary certainly—on which they rely, thinking such alone, without mortifying their desires in other matters, to be sufficient to lead them on to the union of the Divine Wisdom. But this can never be, if the desires be not diligently mortified. If these persons bestowed but half their labour on this, they would make greater progress in a month than they can now make in many years, if they persevere in their present ways. As it is necessary to till the earth that it may bring forth fruit—for otherwise nothing will grow therein but weeds—so also is it necessary to mortify our desires, if we are to make progress towards perfection. Without mortification, I say it boldly, we shall make no progress whatever in the knowledge of God and of ourselves, notwithstanding all our efforts, any more than the seed will grow which is thrown away on uncultivated ground. Neither can the darkness and ignorance of our souls be removed, if the desires are not extinguished: for they are like a mote or cataract in the natural eye, obstructing the vision, until it be taken away.

Inward mortification more necessary than outward.

The Psalmist, considering the blindness of those souls which are under the power of their desires, the impossibility of their clearly beholding the truth, and the greatness of God's anger with them, said, 'Before your thorns could know the briar, He swalloweth them up, as alive, in His wrath.'* Before your thorns, your desires, harden and grow into a thicket, shutting out the sight of God, as the thread of life is frequently broken in the midst thereof, so will God swallow them up in His anger. Those persons in whom their desires live, and hinder the knowledge of God, God will swallow up in His wrath, either in the next life, in the purifying pains of Purgatory, or in this, in afflictions and sufferings, sent to detach them from their desires, or in the mortification of

Necessity, and design of suffering.

* Ps. lvii. 10.

BOOK I.

those very desires voluntarily undergone. God doeth this to take away the false light of desire between Himself and us, which dazzles us, and hinders us from knowing Him; and that, the intellect becoming clear, the ravage of desire may be repaired.

Oh that men knew how great a blessing, that of the Divine Light, this their blindness, the result of their desires, robs them of, and how great the evils they daily fall into, because they do not mortify them. We are not to rely on a clear intellect, or on the gifts received from God, and then imagine that any affections or desires we may indulge in will not blind us, nor cause us to fall into a worse state, little by little. Who would have thought that a man of perfect wisdom, filled with the gifts of God, as Solomon was, could have fallen away in his old age into such blindness and torpor of the will, as to build altars to idols and worship them? His affection for his wives, and his negligence in controlling his desires and the satisfactions of his heart, were alone sufficient to reduce him to this. So he tells us himself, saying, 'Whatsoever my eyes desired, I refused them not, and I withheld not my heart from enjoying every pleasure.'* Such was the effect upon Solomon of unbridled desires, and their gratification, though at first he was cautious; they soon blinded his understanding, and at last put out the light of wisdom within him, so that in his old age he forsook God. And if unmortified desires could produce such a disaster in the case of Solomon, who knew so well the difference between good and evil, what shall they not produce in us who are so ignorant? We are like the people of Ninive, of whom God said, 'They know not how to distinguish between their right hand and their left,'† since, at every step, we take good for evil, and evil for good; and this is as

Example of Solomon.

* Eccles. ii. 10.

† Jon. iv. 11.

it were natural to us. What, then, must it be when our desires are added to our natural blindness, but that which the prophet bewailed, speaking of those who love to follow after their desires: 'We have groped for the wall, and like the blind, we have groped as if we had no eyes, we have stumbled at noon as if in darkness.'* Such is he who is blinded by his desires, for in the presence of the truth and his real interests he cannot see them any more than if he had been utterly blind.

CHAPTER IX.

The desires pollute the soul. Proofs from Scripture.

THE fourth evil which the desires inflict on the soul is that they pollute and defile it, as it is written, 'He that toucheth pitch shall be defiled with it.'† He, then, toucheth pitch who satisfies the desires of the will in any created thing. Observe here that the wise man compareth the creature with pitch: for there is a greater distance between the excellence of the soul and the noblest creature than there is between the glittering diamond or fine gold and pitch. As a diamond or a piece of gold, if placed, heated, in contact with pitch becomes foul and stained in proportion to the heat, so the soul inflamed by the desire it may entertain for the creature, draws corruption therefrom and defilement. And there is a greater difference between the soul and all other created corporeal things than there is between the most pellucid water and the foulest mud. So, then, as such water mingled with mud becomes foul, so the soul whose affections are set on created things becomes polluted; for then it resembles them. As soot defiles the most beautiful face, so the unruly desires of the soul, if indulged in, defile

4. Defilement.

* Is. lix. 10. † Eccles. xiii. 1.

BOOK I.

and pollute that soul, which is in itself the most beautiful and perfect image of God.

The prophet Jeremias, bewailing the ravages of corruption produced by these unruly desires, first of all describes the beauty of the soul and then its defilement: 'Her Nazarites were whiter than snow, purer than milk, more ruddy than the old ivory, fairer than the sapphire; their face is now made blacker than coals, and they are not known in the streets.'* The hair of the Nazarites signify the thoughts and affections of the soul, which, ordered according to the law of God, that is referred all to Him, are 'whiter than snow, purer than milk, more ruddy than the old ivory, fairer than the sapphire.' The whole physical creation in all its beauty and magnificence is signified by these four things, and higher than all is the soul of man and its operations—that is, the Nazarites with their long hair—which, when ordered, not according to the commandments of God, that is, when occupied with created things, is now made blacker than coals. All this and far greater ruin befalls the soul's beauty from the indulgence of unruly desires.

Man nobler than the universe.

Corruptio optimi pessima.

So, then, if my object were to describe the foul and corrupt condition to which the desires reduce the soul, I should not be able to find anything so full of cobwebs and worms, not even corruption itself, wherewith to compare it. For though the disordered soul in its natural substance be as perfect as God has made it, its reasonable substance is foul, filthy, and dark, overladen with all these evils and even more. Even one unruly desire—as I shall hereafter explain—though not a mortal sin, sullies and deforms the soul, and indisposes it for the perfect union with God, until it be cast away. What, then, must be the corruption of that soul which is wholly disordered, which has abandoned itself to

* Lam. iv. 7, 8.

the sway of its desires, and how far removed from the purity of God! No language can describe, no understanding can comprehend, the diverse impurities which diverse desires produce in the soul.

Love in order is virtue, or justice;

If, indeed, any description of this could be given, so that men might understand it, it would be a matter for wonder and for great pity: for each desire, according to its nature and intensity, deposits the filth and sediment of corruption and uncleanness in the soul, everyone in its own way. For as the soul of the just man, in one single perfection, which is the justice thereof, possesses innumerable most rich gifts, and many virtues of exceeding beauty, everyone of them lovely, different from each other according to the multitude and variety of the acts of the love of God; so the disordered soul in the same way, according to the multitude of the desires, the object of which are created things, contracts a miserable diversity of vileness and impurity, with which these desires pollute it.

Desire in disorder is vice.

Vision of the prophet Ezechiel.

These diverse pollutions are described by the prophet Ezechiel, when God showed him the interior of the temple with its walls painted round about with the likenesses of creeping things, and all abominable and unclean beasts: 'I went in,' saith the prophet, 'and saw, and behold every form of creeping things, and of living creatures, the abomination and all the idols of the house of Israel were painted on the wall round about.' * When the prophet had seen this, God said to him, 'Surely thou seest, O son of man, what the ancients of the house of Israel do in the dark, everyone in private in his chamber. Turn thee again; thou shalt see greater abominations.' The prophet turned, and 'behold women sat there mourning for Adonis.' 'Turn thee again,' said God to the prophet, 'and thou shalt see greater abomi-

* Ezech. viii. 10.

BOOK I.

nations than these.' And then the prophet saw 'at the door of the temple of the Lord, between the porch and the altar, five and twenty men having their backs to the temple of the Lord.'*

Interpretation. Three faculties of the soul; 1. Intellect.

The various creeping things and unclean beasts painted on the walls of the temple within are the thoughts and conceptions of the intellect derived from the vile things of earth and of other created things, which, because contrary to those that are eternal, defile the temple of the soul; and the soul by means thereof, embarrasses the intellect, which is its first court. The women in the second court. 'Mourning for Adonis' are the desires of the will, the second faculty of the soul; these weep, as it were, when they covet that on which the will is bent, that is, the unclean things painted on the understanding. The men in the third court are the fancies and imaginations resulting from created objects which the third faculty of the soul, the memory, preserves and dwells on. These had their backs to the temple of the Lord: for when the faculties of the soul have been completely occupied with any object of earth, the soul itself may be said to have turned its back upon God's temple, which is right reason, and which tolerates nothing that is in opposition to God.

2. Will.

3. Memory.

Three hindrances to the Divine Union. 1. Voluntary imperfection. 2. Venial sin. 3. Mortal sin.

Let this suffice for the present to give us some insight into the foul disorder which desires engender in the soul. For were I to treat separately of the impediment to the Divine union which these imperfections and their varieties occasion; of that of venial sin, which is much greater than that of imperfections, and of its varieties; and also of mortal sin, which is complete defilement, and of its various forms, I should never come to an end. What I say — and it is to the purpose — is, that every single desire, though it be but the slightest imperfection, darkens the soul, and hinders its perfect union with God.

* Ezech. viii. 14, 16.

CHAPTER X.

The desires make the soul lukewarm, and enfeeble virtue. Proofs and illustrations.

CHAP. X. — 5. Weakness.

THE fifth evil inflicted on the soul by its desires is lukewarmness and feebleness, so that it has no strength to follow after virtue nor to persevere therein. As the strength of desire is diminished when it is applied to many objects, instead of being concentrated upon one, and the more numerous the objects embraced, the less is the energy with which each is sought, so, philosophers say, is it with virtue, which is more vigorous when united than when it is dispersed. It is, therefore, clear that if the desire of the will be directed to other objects than virtue it must be most ineffectual in the pursuit thereof. The soul whose will is divided among trifles, is like water which never rises, because it has an outlet below, and is therefore profitless. Thus it was that the patriarch Jacob compared Ruben his son to 'water poured out,' because he had given way to his desires in a certain sin: 'Thou art poured out as water, grow thou not;'* that is, because thou art poured out as water in thy desires thou shalt not grow in virtues. As boiling water left uncovered quickly loses its heat, and as aromatic spices exposed to the air gradually lose their fragrance and the strength of their perfume, so the soul not recollected in the love of God alone loses the heat and vigour of virtue. This truth was well understood by the Psalmist when he said, 'I will keep my strength to Thee,'† that is, I will concentrate the strength of my affections on Thee alone.

The desires enfeeble the soul, for they are like the little twigs and suckers which grow on a tree, sapping its strength so that it shall not be so fruitful. Of such souls our Saviour says: 'Woe unto them that are with child, and that give

* Gen. xlix. 4. † Ps. lviii. 10.

BOOK I.

suck in those days.' * This signifies the desires, which, if not cut off, will continually lessen the strength of the soul, and grow to be its ruin, like the suckers on a tree. Our Lord, therefore, warns us, saying, 'Let your loins be girt.' † The loins are the desires; they are also like leeches sucking the blood from the veins, for so the wise man calls them, saying, 'The horse leech hath two daughters,' the desires, 'that say, bring, bring.' ‡

It is, therefore, evident that the desires bring no good at all to the soul, but rather deprive it of what it has, and if we do not mortify them, they will not rest until they have done what the young vipers are said to do to their mother: these, as they grow in the womb, devour the entrails of their mother, and kill her, preserving their own life at the cost of hers. Thus the unmortified desires grow and devour the soul, killing the life of God within it. They alone live in that soul, because that soul has not destroyed them first. This it is that made the wise man pray: 'Take from me the greediness of the belly.' §

The joy of self-restraint.

But even if the desires do not issue in this great calamity, it is lamentable to see how they torture the poor soul in which they dwell—how hateful to itself they render it, how profitless to its neighbours, how dull and slothful in the things of God. There are no corrupt humours which can so bow down a sick man, enfeeble him in his gait, and make him loathe his proper food, as the desire of the creature bows down the soul in sadness, and indisposes it for the practice of virtue. And, in general, the reason why many souls have no love or inclination for virtue is, that they entertain affections and desires which are not innocent nor directed towards our Lord God.

* S. Matt. xxiv. 19. † S. Luke xii. 35.
‡ Prov. xxx. 15. § Eccles. xxiii. 6.

CHAPTER XI.

The necessity of freedom from all desires, however slight, for the Divine union.

CHAP. XI.

Must every desire be mortified?

It seems reasonable here for the reader to ask, whether it be necessary to mortify completely every desire, small and great, before perfection can be reached, or whether it will be enough to have mortified some of them, overlooking others—at least those which seem of less moment—because it is a matter most difficult to attain to such pureness and detachment, as to have no affection for anything remaining in the will.

Answer.

1. Involuntary natural desires harmless.

To this I reply: in the first place, it is true that all the desires are not equally hurtful, neither do they perplex the soul in the same degree. I am speaking of those which are voluntary: for the natural desires, when we do not consent to them, and when they do not pass beyond the first movements, do but slightly or not at all stand in the way of union. By natural and first movements I mean all those in which the natural will had no share, either before or after they arose: for to banish and mortify these completely is, in this life, impossible. The hindrance which these create is not such as to prevent the Divine union, though they may not be wholly mortified; they may remain in our nature, and yet the soul in its spiritual part may be most free from them. For it will sometimes happen that the soul enjoys the profound union of quiet in the will, while these remain in the sensual portion of man's nature, but having no communication with the spiritual portion occupied in prayer.

2. All unruly desires not equally hurtful;

3. Yet all must be banished.

But all the other voluntary desires, whether mortal sins, which are the most grievous, or of venial sins, which are less so, or imperfections only, which are still less so, must be banished away, and the soul which would attain to perfect union must be delivered from them all, however slight they

BOOK I.

Because perfect union requires identity of will.

may be. The reason is this: the estate of Divine union consists in the total transformation of the will into the will of God, in such a way that every movement of the will shall be always the movement of the will of God only. This is the reason why, in this state, two wills are said to be one—my will and God's will—so that the will of God is also that of the soul. But if the soul then cleaves to any imperfection, contrary to the will of God, His will is not done, for the soul wills that which God wills not. It is clear, therefore, that, if the soul is to be united in love and will with God, every desire of the will must first of all be cast away, however slight it may be; that is, we must not deliberately and knowingly assent with the will to any imperfection, and we must have such power over it, and such liberty, as to reject every such desire the moment we are aware of it. I say knowingly, for without deliberation and a clear perception of what we are doing, or because it is not wholly in our power, we may easily give way to imperfections and venial sins, and to those natural desires of which I have just spoken. It is of such sins as these, not so entirely voluntary, that it is written: 'A just man shall fall seven times, and shall rise again.' *

Knowledge and consent necessary for a moral act.

But as to those voluntary and perfectly deliberate desires, how slight soever their objects may be, any one of them, not overcome, is sufficient to prevent this union. I am speaking of the unmortified habit thereof, because certain acts occasionally have not so much power, for the habit of them is not settled; still we must get rid of them, for they, too, proceed from habitual imperfection. Some habits of voluntary imperfections, so far as they are never perfectly overcome, impede not only the Divine union but our progress towards perfection.

One act does not make a habit.

These habitual imperfections are, for instance, much

* Prov. xxiv. 16.

talking, certain attachments, which we never resolve to break through—such as to individuals, to a book or a cell, to a particular food, to certain society, the satisfaction of one's taste, science, news, and such things. Everyone of these imperfections, if the soul is attached and habituated to them, results in such serious injuries to our growth and progress in perfection. Yea, even if we fall daily into many other imperfections greater than these, provided they are not the result of the habitual indulgence of any evil inclination, we should not be so much hindered in our spiritual course as we are by this selfish attachment of the soul to particular objects; for while the soul entertains it, it is useless to hope that we can ever attain to perfection, even though the object of our attachment be but of the slightest importance possible.

Perfection measured by habits.

Does it make any difference whether a bird be held by a slender thread or by a rope, while the bird is bound and cannot fly till the cord that holds it is broken? It is true that a slender thread is more easily broken, still, notwithstanding, if it is not broken the bird cannot fly. This is the state of a soul with particular attachments: it never can attain to the liberty of the Divine union, whatever virtues it may possess. Desires and attachments affect the soul as the remora is said to affect a ship; that is but a little fish, yet when it adheres to the vessel it effectually prevents its progress.

The remora of selfish attachments.

How sad it is to see certain souls, like vessels richly freighted, full of good works, of spiritual exercises, virtues and gifts of God, which, because they have not the courage to break with certain tastes, attachments, or affections—these are all one—never reach the haven of perfect union. And yet it would cost them but a single vigorous flight to break the thread of their attachment or to shake off the remora of desire. It is a matter of deep regret, when God has given them strength to burst other and stronger bonds — those of vanity and sins — merely because they will not detach themselves from trifles, which God has left for them to break away from for love of Him, and which are no more than a single thread — that they should for this neglect their own advancement and the attainment of so great a blessing. And what is still more deplorable, because of such attachments, not only do they not advance, but, so far as perfection is concerned, they fall back, losing in some measure what they had already gained with so much labour. For it is well known that on the spiritual road not to go on overcoming self is to go backwards, and not to increase our gain is to lose.

Not to advance is to fall back.

This is what our Lord would teach us when He says, 'He that gathereth not with me scattereth.'* He who will neglect to repair the vessel that is but slightly cracked, will at last lose all the liquor it may hold; for 'he that contemneth small things shall fall by little and little:'† and 'of one spark cometh a great fire.'‡ One imperfection is enough to beget another, and this other, others again. We shall never see a soul, negligent in overcoming a single desire, which has not also many other desires arising out of the weakness and imperfection from which the first proceeds. There have been many persons who, by the grace of God, had made great progress in detachment and freedom, and yet because they gave way, under the pretence of some good— as of society and friendship — to petty attachments, have thereby lost the spirit and sweetness of God, holy solitude, and cheerfulness, and have injured the integrity of their spiritual exercises, so as to be unable to stop before all was gone. All this has befallen them because they did not root out the principle of pleasure and of the sensual desires, keeping themselves in solitude for God.

* S. Matt. xii. 30. † Eccles. xix. 1. ‡ Ibid. xi. 34.

We must ever walk on this road so as to reach the end; that is, in the constant repression of our desires, and not in their indulgence: and if we do not perfectly repress them we shall never perfectly reach the end. As wood can never be transformed into fire if but one degree of heat necessary for that end be wanting, so the soul that has but one imperfection can never be perfectly transformed in God, as I shall hereafter explain when speaking of the Night of Faith. The soul has but one will; and if this will be occupied or embarrassed, it is not free, perfect, solitary, and pure, as it ought to be for this Divine transformation. This truth is foreshadowed in the Book of Judges, where we read that an angel of the Lord came to the children of Israel and told them that, because they had not destroyed the inhabitants of the land, but had made a league with some of them, those, therefore, would be left among them as their enemies, and an occasion to them of their fall and destruction: 'Wherefore I would not destroy them from before your face, that you may have enemies, and their gods may be your ruin.'*

The soul has but one will.

God is just in thus dealing with those souls whom He has led forth out of the Egypt of this world, for whom he has slain the giants of their sins, and whose enemies he has destroyed, which are the occasions of sin which they meet with in the world, and all this for the sole purpose of their entrance into the promised land of the Divine union. He is just, I say, in thus dealing with them, when he sees them form friendships, and become confederate with the heathen, which are their imperfections; when they do not mortify themselves wholly, but are negligent and slothful in their lives: for this, then, He becomes angry with them, and suffers them to fall through their desires from bad to worse.

This truth is also shadowed forth in the command of God

* Judges ii. 3.

BOOK I.

to Josue when the children of Israel were about to enter into the land of promise. The city of Jericho was to be utterly destroyed and all that was within, man and woman, young and old, together with the cattle; and the people were not to take, nor even to touch any of the spoil thereof.* He, therefore, that will enter into the Divine union must put to death all that lives in his soul, whether small or great, many or few; he must abstain from all desire thereof, and be completely detached therefrom, as if neither existed for the other.

S. Paul, also writing to the Corinthians, says the same thing: 'This therefore I say, brethren, the time is short: it remaineth, that they also who have wives be as if they had none, and they that weep, as though they wept not, and they that rejoice as if they rejoiced not, and they that buy as though they possessed not, and they that use this world as if they used it not.' † The apostle teaches here that we must be detached in spirit from the world if we would walk so as to attain unto God.

CHAPTER XII.

The nature of those desires which suffice to injure the soul.

I MIGHT have entered at greater length on the night of sense according to the extent of evil which the desires occasion, not only in the way described, but in many others as well, Summary. but this is enough for my purpose, because it is now clear why the mortification of them is called night, and how necessary it is to enter into this night in order to draw near unto God.

One thing only remains for discussion before I speak of

* Josue vi. 18, 21.

† 1 Cor. vii. 29–31.

the way by which this night is entered upon, and so conclude this book—namely, a doubt which might be suggested to the reader by the matter in hand. It might be asked, in the first place, whether any desire be enough to produce in the soul these positive and negative evils of which I have spoken, and, in the second place, whether any desire, however slight, and of whatever kind, be enough to produce all these evils together, or whether each desire produces a distinct evil, as one desire weariness, another pain, and another darkness.

What evils in the soul does even one sin produce?

To this I reply as follows:—In the first place, if we are speaking of the negative evil, which consists in the soul's being deprived of God, it is only those voluntary desires which are the matter of mortal sin that can, and do, result in this: for these rob the soul in this life of grace, and in the next of glory, which is the fruition of God. And in the second place that all these desires, those which are the matter of mortal sin, and those voluntary desires, which are matter of venial sin, and those which are imperfections, are, every-one of them, enough to inflict on the soul the positive evils. These evils, though in one sense negative, are here called positive, because they correspond to a turning towards the creature, as the negative evils correspond to a turning away from God.

Answer.

1. One mortal sin inflicts all the negative evils;

2. Any sin the positive evils.

There is, however, this difference: those desires which are matter of mortal sin produce complete blindness, pain, im-pureness, and weakness. But those other desires, matter of venial sin, or known imperfection, do not produce these evils in this perfect and supreme degree, seeing that they do not cast the soul out of the state of grace: for the loss of grace is concurrent with their dominion over the soul, because their life consists in the death of grace. Still they occasion somewhat of these evils, though but remissly, proportional to that weakness and remissness which they generate in the soul; so that the particular desire which most weakens the

But in different degrees.

soul is most fruitful in pain, blindness, and impureness. But it is to be remarked that, though every desire generates all

3. Some sins specific evils, e.g. (1) Sensuality.

these evils, which we here call positive, there are some which chiefly and directly produce particular evils, and other evils incidentally. For though it is true that one sensual desire produces all these evils, yet its chief and proper fruit is the

(2) Avarice.

defilement of soul and body. Though one avaricious desire also produces all these evils, yet its principal and direct

(3) Vainglory.

result is trouble. Though one vainglorious desire, precisely like the rest, produces all these evils, yet its chief and im-

(4) Gluttony.

mediate effect is darkness and blindness. And, though one gluttonous desire issues in the same evils, yet still its primary direct result is weakness in those things that pertain to virtue. The same may be said of all other desires.

Fruits of Virtue.

The reason why any act of voluntary desire produces all these evils in the soul together, is that contrariety which subsists directly between it and those acts of virtue which result in opposite effects. As an act of virtue produces and generates in the soul sweetness, peace, consolation, light, pureness, and fortitude together, so an unruly desire begets pain, fatigue, weariness, blindness, and weakness. All virtues

The force of habit.

increase by the practice of each; so also vices thrive and grow, and their effects are magnified in the soul in the same way. Though all these evils are not visible then when the desire is gratified, because the satisfaction thereof furnishes at the time no opportunity for them, yet afterwards the evil results become clearly visible. For the desire, when it is fulfilled, is sweet, and appears good, but afterwards the effects thereof are found to be bitter, which is the experience of everyone who has suffered himself to be led away thereby. I am not ignorant, however, that there are some so blind and so insensible as not to feel this: they do not walk in the ways of God, and therefore see not that which hinders their drawing near unto Him.

I am not speaking here of those other natural desires which are involuntary, nor of thoughts which do not go beyond the first movements, nor of other temptations to which we consent not, because none of these produce any of the evils I describe. Though a person liable to these trials may imagine that the passion and disturbance thus occasioned darken and defile his soul, in reality it is not so—yea, rather the contrary effects are sometimes the result of them. Because, in proportion to the resistance offered, such an one gains strength, pureness, light, consolation, and many other good things, according to the words of our Lord to S. Paul: 'Virtue is made perfect in infirmity.'* But voluntary desires produce these and more evils. For this cause the chief solicitude of spiritual directors is to mortify the desires of their penitents, and to make them deny themselves in all that is pleasing to them, so as to deliver them from so great misery.

How trials give strength.

CHAPTER XIII.

How the soul enters by faith into the night of sense.

It now remains for me to give some directions by which the soul may be able to enter on this night of sense. Ordinarily, the soul enters in two ways on this night: one is the active way, the other is the passive. The active way is that by which the soul is able to make, and does make, efforts of its own to enter in, assisted by divine grace. Of this I shall speak in the instructions that follow. The passive way is that in which the soul doeth nothing as of itself, neither does it make therein any efforts of its own; but it is God who works in it, giving special aids, and the soul is, as it were,

Two ways. 1. Active. 2. Passive.

* 2 Cor. xii. 9.

BOOK I.

patient, freely consenting thereto. Of this I shall speak when treating of the obscure night, when I shall have to describe those who are beginners. And as I shall have then to give many counsels to such with reference to the many imperfections to which they are liable on this road, I shall not enlarge on that question now. Besides, this is not the place to do so, for I am now concerned only with the reasons why this journey is called night, with the nature and divisions of the same. But as it seems a defect, and not so profitable as it should be, to abstain here from furnishing some help or instructions proper for this night of the desires, I have determined to lay down the brief instruction following. I shall adopt the same course at the conclusion of each of these divisions or causes of this night, of which by the help of our Lord I undertake to speak.

Instructions.

These instructions for the subduing of our desires are, in my opinion, though brief and few, as profitable and effectual as they are brief. He who will reduce them to practice will need none others, for they include everything.

Imitation of Christ.

1. Be continually careful and earnest in imitating Christ in everything, conforming thyself to His life: for this end thou must meditate thereon, that thou mayest know how to imitate it, and conduct thyself in all things as He would have done Himself.

Self-denial.

2. To do this well, every satisfaction offered to the senses, which is not for God's honour and glory, must be renounced and rejected for the love of Jesus Christ, who in this life had, and sought, no other pleasure than doing the will of His Father, which was His meat,* as He tells us Himself. For instance, if the pleasure of listening to anything which tends not to the service of God presents itself, seek not that pleasure, neither give ear to what is said. If thou art offered

* S. John iv. 34.

the sight, pleasurable in itself, of things which do not tend to God's honour, seek not that pleasure, and abstain from that sight. Do the same also in conversation and every other commerce of society. Practise the same mortification with respect to the other senses, as far as possible; and if it be not possible, it will be enough not to seek the pleasure that is offered. Thus the mortification of the senses and the absence of all pleasure must be striven after, so that the soul may be as in darkness. The practice of this counsel will bring with it great profit in a short time.

In order to mortify and calm the four natural passions of joy, hope, fear, and grief, from the concord and tranquillity of which result these and other great advantages, the following instructions are a perfect means of great merit and the source of great virtues: —

Strive always, not after that which is most easy, but that which is most difficult. Mortification of

Not after that which is most pleasant, but that which is most unpleasant. 1. Joy.

Not after that which giveth pleasure, but after that which giveth none.

Not after that which is consoling, but that which is afflictive. 2. Grief.

Not after that which ministers repose, but after that which ministers labour.

Not after great things, but after little things. 3. Hope.

Not after that which is elevated and precious, but after that which is vile and despised.

Strive not to desire anything, but rather nothing. 4. Fear.

Seek not after that which is better, but that which is worse, and desire to be detached from all things, empty and poor for Christ's sake. This state is to be embraced with a perfect heart, and the will must conform thereto. Because if our heart be truly engaged herein, we shall in a short time

BOOK I.

attain to great joy and consolation, doing our work orderly with discretion.

These instructions, well acted upon, are sufficient for our entrance on the night of sense. But still, out of the abundance of the matter, I will give another method of devotion, which teaches us how to mortify truly the desire of honour, from which so many others proceed.

Humility in

1. Deed. 1. Do those things which bring thee into contempt, and desire that others also may do them.

2. Word. 2. Speak disparagingly of thyself, and contrive that others may do so too.

3. Thought. 3. Think humbly and contemptuously of thyself, and desire that others may do so also.

I think it fitting, in conclusion, to insert here certain instructions for ascending to the summit of Mount Carmel, which is the high estate of union. Though the doctrine they contain is spiritual and interior, it relates also to the spirit of imperfection in sensible and exterior things, which may be met in the two roads on either side of the way of perfection. We shall, therefore, take these sentences in this sense, namely, as referring to sensible things, and afterwards, in the second division of the night, we shall take them as referring to that which is spiritual.

Instructions how to enjoy, know, possess, and be like the All, which is God.

1. What to seek. 1. That thou mayest have pleasure in everything, seek pleasure in nothing.

2. That thou mayest know everything, seek to know nothing.

3. That thou mayest possess all things, seek to possess nothing.

4. That thou mayest be everything, seek to be nothing.

2. What to do. 5. That thou mayest attain to that of which thou hast no present perception, thou must walk there where thou hast no perception.

6. That thou mayest attain to that thou knowest not, thou must go through that thou knowest not.

7. That thou mayest attain to that thou possessest not, thou must go through that thou possessest not.

CHAP. XIII.

Desires for 1. Happiness, 2. Knowledge, 3. Gain, and 4. Glory only satisfied in God, who is the All.

8. That thou mayest attain to that which thou art not, thou must go through that which thou art not.

Instructions how not to impede the All.

3. What to avoid.

1. When thou dwellest upon anything, thou hast ceased to cast thyself upon the All.

The creature in itself is nothing, and cannot fill the heart of man.

2. Because in order to arrive from all to the All, thou hast to deny thyself wholly in all.

3. And when thou comest to attain the All, thou must keep it without desiring anything.

4. Because if thou wilt keep anything with the All, thou hast not thy treasure simply in God.

Deus meus et omnia.

In detachment the spirit finds quiet and repose, for coveting nothing, nothing wearies it by elation, and nothing oppresses it by dejection, because it stands in the centre of its own humility; for as soon as it covets anything it is immediately fatigued thereby.

CHAPTER XIV.

Explanation of the second line of the stanza.

With anxious love inflamed.

Recapitulation.

Now that I have explained the first line of the stanza, which relates to the sensual night, and described what the night of sense is, and why it is called night, and that I have also taught how we are to enter on it in the active way, it remains for me here to treat of its wonderful properties and effects. These are comprised in the following lines of this stanza. I touch but lightly upon them, as I promised in the prologue,

BOOK I.

The effects of the night of privation.

and pass on at once to the second book, which describes the other, the spiritual, division of this night.

The words of the soul then are 'with anxious love inflamed.' The soul has passed out and gone forth in the obscure night of sense to the union of the Beloved. For, in order to overcome our desires, and to deny ourselves in all things, our love and inclination for which are wont so to inflame the will that it delights therein, we require another and greater fire of another and nobler love—that of the Bridegroom—so that having all our joy in Him, and deriving from Him all our strength, we may gain such resolution and courage as shall enable us easily to abandon and deny all besides. It was necessary, in order to subdue our sensual desires, not only to have this love for the Bridegroom, but also to be on fire therewith, and that with anxiety. For the fact is, that our sensual nature is influenced by such vehement desires, and attracted by sensible objects, that if our spiritual nature were not on fire with other and nobler anxieties — anxieties for that which is spiritual — we should never overcome our natural and sensible satisfactions, nor be able to enter on the night of sense, neither should we have the courage to remain in the darkness, in the denial of every desire.

1. Love of God.

The nature and varieties of these anxieties of love, which the soul feels in the beginning of the way of union, the carefulness and the contrivances it employs that it may go forth out of its own house, which is self-will, into the night of the mortification of the senses; how easy, and even pleasant, these anxieties make the toils and dangers of that night—this is not the place to explain, neither, indeed, can it be done; for these things are rather to be felt and meditated upon than matters for description: so I shall pass on to the explanation of the other lines in the following chapter.

CHAPTER XV.

Explanation of the last lines.

CHAP. XV.

2. Peace of mind.

'O HAPPY lot! I departed unobserved, my house being now at rest.' This is a metaphor derived from the miserable condition of slaves. He who is delivered therefrom, pronounces his own a happy lot when none of his jailers hinder his release. The soul, because of original sin, is truly a prisoner in this mortal body, in the power of natural passions and desires, and therefore counts it a happy lot when it has gone forth unobserved from this slavery and subjection, that is, unimpeded and unembarrassed by all its desires. To effect this, it was advantageous for the soul to have departed in an obscure night, in the denial of every pleasure, and in the mortification of every desire.

'My house being now at rest,' that is, the sensual part of the soul, the house of the desires being now at rest, because those desires are overcome and lulled to sleep. For until the desires be lulled to sleep by the mortification of sensuality, and sensuality itself be mortified in them, so that it shall be contrary to the spirit no more, the soul cannot go forth in perfect liberty to the fruition of the union with the Beloved.

BOOK II.

PROXIMATE MEANS OF UNION, FAITH. THE SECOND NIGHT OF THE SPIRIT.

CHAPTER I.

STANZA II.

In darkness, and in safety,
By the secret ladder, disguised,
O happy lot!
In darkness and concealment,
My house being now at rest.

BOOK II.

Second part, Purgation of the spirit.

HERE the soul sings of that happy lot, attained by detachment of spirit from all spiritual imperfections, and selfish desires in spiritual things. This was a happiness so much the greater, because of the greatness of the difficulty which the soul had to encounter in tranquillizing the house of the spiritual part, and in effecting an entrance into the interior darkness, which is spiritual detachment from all things, as well sensual as spiritual, leaning only on a living faith—it is of this I speak ordinarily, because I have to do with those who are walking in the way of perfection—and by it ascending upwards unto God.

Explanation of second stanza.

This is here called a secret ladder, because all the steps and divisions of it are secret, hidden from sense and the intellect. Thus the soul is in darkness as to all natural light of sense and intellect, going forth beyond the limits of nature and of reason, that it may ascend by this Divine ladder of the faith which reaches and penetrates into the heights of God. The soul is said to have gone forth in disguise, because its natural condition was Divinely changed, ascending upwards by faith. And this disguise was the cause why it was unobserved, unimpeded by the things of time or reason, and by the devil himself: for none of these can hurt the soul while travelling onwards by living faith.

This is not all: the soul travels in such secrecy and concealment, and the devil with his wiles is so ignorant of its way, that it journeys truly, as it is here said, 'in darkness and concealment,' so far as the evil one is concerned, to whom the light of the faith is more than darkness. Thus the soul, which thus walks, may be said to walk in darkness, hidden from the devil, as I shall more clearly explain hereafter.

This is the reason why it is said that the soul went forth 'in darkness and in safety.' For he to whom is granted the happiness of walking in the darkness of the faith, having faith for his guide, walks in the utmost security when he goeth forth beyond all natural imaginations and spiritual reasonings. And so it is added, that the soul went forth in the spiritual night, 'my house being now at rest,' that is, the rational and spiritual parts. When the soul attains to the Divine union, its natural powers, impulses, and sensible anxieties in the spiritual part, are at rest. It is, therefore, not said here that the soul went forth anxiously, as in the first night of sense, because the anxieties of sensible love were necessary for a perfect departure then, so as to journey in the night of sense, and to be detached from all objects of the same. But in order to perfect the tranquillity of the house of the spirit, no more is required than the confirmation of all the powers of the soul, all its pleasures and spiritual desires, in pure faith. This done, the soul is united with the Beloved in a certain union of simplicity, pureness, love, and resemblance.

In the first stanza, speaking of the sensual part, the soul went forth 'in an obscure night;' and here, speaking of the spiritual part, 'in darkness,' because the darkness of the

BOOK II.

spiritual part is greater, as this darkness is greater than that of the night; for, however obscure the night may be, still something is visible, but in this darkness nothing is visible. Thus, in the night of sense, there remains still some light, because the understanding remains, and the reason also, which are not blind. But in this spiritual night, the night of faith, all is darkness, both in the understanding and the sense. The soul says that it went forth 'in darkness and in safety,' which it said not in the first stanza, and the reason is that the soul, when it makes the least usage of its own proper ability, travels most securely, because it walks most by faith.

I shall explain this matter at great length in the present book, to which I request the benevolent attention of the devout reader, because it will contain things most important to the truly spiritual man. Though they are somewhat obscure, yet one question will open the way to another, so that, as I believe, all will be well understood.

CHAPTER II.

The second part, or cause of this night—Faith. Two reasons why it is darker than the first and third.

II. Faith; the middle and darkest part of the obscure night.

I HAVE now to treat of the second part of this night—Faith—which is that wonderful means of reaching the goal, which is God, who is also to the soul, naturally, the third cause or division of this night. Faith, which is the mean, is compared to midnight, and thus it may be said, that faith is to the soul darker than the first part, and in a way also darker than the third: for the first part, that of the senses, is like the beginning of night, when sensible objects cease to be visible, and is not so far removed from light as midnight is. The third part, that which immediately precedes daybreak, is not so dark as midnight, because the clear light of morning is at hand: this is compared with God.

CHAP. II.

God in Himself is Light.

Though it is true, speaking after the manner of men, that God is as dark a night to the soul as faith, yet because God Himself, when the three divisions of this night are over — which are naturally the night of the soul — illumines it supernaturally with the rays of the Divine Light in a higher and nobler way, experimentally—which is the commencement of the perfect union which ensues when the third night is past—He may be said to be less dark. It is also more obscure than the first part, which relates to the lower, the sensual, nature of man, and consequently the more exterior. The second night, of faith, relates to the higher, to the rational, nature of man, and is therefore more interior and obscure, because it deprives us of the light of reason, or rather, to speak more clearly, makes it blind. Thus the comparison between it and midnight is made good: for that is the most obscure and most perfect portion of the night.

Three points in the second division: 1. Faith, the night of the soul. 2. What contrary to it. 3. Dispositions for it.

I have now to show how this second division—the night of faith—is the night of the spirit, as the first division is the night of sense, and then what those things are which are contrary to it, and how the soul is to be disposed actively for entering into it. For as to the passive way, which is the work of God, I reserve it for another opportunity—for the third book of this treatise.

CHAPTER III.

Faith, the dark night of the soul. Proofs from reason and the Holy Scriptures.

First point. Faith; its definition.

FAITH, according to theologians, is a habit of the soul, certain and obscure. The reason why it is an obscure habit is that it makes us believe the truths which God Himself

BOOK II.

has revealed — truths surpassing the light of reason, and beyond the reach of all human understanding. Hence it is that the excessive light of the faith is obscure darkness to the soul, because it subdues that which is great, and destroys that which is little, as the light of the sun puts out all other lights so that they appear not, and subdues our power of vision. As the sun blinds the eyes and robs them of the vision which it gives, because its own light is out of proportion with, and stronger than, our power of sight, so the light of faith, by reason of its greatness and the mode in which God communicates it, transcends our understanding, which in itself reaches only to natural knowledge, though gifted with the power of obeying in that which is supernatural when it is the will of our Lord to bring it to a supernatural action. The intellect, therefore, can of itself know nothing but in a natural way, the beginning of which is in the senses, and in no other way. For this end it retains the forms and species of objects either in themselves or in their resemblances: for as the philosophers say, knowledge results from an object and the faculty. *Ab objecto et potentia paritur notitia.*

An excess of light.

Faith surpasses 1. Intellect. 2. Knowledge. 3. Experience.

Two analogies.

If a man were told of things he knows nothing of, and the like of which he has never seen, no light could be thrown on them, so far as he is concerned, any more than if they had never been spoken of in his presence. For instance, if you were told that there is in a certain island an animal which you have never seen, and no description of it were given you, so that you might compare it with other animals, your knowledge of it, or what it resembles, is not greater than it would have been if you had never been told of it. I will give another illustration which will make the matter still more clear: if you tell a person blind from his birth that one object is white, another yellow, he would never understand what you mean, though you may speak to him for ever, because he has never seen such colours or anything like them, so as to have any opinion on the subject. The word colour only will remain with him, because that reaches him through the ear, but the form and figure thereof escape him because he has never seen them.

Such is faith to the soul, though the resemblance is not exact in all points; faith tells us of things we have never seen, of things of which we had no previous knowledge, either in themselves or in aught resembling them, and to which we never could have attained but by revelation. The light of natural knowledge cannot inform us of these things, because they are out of proportion with our natural senses. We know them because we have heard of them, believing that which the faith teaches us, subjecting thereto our natural light, and making ourselves blind before it: for 'faith cometh by hearing, and hearing by the Word of Christ.' * Faith is not knowledge that entereth in by any of the senses, but only the assent of the soul to that which cometh by hearing. Faith, therefore, far transcends the foregoing illustrations: for not only does it not produce evidence or knowledge, but, as I have said, it transcends and surpasses all other knowledge whatever, so that perfect contemplation alone may judge of it. Other sciences are acquired by the light of the understanding, but that of faith is acquired without it, by rejecting it for faith, and it is lost in its own light. Therefore is it said, 'If you will not believe you shall not understand.' †

Faith though dark enlightens the soul.

It is evident that the faith is a dark night to the soul, and it is thus that it gives it light; the more it darkens the soul the more does it enlighten it. It is by darkening that it gives light, according to the words of the prophet, 'If you will not believe,' that is, 'if you do not make yourselves

* Rom. x. 17. † Is. vii. 9, according to the Sept.

BOOK II.

Three illustrations from Holy Scripture.

blind you shall not understand'—that is, you shall have no light, the high and supernatural knowledge.

The faith was foreshadowed by the cloud which divided the Egyptians from the children of Israel at the entrance of the Red Sea. 'It was a dark cloud enlightening the night.'* How wonderful a cloud! —its darkness illumines the night. Faith, then, which is a dark cloud, obscure to the soul—and night also, for in the presence of faith the soul is blind, without its own natural light—enlightens with its own obscurity, and illumines the darkness of the soul, so that the master becomes like the disciple. For man who is in darkness cannot be rightly enlightened except by darkness, as the Psalmist saith, 'Day to day uttereth speech, and night to night showeth knowledge.'† The 'day' is God in everlasting bliss, where it is perpetual day, who communicates and reveals His Word, the Son, to the blessed angels and the holy souls, who are also now day, so that they may know Him and rejoice in Him. 'Night,' which is the faith in the Church militant, where it is still night, showeth knowledge to the Church, and consequently to every soul, which is also night, because it does not as yet enjoy the clear beatific vision, and because in the presence of faith its natural light is extinguished. The teaching set before us here then is, that the faith, which is obscure night, illumines the soul which is in darkness, according to the words of the Psalmist, 'Night shall be my light in my pleasures,'‡ that is, in the pleasures of pure contemplation and of union with God. The night of faith shall guide me. The soul, therefore, must be in darkness that it may have light, and be able to journey on the spiritual road.

* Ex. xiv. 20. † Ps. xviii. 3. ‡ Ps. cxxxviii. 11.

CHAPTER IV.

How the soul must be in darkness, in order to be duly guided by faith to the highest contemplation.

CHAP. IV.

Detachment from natural and supernatural goods of the spirit, necessary for Perfection.

I BELIEVE that I have now in some measure explained how faith is the obscure night of the soul, and how also the soul must be obscured, or deprived of its natural light, that it may be guided by faith to this high end of union. But that the soul may know how to effect this, it is necessary that I should explain somewhat more minutely this obscurity, which it must observe that it may enter into the abyss of faith. I shall, therefore, in this chapter, speak of that in general, and by and by, with the favour of God, more particularly of the way which the soul must keep, that it may not go astray in that obscurity, nor put obstacles before its guide.

Second point. What to shun.

In this life union with God is not 1. by the senses;

I say, then, that the soul, to be rightly guided by faith to this estate, must be in darkness, not only as to that part thereof—the sensual and the inferior, of which I have already spoken—which regards temporal and created things, but also as to that part thereof, the rational and the superior, of which I am now speaking, which regards God and spiritual things. Because it is clearly necessary for the soul, aiming at its own supernatural transformation, to be in darkness and far removed from all that relates to its natural condition, the sensual and rational parts. The supernatural is that which transcends nature, and, therefore, that which is natural remains below. Inasmuch as this union and transformation are not cognisable by sense or any human power, the soul must be completely and voluntarily empty of all that can enter into it, of every affection and inclination, so far as it concerns itself. Who shall hinder God from doing His own will in a soul that is resigned, detached, and self-annihilated? The soul, therefore, must be emptied of all such feelings; and,

BOOK II.

however great may be its supernatural endowments, it must be as it were detached from them, in darkness like a blind man, leaning on the obscure faith, and taking it for its light and guide; not trusting to anything it understands, tastes, feels, or imagines—for all this is darkness, which will lead it astray, or keep it back; and faith is above all understanding, taste, and sense.

2. Nor by intellectual vision;

If the soul be not blind herein, and in total darkness as to all such things, it will never reach to those higher things which faith teaches. A blind man, if he be not totally blind, will not commit himself wholly to his guide, but because he sees a little he thinks a certain road secure, not seeing another which is better. Such an one leads his guide astray, because he acts as if he saw, and has more authority in the matter than his guide: so the soul, if it leans upon any understanding, sense, or feeling of its own—all this, whatever it may be, is very little and very unlike to God—in order to travel along this road, is most easily led astray or impeded, because it is not perfectly blind in faith, which is its true guide. This is the meaning of S. Paul when he said, 'He that cometh to God must believe that He is.' * He that will draw near and unite himself unto God, must believe that He is. This is saying in effect, He that will attain to the union of God must not rely on his own understanding, nor lean upon his own imagination, sense, or feeling, but must believe in the perfection of the Divine Essence, which is not cognisable by the understanding, desire, imagination, nor any sense of man, and which in this life can never be known as it is. Yea, in this life, our highest knowledge and deepest sense, perception, and understanding of God is infinitely distant from what He is, and from the pure fruition of His Presence.

3. But by Faith.

Two proofs from Holy Scripture.

* Heb. xi. 6.

Thus the Prophet cries out, 'The eye hath not seen, O God, besides Thee, what things Thou hast prepared for them that wait for Thee;'* and S. Paul repeats his words, 'Eye hath not seen, nor ear heard, neither hath it entered into the heart of man, what things God hath prepared for them that love Him.'† How much soever, then, the soul may desire to be perfectly united by grace in this life to that whereunto it is to be united in glory in the next, which as S. Paul saith, eye hath not seen nor ear heard, and which hath not entered into the heart of man in the flesh, it is evident, that in order to be perfectly united in this life in grace and love, it must live in utter darkness as to all that can enter by the eye, all that the ear receives, all that the fancy may imagine, or the heart conceive, which here signifies the soul. Greatly embarrassed, then, is the soul, on the road of the Divine union, when it leans at all on its own understanding, sense, imagination, judgment, will, or any other habits of its own, or anything peculiar to itself, not knowing how to release and detach itself therefrom. For, as I have said, the goal to which it tends is beyond this, though this may be the highest thing it may know or feel, and it must, therefore, go beyond, passing on to that which it knows not.

Self-reliance hinders the Divine Union.

On this road, therefore, to abandon one's own way is to enter on the true way, or, to speak more correctly, to pass onwards to the goal; and to forsake one's own way is to enter on that which has none, namely God. For the soul that attains to this estate has no ways or methods of its own, neither does it, nor can it, lean upon anything of the kind. I mean ways of understanding, perceiving, or feeling, though it has all ways at the same time, as one who, possessing nothing, yet possesseth everything. For the soul courageously resolved on passing, interiorly and exteriorly,

* Is. lxiv. 4. † 1 Cor. ii. 9.

BOOK II.

beyond the limits of its own nature, enters illimitably within the supernatural, which has no measure, but contains all measure eminently within itself. To arrive there is to depart hence, going away, out of oneself, as far as possible, from this vile estate to that which is the highest of all. Therefore, rising above all that may be known and understood, temporally and spiritually, the soul must earnestly desire to reach that which in this life cannot be known, and which the heart cannot conceive; and, leaving behind all actual and possible taste and feeling of sense and spirit, must desire earnestly to arrive at that which transcends all sense and all feeling.

The flesh and the spirit both to be mortified.

In order that the soul may be free and unembarrassed for this end, it must in no wise attach itself—as I shall presently explain when I treat of this point—to anything it may receive in the sense or spirit, but esteem such as of much less importance. For the more importance the soul attributes to what it understands, feels, and imagines, and the greater the estimation it holds it in, whether it be spiritual or not, the more it detracts from the Supreme Good, and the greater will be its delay in attaining to it. On the other hand, the less it esteems all that it may have in comparison with the Supreme Good, the more does it magnify and esteem the Supreme Good, and consequently the greater the progress towards it.

In this way the soul draws nearer and nearer to the Divine union, in darkness, by the way of faith which, though it be also obscure, yet sends forth a marvellous light. Certainly, if the soul will see, it thereby becomes instantly more blind than he who should attempt to gaze upon the sun shining in its strength. On this road, therefore, to have our own faculties in darkness is to see the light, according to the words of our Lord: 'For judgment I am come into this world, that they who see not may see, and they who see may become blind.' * This relates to the spiritual road: he who is in darkness, blind as to his own proper and natural light, shall see supernaturally, and he who shall rely on any light of his own, the greater will be his blindness, and the more he shall be hindered on the way of the Divine union.

I think it necessary now, in order to avoid confusion, to explain the nature of the soul's union with God. This I intend to do in the following chapter, for if this be clearly understood, a great light will be thrown on what is to follow. This, therefore, seems to me a fit place for the subject. For though it breaks in on the course of the present matter, still it is not beside the question, because it will help us to understand the subject before us. The next chapter then will be a sort of parenthesis, after which I shall return to the special discussion of the three powers of the soul in their relations to the three theological virtues with reference to the second night of the spirit.

CHAPTER V.

The union of the soul with God. A comparison.

Chapter in parenthesis.

WHAT I have hitherto written will, in some degree, explain the nature of that estate which I have called the union of the soul with God, and therefore, what now follows will be so much the more intelligible. It is not my intention at present to describe, in particulars, what is the union of the intellect, of the will, and of the memory; what is the transient, and what the permanent union of these faculties, and what also is the perfect union: of this I shall speak hereafter, and the matter will be more clear when I come to discuss it in its

* S. John ix. 39.

BOOK II.

proper place, having before me a vivid example of it; then the matter will be clear, each particular observed and susceptible of a better decision. Now I am speaking only of the perfect and permanent union in the substance of the soul and its powers, so far as the union is a habit. Because, in reference to actual union, I shall explain hereafter how there is not, and cannot be, any permanent union in this life in the faculties of the soul, but only that which is transient.

Two kinds of union: 1. Substantial.

In order then to understand what this union is, we must remember that in every soul, even that of the greatest sinner in the world, God dwells, and is substantially present. This union or presence of God, in the order of nature, subsists between Him and all His creatures. By this He preserves them in being, and if He withdraws it they immediately perish and cease to be. And so when I speak of the union of the soul with God, I do not mean this substantial pre-

2. Moral;

sence which is in every creature, but that union and transformation of the soul in God by love which is only then accomplished when there subsists the likeness which love begets. For this reason shall this union be called the union of likeness, as the other is essential or substantial union;

Its definition.

this latter one is natural, the other is supernatural, which takes effect when two wills, the will of God and the will of the soul, are conformed together, neither desiring aught repugnant to the other. Thus the soul, when it shall have driven away from itself all that is contrary to the divine will, becomes transformed in God by love.

This is to be understood not only of that which is contrary in act but also in habit, so that not only voluntary acts of imperfection must be got rid of, but the habit thereof as well. And because no creature can, by any actions or capabilities of its own, attain to that which is God, the soul must be therefore detached from all created things, from all actions and capabilities of its own, that is from its own understanding, taste, and feeling, so that passing by everything which is unlike to, and not in conformity with God, it may attain to the receiving of His likeness, and resting upon nothing which is not His will, it may be so transformed in Him. Though it be true, as I have said, that God is always in every soul, bestowing upon it, and preserving to it, by His presence, its natural being, yet for all this He does not always communicate the supernatural life. For this is given only by love and grace, to which all souls do not attain; and those who do, do not in the same degree, for some arise to higher degrees of love than others. That soul, therefore, has greater communion with God, which is most advanced in love, that is, whose will is most conformable to the will of God. And that soul which has reached perfect conformity and resemblance is perfectly united and supernaturally transformed in God. For which cause, therefore, as I have already explained, the more the soul cleaves to created things, relying on its own strength, by habit and inclination, the less is it disposed for this union, because it does not completely resign itself into the hands of God, that He may transform it supernaturally. The soul has need, therefore, to be detached from these natural contrarieties and dissimilarities, that God, who communicates Himself to it naturally, in the order of nature, may also communicate Himself supernaturally, in the order of grace.

Concursus Dei.

This is the meaning of S. John when he said, 'born, not of blood, nor of the will of the flesh, nor of the will of man, but of God.'* It is as if he had said, 'He gave power to be made the sons of God,' that is, to be transformed in God, only to those who are 'born, not of blood,' not of natural temperaments and constitutions, 'nor of the will of the flesh,' nor of our natural free will and capacities, and

* S. John i. 13.

BOOK II.

still less of the will of man, which includes every form of intellectual judgment and comprehension. To none of these gave He power to be made sons of God in all perfection, but only to those who are born of God; to those regenerated by grace, first of all dead to all that is of the old man, rising above themselves to that which is supernatural, and receiving from God their new birth and sonship, surpassing every thought of man. For as our Lord saith, 'Unless a man be born again of water and the Holy Ghost, he cannot enter into the kingdom of God.'* He who shall not have been born again of the Holy Ghost shall not see the kingdom of God, which is the estate of perfection. To be born again of the Holy Ghost in this life perfectly, is to be a soul most like unto God in purity without any stain of imperfection. Thus the pure transformation by participation of union may be effected, though not essentially.

Illustration.

In order that we may have a clearer notion of the one and the other, let us consider the following illustration: the sun, with its rays, strikes a window; but if that window be stained and unclean, the sun cannot shine throughout nor transform it perfectly into itself, as it would have done, had it been clean and unsullied. This depends not on the sun but on the window, so that if the latter were perfectly clean, the rays of the sun would so shine through it, and so transform it as to make it seem identical with the rays and to give forth the light thereof, though in truth the window, while it appears one with the rays of the sun, preserves still its own separate and distinct substance. In this case we might say that the window is a ray or light by participation.

Thus the soul resembles the window; the divine light of the presence of God in the order of nature, perpetually

* S. John iii. 5.

strikes upon it, or rather dwells within it. The soul then by resigning itself — in removing from itself every spot and stain of the creature, which is to keep the will perfectly united to the will of God; for to love Him is to labour to detach ourselves from, and to divest ourselves of, everything which is not God, for God's sake — becomes immediately enlightened by, and transformed in, God; because He communicates His own supernatural Being in such a way that the soul seems to be God Himself and to possess the things of God. Such an union is then wrought when God bestows on the soul that supreme grace which makes the things of God and the soul one by the transformation which renders the one a partaker of the other. The soul seems to be God rather than itself, and indeed is God by participation, though in reality preserving its own natural substance as distinct from God as it did before, although transformed in Him, as the window preserves its own substance distinct from that of the rays of the sun shining through it and making it light.

Dispositions for union; Purity of heart and love.

Hence it becomes more evident that the fitting disposition for this union is, not that the soul should understand, taste, feel, or imagine anything on the subject of the nature of God, or any other thing whatever, but only that pureness and love which is perfect resignation, and complete detachment from all things for God alone. And as there cannot be any perfect transformation without perfect pureness, so in proportion to that pureness will be the enlightenment, illumination, and union of the soul with God, yet not wholly perfect if the soul be not wholly purified and clean. The following illustration will make this plain: conceive a picture painted with exquisite taste and delicate finish, the lines of which are so admirably formed that by reason of their singular fineness they can with difficulty be observed. Now, he whose vision is imperfect will see only the less

An analogy.

BOOK II.

perfect portions of the picture, and he whose vision is clearer will see more of its beauties, and another with still better eyesight will see more, and, finally, he whose vision is the most perfect will see the most delicate excellencies of it, for the painting has so much beauty that the more it is observed the more remains to be seen. All this is applicable to those souls who are enlightened by God and in Him transformed. For though it be true that every soul, according to its measure, great or little, may attain to this union, yet all do not in an equal degree, but only as our Lord shall give unto each; as it is with the blessed in heaven, there some see God more perfectly than others, and yet all see Him and all are satisfied and happy, for each one is filled with the vision according to his merits, greater or less. Hence it comes to pass, that though souls in this life enjoy equal peace and tranquillity in their state of perfection, everyone being satisfied, nevertheless some of them may be more advanced than the rest, in a higher degree of union, and yet all equally satisfied according to their several dispositions, and the knowledge they have of God. But that soul which does not attain to that degree of purity corresponding with the light and vocation it has received from God, will never obtain true peace and contentment, because it has not attained to that detachment, and emptiness of its powers, which are requisite for this pure union.

Different degrees of perfect beatitude.

CHAPTER VI.

The three Theological virtues perfect the powers of the soul, and bring them into a state of emptiness and darkness. Proofs from S. Luke and Isaias.

Third point of the second division. Active dispositions for the spiritual night.

HAVING now to explain how the three powers of the soul, intellect, memory, and will, are to be brought into this spiritual night, which is the means of the Divine union, it becomes necessary, in the first place, to discuss in this chapter how the three theological virtues, Faith, Hope, and Charity — through the instrumentality of which the soul is united to God in its powers — effect this emptiness and darkness, each one in its own power: Faith in the intellect, Hope in the memory, and Charity in the will. Afterwards, I shall show how the intellect is made perfect in the obscurity of Faith, how the memory is made empty in Hope, and how, also, the will is to withdraw and detach itself from every affection that it may ascend upwards unto God. This done, we shall see clearly how necessary it is for the soul, if it will travel securely along the spiritual road, to journey in the obscure night, leaning on these three virtues, which make it empty of all things and blind. For, as I have said, the soul is not united to God in this life by the understanding or feeling or imagination, or any other sense whatever, but only by Faith, in the intellect; by Hope, which may be referred to the memory — though also to the will — in so far as Hope relates to that emptiness and forgetfulness of every temporal and perishable thing which it causes, the soul preserving itself entire for the Supreme Good which it hopes for; and by Love, in the will.

Union with God by 1. Faith in the intellect.

These three virtues render empty all the powers of the soul; Faith makes the intellect empty and blind; Hope takes everything away from the memory, and Charity detaches the will from every pleasure and affection which are not God. Faith teaches us what the intellect cannot reach by the light of nature and of reason, being, as the Apostle saith, 'the substance of things to be hoped for.'* And though the intellect firmly and certainly assents to them, yet it cannot discover them; for if the intellect had discovered them, there would be no room for Faith. And though the

* Hebr. xi. 1.

BOOK II.

intellect derives certainty from Faith, yet it does not derive clearness but rather obscurity. As to Hope, there is no

2. Hope in the memory.

doubt that it renders the memory empty, and brings darkness over it as to all surrounding objects, for hope is ever conversant with that which is not in possession, for if it were already possessed there would be no place for hope; because, as the Apostle saith, 'hope that is seen is not hope, for what a man seeth why doth he hope for?'* This virtue, then, makes empty also, for it is the virtue of that which is not in

3. Love in the will.

possession, and not of that which is. Charity, too, in the same way empties the will of all things, for it compels us to love God above all, which we cannot do without withdrawing our affections from every object, to fix them wholly upon God. Christ our Lord hath said, 'Every one of you that doth not renounce all that he possesseth cannot be My disciple.'† Thus these virtues bring darkness over the soul, and empty it of all created things.

Two illustrations from Holy Scripture.

Consider that parable of our Lord recorded by S. Luke,‡ of the friend who went out at midnight asking for three loaves. These loaves are the three theological virtues. They were asked for at midnight, to teach us that the soul must dispose itself for perfection in these virtues in darkness as to all its powers, and that perfection is to be acquired in this night of the spirit.

The prophet Isaias saw in a vision two seraphim on either side of God, each of them with six wings. With two of their wings they covered their feet. This signifies the quenching and subduing of the will in everything for the sake of God. With two of their wings they covered their faces; this signifies the blindness of the intellect in the presence of God. With two of their wings they flew; this signifies the flight of hope towards those things which we possess not; lifted up on high

* Rom. viii. 24. † S. Luke xiv. 33. ‡ S. Luke xi. 5.

above all possession short of God. 'Upon it stood the seraphim: the one had six wings, and the other had six wings; with two each covered his face, and with two each covered his feet, and with two they flew.'*

We have, therefore, to lead these three powers of the soul unto these three virtues; informing the intellect by Faith, stripping the memory of all that it possesses by Hope, and informing the will by Charity, detaching them from, and making them blind to, all that is beside these three virtues.

Purity of heart to be obtained in the spiritual night.

This is the spiritual night which I have called the active night; because the soul labours, on its own part, to enter into it. When I was treating of the night of sense, I explained how that the sensual powers of the soul are to be emptied of all sensible objects in the desire, so that the soul may go forth from the beginning of its course to the middle, which is faith; so now, while speaking of the night of the spirit, I shall also explain, by the help of God, how that the spiritual powers of the soul are to be emptied and purified of all that is not God, and remain in the darkness of these three virtues, which are the means and dispositions by which the soul becomes united with God. Herein is found every security against the cunning of the devil and the craftiness of self-love with all its ramifications, which is wont most deeply to deceive and hinder the progress of spiritual persons, because they do not know how to be detached, and to guide their steps by these virtues. For this cause they never perfectly reach the substance and pureness of spiritual good, neither do they journey, as they might do, by the straightest and the shortest road. Keep in mind, however, that I am now speaking specially of those who have begun to enter the state of contemplation. For, as to beginners, this must be discussed at greater length, which I shall do when I shall have to treat of what is peculiar to them.

* Is. vi. 2.

CHAPTER VII.

The straitness of the way of life. The detachment and freedom necessary for those who walk in it. The detachment of the intellect.

BOOK II.

THE pureness and detachment of the three powers of the soul require, for their discussion, greater knowledge and abilities than mine, so as to enable spiritual persons to comprehend how strait the way is that leadeth unto life, and that, convinced of this, they may not wonder at the emptiness and detachment wherein we must abandon, in this night, the three powers of the soul. For this end we must ponder well the words of our Lord, applied here to the obscure night, and the way of perfection. Our Lord saith, 'How narrow is the gate and strait is the way that leadeth to life; and few there are that find it.'* Consider the great and significant import of the word 'how.' It is as if He had said, 'In truth it is very narrow, much narrower than you think.' Consider, also, that He began by saying, 'How narrow is the gate.' By this He teaches us that the soul that will enter in by the gate of Christ, which is the beginning of the road, must first of all constrain itself, and detach the will from the things of time and sense, loving God above them all. This refers to the night of the senses.

Perfection requires labour.

Our Lord immediately adds, 'Strait is the way,' that is of perfection. By this He teaches us that He who will walk in the way of perfection must not only enter through the narrow gate, emptying himself of everything that relates to sense, but must also renounce all that he possesses, laying a constraint upon himself, and releasing himself entirely from all attachment even to spiritual things. Thus the narrow gate refers to the sensual nature of man, and the strait way to his spiritual or rational nature.

* S. Matth. vii. 14.

He says also, 'Few there are that find it.' Mark here the reason of this, which is that there are but few who understand how, and desire, to enter into this supreme detachment and emptiness of spirit. For this pathway up the lofty mountain of perfection, in that it ascends upwards and is strait, requires that those who climb it should carry nothing with them which shall press them downwards, or embarrass them in their ascent upwards. And as this is a matter in which we should seek and aim after God alone; so God only ought to be the sole object of our efforts.

In the way of the Cross Christ is 1. Our Teacher.

This clearly shows that the soul must be not only disentangled from all that belongs to the creature, but also detached and annihilated in the things of the spirit. And so our Lord teaching us, and guiding us into this road, gives us this wonderful doctrine, and which is, if I may so say, the less practised by spiritual persons the more it is necessary for them. I shall transcribe it here, because it is so necessary and so much to the purpose, and then explain its real and spiritual meaning. 'If any man will follow Me, let him deny himself, and take up his cross and follow Me. For whosoever will save his life, shall lose it, and whosoever shall lose his life for My sake . . . shall save it.'* O that some one would teach us how to understand, practise, and feel what is involved in this profound lesson of self-denial given us by our Lord Himself, that spiritual persons may perceive how different, on this road, their conduct ought to be from that which many of them think to be right! Some consider any kind of retirement from the world, and any correction of excesses to be sufficient; others are content with a certain degree of virtue, persevere in prayer and practise mortification, but they do not rise to this detachment, and poverty, or self-denial, or spiritual pureness—all these are one—which

* S. Mark viii. 34, 35.

BOOK II.

our Saviour here recommends, because they nourish and clothe their natural self with consolations, instead of detaching themselves therefrom, and denying themselves in all things for God. They think it enough to deny themselves in the things of this world, without annihilating themselves, and purging away all self-seeking in spiritual things. Hence it comes to pass, that when any of this solid devotion presents itself to them, which consists in the annihilation of all sweetness in God, in dryness, in distaste, in trouble, which is the real spiritual cross, and the nakedness of the spiritual poverty of Christ, they run away from it as from death itself. They seek only for delights, for sweet communications, and satisfactions in God, but this is not self-denial, nor detachment of spirit, but rather spiritual gluttony. They render themselves spiritually enemies of the cross of Christ, for true spirituality seeks for bitterness rather than sweetness in God, inclines to suffering more than to consolation, and to be in want of everything for God rather than to possess; to dryness and afflictions rather than to sweet communications, knowing well that this is to follow Christ and deny self, while the other course is perhaps nothing but to seek oneself in God, which is the very opposite of love. For to seek self in God is to seek for comfort and refreshment from God. But to seek God in Himself is not only to be willingly deprived of this thing and of that for God, but to incline ourselves to will and choose for Christ's sake whatever is most disagreeable, whether proceeding from God or from the world; this is to love God.

Spiritual gluttony;—what.

O who can tell us how far God wills that this self-renunciation should reach! In truth it should be as death, a temporal, natural, and spiritual annihilation in all things which the will esteems; herein is all our gain. This is the meaning of our Saviour when He said, 'Whosoever will save his life shall lose it;'* that is, whosoever will possess, or seek anything for himself, he shall lose it. 'Whosoever shall lose his life for My sake, shall save it;' that is, whosoever shall renounce for the sake of Christ whatever is pleasing to his own will, choosing rather the cross—to which our Lord referred when He said, 'He that hateth his life'—he shall gain it.

2. Our Companion.

Our Lord taught this same truth to the two disciples who asked that they might be admitted to sit on His right hand and on His left. He gave no encouragement to them in the matter of their petition, but offered them the chalice which He was about to drink Himself, as something more safe and more precious on earth than the dignity which they sought. This chalice is the death of our natural self by detachment from all that relates to sense, as I have already said, and from all that relates to the spirit, as I shall explain hereafter, so that we may journey onwards on this strait way, that is, detachment from our own understanding, sense, and feelings, and in such a manner that the soul shall renounce itself both in sense and spirit, and more, so that it may not be impeded even by the things of the spirit on the narrow road. For this road admits only of self-denial—as our Lord declares—and the cross, which is our staff to lean on, and which lightens the road and makes it easy. Thus our Lord hath said: 'My yoke is sweet, and My burden light.'† This burden is the cross. For if we are determined to submit ourselves, and to carry the cross—this is nothing else but an earnest resolution to seek and endure it in everything for God—we shall find great refreshment and sweetness therein to enable us to travel along this road, thus detached from all things, desiring nothing. But if we cling to anything whatever, whether it come from God or from the world, we

3. Our Reward.

* S. Mark viii. 35.

† S. Matth. xi. 30.

BOOK II.

are not journeying in detachment and self-denial, and so we shall miss our way, and never be able to ascend the narrow path.

True perfection;—what.

Would that I could persuade spiritual persons that the way of God consisteth not in the multiplicity of meditations, ways of devotion or sweetness, though these may be necessary for beginners, but in one necessary thing only, in knowing how to deny themselves in earnest, inwardly and outwardly, giving themselves up to suffer for Christ's sake, and annihilating themselves utterly. He who shall exercise himself herein, will then find all this and much more. And if he be deficient at all in this exercise, which is the sum and root of all virtue, all he may do will be but beating the air—utterly profitless, notwithstanding great meditations and communications. There is no progress but in the imitation of Christ, Who is the way, the truth, and the life. 'I am the way,' saith He, 'and the truth, and the life. No man cometh to the Father but by Me.'* And again, 'I am the door. By Me if any man enter in he shall be saved.'† That spirituality, therefore, which would travel in sweetness at its ease, shunning the imitation of Christ, is, in my opinion, nothing worth.

No spiritual progress but in the imitation of Christ.

4. Our Model.

And now, having said that Christ is the way, and that the way is to die to our natural self in all that relates to sense and spirit, I proceed to explain how it is to be done in imitation of Christ, for He is our light and our example. In the first place, it is certain that He died spiritually while on earth to all things belonging to sense, and naturally at His death; 'The Son of man,' saith He, 'hath not where to lay His head.'‡ And when He died it was the same. In the second place, it is certain that at the hour of death His soul was desolate and, as it were, brought to nothing, forsaken of

* S. John xiv. 6. † Ib. x. 9. ‡ S. Matth. viii. 20.

His Father, left without comfort in the most distressing dryness, so that He cried out on the cross, 'My God, my God, why hast thou forsaken Me?'* This was the greatest sensible abandonment of His whole life; and it was then that He wrought the greatest work of His whole life of miracles and of wonders, the reconciliation and union with God by grace of all mankind. This He accomplished at that very moment when He was most annihilated in all things, brought lowest in the estimation of men, for when they saw Him dying on the ignominious tree, they showed Him no reverence, yea, rather they stood by and derided Him. Then, too, was He brought lowest in His very nature, for that was as it were annihilated when He died; and as to the protection and consolation of His Father also, for He was then forsaken that He might pay our debt to the utmost, and unite us with God, being Himself annihilated and, as it were, brought to nothing. Therefore it is that the Psalmist saith of Him, 'I am brought to nothing, and I knew not.'† This is for the instruction of the truly spiritual man, in the mystery of the gate and way of Christ, that he may become united with God, and also to teach him that the more he annihilates self for God, in sense and spirit, the more will he be united with God, and the greater the work he will accomplish. And when he shall have been brought to nothing, when his humility is perfect, then will take place the union of the soul and God, which is the highest and noblest estate attainable in this life. This consisteth not in spiritual refreshments, tastes, or sentiments, but in the living death of the cross, sensually and spiritually, outwardly and inwardly.

Mental sorrows of our Saviour.

Salvation and Perfection only in the Cross.

I will not proceed further with this subject, though I could pursue it indefinitely; for I see that Jesus Christ is but little known by those who consider themselves His friends.

* S. Matth. xxvii. 46.

† Ps. lxxii. 22.

BOOK II.

Jesus has few lovers of His Cross.

These, loving themselves very much, seek in Him their own comfort and satisfaction, and not His sufferings and death for love of Him. I am now speaking of those who think themselves His friends, not of those who live at a great distance from Him; men of learning and of dignity, and others who live in the world, slaves of ambition and of honours—of these, we may say, they know not Christ; and their end, however good, will be full of anguish. I am not speaking of these, but they will be remembered in the Day of Judgment, for 'to them it behoveth us first to speak the word of God,'* as to persons whom He has set up as guides to others, by reason of their learning and exalted rank.

But let me now address myself to the intellect of the spiritual man, and in an especial manner of him whom God in His goodness has raised up to the state of contemplation—for I address myself now particularly to him—and instruct him how he is to direct himself in the way of God by faith, and purify himself from all contrary things, girding up his loins that he may enter on this narrow path of obscure contemplation.

CHAPTER VIII.

No creature, no knowledge, comprehensible by the intellect, can subserve as proximate means of union with God.

BEFORE I discuss the proper and fitting means of union with God, which is faith, it is right that I should show how that no created, or imagined, thing can subserve the intellect as a proper means for its union with God; and how everything which the intellect embraces, if it does but cleave to it, becomes a hindrance instead of help. In this chapter I shall show this in general, and afterwards I shall do so in parti-

* Acts xiii. 46.

cular, going through all sorts of knowledge which the intellect may receive through the senses, both exterior and interior; and then the inconveniences and losses it may sustain through all such knowledge, because it does not proceed in reliance on the proper means, which is Faith.

Proportionate means necessary to gain an end.

It is a principle of philosophy that all means must be proportionate to the end, having a certain fitness, and resemblance to it, such as shall be sufficient for the object in view. For instance, a person wishes to reach a certain city: he must necessarily travel along the road, which is the means, leading to it. Likewise, if you wish to combine and unite together wood and fire, in that case, it is requisite that heat, that is the means, should so dispose the wood, and raise it to such a degree of heat that it shall have a great resemblance and proportion to fire. If you attempt this by any other than the proper means, which is heat, as, for instance, by air, water, or earth, it will be impossible to unite wood with fire. So, therefore, if the intellect is to be united with God, so far as that is possible in this life, it must, of necessity, make use of those means which can effect that union, and which are most like unto God.

What means proportionate to God?

Answer. 1. Not creatures.

But remember, among all creatures, the highest and the lowest, there is not one that comes near unto God, or that bears any likeness to His Substance. For, though it be true, as theologians tell us, that all creatures bear a certain relation to God, and are tokens of His Being, some more, some less, according to the greater or less perfection of their nature, yet there is no essential likeness or communion between them and Him; yea, rather the distance between His Divine Nature and their nature is infinite. Hence, then, it is impossible for the intellect to attain perfectly unto God, by means of created things, whether of heaven or of earth, because there is no proportion of similitude between them. Thus David, speaking of the heavenly host, cries out:

BOOK II.

'There is none among the gods like unto Thee, O Lord.'* The 'gods' are the holy Angels and the souls of the Saints. And again, 'Thy way, O God, is in the holy place; who is the great God like our God?'† That is, the way to Thee, O God, is a holy way, namely, pureness of faith. 'Who is the great God like our God?' Who is the Saint so high in glory, or the Angel so exalted by nature, that can be a way proportionate and sufficient for us to attain unto God? The same Prophet speaking of the things of heaven and earth together, saith, 'The Lord is high and looketh on the low, and the high he knoweth afar off.'‡ That is, God high in His own Being, seeth that the things of the earth are in themselves most vile and low, in comparison with Himself; and 'the high,' the heavenly host, He knoweth to be far distant from Him. No creature, therefore, can be a proportionate means of perfect union with God.

2. Not intellectual perception, (1.) Natural;

So also nothing that the imagination may conceive or the intellect comprehend, in this life, is, or can be a proximate means of union with God. For if we speak of natural knowledge; the intellect is incapable of comprehending anything unless it be presented to it under forms and images by the bodily senses; and these forms of things, as I have already said, cannot serve as means, and no natural acts of the intellect can in any way contribute thereto.

(2.) Or supernatural.

Again, if we speak of supernatural acts—as far as possible in this life—the intellect in its bodily prison has neither the disposition nor the capacity requisite for the reception of the clear knowledge of God. This knowledge is not of this life, for we must either die, or remain without it. Thus God said to Moses, 'Man shall not see me and live.'§ And S. John saith the same, 'No man hath seen God at any time.'‖ S. Paul, too, repeats the words of Isaias, 'Eye hath not seen,

* Ps. lxxxv. 8. † Ibid. lxxvi. 14. ‡ Ibid. cxxxvii. 6.
§ Exod. xxxiii. 20. ‖ S. John i. 18.

CHAP. VIII.

nor ear heard, neither hath it entered into the heart of man.'* This is the reason why Moses at the bush 'durst not behold,'† God being there present. He knew that his intellect could not proportionately contemplate God, though this sprung from the deep sense he had of God. Elias, our father, covered his face on the mountain, in the presence of God.‡ By that action he taught us that he made his intellect blind, not venturing to apply an instrument so vile to a matter so high; and that he perceived clearly, that however much he saw or understood, all would be most unlike unto God, and far distant from Him.

Quis sicut Deus?

No knowledge, therefore, and no understanding in this mortal life can serve as proximate means of this high union of the love of God. All that the intellect may comprehend; all that the will may be satisfied with; and all that the imagination may conceive, is most unlike unto God, and most disproportionate to Him. This truth is admirably expressed by the Prophet: 'To whom then have you likened God? or what image will you make for Him? Hath the workman cast a graven statue? or hath the goldsmith formed it with gold, or the silversmith with plates of silver?'§ The workman is the intellect, which fashions our knowledge, and cleanses it from the iron of sensitive impressions and fancy. The goldsmith is the will, which is capable of receiving the forms and figures of pleasure caused by the gold of love wherewith it loves. The silversmith which cannot represent God with plates of silver, is the memory with the imagination, the notions and conceptions of which are well described as plates of silver. The Prophet then says, in other words: The intellect, by speculation, cannot comprehend anything which is like unto God; no delight or satisfaction of the will can resemble that which is God; nor can the memory furnish

* 1 Cor. ii. 9; Is. lxiv. 4.
† Acts vii. 32; Ex. iii. 6.
‡ 3 Kings xix. 13.
§ Is. xl. 18, 19.

BOOK II.

the imagination with any notions or images to represent Him. It is evident, then, from this that the intellect cannot be immediately directed in the way of God by any knowledge such as this, and that, if it is to draw near unto God, it must do so by not understanding rather than by seeking to understand; yea, rather it must be by making itself blind, covering itself with darkness, and not by opening its eyes, that it can attain to the Divine enlightening. Hence it is that Contemplation, by which God enlightens the intellect, is called Mystical Theology, that is, the secret Wisdom of God, because it is a secret even to the intellect which receives it. S. Dionysius calls it a ray of darkness. And the prophet Baruch thus speaks of it: 'The way of wisdom they have not known, neither have they remembered her paths.'* It is therefore clear that the intellect must be blind, as to every path along which it has to travel, in order to be united with God.

3. But the intellect illuminated by Faith.

S. Dionysius.

Aristotle.

Aristotle says, that as the eyes of the bat are with regard to the sun, which wholly blinds them, so is our intellect with regard to the greater Light of God which is to us perfect darkness. He further says, that the more profound and the clearer the things of God are in themselves, the less intelligible and the more obscure they are to us. The Apostle says the same thing, when he teaches us that the deep things of God are not known unto men. I should never end were I to bring forward here all the authorities and reasons which show that, among all created things of which the intellect takes cognisance, there is nothing which can serve as a ladder whereby it may ascend unto God, who is so high. Yea, rather we must acknowledge that all and each of these things, if the intellect will use them as proximate means of union, will prove not only a hindrance,

* Baruch iii. 23.

but the source of many errors and delusions, in the ascent of this mountain.

CHAPTER IX.

Faith is the proximate and proportionate means of the intellect by which the soul may attain to the Divine union of love. Proofs from the Holy Scriptures.

It appears then from what I have written that the intellect, if rightly disposed for the Divine union, must be pure, and empty of all sensible objects, disengaged from all clear intellectual perceptions, interiorly tranquil and at rest, reposing on Faith; for faith is the sole proximate and proportionate means of the soul's union with God, seeing that there is no other alternative, but that God is either seen, or believed in. For as God is infinite, so faith proposes Him as infinite; and as He is Three and One, so faith proposes Him to us as Three and One. And thus by this means alone, that is faith, God manifests Himself to the soul in the Divine light, which surpasses all understanding, and therefore the greater the faith of the soul the more is that soul united to God. This is the meaning of S. Paul when he said, 'He that cometh to God must believe that He is.'* Such an one must walk by faith, with his understanding in darkness, and in the obscurity of faith only; for in this darkness God unites Himself to the intellect, being Himself hidden beneath it, as it is written: 'Darkness was under His feet, and He ascended upon the cherubim, and He flew upon the wings of the winds. And He made darkness His covert, His pavilion round about Him, dark waters in the clouds of the air.'† The darkness 'under His feet,' serving for 'His covert' and 'His pavilion,' and 'the dark waters,' signify the obscurity of faith, which

* Hebr. xi. 6.

† Ps. xvii. 10—12.

BOOK II.

conceals Him. His 'ascending on the cherubim,' and His flying 'on the wings of the winds,' signify that He transcends all understanding. The 'cherubim' mean those who understand or contemplate; the 'wings of the winds' are the sublime and lofty notions or conceptions of the mind, above which His Divine Being is, and which no man can ever comprehend.

In this life the intellect can know God only in the obscurity of Faith. Illustrated by the history of Solomon,

This truth is shadowed forth in the Holy Scriptures, where we read that, when Solomon had finished the Temple, God came down in a cloud, which filled it, so that the people could not see. 'Then Solomon said: The Lord said that He would dwell in a cloud.'* Moses also, on the mount, saw a cloud wherein God was hidden.† And at all times, when God communicated with men, He appeared through a cloud. We read in the Book of Job, that God spoke out of the darkened air: 'The Lord answered Job out of a whirlwind.'‡ These clouds signify the obscurity of faith, in which God is hidden when He communicates Himself to the soul. This will be removed at that time to which S. Paul referred when he said, 'When that which is perfect is come, that which is in part shall be done away;'§ when 'that which is in part,' the obscurity of faith, shall be done away, and when 'that which is perfect,' the Divine light, shall come.

Moses, Job,

Gideon.

This is prefigured in the army of Gideon: the soldiers had lamps in their hands, which they saw not, because they were 'within the pitchers.' But when they had broken the pitchers the lamps gave light. Gideon 'gave them trumpets in their hands, and empty pitchers, and lamps within the pitchers.'‖ So faith, of which these pitchers were a figure, contains the Divine light, that is, the Truth which God is; and at the end of this mortal life, when the work of faith is

* 3 Kings viii. 10—12. † Exod. xix. 9. ‡ Job xxxviii. 1; xl. 1.
§ 1 Cor. xiii. 10. ‖ Judg. vii. 16.

over, and the pitchers are broken, the Light and Glory of God will then shine forth. CHAP. IX.

It is therefore plain that the soul, which would in this life be united with God and commune immediately with Him, must unite itself to Him in the cloud where, according to Solomon, He has promised to dwell; and in the obscure air, wherein He was pleased to reveal His secrets to Job; and take up the pitchers of Gideon, that it may hold in its hands, in the acts of the will, that light which is the union of love—though in the obscurity of faith—so that, as soon as the pitcher of life be broken, it may see God face to face in glory.

It remains for me now to describe particularly those notions and apprehensions which the intellect admits; the hindrance and the injury they may inflict upon us in the way of faith; and how the soul must be disposed with respect to them, so that they may be profitable rather than hurtful, both those which proceed from the sense as well as those which proceed from the spirit.

CHAPTER X.

The divisions of the apprehensions and acts of the intellect.

Two kinds of knowledge; I. Natural: 1. Senses. 2. Reflection. II. Supernatural.

In order to describe specially the profit and the loss, which the notions and apprehensions of the intellect occasion in the soul with respect to Faith, the means of this Divine union, it is necessary to distinguish here between all these apprehensions, natural and supernatural, so that the intellect may be directed with greater accuracy into the night and obscurity of faith. This I shall do with the utmost brevity possible.

There are two ways by which these notions and intelligent

acts enter into the understanding: one is natural, the other supernatural. The first includes all the means by which the intellect receives knowledge, whether through the channel of the bodily senses, or by reflection. The second comprises all that is beyond the natural powers and capacity of the intellect. Some supernatural knowledge is corporeal, and some spiritual. The former is of two kinds: one of them enters the intellect through the exterior bodily senses; and the other through the interior bodily senses, comprehending all that the imagination may grasp, form, and conceive. The spiritual supernatural knowledge is also of two kinds; one distinct and special; the other confused, obscure, and general. The first kind comprises four particular apprehensions, communicated to the mind without the intervention of any one of the bodily senses. These are visions, revelations, interior voices, and spiritual impressions. The second kind, which is obscure and general, has but one form, that of contemplation, which is the work of faith. The soul is to be led into this by directing it thereto through all the rest. I shall begin my instructions with the first of these, showing how the soul is to be detached from them.

Supernatural knowledge divided into, 1. Corporeal. 2. Spiritual. Corporeal into (1) Sensations. (2.) Mental images. Spiritual into (1) Distinct. α. Visions. β. Revelations. γ. Interior voices. δ. Impressions. (2) Obscure; i. e. The Contemplation of Faith.

CHAPTER XI.

Of the hurt and hindrance resulting from intellectual apprehensions supernaturally produced through the instrumentality of the exterior senses. How the soul is to be guided under such circumstances.

First source of supernatural corporeal knowledge,—sensitive perception.

THE first notions, mentioned in the foregoing chapter, are those which relate to the intellect in the order of nature. I shall not speak of them now, because I have discussed them in the first book, while showing how the soul is to be led into the night of sense, where I have given fitting directions concerning them. And therefore the subject of the present chapter will be those notions and apprehensions which relate to the intellect solely in the supernatural order, in the way of the outward bodily senses of seeing, hearing, tasting, smelling, and touching. With respect to these, spiritual men are occasionally liable to representations and objects, set before them in a supernatural way. They sometimes see the forms and figures of those of another life, Saints, or Angels good and evil, or certain extraordinary lights and brightness. They hear strange words, sometimes seeing those who utter them, and sometimes not. They have a sensible perception at times of most sweet odours, without knowing whence they proceed. Their sense of taste is also deliciously affected; and that of the touch so sweetly caressed at times that the bones and the marrow exult and rejoice, bathed, as it were, in joy. This delight is like to that which we call the Union of the Spirit, flowing from Him through all the senses of simple souls. And this sensible sweetness is wont to affect spiritual persons, because of that sensible devotion, more or less, which they feel, every one in his own measure.

Supernatural phænomena of, Sight. Hearing. Smell. Taste, and touch.

Still, though the bodily senses may be thus affected in the way of God, we must never rely on these emotions, nor encourage them; yea, rather we must fly from them, without examining whether they be good or evil. For, inasmuch as they are exterior and in the body, there is the less certainty of their being from God. It is more natural that God should communicate Himself through the spirit — wherein there is greater security and profit for the soul — than through the senses, wherein there is usually much danger and delusion, because the bodily sense decides upon, and judges, spiritual things, thinking them to be what itself feels them to be, when in reality they are as different as body and soul, sensuality and reason. The bodily sense is as ignorant of spiritual things, as a beast of the field is of the

Reasons for repelling them.

1. Less likelihood of their being from God.

BOOK II.

things of reason. He who makes much of these emotions mistakes his way, and exposes himself to the great danger

2. Danger of self-deception.

of delusions; and, at least, places a great obstacle on his road to true spirituality. For all these bodily sensations bear no proportion to spiritual things.

3. Probability of their being from the devil.

There is always ground for fear that these proceed from the devil rather than from God; for the devil has more influence in that which is exterior and corporeal, and can more easily deceive us therein than in what is more interior. And these bodily forms and objects, the more exterior they are, the less do they profit the interior spiritual man, by reason of the great distance and disproportion subsisting between the corporeal and the spiritual. For, although these things communicate some spirituality, as is always the case when they proceed from God, yet it is much less than it would have been, had they been more spiritual and interior; and thus they become more easily and readily occasions of error, presumption, and vanity. As they are so palpable and so material they excite the senses greatly, and the soul is led to consider them the more

4. Loss of Faith as a guide.

important, the more they are felt. It runs after them and abandons the secure guidance of Faith, thinking that the light they give is a guide and means to that which it desires, union with God. Thus the soul, the more it makes of such things, the more it strays from the perfect way and means, that is, Faith. Besides, when the soul perceives itself subject to these extraordinary visitations, self-esteem very frequently enters in, and it thinks itself to be something in the eyes of God, which is contrary to humility. The devil also knows

5. Subtlety of Pride.

too well how to insinuate into the soul a secret, and sometimes an open, self-satisfaction. For this end he frequently presents to the eyes the forms of Saints, and most beautiful lights; he causes voices well dissembled to strike the ear, and delicious odours the smell; he produces sweetness in the mouth, and thrills of pleasure in the sense of touch;

and all to make us long for such things that he may lead us astray into many evils.

For this reason, then, we must always reject and disregard these representations and sensations. For even if some of them were from God, no wrong is offered to Him, because the effect and fruit, which He desires to bring forth in the soul, is not the less accomplished when that soul rejects them and seeks them not. The reason is this: all corporeal visions or emotions of the senses — the same is true of all other interior communications — if from God, effect their chief object at the moment of their presence, before the soul has time to deliberate whether it shall entertain or reject them. For as God begins them in a supernatural way without effort on the part of the soul, and without respect to any capacity for them; so the effect, which He desires to produce by means of them, is wrought without reference to any effort or capacity of the soul; for it is perfected and brought to pass in the spirit passively without its free consent, and therefore does not depend on the will in any way. It is as if a person quite naked came into contact with fire: it matters not whether he wills to be burned or not, the fire necessarily performs its own proper functions.

No wrong thereby done to God; or to the soul.

This is the case with good visions and apparitions: even if the soul wills it not, they produce their effects, chiefly and specially in the soul rather than in the body. So also the visions, which are the work of the devil — without the consent of the soul — bring forth trouble or dryness of spirit, vanity, or presumption, although they are not so effectual for evil, as the visions of God are for good. Diabolic visions do not proceed beyond the primary motions, neither can they influence the will, provided it seeks them not; and the disquiet which they occasion does not last long, unless the soul be negligent and irresolute when they occur. But the visions of God penetrate into the inmost parts of the soul,

BOOK II.

Without detachment even from Divine favours, the soul weakens its Faith;

and produce their effects, a quickened zeal and overpowering joy, which enable and dispose it to assent freely and lovingly to good. Still, even when these outward visions and impressions come from God, if the soul cleaves to them and accepts them readily, six inconveniences follow.

1. The perfect guidance of faith is lessened; because the experience of sense derogates from faith; for faith, as I have said, surpasseth all sense, and thus the soul, by not closing its eyes against every object of sense, turns away from the means of union with God.

refers the gifts to the Giver;

2. They are hindrances in the way of the spirit, if they are not rejected; for the soul rests upon them, and does not regard the invisible. This, too, was one of those causes, of which our Lord spoke to His disciples, that it was expedient for them that He should go away that the Spirit might come. Neither did He permit Mary Magdalene to kiss His feet, after His resurrection, that she, as well as the disciples in the former case, might be the more grounded in faith.

Becomes selfish;

3. The soul clings selfishly to them, and does not advance to true resignation and detachment of spirit.

Loses their fruit;

4. The soul loses the good effect of them and the interior spirit they produce, because it has regard to the sensible part of them, which is the least important. Thus the spirit, which is the proper fruit, is not so abundantly received; because it is most deeply impressed in the soul when we deny ourselves in all things of sense, as they are most at variance with the pure spirit.

And the gifts themselves;

5. The soul loses the gifts of God, because it assumes them for its own, and does not profit rightly by them. To assume them for our own and not to profit by them, is to seek them and to occupy ourselves with them. God does not send them for this end; neither should we easily believe that they come from God.

6. The ready admission of them opens the door to the devil, that he may deceive us by others like them; he knows well how to dissemble and disguise his own visions so that they shall seem to be good; for Satan transformeth himself 'into an angel of light.'* I shall treat this question hereafter, by the grace of God, when I come to describe spiritual gluttony in the first book of the Obscure Night.

And is easily deceived by the devil.

It is therefore expedient that the soul should close its eyes and reject them, come they whence they may. For unless we do so we shall make way for those of the devil, and give him so much power over us, that not only will the evil visions come in the place of those which are Divine, but, when the latter cease, they will also become so numerous, that the devil will have every influence over us, and God none, as it has happened to many incautious and ignorant souls. They so relied on their visions, that many of them had great difficulty in returning to God in pureness of faith, and many never returned at all; so widely and so deeply had the roots of the devil grown within them. For this reason it is good to shut our eyes against these visions and to fear them all. By withdrawing from the evil visions we escape the delusions of the devil; and by withdrawing from those which are good we put no obstacles in the way of faith, and the spirit still derives fruit from them.

When the soul gives admission readily to these visions God withholds them, because it cleaves to them and does not duly profit by them; the devil also insinuates himself and multiplies his own visions, because the soul makes room for them. But when the soul is resigned and not attached to such visions the devil retires, seeing that he cannot injure us then; and, on the other hand, God multiplies His graces in the humble and detached soul, placing it over many

* 2 Cor. xi. 14.

BOOK II.

things, like the good and faithful servant to whom it is said, 'Because thou hast been faithful over a few things, I will place thee over many things.'* The soul that is faithful amid these visitations God will not leave, till He shall raise it up, step by step, to the Divine union and transformation. This is the way our Lord tests and elevates the soul: He visits it first in the senses according to its capacity; so that, having conducted itself then as it ought to do, receiving in all temperance these first morsels for its own strength and nourishment, He may admit it to the better and more abundant feast. If the soul shall overcome the devil in the first combat it shall then pass on to the second; and if it shall be victorious there also, it shall then pass on to the third; and then through the seven mansions, the seven degrees of love, until the Bridegroom shall bring it to 'the cellar of wine'† of perfect Charity.

The spiritual combat.

Blessed is that soul which knoweth how to fight against the beast with seven heads,‡ which he opposes to the seven degrees of love. The beast fighteth against each of these degrees with his seven heads; and with each one of them against the soul in all the seven mansions, wherein the soul is tried and gains each degree of the love of God. And, beyond all doubt, if the soul shall faithfully fight against every one of these heads and obtain the victory, it will deserve to pass on from one degree to another, or from one mansion to the next, until it shall have reached the highest, having destroyed the seven heads by which the beast waged so furious a war against it. So fearful is this war that the Apostle says, 'It was given unto him to make war with the Saints and to overcome them,'§ arraying his weapons and munitions of war over against each of these degrees of love

* S. Matth. xxv. 21. † Cant. ii. 4.
‡ Apoc. xiii. 1. § Ibid. 7.

Many, alas, there are who enter the battle of the spiritual life against the beast, who do not cut off even the first head, by self-denial in the sensible objects of this world. Others, more successful, cut off the first, but not the second—the visions of sense—of which I am speaking. But what is more painful still is, that some who, having cut off not only the first and second, but the third head also, which relates to the interior senses and the passage from the state of meditation into a higher one, are overcome by the beast, when they should enter into the purity of the spirit. Then it is that he returns to the assault with his heads restored to life, and renders 'their latter state worse than the first,' for he bringeth with him 'seven other spirits more wicked than himself.'* The spiritual man must therefore reject all these apprehensions, together with the corporeal satisfactions to which the exterior senses are liable, if he will destroy the first and second head of this beast, by entering into the first and second mansion of love by a living faith, not laying hold of, nor being embarrassed by, the impressions of the exterior senses; for these present the greatest impediment to the spiritual night of Faith.

It is now clear that these visions and apprehensions of sense cannot be the means of the Divine union, for they bear no proportion to God. And this is one of the reasons why Christ would not suffer Mary Magdalene to touch Him, and yet allowed it, as the better and more perfect course, in S. Thomas. The devil greatly rejoices when a soul seeks after revelations and is ready to accept them; for such conduct furnishes him with many opportunities of insinuating delusions, and derogating from faith as much as he possibly can; for such a soul becomes rough and rude, and falls frequently into many temptations and unseemly habits.

* S. Luke xi. 26.

BOOK II.

I have dwelt at some length on these exterior communications in order to throw greater light on the others, which I have soon to discuss. But I have so much to say on this matter that it appears impossible to have done with it. I might sum up what I have said in this single sentence; that these visions should never be admitted, unless in certain rare instances, after examination by a learned, spiritual, and experienced director, and even then there must be no desire for them.

Conclusion.

CHAPTER XII.

Of natural and imaginary apprehensions. Their nature. They cannot be proportionate means of union. The evil results of not knowing how to detach oneself from them in time.

Second source of natural knowledge,—Reflection on mental images.

BEFORE discussing the imaginary visions which are wont to be represented supernaturally to the interior sense, the imagination and the fancy, it is expedient that I should now —to proceed orderly—speak of the natural apprehensions incident to the same interior bodily sense. I adopt this course that we may advance from the less to the greater—from that which is more outward to that which is more inward—to that most interior recollection wherein the soul is united unto God. This too is the course I have hitherto observed. In the first place, I treated of the detachment of the soul from the natural apprehensions of exterior objects, and, consequently, from the natural powers of the desires. This I did in the first book, while speaking of the night of sense. I then treated in detail of detachment from exterior supernatural apprehensions, to which the exterior senses are liable — as in the preceding chapter — so that I may guide the steps of the soul into the night of the spirit in this second book.

Now the first subject of discussion is the interior bodily

sense, the imagination and fancy, out of which we must cast all imaginary forms and apprehensions naturally incident thereto, and show how impossible it is for the soul to attain to union with God until their operations shall have ceased, because they can never be the proper and proximate means of union.

Imagination not a proximate, but a remote means of union with God.

The senses of which I am now speaking particularly are two, bodily and interior, called imagination and fancy, which in their order subserve each other. In the one there is something of reasoning, though imperfect aud in an imperfect way; the other, the imagination, forms the image. For our purpose the discussion of either is equivalent to that of the other, and therefore when I do not mention them both let it be understood that what is said of the one is applicable to the other also, and that I am speaking indifferently of both, without distinguishing between them.

Its two sources: 1. Natural. 2. Supernatural.

All, therefore, that the senses perceive and fashion are called imaginations and fancies—that is, forms represented to the senses in bodily shape and likeness. These may take place in two ways—supernaturally when, without the action of the senses, they may and do become present passively before them. These are imaginary visions wrought supernaturally, of which I shall speak hereafter. The other way is natural, when the senses actively effect them by their own operation, through forms, figures, and images. These two powers serve for meditation, which is a discursive act by means of imagery, forms, and figures, wrought and fashioned in the senses. We picture to ourselves Christ on the cross, or bound to the pillar, or God sitting on His Throne in great majesty. So also we imagine glory as a most beautiful light, and represent before ourselves any other object, human or Divine, of which the faculty of imagination is capable.

Meditation,—what.

All these imaginations and apprehensions are to be emptied out of the soul, which must remain in darkness so far as it

BOOK II.

concerns the senses, in order that we may attain to the Divine union, because they bear no proportion to the proximate means of union with God; as neither do corporeal things, the objects of the five exterior senses.

Imagination can only recombine sensitive perceptions.

The reason is, that nothing enters the imagination but through the exterior senses. The eye must have seen, or the ear must have heard, or the other senses must first have become cognisant of all that is in it. Or at the utmost, we can only form pictures of what we have seen, heard, or felt; and these forms are not more excellent than what the imagination has received through the senses. Though we picture in our imagination palaces of pearls and mountains of gold, because we have seen gold and pearls, yet after all this is nothing more than one piece of gold or a single pearl, even though the imagination ranges them in a certain order. And as all created things cannot have any proportion with the Being of God, it follows that all the conceptions of the imagination, which must resemble them, cannot serve as proximate means of union with Him. Those persons, therefore, who represent God to their minds under any sort of figure, or as a great fire or light, or anything else, thinking Him to be like them, are very far from drawing near unto Him. For though such considerations, forms, and methods of meditation may be necessary for beginners, in order to inflame and fill their souls with love, through the instrumentality of sense, as I shall explain hereafter—and though they may serve as remote means of union, through which souls must usually pass to the goal and resting-place of spiritual repose—still they must so make use of them as to pass beyond them, and not dwell upon them for ever.

No image or picture of God.

If we dwell upon them we shall never reach the goal, which is not like the remote means, neither has it any proximate relation with them. The steps of a ladder have no proximate relation with the goal and place to which we ascend by it, towards which they are but means; so if he who climbs does not leave behind all the steps so that none remain, or if he rests upon one of them, he will never ascend to the summit, to the peaceful resting of the goal. The soul, therefore, that will ascend in this life to the Supreme Good and Rest must pass beyond all these steps of considerations, forms, and notions, because they bear no likeness or proportion to the end, which is God, towards which it tends. 'We must not suppose,' saith the Apostle, 'the Divinity to be like unto gold, or silver, or stone, the graving of art and device of man.'*

Imagination useful for beginners.

Great, therefore, is the mistake of those spiritual persons who, having laboured to draw near unto God by means of imagery, forms, and meditations, such as become beginners—while God would attract them to more spiritual, interior, and unseen good, by depriving them of the sweetness of discursive meditation—do not accept the guidance, neither venture nor know how to detach themselves from these palpable methods to which they have been accustomed. They retain these methods still, seeking to advance by them and by meditation upon exterior forms, as before, thinking that it must be so always. They take great pains in the matter, but find very little sweetness or none—yea, rather dryness, weariness, and disquiet of soul increase and grow the more they search after the sweetness they had before—it being now impossible for them to have it as they had it at first. The soul has no more pleasure in its first food, which was of the senses, but requires another of greater delicacy, interior, and less cognisable by the senses, consisting, not in the travail of the imagination, but in the repose of the soul, and in that quietness thereof, which is more spiritual. The more the soul advances in spirituality, the more it ceases from the operations of its faculties on particular objects; for it then gives itself up to

* Acts xvii. 29.

one sole, pure, and general act; and so its powers cease from the practice of that method by which they once travelled towards the point to which the soul was tending; as the feet cease from movement and are at rest when the journey is over; for if all were movement, there would be no goal to reach, and if all things are means, where or when shall we enjoy the end?

Peace found only in following the guidance of the Holy Spirit.

How sad it is to see men who, when the soul would be at peace in the repose of interior quiet, where God fills it with refreshment and peace, disturb it, draw it away to outward things, compel it to travel again along the road it had passed, and to abandon the goal, where it reposes, for the sake of the means and considerations which guided it to its rest. This is not effected without loathing and repugnance on the part of the soul, which would repose in this tranquillity as in its proper place—as it happens to him who after toilsome labour has attained repose; for when he is made to return to his work he feels it painfully. And as they do not understand the secret of their new condition, they imagine themselves to be idle, doing nothing; and so do not suffer themselves to be at rest, but strive to reproduce their former reflections and discursive acts. They are therefore full of dryness and trouble, because they seek there for sweetness where there is no longer sweetness for them. To them the proverb applies, 'the more it freezes the more it binds;' the more obstinately they cling to this way the worse it becomes for them, because they lead their soul further away from spiritual peace. This is to abandon what is greatest for what is least, to travel backwards along the road they came, and do again what they have done before.

To these my counsel is—learn to abide with attention in loving waiting upon God in the state of quiet; give no heed to your imagination, nor to its operations, for now, as I have said, the powers of the soul are at rest, and are not exercised, except in the sweet and pure waiting of love. If at times they are excited, it is not violently, nor with meditation elaborately prepared, but by the sweetness of love, more under the influence of God than by the ability of the soul, as I shall hereafter clearly explain.

Let this, for the present, suffice to show how necessary it is for those who would make progress, to abandon these methods and ways of the imagination at the proper time, when their growth, in that state wherein they are, requires it. And that we may know when this time is come, I shall describe certain signs which the spiritual man is to observe, that he may thereby recognise the time when he may freely avail himself of the goal already mentioned, and leave behind him all intellectual reflections and all the acts of the imagination.

CHAPTER XIII.

The signs to be observed by the spiritual man that he may know when to withdraw the intellect from imaginary forms and discursive meditations.

When should Meditation give place to Contemplation?

To avoid confusion in my teaching, I find it necessary in this chapter to explain when the spiritual man should abstain from the meditation which rests on imaginary forms and mental representations, in order that he may not abstain from it sooner or later than the Spirit calls him. For as it is necessary to abstain from it at the proper time, in order to draw near unto God, that we may not be hindered by it; so also must we not cease from it before the time, lest we go backwards: for though all that the powers of the soul may apprehend cannot be proximate means of union for those who have made some spiritual progress, still they serve, as remote means, to dispose and habituate the minds of beginners to that which is spiritual by means of the senses, and to clear the way of all other low forms and images,

BOOK II.

Answer,— By observing three signs.

temporal, worldly, and natural. With this view I will mention here certain signs and evidences, three in number, by observing which the spiritual man may know whether the time is come for him to cease from meditation or not.

1. Dryness of spirit.

1. When he finds that he cannot meditate nor exert his imagination, nor derive any satisfaction from it, as he was wont to do—when he finds dryness there, where he was accustomed to fix the senses and draw forth sweetness—then the time is come. But while he finds sweetness, and is able to meditate as usual, let him not cease therefrom, except when his soul is in peace, of which I shall speak when describing the third sign.

2. No play of Imagination.

2. When he sees that he has no inclination to fix the imagination or the senses on particular objects, exterior or interior. I do not mean when the imagination neither comes nor goes—for it is disorderly even in the most complete self-recollection—but only when the soul derives no pleasure from tying it down deliberately to other matters.

3. Desire of repose in God.

3. The third sign is the most certain of the three, namely, when the soul delights to be alone, waiting lovingly on God, without any particular considerations, in interior peace, quiet, and repose, when the acts and exercises of the intellect, memory, and will, at least discursively—which is the going from one subject to another—have ceased; nothing remaining except that knowledge and attention, general and loving, of which I have spoken, without the particular perception of aught else.

Cautions.

The spiritual man must have observed these three signs together, at least, before he can venture with safety to abandon the state of meditation for that of the way of spiritual contemplation. It is not enough for him to observe the first without the second, for it may happen that he cannot meditate on the things of God, as before, because of distractions and the absence of due preparation. He must therefore have regard to the second sign, and see whether he has no inclination or desire to think of other things. For when this inability to fix the imagination and the senses on the things of God proceeds from distraction or lukewarmness, the soul readily inclines to other matters, and these lead it away from God.

Physical causes may blunt our faculties,

Neither is it sufficient to have observed the first and second sign if we do not also discern the third. For though we cannot meditate or think on the things of God, and have no pleasure either in dwelling upon anything else; yet this may be the effect of melancholy or some other oppression of the brain or the heart, which is wont to produce a certain suspension of our faculties, so that we think upon nothing, nor desire to do so, nor have any inclination thereto, but rather remain in a kind of soothing astonishment. By way of defence against this, we must be sure of the third sign, which is a loving knowledge and attention in peace, as I have said. It is, however, true that in the commencement of this estate this loving knowledge is, as it were, imperceptible, because it is then wont to be, in the first place, most subtile and delicate, and as it were, unfelt; and because, in the second place, the soul, having been accustomed to meditation, which is more cognisable by sense, does not perceive, and, as it were, does not feel this new condition, not subject to sense, and which is purely spiritual.

and produce a deceitful softness.

This is the case especially when, through not understanding his condition, the spiritual man will not allow himself to rest therein, but will strive after that which is cognisable by sense. This striving, notwithstanding the abundance of loving interior peace, disturbs him in the consciousness and enjoyment of it. But the more the soul is disposed for this tranquillity, the more will it grow therein continually; and the more conscious it will be of this general loving knowledge of God, which is sweeter to it than all besides,

BOOK II.

because it brings with it peace and rest, sweetness and delight without trouble. To make this matter more clear, I shall explain in the following chapter why these signs are necessary for the direction of the soul.

CHAPTER XIV.

The fitness of these signs. The necessity of observing them for spiritual progress.

Two reasons for the first sign.

As to the first sign, it is to be observed that there are two reasons, comprised as it were in one, why the spiritual man — if he is to enter on the life of the spirit, which is that of contemplation — must abandon the way of the imagination and sensible meditation, when he has no pleasure in it and is no longer able to make his wonted discourse. The first is, that all the spiritual good to be found, by way of meditation in the things of God, has been already in a manner bestowed upon him. This is shown by the fact that he cannot now make his former meditations and reflections, and that he has no pleasure or satisfaction therein as he had before, because he had not then attained to the spiritual life. And, in general, whenever the soul receives a fresh spiritual grace it receives it with pleasure, at least in spirit, in the means whereby it comes, and it profits by it; otherwise its profiting would be miraculous. This is in accordance with the philosophical saying, What is palatable nourishes; and also with the words of Job, 'Can an unsavoury thing be eaten that is not seasoned with salt?'* The reason, then, why meditation is no longer possible, is the little pleasure and profit which the mind now derives from it.

1. No pleasure, no profit.

2. End attained, the means cease.

The second reason is this: the soul has now attained substantially and habitually to the spirit of meditation. For the end of meditation and reflection on the things of God

* Job vi. 6.

is to elicit the knowledge and the love of Him. Each time the soul elicits this, it is an act, and as acts often repeated produce habits, so, many acts of loving knowledge continuously elicited by the soul, beget the habit thereof in the course of time. God is wont at times to effect this without these acts of meditation — at least without many of them — leading souls at once into the state of contemplation. Thus, what the soul elicited before, at intervals, by dint of meditation, in particular acts of knowledge, is now by practice converted into the habit and substance of knowledge, loving, general, not distinct or particular, as before. And, therefore, such a soul betaking itself to prayer — like a man with water before him — drinks sweetly without effort, without the necessity of drawing it through the channel of previous reflections, forms, and figures. And the moment such a soul places itself in the presence of God, it elicits an act of knowledge, confused, loving, peaceful, and tranquil, wherein it drinks in wisdom, love, and sweetness.

Meditation painful,—why.

This is the reason why the soul is troubled and disgusted when compelled, in this state, to make meditations and to labour after particular acts of knowledge. Its condition, then, is like that of an infant at the breast, withdrawn from it while it was sucking it, and bidden to procure its nourishment by efforts of its own; or of one who, having removed the rind, is tasting the fruit it contained, and is bidden to cease therefrom and to peel away the rind already removed, and then finds no rind and loses the fruit he had in his hand — like one who loses a prize already in his power. This is the case with many who have begun to enter upon this state. They think that the whole matter consists in discursive meditations, in the understanding of particulars by means of forms and images, which are the rind of the spiritual life. When they do not find these in that loving and substantial quiet, where the soul desires to dwell, and where nothing distinct reaches the intellect, they suppose themselves to be going astray, wasting their time, and so go in quest of the rind of images and discursive meditation, not now to be found, because long ago taken away. Thus they do not enjoy the substance, neither can they meditate; and so they vex themselves, thinking that they are going backwards, and that they are lost. This is certainly true, but not in the way they mean: they are lost to their own sense, to their first perceptions and understanding, which is nothing else but to gain the spiritual life which is given unto them; for the less they understand, the further do they enter into the night of the spirit, through which they have to pass in order to be united with God, in a way that surpasses all understanding.

Second sign.

There is but little for me to say of the second sign, because it is evident that the soul has necessarily no pleasure at that time in other imaginary representations, those of the world, seeing that it has none, for the reasons already given, in those which are most befitting it, as those of the things of God. Only, as I have said before, the imaginative faculty, in this state of recollection, is wont to come, and go, and vary, but without the consent of the soul and without giving it any pleasure; yea, rather, the soul is then afflicted thereby, because of the interruption of its peace and sweetness.

Involuntary distractions painful.

Third sign.

Nor do I think it necessary here to speak at all of the fitness and necessity of the third sign, whereby we may discern when we are to cease from meditation. That sign is a knowledge of, and attention to, God, general and loving. I have explained this in some degree while speaking of the first sign; and I have to treat of it again directly, when I speak of that general, confused knowledge, after discussing the particular apprehensions of the intellect. But I propose now to mention one reason only, which will make it clear why this attention, or general loving knowledge of God, is necessary, when the spiritual man passes from the state of meditation to that of contemplation.

Without Meditation or Contemplation, the soul idle.

That reason is this: if the soul were without this knowledge or sense of God's presence at that time, the result would be that it would have nothing, and do nothing; for having ceased from meditation, wherein the soul acts discursively, by means of its intellectual faculties — and contemplation not yet attained to, which is that general knowledge, wherein the spiritual powers of the soul, memory, intellect, and will, are exerted, and united in this knowledge, which is as it were effected and received in them — every act of the worship of God must of necessity be wanting; for the soul cannot act at all, nor receive impressions, nor persevere in the work it has before it, but by the action of its intellectual and spiritual faculties. It is through the intellectual faculties that the soul reflects, searches out, and effects the knowledge of things; and through the spiritual faculties that it rejoices in the knowledge thus attained without further labour, search, or reflection. The difference between these two conditions of the soul is like the difference between working, and the enjoyment of the fruit of our work; between receiving a gift, and profiting by it; between the toil of travelling, and the rest at our journey's end; between the preparation of our food, and the eating or enjoyment of it. If the soul be idle, not occupied, either with its intellectual faculties in meditation and reflection, or with its spiritual faculties in contemplation and pure knowledge, it is impossible to say that it is occupied at all. This knowledge is therefore necessary for the abandonment of the way of meditation and reflection.

Contemplation,—what.

But it is to be remembered that this general knowledge, of which I am speaking, is at times so subtile and delicate — particularly when most pure, simple, perfect, spiritual, and interior — that the soul, though in the practice thereof, is not observant or conscious of it. This is the case when that

BOOK. II.

The soul in pure Contemplation,

1. Unconscious of particular thoughts.

knowledge is most pure, clear, and simple, which it is when it enters into a soul most pure and detached from all other acts of knowledge and special perceptions, to which the intellect or the sense may cling. Such a soul, because freed from all those things which were actually and habitually objects of the intellect or of the sense, is not aware of them, because the accustomed objects of sense have failed it. This is the reason why this knowledge, when most pure, perfect, and simple, is the less perceived by the intellect, and the more obscure. On the other hand, when this knowledge is less pure and simple the more clear and the more important it seems to the intellect; because it is mixed up with, clothed in, or involved in, certain intelligible forms, of which the intellect most easily takes cognisance, to its hurt.

Illustrated by the analogy of light.

The following comparison will make this more intelligible. When the rays of the sun penetrate through a crevice into a dark room, the atmosphere of which is full of atoms and particles of dust, they are then more palpable, and more visible to the eye; and yet those rays are then less pure, simple, and perfect, because mixed up with so much impurity: also, when they are most pure and most free from dust, the less are they cognisable by the material eye; and the more pure they are the less are they seen and apprehended. If, again, these rays were altogether pure, clear of every atom, and of the minutest particle of dust, they would be utterly invisible, by reason of the absence of all objects whereon the eye could rest; for pure and simple light is not properly the object of vision, but the means whereby we discern visible things; and so, if there be no visible objects present to reflect the light, nothing can be seen. Hence, then, a ray of light entering in by one crevice and going out by another, unaffected by any material object, cannot be seen; and yet that ray is more pure and clear than when it is most distinctly seen through being mixed up with visible objects.

Such are the conditions of the spiritual light with regard to the eye of the soul, which is the intellect, against which this knowledge and supernatural light strikes so purely and so plainly. So clear is it of all intelligible forms, which are the adequate objects of the intellect, that the intellect is not conscious of its presence. Sometimes, indeed—when it is most pure—it creates darkness, because it withdraws the intellect from its accustomed lights, forms, and fantasies, and then the darkness becomes palpable and visible.

2. Unconscious of time, and place.

At other times, also, the Divine Light strikes the soul with such force that the darkness is unfelt and the light unheeded; the soul seems unconscious of all it knows, and is therefore lost, as it were, in forgetfulness, knowing not where it is, nor what has happened to it, unaware of the lapse of time. It may and does occur that many hours pass while it is in this state of forgetfulness; all seem but a moment when it again returns to itself. The cause of this forgetfulness is the pureness and simplicity of this knowledge. This knowledge, being itself pure and clear, cleanses the soul while it fills it, and purifies it of all the apprehensions and forms of sense and memory through which the soul once acted, and thus brings it to a state of forgetfulness, and unconsciousness of the flight of time. This prayer of the soul, though in reality long, seems to last but for a moment, because it is an act of pure intelligence; for it is that prayer which is said to 'pierce the clouds,'* time being unheeded while it lasts: it pierces the clouds because the soul is then in union with the heavenly Intelligence. This knowledge leaves behind it in the soul, when awake, all the effects it then wrought, without any consciousness on the part of the soul that they were wrought. These effects are the lifting up of the soul to the heavenly Intelligence, the withdrawal and estrangement of it from all things, and from the forms and figures of them.

* Eccles. xxxv. 21.

BOOK II.

Three illustrations from Holy Scripture.

Thus it befell David, who, when he returned to himself, said, 'I have watched, and am become as a sparrow, all alone on the housetop.'* 'Alone' expresses his estrangement and detachment from all things; and the 'housetop' the lifting up of the soul on high. The soul is now, as it were, ignorant of all things, because it knows God only, without knowing how. The Bride also speaks of this ignorance as one of the effects of this sleep or forgetfulness, saying, 'I knew not:'† that is, I knew not how. Though he to whose soul is given this knowledge seems to be doing nothing and to be wholly unoccupied, because the imagination has ceased to act, he still believes that the time has not been lost or uselessly spent: for though the harmonious correspondence of the powers of the soul has ceased, the understanding thereof abides as I say. The Bride in her wisdom answers herself this question, when she says, 'I sleep, and my heart watcheth:'‡ though I sleep in my natural state, and cease from all exertion, my heart watcheth supernaturally, lifted up in supernatural knowledge. A sign by which we may discern whether the soul is occupied in this secret intelligence is, that it has no pleasure in the thought of anything high or low.

God may suspend the faculties of the soul.

Still we are not to suppose that this knowledge necessarily induces this forgetfulness; the reality of it does not depend on this. This forgetfulness occurs when God in a special way suspends the faculties of the soul. This does not often occur, for this knowledge does not always fill the whole soul. It is sufficient for our purpose that the intellect should be abstracted from all particular knowledge, whether temporal or spiritual, and that the will should have no inclination to dwell upon either. This sign serves to show that the soul is in this state of forgetfulness, when this know-

* Ps. ci. 8. † Cant. vi. 11. ‡ Cant. v. 2.

ledge is furnished and communicated to the intellect only. But when it is communicated to the will also, which is almost always the case in a greater or less degree, the soul cannot but see, if it will reflect thereon, that it is occupied by this knowledge; because it is then conscious of the sweetness of love therein, without any particular knowledge or perception of what it loves. This is the reason why this knowledge is called loving and general; for as it communicates itself obscurely to the intellect, so also to the will, infusing therein love and sweetness confusedly, without the soul's knowing distinctly the object of its love. Let this suffice to show how necessary it is for the soul to be occupied by this knowledge, in order that it may leave the way of meditation, and to feel assured, notwithstanding the appearance of doing nothing, that it is well employed, if it observes the signs of which I am speaking. It appears, also, from the illustration drawn from the shining of the sun's rays, full of atoms, that the soul is not to imagine this light to be then most pure, subtile, and clear, when it presents itself to the intellect more palpably and more comprehensibly. For it is certain, according to Aristotle and theologians, that the more pure and sublime the Divine Light is, the more obscure it is to our understanding.

3. Yet not idle, because conscious of God by love.

I have much to say of this Divine Knowledge, both as it is in itself, and in its effects upon contemplatives; but I reserve it for its proper place. The present discussion would not have been so long had it not been requisite that the subject should be left in somewhat less confusion than it is at present, which I must admit to be the case. Over and above the fact that this subject is rarely treated in this way, whether in writing or by word of mouth, because it is in itself strange and obscure, comes also my poor method and little knowledge. I am without confidence in my own capacity to explain it, and therefore grow prolix and wearisome, exceeding the just limits required for the explanation of this division of the subject. I admit that I have done this occasionally on purpose; for a subject that cannot be explained by one view of it may be by another; and also because I consider that I have in this way thrown more light on what is to follow. For this reason, in order to conclude this part of the subject, I think I ought to solve one question concerning the duration of this knowledge, which I propose to do in the following chapter.

CHAPTER XV.

Of the occasional necessity of meditating and exerting the natural faculties on the part of those who begin to enter on the contemplative state.

HERE it may be asked, whether proficients, those whom God has begun to lead into this supernatural knowledge of contemplation, are, in virtue of this commencement, never again to return to the way of meditation, reflections, and natural forms? To this I answer, that it is not to be supposed that those who have begun to have this pure and loving knowledge are never to meditate again or attempt it. For in the beginning of their advancement the habit of this is not so perfect as that they should be able at pleasure to perform the acts of it. Neither are they so far advanced beyond the state of meditation as to be unable to meditate and make their reflections as before, and to find therein something new. Yea, rather, at first, when we see, by the help of these signs, that our soul is not occupied in this quiet, or knowledge, it will be necessary to have recourse to reflections, until we attain to the habit of it in some degree of perfection. Such will be the case when, as often as we apply ourselves to meditation, the soul reposes in this peaceful knowledge,

Meditation,—when to be resumed.

without the power or the inclination to meditate; because, until we arrive at this, sometimes one, sometimes the other, occurs in this time of proficiency in such a way that very often the soul finds itself in this loving or peaceful attendance upon God, with all its faculties in repose; and very often also will find it necessary, for that end, to have recourse to meditation, calmly and with moderation. But when this state is attained to, meditation ceases, and the faculties labour no more; for then we may rather say, that intelligence and sweetness are wrought in the soul, and that it itself abstains from every effort, except only that it attends lovingly upon God, without any desire to feel or see anything further than to be in the hands of God, Who now communicates Himself to the soul, thus passive, as the light of the sun to him whose eyes are open. Only, we must take care, if we wish to receive in pureness and abundance this Divine light, that no other lights of knowledge, or forms, or figures of meditations, of a more palpable kind, intervene, for nothing of this kind bears any resemblance to that serene and clear light. And therefore, if at that time we seek to apprehend and reflect on particular objects, however spiritual they may be, we shall obstruct the pure and limpid light of the Spirit, by interposing these clouds before us, as a man who should place anything before his eyes impedes the vision of things beyond.

They who leave all for God, find all in God.

It appears, then, from all this that the soul, when it shall have purified and emptied itself from all these intelligible forms and images, will then dwell in this pure and simple light, transformed thereto in the state of perfection. This light is ever ready to be communicated to the soul, but does not flow in, because of the forms and veils of the creature which infold and embarrass the soul. Take away these hindrances and coverings, as I shall hereafter explain, and the soul in detachment and poverty of spirit will then, being pure and simple, be transformed in the pure and sincere

BOOK II.

Wisdom of God who is the Son. For then that which is natural having failed, that which is Divine flows supernaturally into the enamoured soul; since God leaves nothing empty that He does not fill.

When the spiritual man is unable to meditate, let him learn to remain in loving attention to God, in the quiet of his understanding, though he may seem to be doing nothing. For thus by little and little, and most rapidly, will the Divine tranquillity and peace from this marvellous and deep knowledge of God, involved in the Divine love, be infused into his soul. Let him not intermeddle with forms, imagery, meditations, or reflections of any kind, that he may not disquiet his soul, and drag it out of peace and contentment into that which can only end in bitterness. And if this inactivity should cause scruples to arise, let him remember that it is not a slight matter to possess his soul in peace and rest, without effort or desire. This is what our Lord requires at our hands, saying, 'Be still, and see that I am God.'* Learn to be interiorly empty of all things, and you will see with delight that I am God.

CHAPTER XVI.

Of imaginary apprehensions supernaturally represented to the fancy. They cannot be proximate means of union with God.

Second means of supernatural corporeal knowledge,—Imagination.

AND now having treated of those impressions which the soul receives in the order of nature, and which exercise the imagination and the fancy, it is necessary to discuss those which are supernatural, called imaginary visions, and which also, inasmuch as they are images, forms, and figures, appertain to this sense, like those which are in the order of nature. Under the designation of imaginary visions, I include every-

* Ps. xlv. 11.

CHAP. XVI.

thing which may be supernaturally represented to the imagination by images, forms, figures, or impressions, and these of the most perfect kind, which represent things, and influence us more vividly and more perfectly than it is possible in the natural order of the senses. For all these impressions and images which the five senses represent to the soul, and which establish themselves within in a natural way, may also have their place there in a way that is supernatural, represented therein without any intervention whatever on the part of the outward senses. The sense of fancy and memory is, as it were, a storehouse of the intellect, where all forms and objects of the intellect are treasured up; and thus the intellect considers them and forms judgments about them.

Interior visions,—what.

We must, therefore, remember that as the five outward senses propose and represent to the interior senses the images and pictures of their objects; so in a supernatural way, without the intervention of the outward senses, may be represented the same images and pictures, and that much more vividly and perfectly. And thus by means of images God frequently shows many things to the soul, and teaches it wisdom, as we see throughout the Holy Scriptures. He showed His glory in the cloud which covered the tabernacle;* and between the Seraphim which covered their faces and their feet with their wings.† To Jeremias He showed 'a rod watching;'‡ and to Daniel a multitude of visions.

Presented to the mind without sensation.

The devil, also, with visions of his own, seemingly good, labours to delude the soul. We have an instance of it in the history of the kings of Israel, where we read that he deceived the prophets of Achab, by representing to them the figure of horns, by which the king was to push Syria till he destroyed it.§ Yet all was a delusion. Such also was the vision of

May come from the devil.

* Exod. xl. 33.
† Is. vi. 4.
‡ Jer. i. 11.
§ 3 Kings xxii. 11, 12.

Pilate's wife concerning the condemnation of Christ, and many others.

In the case of those who have made some spiritual progress, visions of the imagination are of more frequent occurrence than bodily and exterior visions. There is no difference between them and those of the outward senses, considered as images and representations; but there is a great difference in the effect they produce, and in their perfectness: they are more pure, and make a deeper impression on the soul, inasmuch as they are supernatural and at the same time more interior than the exterior supernatural visions, still, notwithstanding, some bodily exterior visions produce a greater effect, for this depends on the will of God; but I am speaking of them as they are in themselves, as being more interior.

The sense of fancy and imagination is ordinarily that to which the devil applies himself with all his cunning, because it is the portal of the soul, and there too the intellect takes up, or leaves, its wares as in a repository. For this reason, therefore, God and the devil too come hither with images and forms to be presented to the intellect; though God does not make use only of this means to instruct the soul, seeing that He dwells substantially within it, and is able to do so directly by Himself, and by other methods. I shall not stop here to explain how it may be known whether certain visions are from God or not, for that is not my object now, my sole purpose being to direct the intellect, so that, in the way of union with the Divine Wisdom, it shall not be embarrassed or impeded by those which are good, nor deluded by those which are evil.

God may move the soul immediately.

I say therefore with respect to all these impressions and imaginary visions, and others of whatever kind they may be, which present themselves under forms or images, or any particular intelligible forms, whether false as coming from the devil, or known to be true as coming from God, that the intellect is not to perplex itself about them, nor feed itself upon them; the soul must not willingly accept them, nor rest upon them, in order that it may be detached, naked, pure, and sincerely simple, which is the condition of the Divine union. The reason of this is that all these forms are never represented so as to be laid hold of but under certain ways and limitations, and the Divine Wisdom to which the intellect is to be united admits of no such limitations or forms, neither can it be comprehended under any particular image, because it is all pureness and simplicity. However, if two extremes are to be united together, such as the soul and the Divine Wisdom, it is necessary that they should meet under a certain kind of mutual resemblance; and hence the soul must be also pure and simple, unlimited, not adhering to any particular intelligence, and unmodified by any forms, figures, or image. As God is not comprehended under any form, or likeness, or particular conception, so the soul also, if it is to be united to Him, must not be under the power of any particular form or conception. God has no form or likeness, as the Holy Ghost tells us: 'You heard the voice of His words, but you saw not any form at all.'* But He also says, 'That there was darkness, and a cloud, and obscurity,'† which is the obscure night in which the soul is united to God. He says further on, 'You saw not any similitude in the day that the Lord God spoke to you in Horeb from the midst of the fire.'‡

Visions not a proximate means of union with God,—why.

Two proofs from Holy Scripture.

The soul can never attain to the height of the Divine union, so far as it is possible in this life, through the medium of any forms or figures. This truth is set before us by the same Spirit of God in the book of Numbers, where we read of the rebuking of Aaron and Mary, because they had murmured against their brother. God then would have them

* Deut. iv. 12. † Ib. iv. 11. ‡ Ib. iv. 15.

BOOK II.

understand the high estate of union and friendship with Himself to which He had raised Moses. 'If there be among you,' said God, 'a prophet of the Lord, I will appear to him in a vision, or I will speak to him in a dream; but it is not so with My servant Moses who is most faithful in all My house, for I speak to him mouth to mouth and plainly, and not by riddles and figures doth he see the Lord.'* It is evident from this, that in the high estate of the union of love, God does not communicate Himself to the soul under the disguise of imaginary visions, similitudes, or figures, neither is there place for such, but mouth to mouth; that is, it is in the pure and naked Essence of God, which is as it were the mouth of God in love, that He communicates Himself to the pure and naked essence of the soul, through the will which is the mouth of the soul in the love of God.

The will effects the Divine union of love.

The soul, therefore, that will ascend to this perfect union with God, must be careful not to lean upon imaginary visions, forms, figures, and particular intelligible objects, for these things can never serve as proportionate or proximate means towards so great an end: yea, rather they are an obstacle in the way, and therefore to be guarded against and rejected. For if in any case we are to admit these visions and esteem them, that must be for the profit and good effects which true visions have on the soul; but it is not necessary, to secure these good effects, that we should admit the visions; yea, rather it is always necessary to reject them that we may profit the more by them. The fruit of these imaginary visions, and also of the exterior bodily visions, is the communication of intelligence, love, or sweetness, but it is not necessary for this result that we should admit them willingly. For as I have already said, when these visions are present to the imagination they infuse into the

* Num. xii. 6, 7, 8.

soul that intelligence, love, or sweetness, according to the good pleasure of God; and thus the soul passively receives their quickening effects without being able on its own part to hinder them any more than it could acquire them, notwithstanding its previous efforts to dispose itself for that end.

The soul in some respects resembles a window, which cannot repel the rays of the sun striking against it, but which is disposed for the reception thereof, and is passively illuminated thereby, without care or effort on its own part. Thus the soul cannot but receive the influx and communications of these representations, because the will, negatively disposed, cannot, in its state of humble and loving resignation, resist the supernatural influence; though, no doubt, its impureness and imperfections are an impediment, as stains in the glass obscure the light.

Fruit of Divine favours in proportion to detachment from them.

It is clear from this, then, that the soul, the more it is detached in will and affections from the stains of impressions, images, and representations, in which the spiritual communications are involved, not only does not deprive itself of these communications, and the blessings of which they are the cause, but is thereby the more disposed for their reception, and that in greater abundance, clearness, liberty of spirit, and singleness of mind; all the impressions, veils, and shadows, which hide the deeper spirituality within, being cast aside. If we feed upon them, sense and spirit are so filled, that spiritual communication cannot freely and in simplicity be made to us; for while we are occupied with the exterior covering, the intellect is not free to receive the substance within. If the soul will admit, and make much of, these impressions, the result will be embarrassment, and resting satisfied with that which is of least importance in them, namely, with all that it can grasp and comprehend, the form, the representation, and the particular conception. The chief part of them, the spiritual part infused, eludes its grasp, and is beyond its comprehension; the soul cannot discern or explain it, because it is wholly spiritual. That only can it perceive, which is of least value, namely the sensible forms which are within the reach of its own understanding; and for this cause I maintain that the soul, passively, without any intellectual effort, and without knowing how to make any such effort, receives through these visions what it can neither understand nor imagine.

Faith better than visions.

For these reasons, therefore, the eyes of the soul must be continually turned aside from these visible and distinctly intelligible things, communicated through the senses, which form neither the foundation nor the security of Faith, and be fixed on the invisible, not on the things of sense but on those of the Spirit which are not cognisable by sense; for it is this that lifts up the soul to union in faith which is the proper medium. And thus these visions will subsequently profit the soul in the attainment of faith when it shall have perfectly renounced all that sense and intellect find in them; and when it shall have duly applied itself to that end which God had in view when He sent them, by detaching itself from them. Because, as I have said before with regard to bodily visions, God does not send them that the soul may admit them and set its affections upon them.

But here arises this doubt; if it be true that these supernatural visions are sent from God, not for the purpose of being received, clung to, and prized by the soul, why then are they sent at all? They are the source of many errors and dangers, and are at least inconveniences, hindering our further advancement. This objection is specially true, for God is able to communicate spiritually to the very substance of the soul that which He thus communicates through the interior senses in visions and sensible forms.

I shall reply to this doubt in the following chapter. The doctrine on this subject is most important, and in my opinion exceedingly necessary as well for spiritual persons as for those who have the direction of them. I shall therein explain the way of God in them, and the end He has in view, the ignorance of which renders many unable to control themselves, or to guide others through these visions along the road of union. They imagine, the moment they have ascertained the visions to be true and from God, that they may lean upon them and cleave to them; not considering that the soul will find in them that which is natural to itself, that it will set its affections upon them and be embarrassed by them, as by the things of this world, if it does not repel them as it repels these. In this state of mind they will think it right to accept the visions, and to reject worldly things, thereby exposing themselves and the souls they direct to great dangers and vexations in discerning the truth or falsehood of these visions. God does not bid them to undertake this labour, nor to expose simple and sincere souls to this hazard; for He has given them the sound and safe teaching of Faith, whereby to direct their steps, which cannot be followed without shutting our eyes against every object of sense, and of clear and particular perception. S. Peter was perfectly certain of that vision of glory which he saw when our Lord was transfigured, yet after relating it, he bids us walk by faith, saying: 'We have the more firm prophetical word: whereunto you do well to attend, as to a light that shineth in a dark place.'* This comparison involves the doctrine which I am teaching. For in saying that we should look to Faith of which the Prophets spoke, as to a light that shineth in a dark place, he bids us remain in darkness, shutting our eyes to all other light, and tells us that this darkness of faith, which is also obscure, ought to be the only light to which we should trust. For if we rely on other lights, clear

* 2 S. Pet. i. 19.

BOOK II.

and distinct, of the understanding, we have ceased to rely on the obscurity of faith, which has therefore ceased to shine in the dark place of which the Apostle speaks. This place is the intellect, which is the candlestick to hold the light of faith. In this life, the intellect must therefore be dark, until the day of our transformation and union with Him, towards Whom the soul is travelling; or until the day of the clear Vision of God shall have dawned in the next life.

CHAPTER XVII.

Of the ends and way of God in communicating spiritual blessings to the soul through the interior senses. Answer to the question proposed.

Visions are dangerous,—why then are they sent?

I HAVE much to say of the end which God has in view, and of the ways He employs, when He sends visions to raise up the soul from its tepidity to the Divine union with Himself. This is treated of in all spiritual books, and I shall therefore confine myself here to the solution of the question before us. That question is this: Why does God Who is most wise, and ever ready to remove every snare and every stumbling-block from before us, send us these supernatural visions, seeing that they are so full of danger, and so perplexing to us in our further progress?

Answer. Because God observes the natural order which He has made.

To answer this we have three principles to take for granted. The first is thus expressed by S. Paul: 'Those that are, are ordained of God.' * That is, all that is done is done according to the ordinance of God. The second is expressed by the Holy Ghost saying of wisdom that it 'ordereth all things sweetly.' † The third is an axiom of Theology, God moveth all things in harmony with their constitution. ‡ Ac-

* Rom. xiii. 1. † Wisd. viii. 1.

‡ Deus omnia movet secundum modum eorum.

cording to these principles, then, it is evident that God, when He elevates the soul from the depths of its own vileness to the opposite heights of His own dignity in union with Himself, worketh orderly, sweetly, and in harmony with the constitution of the soul. As the process by which the soul acquires knowledge rests on the forms and images of created things, and as the mode of its understanding and perception is that of the senses, it follows that God, in order to raise it up to the highest knowledge, orderly and sweetly, must begin with the lower senses, that He may thus raise it up in harmony with its own constitution to the supreme Wisdom of the Spirit which is not cognisable by sense. For this reason He leads the soul first of all through forms, images, and sensible ways, proportionate to its capacity, whether natural or supernatural, and through reflections, upwards to His own Supreme Spirit. This is the cause of His sending visions and imaginary forms, and other sensible and intelligible means of knowledge. Not because He would not in an instant communicate the substance of the Spirit, provided that the two extremes, the human and Divine, that is, sense and Spirit, were ordinarily able to meet together, and to be united in a single act, without the previous intervention of many disposing acts, which orderly and sweetly concur together, one being the foundation and the preparation for the other, as in natural operations where the first subserves the second, that the next, and so onwards. Thus the way in which God leads man to perfection is the way of his natural constitution, raising him up from what is vile and exterior to that which is interior and noble.

Analogy of the natural acquisition of knowledge.

In the first place He perfects him in the bodily senses, moving him to make a right use of good things which in themselves are natural, perfect, and exterior; such as hearing Mass and sermons, veneration of holy things, mortification of the appetite at meals, the maceration of the body by

Four ordinary states of spiritual progress.

1. External mortification.

BOOK II.

penance, and the chastening of the sense of touch by holy austerities. And when the senses are in some measure pre-

2. Sensible sweetness.

pared, God is wont to perfect them still more by granting them certain supernatural favours and consolations that they may be confirmed the more in goodness. He sends to them certain supernatural communications, such as visions of Saints or of holy things in bodily form, delicious odours, Divine locutions accompanied by a pure and singular sweetness, whereby the very senses are greatly strengthened in

3. Meditation.

virtue and withdrawn from the desire of evil things. Besides, He perfects also the interior bodily senses, the imagination and the fancy, at the same time; accustoms them to good, through considerations, meditations, and holy reflections, according to the measure of their capacity, and in all teaches

4. Interior visions.

and informs the mind. And when the interior senses are disposed by this natural exercise, God is wont to enlighten them, and to spiritualise them, more and more, through the instrumentality of certain supernatural visions, which I have called imaginary; from which the mind at the same time derives great profit, and through the interior and exterior visions casts off its natural rudeness and becomes by degrees refined.

God is free and sovereign in dispensing His graces.

This is the way of God in elevating the soul to that which is interior. Not that it is necessary for Him to observe this order and succession of progress, for He occasionally effects one degree without the other, as he sees it expedient for a particular soul, and as it pleases Him to dispense His graces; still His ordinary way is what I have described. This is the ordinary method of God in teaching and spiritualising the soul; He begins by communicating to it spiritual things through things outward, palpable, and appropriate to sense, condescending to its weakness and the slight measure of its powers; so that through the veil of exterior objects, in themselves good, the mind, forming particular acts, and receiving such portions of the spiritual communication, may acquire the habit of spirituality and attain to the Substance of the Spirit, to which sense is a stranger, and which the soul could never reach but by little and little in its own way, through the senses, on which it has always rested. And thus in proportion as it approaches spirituality in its converse with God, does it detach itself from, and empty itself of, the ways of sense, that is, of reflections, meditation, and imagination. And when it shall have attained perfectly to converse in spirit with God, it must of necessity have emptied itself of all that relates to that converse which falls under the cognisance of sense.

Thus, when an object is attracted to one extreme, the more it recedes from the other the nearer it approaches; and when it shall have completely reached the point to which it tends, it will then be completely withdrawn from the other. This is the spiritual maxim so generally known: *Gustato Spiritu, desipit omnis caro.* When we have tasted the sweetness of the Spirit, all that is flesh becomes insipid; that is, it profits us no more, and the ways of sense are no longer pleasing. This maxim refers to all the ways in which sense may be employed about spiritual things. This is evident: for if a thing be spiritual it falls not under the cognisance of the senses, and if it be such as is comprehensible by sense, then is it no longer purely spiritual. For the more anything is comprehended by sense and our natural perceptions, the less it has of the Spirit and of the supernatural.

The full stature of the spiritual man.

The spiritual man, therefore, having attained to perfection, makes no account of sense, receives nothing through it, does not avail himself of it, neither has he any need of it in his converse with God, as was the case before with him when he had not received the increase of the Spirit. This is the meaning of S. Paul when he said: 'When I was a child, I spoke as a child, I understood as a child, I thought as a child. But when I became a man, I put away the things of

BOOK II.

a child.'* I have already said that the objects of sense and the knowledge which results from them are the occupations of a child. That soul which ever clings to these, and which never detaches itself from them, will never cease to be a child; as a child will it always speak, understand, and think of God, because relying on the outward veil of the senses which is childish, it will never attain to the Substance of the Spirit, which is the perfect man. And so the soul ought not to admit revelations, with a view to its own spiritual growth, even though God should send them; for the infant must abandon the breasts if it is to become accustomed to more solid and substantial food.

Should interior visions be rejected even by a beginner?

Is it necessary then, you will ask, that the soul, in its spiritual infancy, should accept these revelations, and abandon them when it has grown; for the infant must seek its nourishment at the breast to be able to leave it when the time is come? My answer is, that with regard to meditation and natural reflections, through which the soul begins its search after God, it must not, it is true, abandon the breast of the interior senses, to support itself, until the time has come when it may do so. That time is come when God raises the soul to a more spiritual converse with Himself, which is contemplation, and of that I spoke in the thirteenth chapter of this book. Still I maintain that these imaginary visions or other supernatural impressions, to which the senses are subject without the assent of the will, are, upon all occasions and at all times, whether in the perfect or less perfect state, and notwithstanding their coming from God, not to be sought after, nor dwelt upon by the soul; and this for two reasons:—

Answer. Yes.

Because they then become;

1. More profitable,

First, because these visions produce their effects passively in the soul, without its being able on its own part to

* 1 Cor. xiii. 11.

hinder them, though it may do something towards hindering the manner of the vision; consequently the secondary effects which it is intended to produce are much more substantially wrought, though not in that way. For in renouncing them with humility and fear, there is neither imperfection nor selfishness, but rather disinterestedness and emptiness of self, which is the best disposition for union with God.

2. less dangerous and troublesome.

Secondly, because we are thereby delivered from the risk and labour of discerning between good and bad visions, and of ascertaining whether the angel of light or of darkness is at hand. The attempt to do so is not profitable at all, but rather waste of time, an occasion of many imperfections and delay on the spiritual journey. That is not the way to direct a soul in matters which are of real importance, nor to relieve it of the vexation of trifles which are involved in particular apprehensions and perceptions, as I have said with respect to bodily visions and to those of the imagination, and as I shall have to say again. Believe me, our Lord would never have communicated the abundance of the Spirit through these channels, so narrow, of forms and figures and particular perceptions, by which, as if by crumbs, He sustains the soul, if He had not to raise up that soul to Himself in the way appropriate to its own constitution. This is the meaning of the Psalmist when he said: 'He sendeth His crystal like morsels.'* The Wisdom of God is His crystal. How sad it is that the soul, whose capacity is as it were infinite, should be fed by morsels through the senses, because of its want of generosity, and because of its sensual weakness. S. Paul also saw with grief this littleness of mind and absence of good spiritual dispositions, when he said to the Corinthians: 'And I, brethren, could not speak to you as unto spiritual, but as unto carnal.

* Ps. cxlvii. 17.

As unto little ones in Christ, I gave you milk to drink, not meat: for you were not able as yet. But neither indeed are you now able, for you are yet carnal.' *

Let us, then, keep in mind that the soul must not regard these figures and objects, which are but the rind, when supernaturally set before it; whether occurring through the exterior senses, as voices and words in the ear, visible visions of the Saints and beautiful lights, odours to the smell, sweetness to the palate, and other delectations of the touch, which are wont to proceed from the Spirit; or through the interior senses as the interior imaginary visions. These things the soul must not regard; yea, rather it must renounce them wholly, having its eyes fixed on that spiritual good alone which they effect, labouring to preserve it in good works, and employing itself in that which is purely for the service of God without reference to these visions, and without seeking for sensible sweetness. In this way we shall reap from these visions that fruit only which God intends and wills, a spirit of devotion, for that is the chief end, and none other, for which He sends them; and we shall also pass by that which He too would have passed by, if we could without it have received the blessings He intends to confer, namely, the usage and appliance of sense.

Conclusion,—Perfection consists in doing the will of God in self-denial, faith, and good works.

CHAPTER XVIII.

How souls are injured because their spiritual directors do not guide them aright through these visions. How these visions, though from God, become occasions of error.

I CANNOT be so concise with respect to visions as I desire, because of the abundance of the matter. And therefore, though I have said enough, in substance, for the instruction

* 1 Cor. iii. 1, 2.

CHAP. XVIII.

of the spiritual man, how he is to order himself when visions occur; and also for the spiritual director who guides him, how he is to demean himself with his penitent: I think it not superfluous to enter further into the details of this doctrine, and to bring into clearer light the evils that may happen to the penitent on the one hand, and his director on the other, should they be too credulous in the matter of visions, even if those visions come from God. What leads me to enlarge upon this subject, is the little discretion which, I think, I have observed among certain spiritual directors, who, having too great a reliance on these supernatural impressions, because they have ascertained them to be good and from God, have fallen, together with their penitents, into great errors, and involved themselves in many difficulties; thereby verifying these words of our Lord, 'If the blind lead the blind, both fall into the pit.' *

How visions are to be treated.

Our Lord does not say they shall fall, but they fall: for it is not necessary for such a fall that it should be one of manifest delusion; the fall is complete in the venturing upon such a mode of direction, and thus, at least, both the director and the penitent fall together. There are some spiritual directors who fall at once into error, because their instructions to those, who are liable to visions, are such as to lead them astray or perplex them with regard to their visions; or they do not direct them in the way of humility. They suffer their penitents to make much of their visions, which is the reason why they walk not according to the pure and perfect spirit of faith; neither do they build them up nor strengthen them in faith, while they attach so much importance to these visions.

This kind of direction shows that they themselves consider visions matters of importance; and their penitents, observing

* S. Matt. xv. 14.

BOOK II.

this, follow their example, dwelling upon these visions, not building themselves up in faith; neither do they withdraw, nor detach themselves from them, so that they may take their flight upwards in the obscurity of faith. All this results from the language and conduct of spiritual directors; for somehow, a certain sense of satisfaction arises from these things—which is not in our own control—that withdraws our eyes from the abyss of faith. The reason why this so easily takes place, must be that the soul is so occupied with them. For inasmuch as they are objects of sense, to which we are naturally inclined, and as we have had experience of them, and are disposed for the apprehension of things distinct and sensible; it is enough to see our confessor or any other person appreciate them, to induce us not only to do the same, but also to indulge our desire for them, to feed upon them unconsciously, to be more and more inclined to them, and to hold them in greater estimation.

Advice to spiritual directors.

This kind of direction is the source of many imperfections at least, for the soul is no longer humble, but thinks itself to be something good, and that God makes much of it; and so it goes on contented and satisfied with itself, which is contrary to humility. The devil also at once applies himself in secret to foster this feeling, while the soul is not aware of it, and suggests to it thoughts about other people, whether they have these visions or not, or whether they are or are not such as they seem to be: all this is contrary to holy simplicity and spiritual solitude. These evils they cannot avoid, because they do not grow in faith. Besides, if souls do not fall into evils so palpable as these, they fall into others of a more subtle nature, and more hateful in the eyes of God, simply because they are not living in detachment.

For the present, I shall pursue this subject no further, as I shall have to resume it when I have to treat of spiritual gluttony, and the other six capital vices. Then, indeed, I

CHAP. XVIII.

shall have much to say of these minute and subtle stains, which defile the mind because of the failure of true direction in detachment. I shall now speak of the method of direction observed by some whose guidance of souls is not good. I wish I could do this well; for, in truth, it is a difficult thing to explain how the mind of the penitent becomes secretly conformed to that of his director. It appears to me that we cannot understand the one without understanding the other. Moreover, as they are spiritual things, the one corresponds with the other.

Weakness, or imprudence in regard to visions injures, 1. Faith, 2. Humility, 3. Peace of mind.

It seems to me—and I believe it to be true—that, if the spiritual director be a man who has a weakness for revelations, who is impressed by them, and feels in them a sort of pleasurable satisfaction, he must communicate, without intending it, the same feelings to the mind of his penitent, unless the latter be more advanced in spirituality than he is himself. But even if that be the case, he must do his penitent grievous harm if he continues under his direction. Out of this weakness of the director for revelations, and his satisfaction in them, arises a certain kind of appreciation of them, which, without the utmost care on his part, he cannot but make manifest to his penitent; and if the penitent have the same inclination, in my opinion this weakness will be increased in both by their mutual intercourse.

I will not enter into minute details on this subject, and will therefore speak of such a director, who, whether having a weakness for visions or not, is not so cautious in his relations with his penitent as he ought to be, so as to relieve him of his embarrassments, and detach him in desire from these visions; but who on the contrary converses with him on the subject, and makes them the chief matter of his spiritual instructions, teaching him how to distinguish between good visions and evil ones. Though this knowledge be good, yet is it not right to inflict on the penitent the labour, anxiety,

BOOK II.

and danger which it involves, unless in a case of pressing necessity; seeing that by giving no heed to them all this is avoided, and everything done that ought to be done. This is not all; for some directors, when they see that their penitents have visions from God, bid them pray to Him, to reveal to them such and such things concerning themselves or others, and the simple souls obey them, thinking it lawful to seek information in that way. They suppose it lawful to desire, and even to pray for, a revelation, because it is the good pleasure of God to reveal something to them in a supernatural way, in a particular manner or for a particular end. And if God grants to them their petition, they become more and more confident on other occasions, and imagine God to be pleased with this mode of conversing with Him; when in truth it is not pleasing to Him, and contrary to His will. And if they are much given to this mode of conversing with God, they attach themselves to it, and the will acquiesces naturally in it; for as this naturally pleases them, they also naturally fall down to the level of their own perceptions, and frequently err in what they say: and when they see that events have not answered their expectations they are astonished; and doubts assail them as to whether their visions were from God or not, because the issues correspond not with their impressions.

Folly of praying for, or trusting in visions.

They seem to have presupposed two things—the first, that the visions came from God, because they had made so deep an impression upon them; and this might be simply the effect of their natural tendency to trust in visions. The second, that as the vision came from God, so the event ought to have answered their expectations or impressions. This is a grand delusion, for the revelations and words of God are not always fulfilled as man understands them, or even in their obvious sense. We must, therefore, not rely upon visions, nor accept them at once, even when we know that they are revelations, answers, or words of God. For though they are certain and true in themselves, it is not of necessity that they should be so in our sense, as I shall show in the next chapter. And I shall further show also that God, though at times supernaturally answering petitions presented to Him, is not pleased with this, and that He is sometimes angry, though He answers.

CHAPTER XIX.

Visions, Revelations, and Locutions, though true and from God, may deceive. Proofs from Holy Scripture.

First reason why Divine visions may deceive,—Misinterpretation.

THERE are two reasons why Divine locutions and visions prove untrue to us, though they are in themselves always true and certain. The first is our defective understanding of them, and the second depends on the cause and ground of them: they are frequently threats, and therefore conditional, depending for their fulfilment on penance done, or abstinence from particular acts; although at the same time expressed in absolute terms. I proceed to illustrate this by certain proofs from the Holy Writings.

God higher than man.

In the first place, it is clear that the prophecies do not always mean what we understand by them, and that the issues do not correspond with our expectations. The reason is that God is infinite and most high, and therefore His prophecies, locutions, and revelations, involve other conceptions, other meanings, widely different from those according to which we measure our own perceptions; and they are the more true and the more certain the less they seem so to our intellect. We have instances of this truth in the Holy Scriptures, where we read that many prophecies and Divine locutions disappointed, in their fulfilment, the expectations of many of the ancient people, because they understood them

BOOK II.

too much according to the letter in their own way. This will become clear if we consider the following examples.

Examples from Holy Scripture.

1. Promise to Abraham.

When God had brought Abraham into the land of Chanaan, He said unto him, 'I brought thee out from Ur of the Chaldees to give thee this land.'* But now that God had said this to Abraham more than once, and as the Patriarch was old, and the land not yet his, he said unto God when the promise was again made, 'Whereby may I know that I shall possess it?'† Then God revealed to Abraham that it was not he, but his children, after the lapse of four hundred years, who were to possess the land. Abraham then understood the promise, which in itself was most true: for God by giving the land to his children, because of the love He bore him, was giving it to him. Thus Abraham deceived himself while he understood the promise in his own sense. And if he had then acted on that understanding, he would have greatly erred, for the time of fulfilment was not come. Those, too, who saw him die before he had entered into possession of the land, knowing the promise which God had made him, would have been put to shame, and would have accounted the prophecy for a false one.

2. Prophecy to Jacob.

Afterwards, when Jacob his grandson was going to Egypt, whither Joseph had sent for him, because of the famine in the land of Chanaan, God appeared to him on the way, and said, 'Fear not, go down into Egypt. I will bring thee back again from thence.'‡ This prophecy was not fulfilled as we should understand it, for the holy old man died in Egypt, and never came back alive. That prophecy was to be fulfilled in his descendants, whom God brought back, after many years, being Himself their Guide. Now anyone who might have heard of this prophecy might have been certain, that as Jacob went down into Egypt by the grace and command of

* Gen. xv. 7. † Ib. 8. ‡ Ib. xlvi. 3, 4.

God, so would he return thence alive without fail; for the same promise extended to his return and protection. Such an one would have been astonished and deceived when he saw the Patriarch die, and the events not answering to his expectation. Thus, while the promise of God was most certain, men might deceive themselves greatly about it.

3. Answer to the Tribes of Israel.

The tribes of Israel assembled together to fight against that of Benjamin, because of a certain evil deed which that tribe had sanctioned. God, too, appointed them a leader in the war. Upon this they were so confident of success that, when they were defeated with the loss of two and twenty thousand men, they were filled with astonishment, and wept before God, not knowing the cause of their discomfiture, for they had understood that victory had been promised them. They asked whether they should return to the fight; God answered them, 'Go up against them and join battle.' They went up the second time with great boldness, confident of victory, but were beaten again, and eighteen thousand of them were slain. In consequence of this they were filled with confusion, and knew not what to do. God had commanded them to fight, and they were always beaten, though they surpassed their enemies in courage and in numbers—being themselves four hundred thousand strong, while the tribe of Benjamin only mustered five and twenty thousand and seven hundred men. They deceived themselves by their own interpretation of the word of God, which in itself was true. God had not said to them, go forth and conquer, but go forth and fight. And His purpose was to chastise them in this way for their negligence and presumption, and so to humble them. At last God said unto them, 'Go up, for to-morrow I will deliver them into your hands,' and then by toil and stratagem they obtained the victory.*

* Judg. xx. 23—28.

BOOK II.

This is the way in which many souls deceive themselves in the matter of revelations and Divine locutions. They understand them in the letter according to their apparent meaning. For, as I have said, the chief purpose of God in sending visions is to express and communicate the Spirit which is hidden within them, and which is very hard to be understood. This is much more abundant than the letter, more extraordinary, and surpasses the limits thereof. He therefore that will rely on the letter of the Divine locution, or on the intelligible form of the vision, will of necessity fall into a delusion, and be put to shame; for he directs himself therein by sense, and does not yield to the Spirit in detachment from sense. 'The letter killeth,' saith the Apostle, 'but the Spirit quickeneth.'* We must therefore reject the literal sense, and abide in the obscurity of faith, which is the Spirit, incomprehensible by sense.

4. Complaint of Isaias.

This is the reason why many of the people of Israel came to disregard and to disbelieve the words of their Prophets. They understood them in a particular sense, according to the letter, and were disappointed at their non-fulfilment. To such an extent did this evil grow among them that they had a current proverb in ridicule of the prophecies. Isaias complains of this, saying: 'Whom shall he teach knowledge? and whom shall he make to understand the hearing? Them that are weaned from the milk, that are drawn away from the breasts. For command, command again; command, command again; wait, wait again; wait, wait again; a little there, a little there. For with the speech of lips, and with another tongue He will speak to this people.'† It is clear from these words, that the people made a jest of the prophecies, and were in the habit of ridiculing them by saying, 'wait, wait again.' Their object was to insinuate

* 2 Cor. iii. 6.

† Is. xxviii. 9—11.

that the prophecies would never be accomplished: for they understood them according to the letter, which is the milk of babes; and in their own sense, which is the 'breasts,' which is in contradiction with the grandeur of the science of the Spirit. The Prophet therefore asks, 'Whom shall he teach the knowledge' of his prophecies, and 'whom shall he make to understand' what they teach? Is it not they who are 'weaned from the milk' of the letter and from 'the breasts' of sense? That nation understood not the prophecies, for it followed after the milk of the letter, and the breasts of sense, saying, 'command, command again; wait, wait again.' For God spoke to them the doctrine of His own mouth, and not of theirs, and that in another tongue than theirs.

5. Prayer of Jeremias.

We are therefore not to consider Prophecy according to our own understanding and our own speech, knowing that the words of God have a meaning different from ours, and very difficult to ascertain. So much so that Jeremias, himself a Prophet of God, seems to have been deceived when he saw the meaning of the Divine words to be so far removed from the ordinary understanding of men; for he thus complains on behalf of the people, saying, 'Alas, alas, alas! O Lord God, hast Thou then deceived this people and Jerusalem, saying, You shall have peace, and behold the sword reacheth even to the soul?'* The peace which God had promised was peace between Himself and man in the Messias, Whom He was to send; but the people understood it of temporal peace; and so, when war and trouble came upon them, they thought God had deceived them, because they were disappointed in their hopes. They then cried out in the words of the Prophet, 'We looked for peace, and no good came.'† It was not possible for them not to be deceived, because they relied on the literal, grammatical sense.

* Jer. iv. 10. † Ib. viii. 15.

BOOK II.

6. Prophecies relating to the Messias.

Is it possible for anyone to escape error and confusion, who should understand in the letter the prophecy of the Psalmist concerning Christ, especially that which says of Him, 'He shall rule from sea to sea, and from the river unto the ends of the earth'?* And again, 'He shall deliver the poor from the mighty, and the needy that hath no helper.'† Now Christ was born in a low estate, lived in poverty, and died in misery: so far was He from ruling over the earth while He lived upon it, that He subjected Himself to the lowest of the people and died under Pontius Pilate. Not only did He not deliver the poor, His own disciples, from the mighty, but He suffered the mighty to persecute them for His name, and to put them to death. The prophecy concerning Christ is to be understood spiritually, for in that sense is it most true. He is not only the Lord of the whole earth, but of Heaven also, for He is God. And the poor, who are to follow Him, are not only redeemed by Him and delivered from the mighty, that is out of the hand of Satan, but also made heirs of the kingdom of Heaven. The prophecy referred to Christ and His followers in the highest sense, to His eternal kingdom and our everlasting salvation; but men understood it in their own way, referring it to that which is of least importance, and of which God makes but little account, a temporal dominion, and a temporal deliverance, which in the sight of God is not a kingdom nor freedom. The Jews, blinded by the letter of the prophecy, and not understanding the true spiritual meaning it involved, put our Lord God to death. 'They that inhabited Jerusalem,' saith the Apostle, 'and the rulers thereof, not knowing Him, nor the voices of the Prophets, which are read every Sabbath, judging Him, have fulfilled them.'‡

The words of God are indeed hard to be understood as

* Ps. lxxi. 8. † Ib. 12. ‡ Acts xiii. 27.

they ought to be. His own disciples, who had been familiar with Him, were themselves deceived. Two of them after His death were journeying sad and desponding to Emmaus, and saying, 'We hoped that it was He who should have redeemed Israel.'* They, too, understood this redemption and dominion in a temporal sense. Our Lord appeared to them, and rebuked them, saying, 'O foolish, and slow of heart to believe in all things which the Prophets have spoken!'† Even on the day of His Ascension some of them were alike ignorant, for they asked Him saying, 'Lord, wilt thou at this time restore again the kingdom to Israel?'‡

Caiphas as a prophet.

Many things have been spoken by the Holy Ghost, the meaning of which is different from that which men conceive. Such were the words of Caiphas concerning Christ: 'It is expedient for you that one man should die for the people, and that the whole nation perish not. And this he spoke not of himself.'§ The words of Caiphas had one meaning to himself, and another, a very different one, to the Holy Ghost.

This shows us that we cannot rely upon visions and revelations, even though coming from God, because it is so easy for us to be deceived by understanding them in our own sense. They are an abyss and a depth of the Spirit, and therefore to limit them to our own sense and apprehension of them, is to grasp the air and the motes floating in it; the air only disperses, and our hand is empty.

True discernment found in detachment of spirit.

The spiritual director must be therefore careful not to make his penitent narrow-minded by attaching any importance to these supernatural visitations; for they are nothing else but the motes of the Spirit, and he who shall give his attention to these alone will in the end have no spirituality at all. Yea, rather let him wean him from all visions and locutions, and guide him into the liberty and obscurity of

* S. Luke xxiv. 21.
† Ib. 25.
‡ Acts i. 6.
§ S. John xi. 50.

BOOK II.

faith, where he shall receive of the abundance of the Spirit, and consequently the knowledge and understanding of the words of God. It is impossible for anyone who is not spiritually-minded to judge, even in a moderate degree, the things of God; and he who judges them according to sense is not spiritual. Though the things of God are presented to men through the senses, they are not to be so understood. 'The sensual man,' saith the Apostle, 'perceiveth not the things that are of the Spirit of God; for it is foolishness to him, and he cannot understand; because it is spiritually examined. But the spiritual man judgeth all things.'* By 'sensual man' is here meant one who understands the Divine locutions in the literal sense; and the 'spiritual man' is he who is neither tied to it, nor directed by it. It is presumption therefore to converse with God in this supernatural way and to allow sense to intermeddle therewith.

The best interpreters,—Faith, and Liberty of Spirit.

Two illustrations.

1. Spiritual Triumph.

For the clearer understanding of this I will give some illustrations of it. Let us suppose a holy man in affliction, persecuted by his enemies, to whom God shall say, 'I will deliver thee out of their hands.' This promise may be verified, and yet the enemies of the Saint triumph, and he die by their hands. Should he understand the word of God in a temporal sense, that would be a delusion; for God may have spoken of the true deliverance and victory, which is salvation, by which the soul is delivered, and by which it conquers all its enemies in a higher and truer sense than that of any temporal victory over them. Thus the prophecy is much more true and comprehensive than the understanding of it by anyone who should have limited its meaning to this life. For God, when He speaks, intends great and profitable things; but man may understand Him in his

* 1 Cor. ii. 14.

CHAP. XIX.

own way, in the lowest sense, and so fall into error. This is exemplified in the prophecy of David concerning Christ: 'Thou shalt rule them with a rod of iron, and shalt break them in pieces like a potter's vessel.'* Here God speaks of that supreme and perfect dominion, which is eternal and now accomplished; not of a dominion which is less perfect, which is temporal, and which was not fulfilled in the earthly life of Christ.

2. Martyrdom of Desire.

Again: let us suppose a man longing for martyrdom, to whom God shall say, 'Thou shalt be a Martyr.' Upon this such an one feels great interior consolation, and hopes of being a martyr. Still he does not die a martyr's death, and yet the promise is fulfilled. But why is the promise not literally performed? Because God keeps it in the highest and substantial sense, bestowing on that soul the essential love and reward of a martyr, making it a martyr of love, granting to it a prolonged martyrdom of suffering, the continuance of which is more painful than death. Thus He bestows really on that soul what that soul desired, and what He had promised. For the substance of that desire was, not any particular kind of death, but rather the oblation to God of the obedience of a martyr, and a martyr's act of love. Martyrdom itself is nothing worth without the friendship of God, Who by other means gives the love, obedience, and reward of a martyr perfectly; and the soul is satisfied as to its desires, though the death of a martyr is withheld from it.

Analogy between fulfilment of Prophecy, and answer to Prayer.

These desires, and others like them, when they spring from true love, though not fulfilled as men may understand them, are nevertheless fulfilled in another and better way, and more for the honour of God than men know how to ask. 'The Lord hath heard the desire of the poor;'† and 'to the just their desire shall be given.'‡ Many Saints have desired

* Ps. ii. 9. † Ib. ix. 17. ‡ Prov. x. 24.

many things for God in this life, and their desires have not been granted; but it is certain that, as their desires were just and good, they will be perfectly fulfilled in the world to come. And as this is true, so also is it true, that God in this life performs His promise of granting their desires, though not in the way they thought.

In this and in many other ways the words and visions of God are true and certain, and yet we may be deceived because we do not rise to the heights of God's purpose and meaning. Thus, the safest course, which directors can take, is to lead souls into a prudent avoidance of these supernatural visitations, accustoming them to pureness of spirit in the obscurity of faith, which is the means of the Divine union

---

CHAPTER XX.

Proofs from Scripture that the Divine Locutions, though always true, are not always certain in their causes.

Second reason why Divine visions may deceive,—their conditional nature.

It is necessary for me now to show why Divine visions and locutions, though always true in themselves, are not always so with regard to us. This depends on the motive on which they are founded; and it is to be understood that they are always true, while the cause remains, which determines God, for instance, to inflict chastisement. God perhaps says, 'Within a year such a kingdom shall be visited with pestilence.' The ground of this denunciation is a certain offence against God committed in that kingdom. Now if that offence ceases or is changed, the punishment will not be inflicted, or it will come in another form. The denunciation was true, because grounded upon actual sin, and would have been verified if the sin had been persisted in. This is a threatening or conditional revelation.

We have an instance of this in the story of Ninive. God

Conditional prophecies of Jonas; and of Elias.

sent Jonas to it to prophesy its ruin: 'Yet forty days and Ninive shall be destroyed.'* The prophecy was not fulfilled, because the reason of it had ceased. The people did penance for their sins; but if they had not done so, the prophecy would have been accomplished. King Achab committed a great sin, and God sent our Father Elias to threaten him and his house and his kingdom with a most grievous chastisement. But when Achab 'rent his garments, and put haircloth on his flesh, and fasted and slept in sackcloth, and walked with his head cast down,' and was humbled, God said to the same Prophet, 'Because he hath humbled himself for My sake, I will not bring the evil in his days; but in his son's days will I bring the evil upon his house.'† Thus we see that, because of the change in Achab, there was a change also of the threatening and sentence of God.

Voluntas Dei conditionata.

It follows, then, from this that God, having once revealed distinctly to anyone, that he was about to bless or punish either that person or any other, may still change his purpose more or less, or cease from it altogether, according to the change in the disposition of those to whom the revelation referred, or the cessation of the cause in view of which the revelation was made. And this being so, the word that He spoke will not be fulfilled according to the expectation of those to whom it was known, and that very often without its being known why, save to God only. God is wont to speak, teach, and promise, many things at different times, not to be understood, or accomplished then; but that they may be understood afterwards, when the time is come, or when they are effectually fulfilled. It was in this way our Lord conversed with His disciples. He spoke to them in parables and dark sayings, the meaning of which they perceived not till the time came when they were to preach them to others.

* Jon. iii. 4.

† 3 Kings xxi. 27—29.

BOOK II.

This time arrived when the Holy Ghost descended upon them, of whom our Saviour had said: 'He will teach you all things, and bring all things to your mind, whatsoever I shall have said to you.'* S. John, speaking of our Lord's entry into Jerusalem, says: 'These things His disciples did not know at the first; but when Jesus was glorified, then they remembered that these things were written of Him.'† Thus, then, many Divine communications, most distinctly made, may be received by us without being understood before the proper time, either by ourselves or by our spiritual directors.

The conditional promise to Heli.

God was angry with Heli the High Priest of Israel, because he knew that his 'sons did wickedly, and he did not chastise them.'‡ He sent a prophet to him to admonish him. 'I said indeed that thy house and the house of thy father should minister in My sight for ever. But now saith the Lord, Far be this from Me: but whosoever shall glorify Me, him will I glorify: but they that despise Me shall be despised.'§ Now the priesthood was instituted for the honour and glory of God, and for that end it had been promised by God for ever to the father of Heli on the due fulfilment of his functions. But when Heli ceased to be zealous for God's honour—as God Himself complains—preferring his children above Him, conniving at their sins that he might not be compelled to punish them—the promise also ceased to be observed; though it would have abided for ever, had they to whom it belonged persevered zealously in the true service of God. We are, therefore, not to imagine that the words or revelations of God, though most true, will be infallibly verified in their obvious meaning; for they are, by the disposition of God Himself, bound up with human causes, which are liable to fluctuation and change. All this is known unto God, but He declares it not. He sends forth

* S. John xiv. 26. † Ib. xii. 16.
‡ 1 Kings iii. 13. § Ib. ii. 30.

His word, and at times makes no mention of the condition; as in the case of Ninive, when He declared distinctly that after forty days the city would be destroyed. At other times He declares the condition, as in the case of Jeroboam, saying, 'If then thou . . . wilt walk in My ways . . . keeping My commandments and My precepts, as David My servant did; I will be with thee and will build thee up a faithful house as I built a house for David.'*

But after all, whether God declares the conditions or not, we must not trust to our understanding of His words; for we cannot comprehend the hidden truths of God, and the manifold meaning of His words. He is high above the heavens, speaking in the ways of eternity; we are blind upon earth, and cannot penetrate His secrets. This is the meaning of Solomon when he said: 'God is in Heaven, and thou upon earth; therefore let thy words be few.'†

Revelations hard to understand,—why sent.

Here, perhaps, an objection may be made: If then we cannot understand the revelations of God, nor enter into their meaning, why does He send them? I have already met this difficulty. Everything will be intelligible in the time appointed by Him who hath spoken, and he whom He hath determined beforehand shall understand: and then all will see that it was right and fitting it should be so: for God doeth nothing but in truth and equity. It is, therefore, most certain that we cannot perfectly understand nor grasp the full meaning of His words, or determine the sense of them to be what it seems to be, without falling into shameful delusions. This truth was well known to the Prophets to whom the word of the Lord was sent. To prophesy to the people was to them a grievous affliction; for, as I have said, much of what they said was not fulfilled in the letter, and this proved an excuse to the multitude to ridicule and mock

* 3 Kings xi. 38.

† Eccles. v. i.

BOOK II.

the Prophets. 'I am become,' saith the Prophet, 'a laughing-stock all the day, all scoff at me. For I am speaking now this long time, crying out against iniquity, and I often proclaim devastation; and the word of the Lord is made a reproach unto me, and a derision all the day. Then I said: I will not make mention of Him, nor speak any more in His name.'*

Examples of Jeremias and Jonas.

Here the holy Prophet, though he speaks with resignation and like a frail man, unable to endure the ways and secrets of God, teaches us clearly the difference between the true fulfilment and the apparent meaning of the word of God. The people treated the heavenly messengers as deceivers, whose afflictions, on account of their prophecies, were so great that Jeremias cried out: 'Prophecy is become to us a fear, and a snare and destruction.'† Jonas fled when God sent him to preach the destruction of Ninive, because he did not perceive the truth, nor wholly comprehend the meaning, of the words of God. He fled, that he might not become an object of derision to the people when they saw the prophecy not fulfilled. He further stayed outside the city for forty days waiting for the accomplishment of his prophecy, and when he saw that it remained unfulfilled, he was greatly affected, and complained, saying: 'I beseech Thee, O Lord, is not this what I said, when I was yet in my own country? Therefore, I went before to flee unto Tharsis.'‡ In his vexation, therefore, he prayed God to take his life from him.

Is it then surprising that the revelations are not fulfilled in our sense? For if God makes known to anyone good or evil, relating to him or to others, and if the revelation thereof be founded on the obedience or disobedience of that person or the others, and if the facts continue the same, no doubt the prophecy will be fulfilled. But it is not, however, certain

* Jerem. xx. 7-9. † Lam. iii. 47. ‡ Jon. iv. 2.

that it will be fulfilled in the letter, because the reasons of it may change. And therefore we must not trust to our own understanding of these revelations, but to faith.

CHAPTER XXI.

God is at times displeased with certain prayers, though He answers them. Illustrations of His anger with such prayers.

Transgression of natural order displeasing to God.

SOME spiritual persons persuade themselves—not reflecting on the great curiosity which they often display when they seek knowledge from God in supernatural ways—because their prayers are sometimes answered, that their conduct in the matter is good and pleasing unto God. Nevertheless the truth is, notwithstanding the answers they receive, that God is offended, and not pleased. And more than this, they provoke Him to anger, and displease Him greatly. The reason is this—no creature may transgress the limits which God hath appointed in the order of its being for its rule and guidance. He has ordained for man's governance certain natural and reasonable laws, the transgression of which is therefore not right: now, to seek anything by supernatural ways is to transgress these laws, and therefore an unholy and unbecoming thing, and displeasing unto God.

God condescends to human weakness.

You will object, and say, Why then does God, if He is displeased, answer such prayers at all? I reply, the answer occasionally comes from the devil. But when God answers, it is out of condescension to the human weakness of him who will walk in that way, that he may not become disconsolate, and go back; or that he may not think that God is angry with him, or that he may not be tempted overmuch; or it may be for other ends known to God, founded on his weakness, in consideration of which God is pleased to answer him, and condescend to him in that way. He deals in the same

BOOK II.

way with many weak and delicate souls, giving them a sensible sweetness in their converse with Himself, not because He delights in this, or because this way is according to His will; but because He deals with everyone according to his capacity.

Extraordinary means permitted, but not expedient.

God is a well from which everyone may draw water according to the measure of his vessel, and He sometimes permits us to draw it through extraordinary channels, but it is not therefore necessarily right to make use of them. It belongs to God alone to determine this, Who gives how, when, to whom, and why He wills, without respect of persons. He sometimes inclines His ear to the prayer of those who cry to Him, and because of their goodness and simplicity succours them, that they may not be made sad, and not because He is pleased with their prayer. The following illustration will make this more clear. A father covers his table with divers meats, some better than others. One of his children asks for one kind, not the best, but the first that presents itself to him: he asks for it because he likes it better than any other. His father seeing that he will not take of the best, even if he offered it, and that he would not have any satisfaction in it, gives him that he asked for. He gives it to him that he might not be left without food and disconsolate, but he gives it sorrowfully. Such was God's dealing with the people of Israel when they demanded a king. He gave them a king unwillingly, for that was not for their good. 'Hearken to the voice of the people,' saith He to Samuel: 'they have not rejected thee but Me, that I should not reign over them.'* He condescends in the same way to certain souls, giving them that which is not for their greater good, either because they will not, or because they cannot, walk with Him in the better way. And if at times these souls have a

* 1 Kings viii. 7.

tenderness and sweetness, spiritual or sensible, He gives it them because they are not disposed to feed on the strong and substantial meat, the sufferings of the Cross of His Son. It is His will that we should cleave thereto rather than to aught else. It is, in my opinion, much worse to seek for the knowledge of events through supernatural ways, than to seek spiritual sweetness in those of sense.

True means,—Reason and Revelation.

I do not see how I can excuse from sin, at least venial, those persons who do this, however good their intentions and great their progress in perfection. I say the same of those who bid them persevere in this way, or who consent to it. There is no necessity for their acting thus, because natural reason, the law and teaching of the Gospel are sufficient for our guidance, and there are no wants or difficulties which cannot be supplied or remedied by them, and that more in accordance with the will of God, and more to the profit of souls. Such is our obligation to make use of our reason and of the teaching of the Gospel, that, whether with or without our concurrence, if anything be revealed to us supernaturally, we may receive that only which is consistent with reason and the evangelical law. And we are bound to examine such things much more carefully than we should do, if no revelation had been made; for the devil, in order to deceive us, utters many things which are true and in conformity with reason.

Prayer and Hope enough for all needs.

There is no better or safer remedy for all our necessities and troubles than prayer and hope, by which God is moved to provide for us by such means as are pleasing unto Him. This is the counsel which the Holy Scriptures furnish us. When King Josaphat was in deepest affliction, hemmed in by his enemies on all sides, he betook himself to prayer, and said, 'As we know not what to do, we can only turn our eyes to Thee.'* When everything fails us, when reason is power-

* 2 Paral. xx. 12.

BOOK II.

less to suggest relief, we can then lift up our eyes to Thee only, that Thou mayest provide for us, as it shall seem best to Thee.

Three examples from Holy Scripture.

God too, though He sends answers to prayers thus offered, is angry. But, notwithstanding the certainty of this, I think it will be well to show it from certain passages of Holy Writ. When Saul desired to consult the prophet Samuel, then dead, the Prophet came at his request; God, however, was angry with Saul, for the Prophet rebuked him, saying, 'Why hast thou disturbed my rest, that I should be brought up?'* We know, too, that God was angry with the people of Israel when they asked Him for meat. He gave them meat, but He also sent fire from heaven to chastise them: 'As yet the meat was in their mouth, and the wrath of God came upon them.'† He was angry also with Balaam, when, at the bidding of Balac, he went to the Madianites, though God had said, 'Arise and go.' Balaam was bent on going, and had asked permission of God; but an Angel stood before him in the way with a drawn sword in his hand, and sought to kill him, and said, 'Thy way is perverse and contrary to Me.'‡ In this, and in many other ways, God condescends, but in anger, to our desires. And the Holy Writings furnish us many other instances of this truth, but on which we have no need to enlarge in a matter so plain.

I have only to add that it is a most perilous thing, and much more so than I can tell, to converse with God by these supernatural ways, and that whosoever is thus disposed cannot but fall into many shameful delusions. He who shall apply himself to these ways will learn by experience the truth of the matter. For over and above the difficulty of not being deceived by the Divine visions and locutions, there is usually the further danger of the devil thrusting himself

* 1 Kings xxviii. 15. † Num. xi. 4, 33; Ps. lxxvii. 30, 31.
‡ Num. xxii. 20, 32.

in among them. Satan, in general, comes to the soul in the ways and methods of God, suggesting to it communications so much resembling those of God, insinuating himself as a wolf in sheep's clothing among the flock, so that he can scarcely be detected. For as the evil spirit announces many things that are true, conformable with reason, and certain, men may be most easily deluded, thinking that, as the prophecy corresponded with the event, it could be none other than God who had spoken. They do not reflect how very easy it is for one, endowed with clear natural light, to understand in their causes many matters, which have been or may be done. Such an one will accurately guess at many things to come. And as the devil is endowed with so clear a light, he is able to infer such results from such causes; though they are not always such as he describes them, because all things depend on the will of God.

Satan has knowledge of physical causes.

Let us make this clear by an illustration: The devil knows that the condition of the earth and the atmosphere, and the position of the sun are such, that at a given time, the combination of the elements must, of necessity, occasion a pestilence. He will also know where the pestilence will be most violent and where least so. He perceives the pestilence in its causes. Is it a great matter for the devil, in this case, to reveal to a particular person that within a year or six months a plague will come, which does come? Yet the prediction is diabolic. He may also foretell earthquakes in the same way. When he sees the caverns of the earth filled with air, he may say an earthquake will come at such a time. This knowledge is natural. Extraordinary events in the providence of God may also be detected in their sources. Seeing that He is most just in His dealings with men, we may be able to see, in the ordinary way, that a given individual, city, or place is come to such a state or difficulty that God, in His providence and justice, must deal

BOOK II.

Future events foretold by natural knowledge. Two instances.

therewith as the cause demands: either in the way of punishment or of reward, according to the nature of the case. Under these circumstances, we may say, at such a time, God will visit, or such things will happen, most certainly. We have an instance of this in holy Judith, who, when she would persuade Holofernes that the people of Israel must certainly perish, told him of their many sins and the calamities they suffered, and added, 'therefore because they do these things, it is certain they will be given to destruction.'*

Here Judith saw the punishment in its cause. It is as if she had said, it is certain that such sins will draw down the chastisements of God, Who is most just. The same principle is taught in the book of Wisdom where it is written, 'By what things a man sinneth, by the same also he is tormented.'† The devil may perceive this not only naturally, but also by his experience of the like dealings of God. He may also announce it certainly beforehand.

Holy Tobias also knew in its causes the chastisement about to fall upon Ninive, for he warned his son thereof, saying, 'Now, children, hear me, and do not stay here; but as soon as you shall bury your mother by me in one sepulchre, without delay direct your steps to depart hence. For I see that its iniquity will bring it to destruction."‡ It is as if he had said, I see clearly that its iniquity must bring on punishment, and that its punishment will be its utter ruin. This might have been foreseen by the devil and Tobias, not only because of the evil deeds of Ninive, but also from their experience of the past, knowing that God had destroyed the old world, on account of the sins of men, by the deluge, and the people of Sodom by fire. But Tobias knew also the ruin of Ninive by the Holy Ghost.

The evil spirit may know that a given individual will die

* Judith xi. 12. † Wisd. xi. 17. ‡ Tob. xiv. 12, 13.

within a certain time in the course of nature, and may announce the fact beforehand. He may also know many other events in divers ways, which I am unable to describe, because they are exceedingly intricate and subtle. There is no escape here, therefore, but in fleeing revelations, visions, and locutions, because God is most justly offended with whosoever seeks them; He sees that it is rashness to expose oneself to so great a risk, and that to seek these things is presumption, curiosity, the fruit of pride, the source and root of vain-glory, contempt of the things of God, and many other evils into which so many have fallen. Such persons have so offended God, that He has deliberately abandoned them to errors and delusions and mental blindness; and has suffered them to go astray from the ordinary course of a well-regulated life, giving way to vanity and imaginations, as the Prophet saith: 'The Lord hath mingled in the midst thereof the spirit of giddiness,' * that is, in common speech, the spirit of understanding things the wrong way. The words of the Prophet are to the point, for he is speaking of those who attempted to know future events by supernatural ways. He says, therefore, that God had mingled in the midst of them the spirit of understanding things the wrong way; not that God willed or sent, in fact, this spirit of delusion, but that they thrust themselves into those things, the knowledge of which is naturally a secret. God, therefore, in His anger allowed them to utter foolish things, giving them no light where it was not His will they should enter. It is therefore said that He mingled, permissively, the spirit of giddiness in the midst of them.

This is the way in which God is the cause of this evil, namely, as the privative cause, which is the withdrawal of His light and grace, the result of which is inevitable error. It

* Is. xix. 14.

BOOK II.

Two examples of self-delusion.

is in this way, too, that He permits the devil to blind and deceive many, whose sins and whose frowardness deserve it. The devil is then able to deceive them, and does deceive them; men believing and accounting him a good spirit, and this to such a degree, that, though convinced that they are under the influence of the evil one, they cannot get rid of their delusions; because, by the permission of God, the spirit of contradiction is so strong within them. This was the case with the prophets of Achab, who, by the permission of God, was deceived by them; for He had allowed the evil spirit to do so, saying, 'Thou shalt deceive him and shalt prevail; go forth and do so.'* So strong was the delusion of the king and the prophets, that they refused to believe Micheas, who prophesied truly in opposition to the lying words of those prophets. They were all deceived, God having permitted their blindness, because they were bent on what they liked themselves, desiring that the event and the answer of God should correspond with their own wishes and desires. This disposition of mind is the most certain road towards being abandoned of God to error and delusions. Ezechiel in the name of God prophesies to the same effect; for speaking against such as seek knowledge, in the way of God, out of vanity of mind and curiosity, he says: 'If he... come to the prophet to enquire of Me by him, I the Lord will answer him by Myself, and I will set My face against that man. . . . And when the prophet shall err. . . . I the Lord have deceived' him.† We are to understand this of the non-concurrence of God's grace, so that delusion follows. God says, 'I will answer him by Myself,' in My anger, that is, I withdraw My grace and protection; then man falls infallibly into delusions, because God has abandoned him. Then, too, the devil comes forward and makes answer ac-

* 3 Kings xxii. 22.

† Ezech. xiv. 7, 8, 9.

cording to that man's wishes and desires, who, taking pleasure therein, the answers and suggestions of the evil one being in unison with his will, falls into many delusions.

I seem to have strayed in some measure from the subject, as I described it in the beginning of this chapter. I undertook to show that God was offended, even though He answered our prayers. Yet, if what I have said be carefully considered, it will be found to prove what I intended: it being clear throughout, that God is not pleased that men should seek after such visions, because they are in so many ways occasions of delusions.

CHAPTER XXII.

It is not lawful, under the New Law, as it was under the Old, to enquire of God by supernatural ways. This doctrine profitable for the understanding of the mysteries of our Holy Faith. Proofs from S. Paul.

Objections answered.

DOUBTS spring up before us, and hinder us from advancing as rapidly as I wish. For as they rise, it is necessary to remove them, that the truth of this doctrine may remain clear and in its full force. These doubts bring with them this advantage, that, notwithstanding the delays they occasion, they subserve my teaching, and make my purpose clear. Such is the present doubt.

I said in the former chapter, it is not the will of God that men should seek for clear knowledge in visions and locutions by supernatural ways. On the other hand, we know that this method was practised under the Old Law, and that it was then lawful; further still, that it was not only lawful but commanded, and that God rebuked men for not having recourse to it. He rebuked the children of Israel, because they had resolved to go down into Egypt before enquiring of Him, saying to them, 'Woe to you . . . who walk to go down into Egypt, and have not asked at my mouth.' * When the people of Israel were deceived by the Gabaonites, the Holy Ghost rebuked them for a like fault, for it is written that 'they took of their victuals and consulted not the mouth of the Lord.' † In the Holy Writings we see that God was consulted continually by Moses, by David, by all the Kings of Israel in their wars and necessities, by the Priests and Prophets of old, and that He answered them, and was not provoked to anger, and that in this all was well done. Yea, moreover, if they had not consulted Him, they would have done amiss: which is true. Why then, may we not, under the New Law and in the state of grace, do what was done under the Old?

What permitted to Jews forbidden to Christians,—why.

To this I reply, the chief reason why the prayers in question were lawful under the old dispensation, and why it was necessary for Prophets and Priests to seek visions and revelations from God was, that the Faith was not then revealed, that the evangelical Law was not established; and therefore that it was necessary for men to enquire of God in this way, and that He should answer them at one time by visions, revelations and locutions, at another by figures and similitudes, and again by other and different ways of communication. For all the answers, locutions, and revelations of old were mysteries of the Faith, or matters pertaining or tending thereto; inasmuch as the objects of faith proceed not from man, but from the mouth of God Himself, who, by His own mouth has revealed them. He therefore rebuked them when they did not consult Him; for it was His will they should do so, that He might answer them, directing all things towards the Faith, of which they had then no knowledge. But now that the Faith of Christ is established, and the evangelical Law promulgated in this day of grace, there is

* Is. xxx. 1, 2.

† Jos. ix. 14.

no necessity to consult Him as before, nor that He should answer and speak. For in giving to us, as He hath done, His Son, who is His only Word, He has spoken unto us once for all by His own and only Word, and has nothing further to reveal.

The Word of God fully spoken in the Incarnation.

This is the meaning of S. Paul in those words, by which he endeavoured to persuade the Jews to abandon the ancient ways of conversing with God, according to the Law of Moses, and to fix their eyes on Christ alone. 'God, who at sundry times and in divers manners spoke, in times past to the fathers by the Prophets, last of all, in these days hath spoken to us by His Son.'* God hath now so spoken, that nothing remains unspoken; for that which He partially revealed to the Prophets He hath now revealed all in Him, giving unto us all, that is, His Son. And, therefore, he who should now enquire of God in the ancient way, seeking visions or revelations, would offend Him; because he does not fix his eyes upon Christ alone, disregarding all besides. To such an one the answer of God is: 'This is My beloved Son, in whom I am well pleased, hear ye Him.'† I have spoken all by My Word, my Son; fix thine eyes upon Him, for in Him I have spoken and revealed all, and thou wilt find in Him more than thou desirest or askest. For if thou desirest partial visions, revelations, or words, fix thine eyes upon Him, and thou shalt find all. He is My whole Voice and Answer, My whole Vision and Revelation, which I spoke, answered, made, and revealed, when I gave Him to be thy Brother, Master, Companion, Ransom and Reward. I descended upon Him with My Spirit on Mount Tabor and said, 'This is My Beloved Son, in whom I am well pleased, hear ye Him.' It is not for thee now to seek new oracles and responses; for when I spoke in former times it was to promise

* Heb. i. 1.

† S. Matth. xvii. 5.

BOOK II.

Voice and Vision of God in Christ.

Christ: and the prayers of those who then enquired of Me were prayers for Christ and expectations of His coming, in whom all good was comprehended, according to the teaching of the Evangelists and Apostles. But, now, he who shall enquire of Me in the ancient way, or hope for an answer at My mouth, or that I should make to him any revelation, shows that he is not content with Christ, and therefore grievously wrongs My Beloved Son. While thou hast Christ thou hast nothing to ask of Me, nothing to desire in the way of visions or revelations. Look well unto Him, and thou wilt find that I have given all this and much more in Christ. If thou desirest a word of consolation from My mouth, behold My Son obedient unto Me and afflicted for My love, and thou wilt see how great is the answer I give thee. If thou desirest to learn of God secret things, fix thine eyes upon Christ, and thou wilt find the profoundest mysteries, the wisdom and marvels of God, hidden in Him: 'In Whom,' saith the Apostle, 'are hid all the treasures of wisdom and knowledge.'* These treasures will be sweeter and more profitable to thee than all those things thou desirest to know. It was in these that the Apostle gloried when he said, 'I judged not myself to know anything among you but Jesus Christ and Him crucified.'† If thou desirest other visions and revelations, Divine or bodily, look upon His Sacred Humanity, and thou wilt find there more than can ever enter into thy thoughts, 'for in Him dwelleth all the fulness of the Godhead corporally.'‡

It is, therefore, unbecoming to enquire of God by supernatural ways, and there is no necessity that He should reply, for having spoken by Christ, we ought to desire nothing more. He who shall now desire to know anything by extraordinary supernatural ways, implies a defect in God, as if

* Coloss. ii. 3. † 1 Cor. ii. 2. ‡ Coloss. ii. 9.

CHAP. XXII.

He had not given us enough when He gave us His only Son. For though we should enquire of Him, admitting the Faith and believing it, we should be guilty of curiosity showing but little faith. If we are thus curious we cannot expect to be taught, nor receive any other help in the supernatural way. For at that moment when Christ, dying on the cross cried out, 'it is consummated,'* not these forms of prayer only, but all the rites and ceremonies also of the Old Law were done away with.

Knowledge of God through the Church.

We must, therefore, be guided now by the teaching of Christ, of His Church and ministers, and through it seek the remedy for all our spiritual ignorance and infirmities. It is in this way that we shall obtain an abundant relief; all that goes beyond this, or neglects it, is not curiosity only, but great rashness; and we are to rely upon nothing supernatural which does not rest on the teaching of Christ, God and man, and of His ministers. So great is the obligation to do this, that S. Paul said: 'Though we, or an Angel from Heaven, preach to you a gospel, beside that which you have received, let him be anathema.† Seeing, then, that it is true that we must abide in the teaching of Christ, that all beside is nothing and not to be believed, unless it be in harmony therewith, he laboureth in vain who attempts to converse with God according to the way of the ancient dispensation. Moreover, it was not lawful in those days for everyone to enquire of God—neither did God answer everyone—but only for the Priests and the Prophets, for it was at their mouth that men were to seek for the law and knowledge. Whenever, therefore, anyone enquired of God, he did so through a prophet or a priest, and not by himself. And if David from time to time enquired of God, it was because he was himself a prophet, and even then he did not do so

* S. John xix. 30.

† Galat. i. 8.

without assuming the priestly robe; as we learn from his words to Abiathar, 'bring me hither the Ephod,'* which was one of the chief sacerdotal vestments. When the Ephod was brought, then it was he enquired of God. But at other times he made use of the services of Nathan and other prophets. Men were to believe that what the priests said to them came from God, because it was spoken by the mouth of prophets and of priests, and not because they themselves judged it safe. The words of God in those days were not meant by Him to be fully relied on, unless uttered by the mouth of priests and prophets; for it is the will of God that man should be governed and directed by another man like himself, and that we should not give entire belief to His own supernatural communications, nor rely securely upon them, until they shall have passed through the human channel of another man's mouth. And so it is, whenever He reveals anything to the human soul, He does so by inclining that soul, and him to whom it should be made known, to the matter of His revelation. Until then, the soul will be destitute of entire satisfaction therein, in order that man may obtain it through another like himself, and whom God has appointed to stand in His place.

God appoints ministers, from whom men must learn His Truth and Will.

Such was the case with Gideon, to whom God had more than once promised victory over the Madianites. He continued, nevertheless, to hesitate and fear, God having left him in this weakness, until he heard from the mouth of men that which God had announced Himself. So when God saw him hesitate, He said unto him, 'Arise, and go down into the camp. . . . and when thou shalt hear what they are saying, then shall thy hands be strengthened, and thou shalt go down more secure into the enemies' camp.'† So, when he had penetrated within the camp of the Madianites, he

* 1 Kings xxx. 7.

† Judg. vii. 9, 11.

heard one of them tell another how he had dreamed that Gideon conquered them. Upon this he took courage, and with great joy made his preparations for battle. It appears from this, that God's will was that he should not feel secure till he heard from another, what God had revealed Himself.

Hesitation of Gideon and of Moses.

A like event in the life of Moses is more wonderful still. God sent him with many instructions, confirming them by miracles—the rod he had was changed into a serpent, and his hand became leprous—to be the deliverer of the people of Israel. But Moses was so weak, hesitating, and doubtful of his course, that, notwithstanding God's being angry with him, he could not resolve to undertake his work until God encouraged him by the mouth of Aaron his brother: 'Aaron the Levite is thy brother; I know that he is eloquent; behold, he cometh forth to meet thee, and, seeing thee, shall be glad at heart. Speak to him, and put My words in his mouth, and I will be in thy mouth and in his mouth.'* When Moses heard this he took courage, in the hope of that comfort which he was to receive from the counsels of his brother Aaron.

Mutual counsel a means of Divine light and strength.

Such, too, is the conduct of the humble soul: it will not presume to converse with God by itself, neither can it satisfy itself without human counsel and direction. Such, also, is the will of God, for He draws near to those who come together in the way of truth, to make it clear, and to strengthen them in it, as He promised to do in the case of Moses and Aaron—namely, to be in the mouth of them both. He has promised us in His Gospel to help us in the same way, saying, 'Where there are two or three gathered together in My Name, there am I in the midst of them.'† Where two or three meet together, to consider what is for the greater glory and honour of My Name, there am I in the midst of

* Ex. iv. 14, 15.

† S. Matt. xviii. 20.

BOOK II.

Submission to the Church the security against deception.

them, enlightening them, and confirming the truths of God in their hearts. Remember, He does not say: Where one is, but where two are, at the least. He would have us know that it is not His will that anyone should, trusting to himself, rely on the Divine communications; and that He will not establish us therein without the authority and direction of the Church or His ministers. God will not enlighten him who is alone, nor confirm the truth in his heart: such an one will be weak and cold.

Peril of self-guidance.

This truth is insisted on by the Preacher, saying, 'Woe to him that is alone, for when he falleth, he hath none to lift him up. And if two lie together, they shall warm one another: how shall one alone be warmed? And if a man prevail against one, two shall withstand him.'* They shall 'warm one another' in the fire of God; and he that is alone cannot be but cold in the things of God. If the evil one prevail against those who are alone in their spiritual affairs, two, that is the penitent and his director, shall resist him when they come together to learn and practise the truth. And in general, until this be done, he who is alone is weak and tepid in it, notwithstanding he may have heard it of God more than once. S. Paul himself, having preached the Gospel for some time, and having received it, not from man, but from God, would not proceed further without conferring with S. Peter and the other Apostles, lest he should 'run, or had run in vain.'†

Prudence of S. Paul.

It is clear from these words of the Apostle, that it is not safe to rely on what seems to be a revelation from God, except under the conditions I have described. For even if a person were certain that a particular revelation is from God, as S. Paul was of the Gospel—for he had begun to preach it —still such an one might err in the execution of his work and in matters pertaining to it. For God does not always

* Eccles. iv. 10, 11, 12.

† Gal. ii. 2.

reveal the one, while He reveals the other; frequently He reveals a matter without revealing how it is to be brought about—because, in general, all that is within the province of human sagacity and skill He does not Himself perform nor declare, though He may have conversed familiarly for a long time with him to whom the revelation is made. S. Paul understood this well, for though he knew that the Gospel he preached was a Divine revelation, he 'conferred' with S. Peter.

Counsel of Jethro.

We have a most clear illustration of this truth in the life of Moses. Though God conversed so familiarly with him, He never gave him the salutary counsel which Jethro suggested, that he should appoint other judges to assist him, that the people might not 'wait from morning till night.' 'Provide out of all the people able men, such as fear God, in whom there is truth . . . who may judge the people at all times.'* God approved of the counsel of Jethro, but He gave it not, because the matter was within the limits of human prudence and discretion.

In the same way, too, all things relating to visions and Divine locutions, which are within the compass of human prudence and discretion, are not made known to us by God: it being always His will, that we should make use of our natural endowments, so far as possible; except in matters of Faith, which transcend the province of Judgment and Reason, though they are not contrary to them. Let no man, therefore, imagine, although God and His Saints converse familiarly with him about many things, that they will also reveal to him the faults he commits with respect to the matter of the revelation; for he may ascertain these in another way. We must not be too confident in this matter; for S. Peter himself, the Prince of the Church, and immediately taught of God, fell into error in his intercourse with the Gentiles. God was silent, and

Harmony of Reason and Faith.

* Ex. xviii. 21, 22.

BOOK II.

S. Paul rebukes S. Peter.

S. Paul rebuked him, as he tells us himself: 'When I saw that they walked not uprightly unto the truth of the Gospel, I said to Cephas, before them all: If thou, being a Jew, livest after the manner of the Gentiles, and not as the Jews do, how dost thou compel the Gentiles to live as do the Jews?'* God did not warn Peter of his fault, because he might have known it in the ordinary way. In the Day of Judgment God will punish many for sins and errors, with whom He holds familiar intercourse now, and to whom He gives much light and strength; because they are negligent in what they know they ought to do — relying on their converse with Him, and disregarding all besides. Such persons will then be astonished, as our Lord tells us; and they will cry, 'Lord, Lord, have not we prophesied in Thy Name, and cast out devils in Thy Name, and done many miracles in Thy Name?' The answer of the Judge will be, 'I never knew you; depart from Me, you that work iniquity.'† Of the number of these was Balaam, and others like him, who were sinners, even though God held converse with them. God will also rebuke the Elect, His own friends, with whom he conversed familiarly in this life, for the faults and negligences of which they are guilty. It is not necessary for Him to warn them now directly, because He has given them Reason and the Natural Law to remind them of their errors.

Obedience better than miracles.

God the Author of Reason and the Natural Law.

In conclusion, then, I say—and I gather it from the foregoing principle—that all communications made to the soul, of whatever kind and in whatever form, ought to be clearly, distinctly, and simply revealed to our spiritual director forthwith, and in all truthfulness. Though such communications seem to us of no moment, and not worth the time they take up in recounting them—seeing that the soul, by rejecting them and making no account of them, remains secure, as I

* Gal. ii. 14.

† S. Matt. vii. 22, 23.

have said; and more especially if they are visions or revelations or other supernatural visitations, whether clear or not, or whether it be of no importance or not that they should be so — still it is absolutely necessary to reveal them, though we may think otherwise ourselves. There are three reasons why it should be done:

Three fruits of openness with Spiritual Director:—

1. Clear understanding.

1. God reveals many things, the fruit, meaning, and certainty of which He does not establish in the soul until he, whom God has constituted the spiritual judge of that soul, has had them before him; for it is he who has the power to bind and to loose, to approve and reject, those communications, as I have shown by the illustrations I have given. Daily experience teaches us the same truth; for those humble souls, to whom these visitations are made, attain to renewed satisfaction, strength, enlightenment, and security, as soon as they have revealed them to the rightful person. Yea, such is the fruit of this submission, that some who, until they had revealed them, thought they had received them not, and that they were not theirs, after revealing them receive them as it were anew.

2. Detachment of spirit.

2. In general the soul to whom these communications are made requires instruction therein, that it may be directed in that way to poverty of spirit and detachment, which is the Obscure Night. For if the necessary instructions fail — even when the soul does not seek these things — the result will be an unconscious rudeness in the spiritual way, and a falling back upon the way of sense.

3. Humility.

3. An unreserved communication is necessary for humbling and mortifying the soul, though we make no account of these visions, and regard them not. For there are some souls who have a great repugnance to reveal these matters, because they think them to be of no importance, and do not know how their spiritual director may deal with them. This is a want of humility, and therefore such persons must

BOOK II.

submit to reveal them. On the other hand, there are some who are ashamed to make known these things, lest they should seem to be like the Saints, or for other reasons which fill them with pain when they speak. These, therefore, think themselves dispensed from manifesting their state, because they attribute no importance to it. But this is the very reason why they should mortify themselves, and reveal what has passed within them, until they become humble, gentle, and ready in this, and ever afterwards reveal with facility their interior state.

Advice to Spiritual Directors.

But remember, though I say that these communications are to be set aside, and that confessors should be careful not to discuss them with their penitents, it is not right for spiritual directors to show themselves severe in the matter, nor betray any contempt or aversion; lest their penitents should shrink within themselves, and be afraid to reveal their condition, and so fall into many inconveniences, which would be the case if the door were thus shut against them. For, as I have said before, these supernatural visitations are means in the hands of God for guiding souls, and, being such, they must not be lightly regarded by spiritual directors, who are not to be surprised nor scandalised at them; yea, rather, they must treat them with gentleness and calmness, encouraging their penitents, and giving them every opportunity to explain them. And, if it be necessary, they must enjoin upon them this manifestation, for at times, everything is necessary in the difficulty, which penitents experience when they have to reveal their state. Let them direct them by faith, carefully instructing them to turn away from these supernatural visitations, showing them how to be detached therefrom in mind and desire, so that they may advance, and understand that one good work, or act of the will, wrought in charity is more precious in the eyes of God, than that which all the visions and revelations of Heaven might effect; and

Works of love better than visions of Heaven.

that many souls, to whom visions have never come, are incomparably more advanced in the Way of Perfection, than others to whom many have been given.

CHAPTER XXIII.

Of the purely Spiritual Apprehensions of the Intellect.

First kind of supernatural spiritual knowledge,—Distinct.

I HAVE been somewhat concise in the discussion of those intellectual apprehensions which are derived from the senses, if we regard the abundance of the matter, and I am unwilling to pursue it at greater length; because, so far as my purpose is concerned—which is the extrication of the intellect from them, and the direction of it into the Night of Faith—I think I have said more than enough. I shall now, therefore, enter on the discussion of the other four apprehensions of the intellect, which, in the tenth chapter, I said were purely spiritual—namely, Visions, Revelations, Locutions, and Spiritual Impressions. I call these purely spiritual, because they do not reach the intellect, like those which are corporeal and imaginary, by the way of the senses of the body; but because they reach it independently of every bodily sense, interior or exterior, clearly and distinctly in a supernatural way, and passively; that is, irrespectively of, at least, any active operation on the part of the soul itself.

Comprising purely spiritual— 1. Visions. 2. Revelations. 3. Locutions. 4. Impressions.

Speaking generally, we may say that these four apprehensions may be called visions of the soul; for we say that the soul sees when it understands. And inasmuch as all these apprehensions are intelligible to the intellect, we say that they are spiritually visible; and therefore the particular intelligence of them, formed in the intellect, may be called intellectual vision. And as all the objects of the senses—of seeing, hearing, smelling, tasting, and touching—in so far as

The Intelligible seen by the Eye of the Soul.

they are true or false, are objects of the intellect, it follows that, as all that is bodily visible is an occasion of corporeal visions to the bodily eyes; so all that is intelligible is an occasion of spiritual vision to the spiritual eye of the soul, which is the intellect; for, as I have said, to understand is to see. And thus, speaking generally, these four apprehensions may be called visions. The other senses, however, cannot be thus applied, for not one of them is capable of receiving, as such, the subject-matter of another.

Explanation of terms.

But as these apprehensions are represented to the soul in the same manner as to all the senses, it follows, to use the proper and specific terms, that all which the intellect receives by the way of seeing—for it can see spiritually, as the eyes see bodily—may be called Vision; that which it receives by apprehending and perceiving new things, Revelation; that which it receives by the way of hearing, Locution; and that which it receives in the way of the other senses, such as spiritual odour, taste, and delectation, of which the soul is supernaturally conscious, may be called Spiritual Impressions. From all this the intellect elicits an act of intelligence or spiritual vision, as I have said, without perceiving any form, image, or figure whatever of the natural imagination or fancy, which could furnish any foundation for it: for these things are communicated directly to the soul by a supernatural operation and by supernatural means.

The intellect, therefore, must be extricated from these things also — precisely as from the corporeal and imaginary apprehensions — by being guided and directed into the spiritual Night of Faith to the Divine and substantial Union of the love of God. For if this be not effected, the intellect will be perplexed and rude; and that solitude and detachment from them, which is requisite for travelling on the Way of Union, will be prevented. For, admitting that these apprehensions are more exalted, more profitable and safe,

CHAP. XXIII.

than those which are corporeal and imaginary — inasmuch as they are interior, purely spiritual, and less liable to the intrusions of Satan — because they are communications of God to the soul, in the greatest pureness and subtlety, independent of, at least, any active operations of the soul or of the imagination; still the intellect may be not only embarrassed by them, but, by its incautiousness, greatly deluded.

I might now finish with these four apprehensions together, by giving advice common to them all, as I have already done with the others — namely; let no man seek them or desire them: still, inasmuch as a different course will enlighten us how to do so, and as there is something still to be said with reference to them, I think it well to treat of each one of them in particular. With this view I now proceed to speak of the first of them—Spiritual or Intellectual Visions.

CHAPTER XXIV.

Of the two kinds of Spiritual Visions which come by the supernatural way.

First source of distinct supernatural spiritual knowledge,—Intellectual Vision.

I SAY, then, speaking directly of the Spiritual Visions, independent of any bodily sense, that there are two kinds to which the intellect is liable: one of corporeal substances, another of abstract or incorporeal substances. The corporeal visions are visions of all material things in heaven and earth, visible to the soul in a certain light emanating from God, in which distant things of heaven and earth may be seen. The other visions of incorporeal things require a higher light: thus visions of incorporeal substances, as of Angels and of souls, are not frequent or natural in this life; and still less so is the vision of the Divine Essence, which is

Two kinds. 1. Of the Corporeal. 2. Of the Spiritual.

BOOK II.

Spiritual Visions of incorporeal substances.

Examples of S. Paul, Moses, and Elias.

peculiar to the Blessed, unless it be communicated transiently by a dispensation of God, or by conservation of our natural life and condition, and the abstraction of the spirit; as was perhaps the case of S. Paul when he heard the unutterable secrets in the third heaven, 'Whether in the body,' saith he, 'I know not, or out of the body, I know not; God knoweth.' * It is clear from the words of the Apostle that he was carried out of himself, by the act of God, as to his natural existence.

It is also believed that God showed His own Essence to Moses, for He said unto him that He would set him in a hole of the rock, and protect him with His right hand, that he might not die when His glory passed by.† This passing by was a transient vision, God upholding with His right hand the natural life of Moses. But these Essential Visions, such as those of S. Paul, Moses, and our father Elias, when, at the whistling of a gentle air, he 'covered his face with his mantle,'‡ are transient and of most rare occurrence, and scarcely ever granted, and to very few; for God shows them only to those who, like these, are the mighty ones of His Church and Law.

Now, though, in the ordinary course, these visions cannot be clearly and distinctly seen in this life, the effect of them may be felt in the very substance of the soul, through the instrumentality of a loving knowledge, in the most sweet touch and union pertaining to the spiritual impressions, of which, by the grace of God, I shall speak hereafter. The end I have in view is the Divine Embracing, the Union of the soul with the Divine Substance. I shall speak of it when I treat of the mystical, confused, or obscure intelligence, and explain how, in this loving and obscure knowledge, God unites Himself with the soul, eminently and Divinely. For

* 2 Cor. xii. 2. † Ex. xxxiii. 22. ‡ 3 Kings xix. 13.

this loving obscure knowledge, which is Faith, serves, in a manner, in this life as means of the Divine union, as the light of glory hereafter serves for the Beatific Vision.

Spiritual Visions of corporeal substances.

Let me now, then, speak of visions of corporeal substances, spiritually presented to the soul, after the manner of bodily visions. As the eyes behold bodily things in natural light, so the intellect, in light supernaturally derived, beholds interiorly the same natural things, and others also such as God wills; the vision, however, is different in kind and form, for spiritual or intellectual visions are much more clear and subtle than bodily visions. When God grants this favour to any one, He communicates to him that supernatural light, wherein he beholds what God wills, most easily and most distinctly, whether they be things of heaven or of earth; neither is their presence nor absence any impediment to the vision.

1. Their nature.

When these visions occur, it is as if a door were opened into a most marvellous light, whereby the soul sees, as men do when the lightning suddenly flashes in a dark night. The lightning makes surrounding objects visible for an instant, and then leaves them in obscurity, though the forms of them remain in the fancy. But in the case of the soul the vision is much more perfect; for those things it saw in spirit in that light are so impressed upon it, that whenever God enlightens it again, it beholds them as distinctly as it did at first, precisely as in a mirror, in which we see objects reflected whenever we look upon it. These visions once granted to the soul never again leave it altogether; for the forms remain, though they become somewhat indistinct in the course of time.

2. Their permanent character.

The effects of these visions in the soul are quietness, enlightenment, joy like glory, sweetness, pureness, love, humility, inclination or elevation of the mind to God, sometimes more, sometimes less, sometimes more of one, some-

3. Their effects.

BOOK II.

times more of another, according to the disposition of the soul and the will of God.

Diabolic spiritual visions.

The devil, too, can produce or mimic these visions by means of a certain natural light. He employs therein the fancy, in which, by spiritual insinuations, he presents clearly before the mind either present or distant things. And some Doctors, commenting on that place in the Gospel where it is written that the devil 'showed' our Lord 'all the kingdoms of the world,'* say that he did so by a spiritual insinuation, because it was impossible to see at once 'all the kingdoms of the world and the glory of them' with the bodily eyes. But there is a great difference between the visions of God and those of the evil one. For the effect of the latter is not like that of the former: those of Satan result in dryness of spirit, in a tendency to self-esteem, to accept and make much of visions: and in no degree whatever do they produce the gentleness of humility, and love of God. Again, the forms of the diabolic visions do not remain impressed on the soul with the sweet clearness of the others, neither do they endure, yea, rather, are immediately effaced, unless it be when the soul attaches itself to them: in that case the importance attached to them causes them to be remembered naturally, but with great dryness of spirit, and without the fruit of humility and love, which issue out of the good visions, whenever they recur to the memory.

How distinguished from those of God.

These visions, inasmuch as they are visions of created things, between which and God there is no congruity or proportion, cannot subserve the intellect as proximate means of the Divine union. It is, therefore, necessary for the soul to be negatively disposed with respect to them, as well as to the others, if it is to advance by the proximate means,

* S. Matt. iv. 8; vide S. Thom. 3, p. q. 41, a. 2, 3; Abulensem in Matt. iv. q. 49.

which is Faith. And therefore the forms which these visions show, and which remain impressed on the soul, must not be treasured up nor preserved, neither must we trust to them; for this would be to embarrass ourselves by dwelling on forms, images, and persons, which relate to the interior life, and not to advance in the denial of all things onwards unto God. For supposing that these forms are continually present, that would be no great hindrance, if we make no account of them. Though it be true that the recollection of them excites the soul to a certain love of God, and to Contemplation, yet pure faith and detachment in darkness excites it much more, without the soul's knowing how or whence it cometh. The end of this will be that the soul goes forward, on fire with the anxieties of the most pure love of God, without knowing whence they come or on what foundations they rest. In short, as faith is rooted and infused more and more into the soul, in this emptiness and darkness, in detachment from all things, in poverty of spirit — these are different expressions of one and the same thing — so also the Charity of God is the more rooted and infused into the soul. And therefore the more the soul strives to become blind and annihilated as to all interior and exterior things, the more it will be filled with Faith and Love and Hope. But this love at times is neither comprehended nor felt, because it does not establish itself in the senses with tenderness, but in the soul with fortitude, with greater courage and resolution than before; though it sometimes overflows into the senses, and shows itself tender and gentle.

Effective and affective love.

In order, then, to attain to this love, joy, and delight which visions effect, it is necessary that the soul should have fortitude, and be mortified; so as to abide willingly in emptiness and darkness, and to lay the foundation of its love and delight on what it neither sees nor feels, on what it cannot see nor feel—namely, on God Incomprehensible and Supreme. Our way to Him is therefore, of necessity, in self-denial. Even if a soul were so wise, strong, and humble that the devil could not delude it by visions, nor make it presumptuous, as he generally does, it will make no progress, because it puts obstacles in the way of spiritual detachment and poverty of spirit, and emptiness in faith, the essential conditions of the Divine union.

As the principles established in the nineteenth and the twentieth chapters, concerning the visions and supernatural apprehensions of the senses, are applicable to these visions also, I shall not spend further time now in treating of them at greater length.

CHAPTER XXV.

Of Revelations: their nature and division.

Second source,—Spiritual Revelations,—what.

I HAVE now to speak, in the order laid down, of the spiritual apprehensions, which I have called Revelations. Of these, some properly belong to the spirit of Prophecy. In the first place, a revelation is nothing else but the disclosure of some hidden truth, or the manifestation of some secret or mystery. For instance, God permits a certain soul to understand a particular matter, declaring the truth of it to the intellect, or makes known certain things that He hath done, is doing, or intends to do. This being so, we may say that there are two kinds of revelations: one, the disclosure of truths to the intellect, properly called intellectual knowledge or intelligence; the other, a manifestation of secrets, and this is called revelation with more propriety than the former. The first kind, strictly speaking, cannot be called revelation, because it consists in God's making the soul to understand pure truths, regarding not only temporal but also spiritual things, showing them openly and distinctly. I have resolved to treat of them under the term Revelations — first, because of their mutual connection and proximity, and, secondly, because I would not multiply distinctions.

I distinguish revelations therefore into two kinds of apprehensions — intellectual knowledge, and the manifestation of the secrets and hidden mysteries of God. I shall conclude the subject, with the utmost brevity, in two chapters; and, first, of intellectual knowledge.

CHAPTER XXVI.

The Intelligence of pure truths. Two kinds thereof. The conduct of the soul therein.

First kind of Revelations, —Intelligence of pure truths.

THE intelligence of pure truths requires, for its proper explanation, that God should hold the hand and wield the pen of the writer. Keep in mind, my dear reader, that these matters are beyond all words. But as my purpose is not to discuss them, but to teach and direct the soul through them to the Divine union, it will be enough if I speak of them concisely within certain limits, so far as my subject requires it.

This kind of visions, or rather of knowledge of pure truths, is very different from that described in the twenty-second chapter, for it is not the same with the intellectual visions of bodily things. It consists in understanding or seeing with the intellect the truths of God, or of things, or concerning things which are, have been, or will be. It is most like to the spirit of Prophecy, as I shall perhaps hereafter explain.

Its definition and division.

This kind of knowledge is twofold: one relates to the Creator, the other to creatures. And though both kinds are most full of sweetness, the delight produced by that which relates to God is not to be compared to aught beside; and there are

BOOK II.

neither words nor language to describe it, for it is the knowledge of God Himself and His delights; as the Psalmist saith, 'There is no one like to Thee.'*

1. Supernatural intuition of God and His Attributes.

This knowledge relates directly unto God, in the deepest sense of some of His Attributes; now of His Omnipotence, now of His Might, and again of His Goodness and Sweetness; and whenever the soul feels it, it is penetrated by it. In so far as this becomes pure Contemplation, the soul sees clearly that it cannot describe it otherwise than in general terms, which the abundance of delight and happiness forces from it; but still those are not adequate expressions of what it feels within. Thus David, having had experience of this state, makes use of ordinary words, saying, 'The judgments of the Lord,' that is, what we judge and feel about God, His Might and His Attributes, 'are true, justified in themselves, more to be desired than gold and many precious stones, and sweeter than honey and the honeycomb.'†

Examples of David, Moses, and S. Paul.

When God gave Moses the knowledge of Himself, while passing by, all that Moses could say was uttered in ordinary words. For when the Lord passed before him he fell prostrate on his face, and said, 'O the Lord, the Lord God, merciful and gracious, patient and of much compassion and true, Who keepest mercy unto thousands!'‡ It is evident from this that Moses was unable to describe what he learned of God in that particular knowledge, and so gave utterance to these words. And though at times, when this knowledge is vouchsafed to the soul, words are uttered, yet the soul knows full well that it has in nowise expressed what it felt, because it is conscious that there are no words of adequate signification. Thus S. Paul, admitted to this knowledge of God, did not attempt to express it, only saying that he had 'heard secret words which it is not granted to man to utter.'§

* Ps. xxxix. 6. † Ps. xviii. 11.
‡ Ex. xxxiv. 6, 7. § 2 Cor. xii. 4.

This Divine knowledge concerning God never relates to particular things, because it is conversant with the Highest, and therefore cannot be explained unless when it is extended to some truth less than God, which is capable of being described; but this general knowledge is ineffable. It is only a soul in union with God that is capable of this profound loving knowledge, for it is itself that union. This knowledge consists in a certain contact of the soul with the Divinity, and it is God Himself Who is then felt and tasted, though not manifestly and distinctly, as it will be in glory. But this touch of knowledge and of sweetness is so deep and so profound that it penetrates into the inmost substance of the soul, and the devil cannot interfere with it, nor produce anything like it—because there is nothing else comparable with it—nor infuse any sweetness or delight which shall at all resemble it. This knowledge savours, in some measure, of the Divine Essence and of everlasting life, and the devil has no power to simulate anything so great.

Bliss and Power of the Touches of God.

Nevertheless, the devil is able to produce certain pretended imitations of it, by representing to the soul a certain grandeur and sensible fulness, striving to persuade it that this is God; but he cannot so do this that his influence shall penetrate into the interior part of the soul, renew it, and fill it with love profoundly, as the knowledge of God does. For there are some acts of knowledge and touches of God, wrought by Him in the substance of the soul, which so enrich it that one of them is sufficient, not only to purge away at once certain imperfections, which had hitherto resisted the efforts of a whole life, but also to fill the soul with virtues and Divine gifts. Such is the sweetness and deep delight of these touches of God, that one of them is more than a recompense for all the sufferings of this life, however great their number. They render the soul so generous and so courageous in the endurance of afflictions for God, that it becomes a special pain to see its tribulations diminished.

Now the soul can never ascend to the height of this knowledge by any reflections or imagination, because it transcends all these, and so God effects it without the cooperation of the soul. Sometimes, when the soul least thinks of it, and when it least desires it, God touches it divinely, causing certain recollections of Himself. Sometimes, too, the Divine touches are sudden, occurring even while the soul is occupied with something else, and that occasionally of trifling moment. They are also so sensible and efficacious, that at times they make not only the soul, but the body also, to tremble. At other times they come gently, without any agitation whatever, accompanied by a deep sense of delight and spiritual refreshing.

On other occasions, they come at the hearing or utterance of particular expressions, whether taken from the Holy Scripture or elsewhere. But they are not always equally sensible and efficacious, for they are very often exceedingly slight; but however slight they may be, one of these recollections and touches of God is more profitable to the soul than any other knowledge of, or meditation on, the creatures and works of God. And as this knowledge is communicated suddenly, and independently of the will, the soul must not strive to receive it, or strive not to receive it, but be humble and resigned; for God will do His own work, how and when He will. I do not say that the soul is to conduct itself negatively here, as in the case of the other apprehensions; because the Divine touches are a part of the Union, to which I would direct the soul, and for attaining unto which I teach it to withdraw and detach itself from all besides. The means by which God effects this great work must be humility and patient suffering for love of Him, with resignation and indifference as to all reward. These graces are not bestowed

Harmony of Desire and Resignation.

on the soul which cleaves to anything of its own, inasmuch as they are wrought by an especial Love of God towards the soul, which also loves Him in perfect detachment and pure disinterestedness. This is the meaning of those words of our Lord, 'He that loveth Me shall be loved of My Father: and I will love him, and will manifest Myself to him.'* These words refer to this knowledge and these touches, of which I am speaking, and which God manifests to the soul that truly loves Him.

2. Supernatural Intuition of Creatures,—its certainty.

The second kind of knowledge, or of visions of interior truths, is very different from this, being of things greatly lower than God. It includes the perception of the truth of things in themselves, of actions and events in the world. Such is the nature of this knowledge, whenever it is given, that it compels assent, without regard to any assertion on the part of others; even if the matter be told otherwise, the soul is unable to assent interiorly to that account, though it may do violence to itself for that end. The mind perceives something else in that which had been spiritually presented to it, and sees it, as it were, clearly. This may belong to the spirit of Prophecy, or to that gift which S. Paul calls 'the discerning of spirits.'† Still, though the soul may hold what it perceives to be certain and true, it must not on that account refuse belief and obedience to its spiritual director, though his counsels contradict the impressions received. This must be done in order that the soul may be directed in Faith to the Divine union, towards which it should journey by believing rather than by understanding.

The Holy Scriptures furnish clear evidence of both the one and the other. The particular knowledge of things is thus spoken of by the Wise Man: 'He hath given me the true knowledge of the things that are: to know the disposition of the whole world and the virtues of the elements. The

* S. John xiv. 21.

† 1 Cor. xii. 10.

BOOK II.

Infused knowledge of Solomon.

beginning and ending, and midst of the times; the alterations of their courses, and the changes of seasons; the revolutions of the year, and the dispositions of the stars; the natures of living creatures, and the rage of wild beasts; the force of winds, and reasonings of men; the diversities of plants, and the virtues of roots; and all such things as are hid and not foreseen, I have learned: for Wisdom, which is the worker of all things, taught me.'* And though this knowledge of all things, which the Wise Man says he had received from God, was infused and general, the passage before us is sufficient evidence for all the particular knowledge which God infuses into souls supernaturally, according to His good pleasure: not that He gives a general habit of knowledge, as He gave to Solomon, but that He reveals occasionally certain truths concerning those matters which the Wise Man speaks of.

Gratiæ gratis datæ.

Though our Lord infuses into many souls habits of knowledge relating to many things, still He does not infuse them so generally as in the case of Solomon. There is a difference like that between the gifts, mentioned by S. Paul, which God distributes; among these are wisdom, knowledge, faith, prophecy, discerning of spirits, divers kinds of tongues, and interpretation of speeches: 'To one indeed, by the Spirit, is given the word of wisdom. . . . and to another the word of knowledge, . . . to another faith, . . . to another prophecy, to another the discerning of spirits, to another divers kinds of tongues, to another interpretation of speeches.'† All these kinds of knowledge are infused graces *gratis datæ*, gratuitously given of God to whom He will, as He gave them to the holy Prophets and the Apostles, and to other Saints.

But over and above these gifts, or graces *gratis datæ*, perfect persons, or those who are advancing to Perfection,

* Wisd. vii. 17–21.

† 1 Cor. xii. 8–10.

very frequently receive the knowledge of things present or distant, in a certain illumination of their purified and enlightened mind. The following words are applicable in this sense: 'As the faces of them that look therein, shine in the water, so the hearts of men are laid open to the prudent.'* This is to be understood of those who have attained to the Science of the Saints, in Holy Scripture called Prudence.† In the same way, too, spiritual persons understand other things, though not always when they will: for this gift is theirs only who have the habit of this knowledge, and even they sometimes are at fault, because all this depends on the good pleasure of God.

Science of the Saints.

Those persons, whose minds are purified, ascertain with great facility, some better than others, what is passing in the hearts of men, their inclinations and their capacities; and this from certain outward signs, however slight they may be, such as expressions, motions, or gestures. As the devil, being a spirit, can do this, so also the spiritual man, according to the words of the Apostle: 'The spiritual man judgeth all things,'‡ and 'the Spirit searcheth all things, even the deep things of God.'§ Therefore, though spiritual men cannot, in the order of nature, know the thoughts and intentions of others, yet by supernatural enlightenment, through certain signs, they may well do so. And though they may be often deceived in their interpretation of these signs, yet for the most part they will be correct. But we are not to rely on any of these means, for the devil may insinuate himself herein with exceeding cunning, as we shall presently see, and in consequence of this, we must renounce this method and form of knowledge.

Spiritual persons are able to see, though distant, what

* Prov. xxvii. 19.
† Ib. ix. 10.
‡ 1 Cor. ii. 15.
§ Ib. 10.

BOOK II.

Infused knowledge of Eliseus.

other men are doing. We have an instance of this in our holy Father Eliseus, who saw his servant Giezi hide the gifts he had received from Naaman. 'Was not my heart present,' saith the Prophet, 'when the man turned back from his chariot to meet thee?'* Eliseus saw in spirit the act, as if he had been present on the spot. The same Prophet saw also what passed in the council of the King of Syria, and revealed it to the King of Israel, thereby frustrating the devices of the former. So when the King of Syria saw that his plans became known to his enemy, he complained to his people, saying: 'Why do you not tell me who it is that betrays me to the King of Israel? And one of his servants said, No one, my Lord O King; but Eliseus the prophet that is in Israel, telleth the King of Israel all the words, that thou speakest in thy privy chamber.'†

Both the one and the other kind of this knowledge of events are granted to the soul passively, without effort on its part. For it sometimes occurs that a person, while not thinking at all of the matter, receives in spirit a vivid perception of what he hears or reads, and that with greater distinctness than the words involve; and sometimes, too, even when he knows not the language to which the words belong, the knowledge of the matter is conveyed to him without his being able to explain the terms that imply it.

As to the delusions which the devil is able to effect, and does effect, with reference to this knowledge, I have much to say. Those delusions are very great and very difficult of detection; for the devil, by way of suggestion, is able to represent much intellectual knowledge to the soul, by the use of the bodily senses, and is able to establish that knowledge so firmly as to make it appear true; and if that soul be not humble and cautious, he will no doubt cause it to believe

* 4 Kings v. 26. † Ib. vi. 11, 12.

CHAP. XXVI.

an infinity of lies. For the suggestions of the devil offer great violence to the soul at times, especially because the senses are weak; and he plays on that weakness with such force, persuasiveness, and determination, that much prayer and repeated efforts become necessary, in order to shake off his influence.

He is wont occasionally to reveal, falsely, but with great distinctness, the sins of others, evil consciences, and corrupt souls, with a view to detraction, and to induce him, to whom the revelation is made, to publish the sins in question, so that other sins may be added to them. He excites a false zeal, deluding him, in whom he excites it, into the belief that these revelations are intended to lead him to pray for the souls of those whom he thus traduces. It is indeed true that God sometimes represents to holy souls the necessities of their neighbours, that they may pray for them, or relieve them. He revealed to Jeremias the weakness of Baruch, that he might advise him therein.* But most frequently it is the devil that doeth this, and that falsely, that persons may be accused of sin, and afflicted: of this we have many proofs. At other times, he communicates with much certainty other kinds of knowledge, and induces men to believe them.

Detachment from supernatural intuitions necessary for Perfection.

All such knowledge as this, whether it comes from God or not, can be but of little profit to the soul in the Way of Perfection, if it trusts to it: yea, rather, if it is not careful to reject it, it will not only hinder it on its road, but will inflict upon it great evil, and cause it to fall into many delusions; for all the dangers and inconveniences of the Supernatural Apprehensions, and many more, are to be found here. I shall, therefore, not enlarge further on this point; seeing that I have already given sufficient instruction on this

* Jerem. xlv.

BOOK II.

matter, and shall say but this, that the penitent must be careful to reject this knowledge, walking with God in the way of knowing nothing, and to give account to his director of it all, and abide constantly by his advice.

Let the director guide his penitent quickly past this, and not suffer him to dwell upon it, because it is of no help to him on the road to the Divine union. For as I have said of those things which are passively wrought in the soul, the fruit which God wills, remains behind. I do not, therefore, think it requisite to describe the effects of this knowledge, whether true or false, for my task in such a case would be wearisome and endless. The effects in question cannot be described within reasonable limits, for as the knowledge is manifold, so are the effects of it. The true knowledge brings forth good issues, tending to good; and the false knowledge evil, tending to evil. When I say that this knowledge is to be rejected, and how it is to be done, I have said enough.

CHAPTER XXVII.

Of the second kind of Revelations, the disclosure of secrets and hidden mysteries. How they may subserve and hinder the Divine union. Of the many delusions of the devil incident to them.

Second kind of Revelations,—Disclosure of Mysteries.

I EXPLAINED the second kind of revelations to be the manifestation of secrets and hidden mysteries. This again is twofold. One relates to God Himself, and includes the revelation of the Mystery of the Most Holy Trinity and the Divine Unity. The second relates to God in His operations, and includes all the other articles of the Holy Catholic Faith, and the truths explicitly resulting therefrom. It includes also a great number of prophetic revelations, promises, and threatenings of God, and other matters which have already been accomplished, and which shall hereafter occur. We may also refer to this second kind of revelations, many other particular events which God ordinarily reveals, as well concerning the world in general, as also concerning particular Kingdoms, Provinces, States, families, and persons. We have abundant evidence of all this in the Holy Scriptures, especially in the books of the Prophets, where we meet with revelations of all kinds.

Revelations divided into 1. De Deo ad intra. 2. De Deo ad extra.

But as this matter is perfectly plain and clear, I will not spend my time in adducing the proofs; but content myself with saying, that these revelations are not always expressed in words, for God makes them in many and in divers ways. Sometimes He makes them by words alone, and sometimes by signs alone, figures, images, and resemblances, and at other times by both signs and words together; as we see in the Prophets, particularly in the Apocalypse, where we find not only the kinds of revelations here spoken of, but also the divers modes by which they are made.

God still in our day makes revelations of the second kind. He reveals to some individuals how long they shall live, what trials they have to endure, or what will befall such and such a person, such or such a kingdom. And even with regard to the mysteries of our Faith, He is wont to reveal the truths thereof by a special light and meaning. This, however, is not properly a revelation, because the matter of it has been already revealed, but rather a manifestation and explanation of it.

Revelations tested by the Catholic Faith.

In those things, therefore, which we call revelations — I am not now using the word as relating to the Revelation of the mysteries of Faith—the devil may interfere on a great scale. For as these revelations are generally expressed by words, figures, and similitudes, the devil may also imitate the same most easily. If, however, in the first and second kind, in that which touches the Faith, any new or different revelation be made, we are in no wise to give heed to it; no, not

BOOK II.

The Catholic Faith always the same.

even if we learned it from an angel from Heaven. 'Though we or an angel from Heaven,' saith the Apostle, 'preach a gospel to you beside that which you have received, let him be anathema.'* No new revelations are to be admitted in the matter of that once made, beyond what may be consistent with it, lest we should go astray by admitting contradictions, and lose the purity of Faith. We must captivate the intellect, and cleave in simplicity to the Faith and teaching of the Church, 'for faith,' saith S. Paul, 'cometh by hearing.'† No man will give heed or credit easily to new revelations, unless he has a mind to be deceived.

The devil likened to a cobbler.

The devil with a view to deceive mankind, and propagate delusions in the world, begins by publishing truth, and what is likely to be true, in order to gain our confidence. He resembles herein a cobbler, who with the sharp bristle at the end of his thread penetrates the leather, and then draws after it the soft and waxened part, which never could have penetrated the leather by itself, without being preceded by the hard bristle. Great circumspection is necessary here; for though it were true that the soul ran no risk of delusion, yet is it more becoming that it should not desire clear knowledge, so that it may preserve the merit of its faith in its purity and integrity, and come in this Night of the Intellect to the Divine light of Union.

It is of the utmost moment for us to close the eyes of our intellect, when a new revelation is brought to us, and rest on the ancient prophecies. The Apostle himself, though he had seen the glories of Tabor, writes, 'We have the more firm prophetical word, whereunto you do well to attend.'‡ Though the vision which we saw on the Mount was true, yet the more certain and more firm is the word of revealed Prophecy, on which you do well to rest your souls.

* Galat. i. 8. † Rom. x. 17. ‡ 2 S. Pet. i. 19.

If it be true, for these reasons, that we ought not to regard with curiosity any new revelations on the subject-matter of the Faith; how much more ought we also, not to admit, or to give heed to, other revelations relating to other matters? It is in these that the devil in general is so strong, that I think it impossible to escape his delusions in many of them, if we do not strive to repel them; such appearance of truth and certainty does the devil throw around them. He unites together so many probabilities, and all so consistently arranged, in order to gain credit, and roots them so firmly in the senses and the imagination, that the subject of them believes them without any hesitation whatever. He makes the soul trust to them so completely, that if it were not humble, it could scarcely be persuaded of their falsehood and disentangled from his delusions.

For this cause, therefore, the pure, simple, cautious, and humble soul ought to resist and reject these revelations and other visions; for it is not necessary to seek them, yea rather it is necessary to reject them, if we are to attain to the Union of Love. This is the meaning of Solomon when he said, 'What needeth a man to seek things that are above him?'* That is, it is not necessary for Perfection, by supernatural and extraordinary ways, to seek supernatural things which are beyond our reach.

Having, in the nineteenth and twentieth chapters, replied to the objections that may be brought forward, I now refer the reader thereto, and conclude the discussion of revelations of this sort: it being sufficient to have said that the soul ought to be very prudent in the matter, that it may walk in pureness, without illusions, in the Night of Faith, to the Divine union.

* Eccles. vii. 1.

BOOK II.

CHAPTER XXVIII.

Of the interior Locutions which occur supernaturally. Their different kinds.

Third source of supernatural knowledge,—Spiritual Locutions.

It is necessary for the reader to keep in mind continually the end and object which I have in view — namely, the direction of the soul, through all its natural and supernatural apprehensions, without illusion or perplexity, in pureness of faith to the Divine union with God — that he may perceive that I am not too concise; though I do not enter into divisions and subdivisions of the subject, while treating of the apprehensions of the soul, as, perhaps, the intellect might require. On the whole, I think I have furnished sufficient advice, information, and warning, to enable the soul, by a prudent behaviour, in all these interior and exterior matters, to make progress onwards. This is the reason why I have so soon dismissed the subject of Prophecy like the rest, having at the same time much to say of each kind according to their distinctive characteristics, which are so many that I should never accomplish my task. I am satisfied that I have said enough about them, and that I have given the true doctrine and the requisite cautions with reference to them, and to every other matter of a like nature that may pass within the soul.

Three kinds: 1. Successive. 2. Formal. 3. Substantial.

I shall pursue the same course with the third kind of apprehensions, the Supernatural Locutions of spiritual men, which are effected without the instrumentality of the corporeal senses. These locutions, notwithstanding their variety, may be comprised under three designations: Successive, Formal, and Substantial Words. By Successive Words I mean certain words and considerations which the mind, self-recollected, forms and fashions within itself. By Formal, I mean certain distinct and definite words, which the mind receives not from itself but from a third person, sometimes while in a state of self-recollection, and at other times while not. By Substantial, I mean other words which are also formally in the mind, sometimes while it is recollected, and sometimes while it is not. These words produce and effect in the innermost soul that substance and power of which they are the expression. I shall speak of these in the order I have named them.

CHAPTER XXIX.

Of the first kind of words formed by the mind self-recollected. The causes of them. The advantages and disadvantages of them.

First kind of interior words,—Successive.

At all times when Successive Words take place, it is when the mind is collected and absorbed by some particular subject; and while attentively considering the matter which occupies its thoughts, it proceeds from one part of it to another, puts words and reasonings together so much to the purpose, and with such facility and clearness discovers by reflection things it knew not before, that it seems to itself as if it was not itself which did so, but some third person which addressed it interiorly, reasoning, answering, and informing. And in truth there is good ground for such a notion; the mind then reasons with itself as one man does with another, and to a certain extent it is so. For though it be the mind itself that thus reasons, yet the Holy Ghost very often assists it in the formation of these conceptions, words, and reasonings. Thus the mind addresses itself to itself as if to some other person.

For as the intellect is then united, and intently occupied, with the truth of that whereof it thinks, and as the Holy Spirit is also united with it; the intellect in this communion with the Divine Spirit, through the channel of that particular truth, forms successively within itself those other truths which

BOOK II.

The Holy Ghost may teach a truth, which the mind puts into words.

relate to the matter before it; the Holy Ghost, the Teacher, opening the way and giving light. This is one way in which the Holy Ghost teaches us. The understanding, being thus enlightened and instructed by the great Teacher, while perceiving these truths, forms at the same time the words in question about those truths which it receives from another source. We may apply to this the saying of Isaac, 'The voice, indeed, is the voice of Jacob; but the hands are the hands of Esau.'* He who is in this state cannot believe that the words and expressions do not proceed from some third person, not knowing how easily the intellect can form words about conceptions and truths which it derives from another person.

Error may occur in Expression and Deduction.

Now, though it is true that there can be no illusion in this communication, and in the enlightenment of the intellect; still illusions may, and do, frequently occur in the formal words and reasonings which the intellect forms about them. Inasmuch as the light then bestowed is most subtle and spiritual, so much so that it is beyond the capacity of the intellect, the result is that the intellect in its own strength forms these reasonings which in consequence are often false, apparently true, or imperfect. When a man has the clue of a true principle and then deals with it by his own abilities, or in the ignorance of his weak understanding, it is an easy thing for such an one to fall into delusions, and that too, in this way, as if a third person were addressing him. I have known one who had these Successive Locutions, but who, on the subject of the Most Holy Sacrament of the Eucharist, amid some most true, had others full of error.

I am terrified by what passes among us in these days. Anyone, who has barely begun to meditate, if he becomes conscious of these locutions during his self-recollection, pronounces them forthwith to be the work of God, and,

* Genes. xxvii. 22.

considering them to be so, says, God has spoken to me, or, I have had an answer from God. But it is not true: such an one has been only speaking to himself. Besides, the affection and desire for these locutions, which men encourage, cause them to reply to themselves, and then to imagine that God has spoken. The consequence is that they fall into great disorders, if they do not restrain themselves, and if their spiritual director does not command them to abstain from these interior discourses; for the fruit of them is foolishness and impureness of soul, and not the spirit of humility and mortification. They think that these locutions are great things, that God has been speaking to them, when in truth all was little more than nothing, or nothing, or less than nothing. For what is that worth which does not beget humility and charity, mortification, and holy simplicity and silence? These locutions, then, may prove a great impediment to the Divine union, because they lead astray the soul, that thinks much of them, from the abyss of Faith, where the intellect ought to abide in obscurity, and in obscurity advance by faith in love, and not by much reasoning.

Men deceived by their own words.

True test of worth,—what.

You will object, and say, Why must the intellect deny itself in these truths, seeing that the Spirit of God enlightens it in them, and that they cannot for that reason proceed from the evil one? I answer, the Holy Ghost enlightens the recollected intellect, and in proportion to its recollection; and, as there can be no greater recollection of the intellect than in Faith, the Holy Ghost will not enlighten it in any other way more than in that of Faith. For the more pure and complete the soul in the perfection of a living Faith the greater is the infusion of Charity, and the greater the Charity the greater the illumination, and the more abundant the graces. Though it be true that in this illumination some light is given to the soul, yet the light of Faith, wherein nothing is clearly seen, is in kind as different from it as refined

Faith, the greatest Light of the Holy Ghost.

BOOK II.

gold from base metal, and in quantity as the sea exceeds a drop of water. In one way the soul receives the knowledge of one, two, or three truths; but in the other the Wisdom of God generally, which is His Son, in one simple universal knowledge communicated to the soul by Faith.

Faith and Love better than Interior Voices.

If, again, you object and say that this is all good, and that it hinders not the other; my answer is, that it hinders it very much if the soul makes any account of it; for by doing so the soul occupies itself with evident matters and of little moment, which impede the communication of the abyss of faith, wherein God supernaturally and secretly teaches the soul, and trains it up, in a way it knows not, in virtues and in graces. We shall never profit by these Successive Locutions if we deliberately contemplate them with the intellect, for if we do this we shall lose all the good of them, as it is written, 'Turn away thy eyes from me, for they have made me flee away.'* We must therefore simply and sincerely, without applying the intellect to the matter of these supernatural communications, direct the will lovingly to God, because it is by love that these blessings are bestowed, and that in greater abundance than before. If the powers of the intellect, or of our other faculties, be actively applied to these things which are supernaturally and passively received, we shall find that our incapacity and ignorance will not reach them. They will therefore be modified and changed, and so we shall of necessity incur the hazard of delusions while forming these reasonings within ourselves. This will be neither supernatural itself, nor will in any respect resemble it, but will be something most natural and common.

There are some men whose intellect is so quick and penetrating that their conceptions, when they are self-recollected, naturally proceed with great facility, and form

* Cant. vi. 4.

themselves into these locutions and reasonings so clearly as to make them think that God is speaking. But it is not so. All this is the work of the intellect, somewhat disengaged from the operations of sense; for it may do this and even more without any supernatural help whatever, by its own natural light. This is a state of things of frequent occurrence, and many delude themselves into the belief that they have acquired the gift of prayer, and that God converses with them: they write down, or cause others to write for them, what they have experienced. And after all it is nothing: without the substance of virtue, and serving to no other end than to minister food to vanity.

Let such persons learn to disregard these locutions, and to ground the will in humble love; let them practise good works, and suffer patiently, imitating the Son of God, and mortifying themselves in all things: this, and not the abundance of interior discourses, is the road unto spiritual good.

Satan as a logician.

These Interior Successive Locutions furnish occasions to the evil spirit, especially when persons have an inclination or affection for them. For when they begin to recollect themselves, the devil offers to them materials for discursive reflections, suggesting thoughts and expressions to the intellect; and then, having deceived them by things that appear to be true, casts them down to the ground. Such is his dealing with those, who have entered into a compact with him, tacit or expressed. Thus he converses with some heretics, especially with heresiarchs; he informs their intellect with most subtle thoughts and reasonings, false, however, and erroneous.

It appears, then, that these Successive Words may proceed from three sources: from the Holy Spirit, moving and enlightening; from the natural light of the intellect; and from the evil spirit suggesting. It will be rather a difficult matter to describe the signs and tokens, by which it may be known

BOOK II.

Three Spirits; 1. Divine. 2. Human. 3. Diabolic.

from which of these sources particular locutions proceed, but some general notions may be given. When the soul loves, and at the same time is humbly and reverently conscious of that love, it is a sign that these locutions come from the Holy Ghost, Who, whenever He grants us these graces, grants them through love. When they come from the vivacity and light of the intellect only, it is that which effects them without any operation of virtue—though the will may love naturally in the knowledge and light of those truths—and, when the meditation is over, the will remains cold, though not inclined to vanity or evil, unless the devil shall have tempted us anew. The Locutions of the Holy Ghost cannot issue in this, for when they are over, the will is usually affectionately disposed towards God, and inclined to good, though sometimes, certainly, the will may be dry, even after the communications of the Holy Spirit, God thus ordering it for the profit of particular souls. At other times, too, the soul will not be very sensible of the operations or motions of these virtues, and yet what passes within will have been good. This is why I have said that it is sometimes difficult to distinguish one from another, because of the various effects which they sometimes have. The effects I have mentioned are the most common, though sometimes more, and sometimes less abundant.

Their distinctive marks.

The evil Locutions are occasionally hard to distinguish, for, though they dry up the love of God in the will, and incline men to vanity, self-esteem, or complacency; still they beget at times a certain false humility and fervent affection of the will founded on self-love, which requires for its detection great spirituality of mind. This the devil brings about, the better to conceal his presence. He is able perfectly well to produce tears by the impressions he makes, and he does so that he may inspire the soul with those affections, which he desires to excite. But he always labours to move the will so that men shall esteem these interior communications, and make much account of them, in order to induce them to give themselves up to them, and occupy themselves with what is not virtue, but rather an occasion of losing what virtue they may have.

Let us, therefore, abide by this necessary caution, in order to escape all perplexity and delusions; never to make any account of these Locutions, from whatever source they may come, but learn how to direct our will courageously to God in the perfect fulfilment of His law and holy counsels, which is the Wisdom of the Saints, content with the knowledge of those truths and mysteries, in simplicity and sincerity, as the Holy Church sets them forth, for these are sufficient to inflame our will; without thrusting ourselves into deep and curious investigations, where the absence of danger is a miracle. It was with reference to this that S. Paul exhorts us 'not to be more wise than it behoveth to be wise.'* Let this suffice on the subject of successive words.

CHAPTER XXX.

Of Interior Words formally wrought in a Supernatural way. Of the dangers incident thereto; and a necessary caution against delusions.

Second kind of interior Words,—Formal.

THE second kind of interior locutions are Formal Words, uttered in the mind sometimes supernaturally, without the intervention of the senses, whether in a state of recollection or not. I call these Formal Words, because the mind formally perceives they are spoken by a third person, independently of its own operations. For this reason they are very different from those of which I have just spoken. They differ from them, not only because they take place without any effort of

* Rom. xii. 3.

BOOK II.

Explanation of Formal Words.

the mind, but sometimes even when the mind is not recollected, but far from thinking of what is uttered within it. This is not so in the case of Successive Words, for these always relate to the matter which then occupies the mind. The locutions of which I am now speaking are sometimes perfectly formed, sometimes not, being very often, as it were, conceptions, by which something is said, at one time in the way of an answer, at another by another mode of speaking. Sometimes it is one word, at another two or more, and occasionally successive words, as in the former case: for they continue in the way of instruction to the soul, or of discussion with it. Still all takes place without the active participation of the mind, for it is as if another person were then speaking, as we read in Daniel, who says that an Angel instructed him and spoke. This was formal successive reasoning and instruction: the Angel says, 'I am now come forth to teach thee.' *

1. Their objective character.

2. Their constraining power.

When these Locutions are no more than formal, the effect on the mind is not great. They are in general sent only to instruct and enlighten us on a particular subject; and it is not necessary for this purpose, that they should have another effect different from that, for which they are sent. And so whenever they come from God, they effect their object in the soul; for they render it ready to accomplish what is commanded, and enlighten it so that it understands what it hears. They do not always remove the repugnance which the soul feels, but rather increase it; and this is the operation of God, the end of which is the more perfect instruction, humiliation, and profit of the soul. This repugnance is in general the result, when great and noble deeds are commanded; and there is greater promptitude and facility, when vile and humiliating things are enjoined. Thus when Moses was

God increases repugnance, to perfect the Will.

* Dan. ix. 22.

commanded to go unto Pharao, and deliver the people of Israel, he felt so great a repugnance for his task, that God was obliged to command him three times, and show him signs. And after all, this was not sufficient until God gave him Aaron, as his partner in the work, and a partaker of his dignity.

God exalts the Humble.

On the other hand, when these locutions are from the evil spirit, great things are readily undertaken, but humble occupations become repugnant. God hates to see men inclined to greatness and honour; for when He bids them accept dignities, and when He bestows them Himself, He wills not that they should be accepted with readiness and willingness. Formal Words differ, as to that readiness which God communicates, from the other Successive Words: these do not influence the mind so much, neither do they communicate to it so much readiness; that is an effect of the former, by reason of their greater formality, and because the intellect has less to do with them. Still this does not prevent successive locutions from having occasionally a greater influence, because of the great intercourse, that takes place at times, between the human spirit and the Divine. But there is a great difference in the manner. In the formal locutions the soul has no doubt about them, whether they come from itself or not; for it sees clearly that they do not—especially when it was not thinking of the subject to which they relate; and even when that subject occupied its thoughts, it sees most clearly and distinctly, that the locutions proceed from another.

We must not make much of these Formal Locutions any more than of the Successive. For over and above the occupation of the mind with that, which is not the legitimate and proximate means of Union with God, namely Faith, there is also the too certain risk of diabolical delusions. We can scarcely distinguish at times what locutions come from a good, and what from an evil, spirit. And as the effects of them are not great, we can hardly distinguish them by that test; for sometimes the diabolic locutions have a more sensible influence on the imperfect, than the Divine locutions on spiritual, persons. We must, also, not obey them at once, whether they come from a good or evil spirit. But we must not neglect to manifest them to a prudent confessor, or to some discreet and learned person, who shall teach us, and decide for us, what we ought to do; and when we have had his decision, we must be resigned and indifferent in the matter. If we cannot find such a person, a man of experience, it is better in that case, accepting the substance of them, and what is safe, to disregard the rest, and to reveal the matter to no one; for it is easy to find persons who destroy souls instead of edifying them. It is not everyone who is fitted for the direction of souls, it being a matter of the last importance to give right or wrong advice in so serious an affair as that.

Cautions.

Remember, too, that we must never do of our own head, or accept, anything told us in these locutions, without great deliberation and reflection. So subtle and so singular are the illusions incidental to them that, in my opinion, no soul, who does not deal with them as with an enemy, can possibly escape delusions in a greater, or less degree, in many of them. Having in the seventeenth, eighteenth, nineteenth, and twentieth chapters of this book, deliberately discussed these illusions and dangers, and the cautions to be observed, I shall not enlarge upon them here. I content myself with saying, that the real and secure teaching on the subject is, not to give heed to them, however plausible they may be, but to be governed in all by Reason, and by what the Church has taught and teaches us every day.

CHAPTER XXXI.

Of the Interior Substantial Locutions: the difference between them and the Formal. The profitableness of them. The resignation and reverence of the soul in respect of them.

CHAP. XXXI.

Third kind of interior words,—Substantial.

THE third kind of interior locutions are the Substantial Words. Though these are also formal, inasmuch as they are formally impressed on the soul, they differ from them in this; the substantial locutions produce a vivid and substantial effect in the soul, while those locutions which are only formal do not. Though it be true that every substantial locution is also formal, yet every formal locution is not substantial; but only that which really impresses on the soul what it signifies. Thus, if our Lord were to say formally to a particular soul, Be thou good; that soul would immediately be good. Or, Love thou Me; that soul would at once have and feel in itself the substance of love, that is, a true love of God. Or, again, if He were to say to a timid soul, Be not afraid; that soul would on the instant become courageous and calm. For 'The Word of God,' saith the wise man, 'is full of power.'* Thus, what the locution meaneth is substantially accomplished in the soul. This is the meaning of those words of David: 'He will give to His voice the voice of power.'† Thus, also, dealt He with Abraham, when He said unto him, 'Walk before Me, and be perfect.'‡ Abraham was then perfect, and ever walked reverently before God.

1. They work what they signify.

This is the power of His word in the Gospel, by which He healed the sick and raised the dead, by a word only. Such, too, are His Substantial Locutions; they are of such price and moment, as to be the life and strength and the

* Eccles. viii. 4. † Ps. lxvii. 34. ‡ Genes. xvii. 1.

BOOK II.

incomparable good of souls; for one location of God does for the soul far more at once, than that soul has done for itself in its whole past life.

2. Their independence of the Will.

The soul is not called upon to do or attempt anything with regard to these locutions, but to be resigned and humble. It is not called upon to undervalue or fear them, nor to labour in doing what they enjoin it. For God by means of these substantial locutions works in and by the soul Himself. And herein they differ from the formal and successive locutions. The soul need not reject these locutions, for the effect of them remains substantially in the soul, and full of blessing; and therefore the action of the soul is useless, because it has received them passively.

3. Their freedom from illusions.

Neither need the soul be afraid of illusions here, for these locutions are beyond the reach of the intellect or the evil spirit. The devil cannot passively produce this substantial effect in any soul whatever, so as to impress upon it the effect and habit of his locution; though he may, by his suggestions, lead those souls in whom he dwells as their lord, in virtue of their voluntary compact with him, to perform deeds of exceeding malignity. For he is able to influence them easily, because they are united to him voluntarily in the bonds of iniquity. We see, by experience, that even

Not Satan, but the Will enslaves the soul.

good men suffer violence from his suggestions, which are exceedingly strong; but if men are evilly disposed, his suggestions then are more efficacious.

But the devil cannot produce any effects resembling those of the Divine Locutions, for there is no comparison possible between his locutions and those of God. All his are as if they were not, in presence of the Divine, and their effects as nothing compared with the effects of God's locutions. This is the meaning of those words of the Prophet: 'What hath the chaff to do with the wheat? . . . Are not My words as a fire, and as a hammer that breaketh the rock in pieces?'* Thus the Substantial Locutions conduce greatly to the Union of the soul with God; and the more interior they are, the more substantial are they and the more profitable. Blessed then is that soul to which God sends His locutions: 'Speak Lord, for Thy servant heareth.'†

CHAPTER XXXII.

Of Intellectual Apprehensions resulting from the Interior Impressions supernaturally effected. The sources of them. The conduct to be observed by the soul, so that these apprehensions shall not hinder it on the Way of Union.

Fourth source of supernatural knowledge,—Spiritual Impressions.

It remains for me now to discuss the fourth and last kind of apprehensions, which those spiritual impressions, frequently effected supernaturally in spiritual men, produce in the intellect. Those impressions I have reckoned among the distinct apprehensions of the intellect.‡

Of two kinds.

There are two kinds of these Distinct Spiritual Impressions. The first kind is in the affection of the will. The second, though also in the will, yet because it is most intense, high, profound, and secret, seems not to touch the will, but to have been wrought in the very substance of the soul. Both the one and the other are extremely diversified. The first, when from God, is very high; but the second is the highest, of great profit and advantage. But neither the soul that receives them, nor its director, can ever know their sources, or why God effects them; they do not depend in any way upon good works or meditation, though these dispose us for them. God sends them to whom, and why, He wills.

Sometimes a person who has done many good works will never have these touches, and another of inferior merit, will

* Jerem. xxiii. 28, 29. † 1 Kings iii. 10. ‡ Bk. ii. c. 10.

BOOK II.

The Spirit breathes where He will.

have them most profoundly and most abundantly. It is not necessary, therefore, for the soul to be actually occupied with spiritual things — though that is the better state — in order to be the object of the Divine touches, of which these impressions are the result, for they frequently occur when the soul is heedless of them. Some of these touches are distinct, and pass rapidly away; others less so, but of longer continuance.

Discussion of Spiritual Impressions postponed.

These Impressions — so far as they come under this description of them — do not appertain to the intellect but to the will. I shall therefore not discuss them now, but reserve them for the treatise on the Night, or Purgation of the Will in its affections, which will form the third book. As in general, and even very frequently, a more express and perceptible apprehension, knowledge, and understanding, flow from these impressions into the intellect, it is necessary to mention it here only for that purpose.

We must, therefore, remember that, from all these impressions, whether the Divine touches which cause them, be rapid, or continuous and successive, there flows frequently into the intellect the apprehension of knowledge or understanding; which is usually a most profound and sweet sense of God, to which, as well as to the impression from which it flows, no name can be given. This knowledge comes, sometimes in one way, sometimes in another, now most deep and clear, again less so, according to the nature of the Divine touches, which occasion the impressions, and according to the nature of the impressions, of which it is the result.

It is not necessary to waste words here in cautioning and directing the Intellect, amid this knowledge, in Faith to the Divine union. For as these impressions are passively wrought in the soul, without any cooperation on its part; so also the knowledge which results from them, is passively received by the intellect—Philosophers apply the term passible to the intellect—independently of its own exertions. In order, therefore, to escape delusions here, and not to hinder the benefits of these impressions, the intellect ought not to meddle with them, but to remain passive, inclining the will to consent freely and gratefully, and not interfering itself. For, as in the case of the Successive Locutions, the activity of the intellect can very easily disturb and destroy this delicate knowledge, which is a sweet supernatural intelligence, which no natural faculty can reach or comprehend otherwise than by the way of recipient, and never by that of agent. No effort, therefore, should be made, lest the intellect should fashion something of itself, and the devil at the same time effect an entrance into the soul with false and strange knowledge. He is well able to do this, through the channel of these impressions, by taking advantage of the bodily senses. Let the soul be resigned, humble and passive, for as it receives passively from God this knowledge; so will He communicate it, of His own good pleasure, when He sees it humble and detached. By so living, the soul will put no obstacles in the way of the profitableness of this knowledge for the Divine union: and that profitableness is great. All these touches are touches of Union, which is passively effected in the soul.

Recapitulation.

The whole teaching of this book on the subject of total abstraction and passive Contemplation, whereby we abandon ourselves into the hands of God—in the forgetfulness of all created things, in detachment from images and figures, and dwelling on the supreme truth in pure contemplation—is applicable, not only to the act of most perfect contemplation —the profound and altogether supernatural repose of which is disturbed by 'the daughters of Jerusalem,'* namely, good meditations and reflections, if we then attempt them—but

* Cant. iii. 5. See Spiritual Canticle, stanza 29, Introd., and Flame of Love, stanza 3, § xi.

also to the whole of that time, in which our Lord communicates the simple, general, and loving attention, of which I have made mention before, or when the soul, assisted by grace, is established in that state. For then we must contrive to have the intellect in repose, undisturbed by the intrusion of forms, figures, or particular knowledge, unless it were slightly and for an instant, and that with sweetness of love, to enkindle our souls the more. At other times, however, in all our acts of devotion and of good works, we must make use of good recollections and meditations, so that we may feel an increase of profit and devotion; most especially applying ourselves to the life, passion, and death of Jesus Christ our Lord, that our life and conduct may be an imitation of His.

Let this suffice for the Supernatural Apprehensions of the intellect, so far as the guiding thereof through them, in faith, to the Divine union, is concerned. I think I have said enough on the subject: for the instructions and cautions already given will be found ample with regard to all that may occur in the intellect. And if anything should be met with of a different nature, and not comprised in the distinctions laid down—though I do not imagine that there can be anything which cannot be referred to one of the four kinds of distinct knowledge—what I have said of those that resemble them will suffice.

Advice to the Reader to be simple and candid.

I now proceed to the third book; where, by the help of God, I shall speak of the interior spiritual purgation of the will from its interior affections. This is the Active Night. I therefore entreat the discerning reader to consider what I write in simplicity and candour: for when these qualities are wanting, however perfect and profound the teaching may be, he will not profit by it, neither will he value it as it deserves. And much more will this be the case in the present instance, because of the deficiencies of my way of writing.

BOOK III.

THE PURGATION AND ACTIVE NIGHT OF THE MEMORY AND THE WILL.

ARGUMENT.

The Intellect, which is the first power of the soul, being now instructed, with regard to all its apprehensions, in the first Theological Virtue, namely Faith, so that the soul, according to this power, may be united to God in pureness of faith; it remains for me now to do the same with respect to the two other powers, Memory and Will, showing how they too are to be purified in all their acts, so that the soul, according to them also, may be united to God in perfect Hope and Charity. I shall do this briefly in this third book. For having concluded that which relates to the Intellect, the receptacle of all objects that pass through the Memory and the Will—and that goes a great way towards the full execution of my purpose—it is not so necessary to enlarge on the subject of these two powers; because, in general, the spiritual man who shall have well directed his Intellect in Faith, according to my teaching, will also, by the way, have done as much for the Memory and the Will in the matter of Hope and Charity: for the operations of these virtues are mutually dependent the one on the other. But, as it is necessary—that I may observe the same order, and be the better understood—to speak of the proper and determinate matter, I shall treat of the acts of each of these two faculties, distinguishing between them according to the method of my subject. That distinction arises out of the distinction between their objects, which are three, Natural, Supernatural Imaginary, and Spiritual. The knowledge of the Memory, following these distinctions, is also threefold: Natural, Supernatural Imaginary, and Spiritual. I shall treat of these here, by the grace of God, beginning with natural knowledge, which is conversant with the most exterior objects; and I shall afterwards speak of the affections of the Will, and then conclude this third book, the subject of which is the Active Spiritual Night.

CHAPTER I.

Of the Natural Apprehensions of the Memory: which is to be emptied of them, that the soul, according to that faculty, may be united with God.

BOOK III.

The Reader cautioned.

IT is necessary to keep in mind the special object of each of these books; for otherwise the reader will be perplexed by what he reads, as he may have been by what I said about the Intellect, and as he may be now by what I say of the Memory, and what I have to say hereafter of the Will. For when he observes, that I teach the annihilation of these powers in the matter of their operations; he will perhaps imagine, that I am destroying, and not building up, the spiritual edifice. This objection would be valid, if my purpose here was to instruct only beginners, who are to be conducted onwards by means of these discursive and tangible apprehensions. But as I am teaching how to advance by Contemplation to the Divine union—for which end all these means, and the sensible exertion of the powers of the soul must cease and be silent, in order that God in His own way may bring that Union to pass—it is necessary to release the faculties and to empty them, and to make them renounce their natural jurisdiction and operations, in order that the Supernatural may fill and enlighten them; seeing that the ability of them cannot compass so great a matter, but rather, unless suppressed, prove a difficulty in the way. And as it is most true that the soul knoweth God, rather by what He is not, than by what He is; it follows of necessity that if we are to draw near unto Him, it must be by denying and renouncing to the uttermost, all that may be denied, of our apprehensions, natural and supernatural alike. We shall, therefore, apply this process to the Memory: driving it away out of its natural position and elevating it beyond itself, that is, beyond all distinct knowledge and palpable comprehension, to the highest hope of God Who is Incomprehensible.

First kind of knowledge of the Memory,—Natural.

I begin with Natural Knowledge. The natural knowledge of the Memory is all that knowledge it can form about the objects of the five bodily senses: hearing, seeing, smelling, tasting and touching, and all else of the like kind. The Memory must be denuded and emptied of all this knowledge and of all these forms; it must labour to destroy all apprehension of them, so that no impression whatever of them shall be left behind; it must forget them, and withdraw itself from them, and that as completely as if they had never entered into it. Nothing less than the annihilation of the Memory as to all these forms will serve, if it is to be united with God. For that union can never take place without a total disunion from these forms which are not God, for God is without form; neither is He the object of any distinct knowledge whatever, as I have said while treating of the Night of the Intellect.

The Memory to be purified, and elevated.

'No man,' saith our Redeemer, 'can serve two masters,'* so the Memory cannot be perfectly united with God, and at the same time with forms and distinct knowledge. And as God is without form or image, on which the memory may dwell, so when the Memory is united with God—as we see by daily experience—it remains without form or figure, with the imagination destroyed, and itself absorbed in supreme felicity, in profound oblivion, remembering nothing. The Divine union expels every fancy, and shuts out all forms and knowledge; it elevates the Memory to that which is supernatural, leaving it in such deep forgetfulness that it must do violence to itself, if it will remember anything at all. Such at times is this forgetfulness of the Memory, and

* S. Matt. vi. 24.

BOOK III.

suspension of the imaginative powers, because of the union of the memory with God, that time passes by unheeded, and what took place in the interval cannot be known. When the imaginative powers are held in suspense, there is no sense of pain even when pain is inflicted; for without imagination there is no sense, not even in thought, because it exists not. If God is to bring about this Perfect Union, the Memory must be severed from all acts of knowledge of which it is capable. But it is to be observed, that this suspension never occurs thus in those who are perfect, because they have attained already to the perfect union, and this suspension relates to the commencement of that estate.

Does God destroy Nature?

You will, perhaps, object and say: All this is very well, but the principle involves the destruction of the natural usage and course of our faculties, and reduces man to the level of a brute beast, forgetful of all things, and what is worse, without reflection or recollection of his natural wants and functions. Surely God does not destroy nature, but rather perfects it; but its destruction is the natural issue of this doctrine, for man forgets all moral and rational motives, and all natural acts; he remembers nothing, because he regards not the forms and knowledge in question, which are means of recollection.

No; the natural powers are perfected in God.

To this I reply: the more the Memory is united to God the more it loses all distinct knowledge, and at last all such fades utterly away, when the State of Perfection is reached. In the beginning, when this is going on, great forgetfulness ensues, for these forms and knowledge fall into oblivion, men neglect themselves in outward things, forgetting to eat or drink; they do not remember whether they have done or left undone a particular work, whether they have seen such things or not, or whether such and such things have been mentioned to them; and all this because the Memory is lost in God. But he who has attained to the habit of Union does not forget, in this way, that which relates to moral and natural Reason; he performs with much greater perfection all necessary and befitting actions, though by the ministry of forms and knowledge, in the memory, supplied in a special manner by God. In the State of Union, which is a supernatural state, the memory and the other faculties fail as to their natural functions, and rise beyond their natural objects upwards unto God, Who is Supernatural.

Memory possessed by God.

And thus, then, when the Memory is transformed in God, no permanent forms or knowledge can be impressed upon it; the operations of the memory, therefore, and of the other powers in this state are, as it were, Divine; God has entered into possession, by this transformation, as their absolute Lord; guides and governs them Himself divinely by His own Spirit and Will, as it is written, 'He who is joined to the Lord is one spirit;'* and therefore the operations of the soul in the State of Union are the operations of the Holy Ghost, and, consequently, Divine.

Now, the actions of such souls only are what they ought to be, and reasonable, and not what they ought not to be; because under the influence of the Holy Ghost they know what they ought to know, are ignorant of what they ought to be ignorant, remember what they ought to remember, forget what they ought to forget, love what they ought to love, and love not that which is not God. Thus in general the first motions of the faculties of these souls are, as it were, Divine. There is nothing wonderful in this, seeing that they are transformed in the Divine Nature.

I will explain my meaning by the following illustration. A person in the State of Union is requested to pray for a certain individual. Now he will never remember to do what

* 1 Cor. vi. 17.

BOOK III.

is asked of him, by reason of anything whatever remaining in his memory; but if it be right so to pray — which it will be when God shall be pleased to hear that prayer — God will then move the will and excite a desire to pray. On the other hand, if it be not the Will of God to hear that prayer; let that person do what he may, he will never pray as he was requested, neither will he have any desire to do so. Sometimes God will make him pray for others, whom he never knew or heard of. This is the effect of a particular influence of God exerted over these souls, whom He directs to perform certain actions according to the disposition of His Will. The actions and the prayers of such souls always attain their end.

Prayer and Work of the perfect man.

Example of the Blessed Virgin.

So it was with the Glorious Mother of God. Perfect from the first, there was no impression of created things on her soul, to turn her aside from God, or in any way to influence her; for her every movement ever proceeded from the Holy Ghost.

Again. A perfect man has at a given time a certain indispensable business to transact. He has no recollection whatever of it; but in some way he knows not, it will present itself to his mind, through that stirring of his Memory of which I speak, at the time and in the way it ought, and that without fail. It is not only in these matters that the Holy Ghost enlightens the soul, but in many others, present, future, and distant—men knowing not how the knowledge thereof comes to them. But it comes from the Divine Wisdom, because they exercise themselves in knowing or apprehending nothing, which can obstruct their course. It comes to them in general, as I said in the beginning, while speaking of the Mount, so that they do all things; as it is written, 'Wisdom, which is the worker of all things, taught me.'*

* Wisd. vii. 21.

You will say, perhaps, that the soul cannot so empty and deprive the Memory of all forms and fantasies, as to reach a state so high; for there are two things to be done which are beyond the forces and abilities of man; namely, to cast what is natural aside, and touch, and unite with, the Supernatural, which is the most difficult, and, in truth, impossible for mere natural strength. God, indeed, must raise it up into this supernatural state; but the soul, so far as it can, must also be in good dispositions, which it may acquire by the help which God supplies. And so when the soul rejects these forms and empties itself of them, God causes it to enter into the enjoyment of this Union. When God does this, the soul is passive, as I shall explain in speaking of the Passive Night; and He will then bestow upon it the habit of Perfect Union, proportional to its good dispositions, when it shall seem to Him good to do so. I do not speak of the Divine effects of the perfect union, as they relate to the Intellect on the one hand, to the Memory and the Will on the other, in connection with this Night and Active Purgation, for the Divine union is not here complete; but I will do so in connection with the Passive Night, in which the soul is united with God.

God the Author of the Supernatural.

Hindrances to be removed by Man.

I speak here only of the necessary means of purifying the Memory, so that, so far as itself is concerned, it may enter actively upon this Night and Purgation. The spiritual man must observe this precaution: never to treasure up or retain in the memory anything he may see, hear, taste, touch, or smell; but to let them pass away, forgetting them, and never reflecting upon them, unless when it may be necessary to do so in order to a good meditation. But this deliberate forgetfulness, and rejection of all knowledge and of forms, must never be extended to Christ and His Sacred Humanity.

Sometimes, indeed, in the height of Contemplation and pure intuition of the Divinity, the soul does not remember

BOOK III.

The Sacred Humanity to be kept in Memory.

the Sacred Humanity, because God elevates the mind to this, as it were, confused and most supernatural knowledge; but for all this, studiously to forget It is by no means right, for the contemplation of the Sacred Humanity, and loving meditation upon It, will help us up to all good, and it is by It we shall ascend most easily to the highest state of Union.

It is evident at once that, while all visible and bodily things ought to be forgotten, for they are an impediment in our way, He, who for our salvation became man, is not to be accounted among them, for He is the Truth, the Door, and the Way, and our Guide unto all good.

Let the spiritual man, then, take this for granted. Let him aim at complete abstraction and forgetfulness; so that, as much as possible, no knowledge or form of created things —as if they existed not—shall remain in his Memory, so that the memory thus emptied and free may be wholly for God, lost as it were, in holy oblivion.

If, again, doubts are raised and objections made, as before with regard to the Intellect, to the effect that in this way we shall be doing nothing, losing our time and depriving ourselves of those spiritual blessings, of which the Memory serves as a channel; I can but answer that I have replied to them here as I did before, and that there is no reason why I should dwell longer upon them at present. Only let us remember, that if for a time this forgetfulness of all knowledge and forms is not felt to be profitable, the spiritual man must not therefore grow wearied; for God will draw near in His own time, and that for so great a blessing we ought to wait long, and patiently persevere in Hope.

God abides in those who abide in Him.

Though it is true that we shall scarcely meet with anyone, who in all things and at all times is under the direct influence of God, whose union with Him is so continuous that his faculties are ever Divinely directed; still there are souls, which for the most part in their operations are under the guidance of God, and these are not souls which move themselves; this is the sense of S. Paul, when he said that the sons of God—those who are transformed, and united in Him—'are led by the Spirit of God,'* to accomplish Divine actions in their faculties. This is nothing strange, for these operations must be Divine, seeing that the union of the soul is Divine.

CHAPTER II.

Three kinds of Evils to which the soul is liable, when not in darkness, with respect to the knowledge and reflections of the Memory. Explanation of the first.

THE spiritual man is subject to three evils and inconveniences, if he persists in the use of the natural knowledge of the Memory, with a view to drawing near unto God, or for any other purpose. Two of them are positive, and the third is negative. The first proceeds from the things of this world; the second from the devil; and the third, which is negative, consists in the hindrance to the Divine union, which this knowledge brings with it.

First evil,—a worldly Memory.

The first, proceeding from the things of this world, is a subjection to many kinds of evils, the result of this knowledge and reflection, such as falsehoods, imperfections, desires, opinions, waste of time, and many other things which greatly defile the soul. It is clear, that in yielding to these notions and reflections, we must fall into many errors; for very often what is false seems to be true, what is certain, doubtful, and the contrary; seeing that we can scarcely ever ascertain thoroughly a single truth. From all these we shall escape, if we make the memory blind to these notions and reflections.

* Rom. viii. 14.

BOOK III.

Creatures to be banished from Memory.

Imperfections beset the Memory at every step in all we hear, see, smell, touch, and taste; for these touch certain affections, such as pain and fear and hatred, useless hopes, empty joy, or vain glory. All these at least are imperfections, and sometimes undoubted venial sins; things which disturb perfect purity and simple union with God. Desires also are certainly excited, for the knowledge and reflections in question naturally produce them, and a mere disposition to retain these reflections furnishes food for desire. We are also liable to many a trial through our own opinions, because the memory must err in the recollection of the good and evil of others; for sometimes evil is taken for good, and good for evil. No man, as I believe, can ever escape these evils, who does not blind his memory as to all such matters.

If you say that a man may easily overcome all these trials, when they come upon him, I answer, that it is utterly impossible, if he gives heed to these reflections; for they involve innumerable follies, and some of them so subtle and minute that they cling to the soul unawares, like pitch to the hand that has touched it. I repeat, then, that the best way to overcome them is to do so at once, banishing them utterly out of the memory.

The purely good to be held in Memory.

You will further object and say, that the soul thus deprives itself of many good thoughts and meditations about God, and which are most profitable to it in the blessings they bring with them. I answer, all that is purely God and promotes this pure simple general and confused knowledge, is not to be rejected, but only what detains the Memory on images, forms, figures, and similitudes of created things. And in order that God may accomplish this purgation, pureness of soul is most profitable—that pureness which consists in not setting the affections thereof on any created or transitory things, and in not regarding them; for in my opinion, the opposite conduct will not fail to make a deep impression because of the imperfection, which cleaves to the powers of the soul in their operation. It is, therefore, much better to impose silence on the faculties, that God may speak. In order to attain to this state, the natural operations must cease. This takes place, as the Prophet saith, when the soul comes into solitude with its faculties, and when God speaks to the heart: 'I . . . will lead her into the wilderness, and I will speak to her heart.'*

Spiritual silence,—Remedy for distractions.

But if you still object and say, that the soul will profit nothing, if the Memory does not reflect and dwell upon God, and that it will be liable to much tepidity and distraction—I answer, it is impossible; for if the memory be entirely withdrawn from the things of this life and of the next, no evil, no distraction, no folly or vice can enter within it—such things insinuate themselves through the wandering of the memory—for then there is no way by which they can enter, nor anything to give occasion to them. This certainly would be the case, if we opened the door to the consideration of earthly things, while it is shut against that of heavenly things: but we shut the door against everything which is prejudicial to Union, and out of which distractions may come, bringing the memory into silence, that the Spirit only may be heard; and saying with the Prophet, 'Speak, Lord, for Thy servant heareth.'† Such also is the state of the Bride; for the Bridegroom saith of her, 'My sister, my spouse is a garden enclosed, a fountain sealed up,'‡ so that nothing may enter within.

The River of Peace.

Let the soul, therefore, be 'enclosed' without anxiety or alarm; and He Who, when the doors were shut, entered bodily in among His disciples, and said, 'Peace be unto you,'§ in an unexpected and inconceivable way, will enter spiritually into the soul without its knowledge or cooperation, when

* Os. ii. 14.
† 1 Kings iii. 10.
‡ Cant. iv. 12.
§ S. John xx. 19.

BOOK III.

the doors of Memory, Intellect, and Will are shut, and will fill it with His peace, turning into it the river of peace, as it is written, 'O that thou hadst hearkened to My commandments; thy peace had been as a river.'* And He will take away all misgivings, and suspicions, all uneasiness and darkness, which made the soul afraid that it was already, or on the point of being, lost. Be, therefore, earnest in prayer, and hope in detachment and emptiness: thy good will not tarry.

CHAPTER III.

Of the second evil, coming from the evil spirit through the Natural Apprehensions of the Memory.

Second evil, — caused by the devil.

THE second positive evil, to which the soul is liable from the notions of the Memory, comes from the devil, who by these means has great power over it. For he can heap forms upon forms, and thereby infect the soul with pride, avarice, envy, and hatred. He can also excite unjust enmities, vain love, and delude us in many ways. Besides, he is wont so to impress matters on the fancy, that falsehood seems true, and truth false. Finally, all the greatest delusions of Satan, and the evils of the soul, enter in through these notions and forms of the memory. Now if the memory were blind to these things, and annihilated in forgetfulness of them, it would shut the door against the evil spirit, so far as this evil is concerned, and free itself wholly from these things, which would be a great blessing. The evil spirit cannot molest the soul but through the operations of its faculties, and chiefly by the help of forms and fancies: for upon these depend, more or less, all the operations of the other faculties. And, therefore, if the memory annihilates itself as to them, the

* Is. xlviii. 18.

devil can do nothing; because he can find nothing to lay hold of, and without something of that kind he can do nothing whatever. CHAP. III.

Would that spiritual directors could clearly see, how great are the evils, which the wicked spirits inflict upon souls through the Memory, when they make use of it; what sadness and affliction and vain joys they occasion, both with regard to the things of God and the things of the world; what impurities they leave rooted in the mind, distracting it so profoundly from that supreme self-recollection, which consists in fixing all the powers of the soul on the One Incomprehensible Good, and withdrawing them from all objects of sense. This emptying of the memory, though the advantages of it are not so great as those of the State of Union, yet, merely because it delivers souls from much sorrow, grief, and sadness, besides imperfections and sins, is in itself a great good.

CHAPTER IV.

Of the third evil, proceeding from the Distinct Natural Knowledge of the Memory.

THE third evil, to which the soul is liable from the Natural Apprehensions of the Memory, is negative. These apprehensions can impede moral, and deprive us of spiritual, good. And, first of all, to show how they impede moral good, we must keep in mind, that moral good consists in curbing the passions, and in restraining our disorderly appetites; the result of which is peace, tranquillity, and rest, which appertain unto moral good. But this curbing and restraining of the passions is impossible for any soul, that does not forget and withdraw from all those things, by which its affections are excited; and no trouble is ever produced in the soul but

Third evil—negative.

1. Deprives of Moral good.

BOOK III.

by the apprehensions of the memory. For if we forget all things, there is then nothing to disturb our peace or to excite our desires; seeing that, as they say, what the eye has not seen the heart does not desire.

Means and fruits of the Moral Order of the Soul.

This is a truth of daily experience: whenever the soul broods over anything, it is changed or disturbed, be it much or little, according to the measure of its apprehension. If the subject of its thoughts be serious and disagreeable, it elicits feelings of sadness or dislike; if, on the other hand, the subject be pleasant, its feelings are those of joy and desire. The inevitable result of these changing apprehensions is interior disorder: joy and grief, hate and love succeed each other, and there is no possibility of preserving a uniform state—which is an effect of moral tranquillity—but by the studious oblivion of all these. It is, therefore, quite clear that this knowledge of the memory greatly impedes the good of the moral virtues.

2. Deprives of Spiritual good.

A cumbered Memory also impedes the mystical or spiritual good; for the disturbed soul, having no foundation of moral good is, so far, incapable of that which is spiritual, because this enters into no soul, that is not under control and ordered in peace. Besides, if the soul cleaves and gives heed to the apprehensions of the memory—it can attend to but one thing at a time—if it occupies itself with apprehensible things, for such are the notions of the memory, it is impossible that it can be at liberty for the Incomprehensible, which is God. For, as I have already said,* the soul that will draw near unto God must do so by not comprehending, rather than by comprehending; it must change the mutable and the comprehensible for the Immutable and Incomprehensible.

Moral Justice the foundation of Spiritual Perfection.

* Book ii. ch. 8.

CHAPTER V.

The profitableness of forgetfulness, and emptiness with regard to all thoughts and knowledge, which naturally occur to the Memory.

CHAP. V.

Three benefits of self-restraint in Memory.

THE evils which flow into the soul, through the Apprehensions of the Memory, suggest to us the opposite benefits, which result from forgetting them and emptying ourselves of them; because, as natural Philosophers say, the doctrine of contraries is the same.

1. Peace of mind.

In the first place, the soul enjoys tranquillity and peace of mind, because it is delivered from the harassing vexations of thoughts and notions of the memory; and, in consequence, what is of more importance, the conscience is pure. This state is a preparation for human and Divine wisdom, and for the acquisition of virtue.

2. Victory over Satan.

In the second place, it is delivered from many suggestions, temptations, and assaults of Satan, who, through these thoughts, insinuates himself into the soul, and at least causes it to fall into many impurities and, as I have said, into sin; as it is written, 'They have thought and spoken wickedness.'* So when these thoughts are driven away, the devil has no weapon wherewith to assail the soul.

3. Preparation for the Holy Spirit.

In the third place, while the soul is self-recollected, and forgetful of all things, it is then prepared for the influence and teaching of the Holy Ghost, Who 'will withdraw Himself from thoughts that are without understanding.'† Even if we derived no greater benefit, from this forgetfulness and emptiness of the memory, than our deliverance from pain and trouble, that of itself is a great gain and blessing; because the pain and troubles, occasioned by the adversities of this life, bring no relief with them, but rather aggravate those

* Ps. lxxii. 8. † Wisd. i. 5.

BOOK III.

adversities in general, and hurt the soul. For this it was that made David say, 'Surely man passeth as an image, yea, and he is disquieted in vain.'* And in truth, every man disquieteth himself in vain; for it is clear that disquietude is always vanity, because it serves to no good. Yea, even if the whole world were thrown into confusion, and all things in it, disquietude on that account is vanity, for it hurts us more than it relieves us. To endure all things, with an equable and peaceful mind, not only brings with it many blessings to the soul; but it also enables us, in the midst of our difficulties, to have a clear judgment about them, and to minister the fitting remedy for them.

The cure for the ills of life.

Solomon knew well the advantage of this disposition. 'I have known,' saith he, 'that there was no better thing than to rejoice, and to do well in his life;' †—that is, in all the events of this life, however adverse they may be, the Wise Man bids us rejoice rather than be sad, that we may not lose that greatest good, peace of mind in adversity as well as in prosperity, bearing all things alike. This peace of mind no man will ever lose, if only he will forget these notions and cast aside thoughts, and withdraw from the sight, and hearing, and discussion of matters so far as it is possible for him. We are naturally so frail and weak, that, in spite of all self-discipline, we can scarcely avoid stumbling on the recollection of many things, which disturb and disquiet our mind; though it may have been once established in peace and tranquillity, oblivious of all things. This is the meaning of the Prophet when he said, 'I will be mindful and remember, and my soul shall languish within me.'‡

* Ps. xxxviii. 7. † Eccles. iii. 12. ‡ Lam. iii. 20.

CHAPTER VI.

Of the second kind of Apprehensions: the Imaginary and Supernatural.

CHAP. VI.

Second kind of Apprehensions,—Memory of the Supernatural.

THOUGH, while treating of the first kind of Natural Apprehensions, I also sufficiently explained the Imaginary, which are also natural, it was necessary to make this division, because of the attachment of the Memory to other forms and notions of Supernatural things: such are Visions and Revelations, Locutions and Impressions, which come upon us in a supernatural way. When these things have happened to the soul, the image, form, or figure of them remains impressed upon it, in the memory or the fancy; and sometimes that impression is exceedingly vivid. It is necessary to caution men on this subject: that the memory may not be perplexed by these images, and that they may not prove an impediment to union with God in the purity and integrity of Hope.

I say, then, that in order to attain that blessing, the soul must never reflect upon those objects, which have been clearly and distinctly present to it in a supernatural way, so as to preserve the forms, notions, and figures of them. We must always keep this principle before our eyes; the more the soul attends to any clear and distinct apprehension, natural or supernatural, the less will be its capacity and disposition for entering into the abyss of Faith, wherein all things else are absorbed. For, as I have before maintained, no supernatural forms or knowledge, of which the memory takes cognizance, are God: they bear no proportion to Him, neither can they serve as proximate means of union with Him. The soul, if it is to draw near unto God, must empty itself of all that is not God; and the memory, therefore, must also get rid of all forms and knowledge, in order to be united to Him in the way of perfect and mystical Hope.

BOOK III.

Detachment gives Hope; Hope obtains God.

This must be done, for all possession contradicts Hope, which, as the Apostle writes, is of things not in possession: 'Faith is the substance of things to be hoped for, the evidence of things that appear not.'* Consequently, the more the Memory divests itself, the greater its Hope; and the greater its hope, the greater its union with God. For with respect to God, the more the soul hopes, the more it obtains, and it then hopes most when it is most divested; and when it shall be perfectly divested, it will then have the possession of God, such as is possible on earth in the Divine union. But there are many souls, who will not deprive themselves of that sweetness and delight, which the memory finds in these things, and who, consequently, never attain to this supreme possession and perfect sweetness; for he 'that doth not renounce all that he possesseth, cannot be a disciple'† of Christ.

CHAPTER VII.

The Evils inflicted on the soul by the knowledge of Supernatural things if reflected upon. Their number.

Five evils of reflection on the Supernatural.

THE spiritual man exposes himself to five kinds of evils, if he attends to, and reflects on, that knowledge, and those forms, which are impressed upon his mind by the things which pass through it in a supernatural way.

1. Illusions. 2. Pride. 3. Temptations. 4. Union weakened. 5. God dishonoured.

The first is frequent illusions, mistaking one thing for another.

The second is proximate occasions of presumption or vain glory.

The third is the opportunities of deceiving, which they furnish to the devil.

* Hebr. xi. 1. † S. Luke xiv. 33.

The fourth is impediments to union with God in Hope.

The fifth is low views of God for the most part.

First evil of self-reflection in Supernatural matters.

As to the first evil, it is clear that if the spiritual man attends to, and reflects upon, these notions and forms, he must be frequently deceived in his judgment about them.

Liability to deception.

For as no man can thoroughly comprehend what passes, in the order of nature, into his imagination, or have a sound and certain opinion about it; much less will he be able to decide correctly about Supernatural things, which are beyond our understanding and of rare occurrence. He will frequently attribute to God what is after all but fancies, and to the evil spirit what is from God, and to God what is from Satan. Very frequently, good or evil to others or to himself will be present to him through these forms or figures: and he will consider them most certain and true, and yet they are nothing less than utterly false. Other impressions made upon him he will consider false, though they are true; this, however, I consider the safer course of the two, for it usually proceeds out of Humility.

But if he is not deceived as to their truth, he may be as to their kind and the value to be set upon them; he may look upon that which is trifling as important, and on what is important as trifling. And as to their quality, he may consider what his imagination presents to him to be of this or that kind, when it is not; putting 'darkness for light, and light for darkness, bitter for sweet, and sweet for bitter.'* Finally, if he escapes delusion in one thing, it will be surprising if he does in the next; for even if he abstains from determining anything in the matter, it is sufficient, if he attends to it at all, to bring some detriment upon himself, if not the precise one of which I am now speaking, yet some one of the others of which I shall immediately speak.

* Is. v. 20.

BOOK III.

The duty, therefore, of the spiritual man is, if he wishes to escape from the delusions of his own judgment, not to decide himself upon his own state or feelings, or what such Visions, Knowledge, or Impressions may mean. He ought not to desire to know anything about them, nor give heed to them, except for the purpose of manifesting them to his confessor, that he may learn from him how to empty his memory of these apprehensions, or what in every case may be most expedient for him, in the same spirit of detachment. For be these things what they may, they cannot help us to love God so much as the least act of earnest Faith and Hope done in the emptiness of all things.

CHAPTER VIII.

Of the second evil: the danger of self-conceit and presumption.

Second evil,—Spiritual Pride.

THESE Supernatural Apprehensions of the Memory, if attended to, or regarded at all, are to spiritual men occasions of vanity or presumption. For as he who has no experience of them, is exceedingly free from this vice, because he sees nothing in himself whereon to presume; so on the other hand he, to whom they are familiar, has an ever-present reason for thinking himself to be something, seeing that he is the object of these visitations. It is very true that he may attribute all to God and give thanks, looking upon himself as utterly unworthy; nevertheless a certain secret self-satisfaction and conceit, on the subject of these Apprehensions, will grow up in the mind, out of which, unawares, great spiritual pride will arise. Men might see this very clearly, if they would but reflect on that feeling of dislike and aversion produced in them by those, who do not commend their spirit, or attribute no value to their experiences, and on that feeling of distress, which they have when they are told that others also have the like or greater gifts. All this is the fruit of secret self-esteem and pride, and they cannot be made to understand that they are steeped in it up to their very eyes.

The Pharisee and the Publican.

They think that a certain recognition of their own wretchedness is sufficient, while at the same time they are filled with secret self-esteem and personal satisfaction, taking more delight in their own spirit and gifts than in those of another. They are like the Pharisee who thanked God that he was 'not as the rest of men,' and that he practised such and such virtues: he was satisfied with himself, and presumed upon his state. 'O God, I give Thee thanks,' said he, 'that I am not as the rest of men, extortioners, unjust, adulterers . . . I fast twice in a week, I give tithes of all that I possess.'* Now these men do not say this in so many words, as the Pharisee did, but they habitually think so; and some of them even become so proud as to be worse than devils. When they are conscious of certain feelings, and devotional sweetness in the things of God, as they imagine, they become so self-satisfied, that they look upon themselves as most near unto God, and upon others, unconscious of the like feelings, as most unworthy, and they despise them as the Pharisee did the Publican.

Two remedies. 1. Perfection not found in high thoughts or sweet feelings;

To avoid this pestilent evil, abominable in the sight of God, there are two considerations to help us. The first is that virtue does not consist in these apprehensions and feelings about God, however sublime they may be, nor in any personal experiences of this kind, but, on the contrary, in that which is not matter of feeling at all,—in great humility, contempt of ourselves and of all that belongs to us, profoundly rooted in the soul; and in being glad that others

* S. Luke xviii. 11, 12.

BOOK. III.

have the same opinion of us, and in not wishing to be thought well of by others at all.

2. But in Humility, and in Charity unconscious of self.

The second is, that all visions, revelations, and heavenly feelings, and whatever else is greater than these, are not worth the least act of Humility bearing the fruits of that Charity which neither values nor seeks itself, which thinketh no evil except of self, and which thinketh well not of self, but of all others. Let men, therefore, cease to regard these supernatural apprehensions, and labour rather to forget them, that they may be free.

CHAPTER IX.

Of the third evil: the work of the devil through the Imaginary Apprehensions of the Memory.

Third evil,—Snares of the devil.

FROM what I have already written, we may gather and learn how great is that evil which the devil inflicts on the soul through these Supernatural Apprehensions. Not only can he represent to the memory and the fancy many false notions and forms which shall seem good and true, impressing them on the mind and senses with great effect and certainty by his suggestions—and this in such a way as to make his representations be taken for what they pretend to be, for as he changes himself into an angel, he will seem to be light to the soul—but also in the very truths of God he can tempt us in divers ways, by communicating unruly motions about them to our desires and affections, whether spiritual or sensual. For if the soul takes pleasure in these apprehensions, it is very easy for Satan to increase our affections and desires, and to plunge us into spiritual gluttony and other evils.

And that he may succeed the better, he is wont to inspire and fill the senses with delight, sweetness, and pleasure, in the things of God; so that the soul, dazzled and enervated by that sweetness, may become blind through pleasure, and set itself more upon sweetness than upon love—at least not so much upon love—and attach greater importance to these apprehensions than to that detachment and emptiness, which are to be found in Faith and Hope and the Love of God. He doeth all this that, starting from that point, he may, by little and little, delude the soul, and bring it to believe, with great readiness, all his lies. For the soul that is blind considers falsehood to be falsehood no longer, evil not to be evil, because it puts darkness for light, and light for darkness, and falls into endless disorders. That which was once wine is turned into vinegar, as well in the natural as in the moral and spiritual order. All this comes upon the soul, because it did not in the beginning deny itself in the pleasure ministered by supernatural things. And as this pleasure was at first not great or not so hurtful, the soul was not sufficiently afraid of it, but suffered it to remain and grow, as the grain of mustard grows into a great tree. For a slight error in the beginning becomes a great error in the end.

Blindness caused by spiritual gluttony.

The soul that will escape this evil, the work of the devil, must not take any pleasure in these apprehensions, for if it does the result will most certainly be blindness, and then a fall; for delight and sweetness, of their own proper nature, brutalise and blind the soul. This is the meaning of David when he said, 'Perhaps darkness shall cover me; and night shall be my light in my pleasures;'* that is, perhaps darkness shall cover me in my pleasures, and I shall take night for my light.

* Ps. cxxxviii. 11.

BOOK III.

CHAPTER X.

Of the fourth evil of the Distinct Supernatural Apprehensions of the Memory: the impediment to Union.

Fourth evil, —Divine Union weakened.

THERE is not much to be said here about the fourth evil, because I have been speaking of it throughout this book: I have said that the soul, in order to be united with God in Hope, must renounce all possession in the Memory; because nothing that is not God must remain in the memory, if our hope in God is to be perfect. No form or figure or image, natural or supernatural, of which the memory takes cognisance can be, or resemble, God, as it is written, 'There is none among the gods like unto Thee, O Lord;'* and therefore if the memory dwells upon any such it impedes the Divine union. In the first place, because it perplexes itself; and in the next, because the greater its occupation the less perfect is hope. It is therefore necessary for the soul to forget, and detach itself from, all distinct forms and knowledge of supernatural things, that it may not impede, in the Memory, the Divine union in perfect Hope.

CHAPTER XI.

Of the fifth evil, resulting from the Imaginary Supernatural Apprehensions: low and unseemly views of God.

Fifth evil,—God dishonoured.

THE fifth evil is no less hurtful to the soul. It flows from the willing retention, in the imaginative Memory, of the forms and images of those things which are supernaturally communicated to the soul, but especially then, when we would apply them as means to the Divine union. It is a very easy thing for us to form notions about the nature and

* Ps. lxxxv. 8.

greatness of God, unworthy of and unbecoming His Incomprehensible Being. Though our Reason and Judgment may withhold us from forming any express decision that God is like any one of these similitudes; still the mere consideration of these apprehensions generates in the soul a certain esteem and sense of God which are not so high as Faith teaches; namely, that He transcends all comparison and all comprehension. For over and above that the soul takes from God that which it gives to the creature, the mere consideration of these apprehensions naturally produces within it a certain comparison of them with God, which will not leave it to judge of God as it ought to do. For, as I have said before, no creature whatever, in Heaven or on earth, no forms or images, natural or supernatural, cognisable by our faculties, however noble they may be, present any comparison or proportion with the Being of God; because neither genus nor species includes Him. And in this life the soul of man is incapable of comprehending clearly and distinctly anything that cannot be classed under genus and species. This is why S. John said, 'No man hath seen God at any time;'* and Isaias and S. Paul, 'Neither hath it entered into the heart of man.'† Yea, God Himself hath said, 'Man shall not see Me and live.'‡ He, therefore, who shall perplex his Memory and the other powers of his soul with matters that they can comprehend, will never think and feel about God as he ought to do.

Analogy of a king and his courtiers.

I will explain my meaning by a somewhat low comparison. The more we fix the eyes of our regard upon the courtiers of a king, and the more we consider them, the less will be our reverence and respect for that king; for, even if our disesteem of him be not formally and distinctly recognised by the intellect, it is nevertheless visible in our conduct.

* S. John i. 18. † Is. lxiv. 4.; 1 Cor. ii. 9. ‡ Ex. xxxiii. 20.

BOOK III.

The more we attribute to the courtiers the more we rob their king; and we cannot have a high opinion of that king then, because his courtiers are so respected in his presence. This is the soul's treatment of God whenever the soul gives heed to these apprehensions. This illustration is a very mean one: for God is of another nature than all His creatures, infinitely different from them all.

These apprehensions, therefore, must be put out of sight, and the eyes must regard none of them, but be fixed upon God in Faith and perfect Hope. Hence those who not only give heed to these apprehensions, but also think that God is like unto some of them, and that by their help they may attain unto Union with Him, are already fallen into grievous error; they do not profit by the light of Faith in the Intellect, which is the means by which this faculty is united with God, neither also will they grow up to the heights of Hope, which is the means of union for the Memory; that Union must be effected by the severance of the Memory from all imaginations whatever.

CHAPTER XII.

The benefits of withdrawing the soul from the Apprehensions of the Imagination. Answer to an objection. The difference between the Natural and Supernatural Imaginary Apprehensions.

Benefits of self-denial in Memory.

THE benefits that result from emptying the imaginative faculty of these imaginary forms become manifest by the consideration of the five evils which they inflict on the soul, if it would retain them, as I said before of the natural forms. But, beside these benefits, there are others of perfect rest and tranquillity of mind. For, putting aside that natural rest which the soul enjoys when it has set itself free from the dominion of images and forms, it is also delivered

CHAP. XII.

from the anxiety of ascertaining whether they are good or evil, and what conduct it ought to observe with reference to the one and the other. It also escapes from troubling and wasting the time of its confessors, for it does not require them to determine whether these things are good or evil, or the nature of them,— matters the knowledge of which is not necessary for it, for all it has to do is to reject them in the sense I have already explained, and to give no attention whatever to them. The time and strength, thus wasted, will be then employed in a better and more profitable way, in conforming the will to God, in earnestly striving after detachment, poverty of sense and spirit, which consists in a willing real privation of all consoling and tangible support, interior as well as exterior. This we practise well when we seek and strive to separate ourselves from these forms; the issue of which will be that inestimable blessing of drawing near unto God, who has neither image, form, nor figure; and that blessing will be proportional to our estrangement from all forms, images, and figures.

How penitents waste the time of their confessors.

You will here perhaps object, and say, Why, then, do many spiritual directors counsel us to profit by these Divine communications and impressions, and to desire the gifts of God that we may have wherewithal to give to Him in return, for if He gives nothing, we too have nothing to give unto Him? Why does S. Paul say, 'Extinguish not the Spirit'?* Why does the Bridegroom say to the Bride, 'Put Me as a seal upon thy heart, as a seal upon thy arm'?† This seal signifies some apprehensions. And yet, according to this teaching, we are not only not to seek them, but, even if God sends them, to reject them. It is also certain that God, when He sends them, sends them for our good, and that their effects will be good. Pearls are not to be thrown

Why must the good gifts of the Spirit be repelled?

* 1 Thess. v. 19.

† Cant. viii. 6.

BOOK III.

away. Yea, it is even a sort of pride not to yield a willing reception to God's communications, as if we could do without them in our own strength.

Answer.

Action of will unnecessary, save to consent.

I refer the reader, for a solution of this difficulty, to the fifteenth and sixteenth chapters of the second book, where the objection has been in great measure replied to. I said there that the benefits of the Supernatural Apprehensions, when they are from God, are passively wrought in the soul, at the time of their presentation to the senses, without the cooperation of our faculties. An act of the will admitting them is therefore unnecessary, for, as I have said, if the soul will then exert its own faculties, the effect of that natural and inferior exertion will be to impede the supernatural effects then wrought by God through their intervention, rather than any profit from that active exertion. Yea, rather, inasmuch as the fruit of these Imaginary Apprehensions is passively communicated to the soul; so the soul on its part must be passively disposed in their regard without any interior or exterior acts, as I have already explained. This is really to preserve the Divine impressions, for by this conduct we shall not destroy them by inferior actions of our own. This, too, is the way not to extinguish the Spirit, for we should extinguish Him if we attempted to walk in a way along which God does not lead us. We should be doing that if, when God communicates His Spirit to us passively, as He does in these apprehensions, we should then actively exert our intellect, or seek anything in them beside and beyond that which God communicates through them.

This is evident; for if the soul then exerts itself its action will be only natural, or, at the utmost, if supernatural, far inferior to that which God wills. In its own strength the soul cannot do more, seeing that it neither does, nor can, influence itself supernaturally; it is God that so influences it, but with its own consent. If, then, the soul will do anything itself, it will, necessarily, so far as itself is concerned, impede the communication of God, that is, the Spirit; because it has recourse to its own operations, which are of another kind and far inferior to those of God. This, then, is to extinguish the Spirit. The inferiority of this exertion is clear, for the powers of the soul, in their ordinary and natural course, cannot act or reflect but upon some figure, form, or image; and these are but the rind and accidents of the substance and of the Spirit hidden beneath them. This substance and Spirit unite not with the powers of the soul in true intelligence and love, until the reflex and imperfect action of those powers shall have ceased. The end and aim of the soul in this exertion is to receive in itself the substance, understood and loved, which those forms involve. The difference therefore between the active and passive operation, and the superiority of the latter, is the same as that between a work in the course of performance, and the same work already performed; between the search after an object, and that object sought and found.

Superiority of the passive soul.

If the soul, then, will actively exert its faculties on those Supernatural Apprehensions, in which God, as I have said, communicates passively the spirit of them, it will do nothing else but forsake what is already done, in order to do it anew; and so will have no enjoyment of it, neither will its own exertions have any other effect than to frustrate what God hath wrought. Because, as I have said, the powers of the soul can never of themselves attain to the Spirit, which God communicates independently of them. If we were to attach any importance to these Imaginary Apprehensions, we should directly extinguish the Spirit which God infuses through them into the soul: we must therefore put them aside, and observe a passive conduct in their regard, for God is then lifting up the soul to things above its power and its knowledge. This is the meaning of the Prophet when he said, 'I

BOOK III.

will stand upon my watch, and fix my foot upon the tower; and I will watch to see what will be said to me.'* That is, I will keep guard over my faculties, and will not suffer them to move a step, and so shall I be able to see what will be said to me; that is, I shall understand and enjoy what God will communicate to me supernaturally.

Gifts of the Spirit as motives of Love.

As to the objection founded on the words of the Bridegroom, those words refer to that love which He demands, the function of which is to make the beloved ones resemble each other. And therefore He saith to her, 'Put Me as a seal upon thy heart'†—where the arrows strike that are shot forth from the quiver of love, that is, the actions and motives of love—so that all the arrows of love might strike Him, being there as a target for them, and that all may thus reach Him, and the soul become like unto Him through the actions and motions of love until it becomes transformed in Him. He says also, 'as a seal upon thy arm.' The arm implies the exercise of love, for it is that which comforts and sustains the Beloved. Therefore all we have to do with these Apprehensions, which come upon us from above, as well imaginary as of every other kind, whether Visions, Locutions, Impressions, or Revelations, is, making no account of the letter or the outward veil—that is, the significative and intelligible fact—to attend only to the preservation of the Love of God which they cause interiorly in the soul. It is in this sense that we are to make much of these impressions; not of the sweetness and delight of them, nor of the figures, but of the impressions of love which produce it. And with this object only in view we may probably at times call to mind that image and apprehension, which have been the occasion of love, in order to furnish ourselves with motives of love. For though the

* Habac. ii. 1.

† Cant. viii. 6.

effect of that apprehension be not so great when recalled to mind as it was when it was first communicated, still at the recollection of it our love is renewed and our minds elevated unto God; especially when the recollection is of one of those supernatural images, figures, or impressions which usually so impress themselves on the soul that they continue for some time there, and can scarcely be driven away.

These images, thus imprinted on the soul, produce, whenever they are adverted to, the Divine effects of love, sweetness, and light, sometimes more, sometimes less, for that is the end for which they are impressed. He with whom God thus deals receives a great gift, for he has a mine of blessings within himself. The images which produce such effects as these are vividly grounded in the spiritual memory, and resemble not those which the fancy preserves. It is not therefore necessary when we would remember them to have recourse to the fancy, because we have them in ourselves, as an image seen in a mirror. And whenever a soul has them formally, it may then profitably recall them to that effect of love; because they will not impede the Union of Love in Faith, when we do not dwell upon them, but make use of them, towards exciting our love, and, when that is done, instantly dismiss them: in this way they will be of service to us towards the attainment of the Divine union.

Difference between Spiritual, and Imaginative Memory.

It is difficult to determine when these images touch directly the spiritual part of the soul, and when they are only in the fancy. Those of the fancy are usually very frequent, for the imagination and the fancy of some people are full of imaginary visions, abundantly present in one form; whether it be the result of the great vigour of that organ which, after the slightest effort of thought, represents at once and portrays in the fancy the usual forms, whether it be the work of Satan, or whether it be the work

BOOK III.

of God, but not formally impressed on the soul. But, however, we may determine their nature by their effects. Those that are natural or diabolic in their origin, however accurately remembered, produce no good effect, neither do they spiritually renew the soul, and the recollection of them issues only in dryness; while those which are from God produce, whenever remembered, some good effect, as at the first when originally presented to the soul. The formal images, those which are impressed on the soul, almost always when remembered, produce some effect. He who has these will easily distinguish the one from the other, for the difference between them will be most evident after experience. I have one thing, however, to say; those which are formally and durably impressed on the soul are of very rare occurrence. But of whatever kind they may be, the good of the soul consists in not seeking to comprehend anything save God alone by Faith in Hope.

Finally as to that objection which charges him with pride who rejects these things when they are good, I reply that it is a prudent humility to use them in the best way, as I have shown, and to guide our steps by the road that is safest.

CHAPTER XIII.

Of Spiritual Knowledge as it relates to the Memory.

Third kind of Apprehensions,—Memory of the purely Spiritual.

THE third kind of Apprehensions of the Memory is Spiritual Knowledge: not because it belongs to the bodily sense of the fancy, like the rest, but because it is also cognisable by the spiritual reminiscence and Memory. When the soul has once had one of this kind, it may, when it wills, call it to mind, not by reason of the figure and image which the apprehension thereof may have left behind in the bodily sense—for that is incapable of receiving spiritual forms—

but because it intellectually and spiritually remembers it by that form of it which remains impressed on the soul—which is also a form, or image, or knowledge spiritual or formal, by which the soul remembers it—or by the effect it has wrought. This is the reason why I place these apprehensions among those of the Memory, though not belonging directly to the fancy.

The nature of this knowledge, and the conduct to be observed by the soul with reference to it, in order to be united with God, has been sufficiently explained in the twenty-fourth chapter of the second book, where I treated of it as an apprehension of the Intellect. You will there find that there are two kinds of them, one of Uncreated Perfections, another of creatures. I am now speaking only so far as it touches this part of my subject; namely, the conduct of the Memory in the matter. I say again, as I did of the formal impressions in the preceding chapter—for these are of the same kind, being of created things—that they may be remembered when the effect of them is good, not, indeed, for the purpose of dwelling upon them but for quickening our love and knowledge of God. But if the recollection of them produces not this effect, the memory should never busy itself with them. But as to the knowledge of the Uncreated Perfections, that may be remembered as often as we can, for it will produce great results; for that is, as I said before, touches and impressions of the Divine union towards which I am directing the soul. The memory does not remember these by the help of any form, image, or figure that may have been impressed on the soul—for none such belong to the touches and impressions of Union with the Creator—but only by their effects of light, love, joy, and spiritual renewing, some of which, as often as they are remembered, are wrought anew in the soul.

Continual Remembrance of the Perfections of God.

CHAPTER XIV.

General directions for the guidance of the spiritual man in relation to the Memory.

Recapitulation.

To conclude, then, this subject of the Memory, it may be as well here to furnish the spiritually-minded reader with certain brief directions, of universal application, how he is to unite himself, in the memory, with God. For, notwithstanding that the matter has been sufficiently discussed, it will be more easily grasped, if I repeat it here concisely. Having this in view, then, we must remember, that my object is the Union of the soul with God in the Memory by Hope. Now, that which we hope for is what we possess not, and the less we possess the greater scope we have for hoping, and, consequently, the greater the perfection of hope; while, on the other hand, the more we possess the less room is there for hope, and, consequently, the less is the perfection of hope. Accordingly the more the soul strips the memory of forms and reminiscible matters, which are not the Divinity or God Incarnate — the recollection of Him always subserves our true end, for He is the Way, the Guide, and the Source of all good — the more it will fix the memory on God, and the more empty it will make it, so that it shall hope for Him who is the Fulness of it.

What we have to do, then, in order to live in the simple and perfect Hope of God, whenever these forms, knowledge, and distinct images occur, is, not to fix our minds upon them but to turn immediately to God, emptying the Memory of all such matters, in loving affection, without regarding or considering them more than suffices to enable us to understand and perform our obligations, if they have any reference thereto. We must do this without taking any satisfaction in them, in order that they may leave no disturbing effects behind. And therefore we must not omit to think of, and remember, those things which it is our duty to do and to know; for in that case, provided no selfish attachments intrude, these recollections will do no harm. Those sentences of the thirteenth chapter of the first book will be profitable to us in this matter.

The Author's principles different from those of the Reformers.

But, my dear Reader, bear in mind that I have nothing, and will have nothing, in common with the opinions of those pestilent men who, full of the pride and hate of Satan, labour to destroy among the Faithful the holy and necessary use, and noble worship, of the Images of God and the Saints. My principles are very different from theirs; for I am not saying that Images ought not to be allowed, and worshipped, as they do; but I only show the difference between them and God, teaching men to make use of the sign in such a way as that it shall not hinder their progress to the reality, by resting upon it more than is sufficient for their spiritual advancement.

Images are means to remember and to love God.

Means are necessary to the end; such are Images, for they remind us of God and of His Saints. But when we dwell upon the means more than the nature of such means demands, we are then hindered and perplexed. How much more, then, must this be the case with those interior images and visions which are formed within the soul? These are liable to innumerable risks and illusions. But with regard to the memorial, worship, and veneration of those Images, which our Holy Mother the Church sets before us, there can be neither risk nor delusion; and the recollection of them cannot fail to be profitable, because it is always connected with love of what they represent. And when the Memory makes this use of images they will always help it on towards the Divine union, if it permits the soul to fly upwards, when God grants this grace, from the image to the reality, in forgetfulness of the creature and all that belongs to it.

BOOK III.

CHAPTER XV.

Of the Obscure Night of the Will. Proofs from Deuteronomy and the Psalms. Division of the affections of the Will.

Reformation of the Intellect in Faith; of the Memory, in Hope; of the Will, in Charity.

WE have done nothing by the purification of the Intellect towards grounding it in Faith, and that of the Memory in Hope—according to the sense explained in the sixth chapter of the second book—if we have not also purified the Will in the order of Charity, which is the third virtue, and by which works done in Faith are living and meritorious, and without which they are nothing worth. For as S. James saith, 'Faith without works is dead.'* That is, without the works of Charity Faith is dead.

The greatest of these, Charity.

And now that I have to treat of the Night and active detachment of the Will, with a view to its perfect establishment in this virtue of the Love of God, I cannot find a better authority than that contained in the Book of Deuteronomy: 'Thou shalt love the Lord thy God with thy whole heart, and with thy whole soul, and with thy whole strength.'† This is all that the spiritual man ought to do—and all that I am teaching him—that he may truly draw near unto God in the Union of the will with God in Love. Man is here bidden to employ for God all his faculties and desires, all the functions and affections of his soul, so that all the skill and all the strength of the soul may minister to no other end than this, as the Psalmist says: 'I will keep my strength to Thee.'‡ The strength of the soul consists in its powers, passions, and desires, all of which are governed by the Will. But when the Will directs these powers, passions, and desires to God, and turns them away from all that is not God, it then keeps the strength of the soul for God, and

Love the fulfilment of the Law.

* S. James ii. 20. † Deuter. vi. 5. ‡ Ps. lviii. 10.

loves Him with its whole strength. And that the soul may be able to do this, I purpose here to show how the Will is to be purified from all unruly affections; which are the cause why our strength is not wholly kept for God.

Reformation of the Passions, Joy, Hope, Grief, and Fear.

These affections or Passions are four in number:—Joy, Hope, Grief, and Fear. If these passions are excited only according to Reason, in the way of God, so that we feel no joy except in that which is simply for the honour and glory of our Lord God, nor hope except in Him, nor grief except in what concerns Him, nor fear but of Him only, it is clear, then, that the strength and skill of the soul are directed to, and kept for, God. For the more the soul rejoices in aught beside Him, the less effectively will it rejoice in God, and the more it hopes in aught else, the less will it hope in God. The same applies to the other passions also.

In order to a more complete explanation of this I shall, as usual, speak of each of these passions and desires of the will separately, for the whole matter of Union with God consists in purging the will of its affections and desires, so that the vile and human will may become the Divine Will, being made one with the Will of God.

In disorder they cause Vice: In order, Virtue.

These four Passions domineer over the soul, and assail it with the more vigour, the less the will is attached to God, and the more dependent it is on created things; for it then rejoices easily in those things which do not deserve to be rejoiced in, hopes in that which is valueless, grieves over that for which perhaps it ought to rejoice, and fears where there is nothing to be afraid of.

It is from these affections, when disorderly, that all the vices and imperfections of the soul arise; and all its virtues also, when they are well governed and restrained. Let us remember that if but one of them be under the control of Reason, so will the others be also; for they are so intimately bound together, that the actual course of one is the virtual

BOOK III.

Mutual relations of the Passions to each other; and to the Will.

course of the rest, and if one of them be actually restrained, the others will be proportionately restrained also. For if the Will rejoices in anything, it will consequently hope in the same measure, and there grief and fear are virtually present; and as that joy ceases, in the same proportion cease also grief and fear and hope.

The Will with its four Passions may be said, in some sense, to be represented in the vision which Ezechiel saw of the four living creatures with one body; 'They had faces and wings on the four sides. And the wings of one were joined to the wings of another. They turned not when they went, but every one went straight forward.'* The wings of each one of these four affections are joined to the wings of the others, and whithersoever one of them goes there also of necessity go virtually the others. When one of them goeth on the earth so do the others, and when one is lifted up, so the others also. Where hope is, there also will be joy and fear and grief; and when one has retired, the others retire also.

Remember, therefore, O thou who art spiritual, that the whole soul, with the Will and its other powers, will follow in the wake of every one of these passions; that they will be all captives to it, and that the three other passions also will live in it, afflicting the soul and preventing its flight to the liberty and repose of sweet Contemplation and Union. And so Boethius says: Wilt thou contemplate Truth in clear light? Drive away joy and hope and fear and grief.† For while these passions have dominion over thee, they will not suffer the soul to enjoy that tranquillity and peace which are necessary for the attainment of wisdom, either natural or supernatural.

Boethius quoted.

* Ezech. i. 8, 9.

† 'Tu quoque, si vis lumine claro cernere Verum,
. . . Gaudia pelle, pelle timorem, spemque fugato,
Ne dolor assit.' Boet. *de Cons. Phil.* lib. I. metr. vii.

CHAPTER XVI.

Of the first affection of the Will. What Joy is. Its diverse sources.

THE first of the Passions of the soul and of the affections of the Will is Joy, which, in the sense I speak of, is nothing else but a certain satisfaction of the will joined to the appreciation of the object it regards; for the will has no joy except when it appreciates an object and is satisfied with it. This refers to active joy, to that joy which the soul feels when it clearly and distinctly perceives why it rejoices, and when it is in its own power to rejoice or not. For there is another joy, which is passive: when the soul finds itself rejoicing, without clearly perceiving—and sometimes even perceiving—why it rejoices, it being out of its power at that time to control, or not control, that joy. I shall speak of this hereafter. I am now speaking of that joy, active and voluntary, which is derived from clear and distinct perceptions of things.

First Affection of the Will; Joy,— 1. Its Definition.

2. Its twofold division.

Joy arises out of six different sources: temporal, natural, sensual, moral, supernatural, and spiritual good. I shall speak of these successively, for we have so to order the Will with regard to them, that, unembarrassed by them, it may not omit to place the strength of its Joy in God. And with this there is one truth which we must take for granted, and lean upon it as upon a staff. And we must understand it thoroughly, for it is the light by which we are to be guided, in which this doctrine is to be regarded, and by which our joy in all these goods is to be directed unto God. That truth is this: The Will ought to rejoice in nothing but in that which tends to the Honour and Glory of God; and that to serve Him in Evangelical Perfection is the greatest honour we can render Him: whatever is beside this is of no value nor of any use to man.

3. Its six sources; 1. Temporal. 2. Natural. 3. Sensual. 4. Moral. 5. Supernatural. 6. Spiritual.

Ad majorem Dei Gloriam.

BOOK III.

CHAPTER XVII.

Of Joy in Temporal Goods. How it is to be directed.

First source of Joy,—Temporal Goods.

THE first source of Joy I mentioned is Temporal good; by which I mean riches, rank, office, and other dignities; children, relations, and alliances. All these are matters in which the Will may rejoice. But what vanity to rejoice in riches, rank, titles, office, and the like, after which men are striving! If a man's wealth made him a better servant of God, he might rejoice in his riches; but riches are rather occasions of sin, as the Wise Man saith: 'My son . . . if thou be rich, thou shalt not be free from sin.'* It is very true that temporal goods are not necessarily, in themselves, occasions of sin, yet generally, by reason of our frailty, the heart sets itself upon them, and falls away from God, which is sin. The wise man therefore says, that the rich shall not be free from sin.

Indifferent in themselves. Should be chosen or rejected for God's sake.

1. Riches.

Our Lord Jesus Christ, in the Gospel, calls riches thorns,† that we may learn that he who shall set his Will upon riches will be wounded by sin. Those fearful words recorded by S. Matthew, 'Amen, I say to you, that a rich man shall hardly enter into the kingdom of Heaven,'‡ show us plainly that a man ought not to rejoice in his riches, because they expose him to so great a danger. David also bids us withdraw ourselves from riches, saying, 'If riches abound, set not your heart upon them.'§ I will not allege further proof in a matter so clear, for when shall I have said all the evils of them that Solomon hath said? Solomon was a man full of wisdom and of great riches, and he knew well what they were when he said, 'I have seen all things that are done under the sun, and behold all is vanity and vexation of spirit

* Ecclus. xi. 10.
† S. Matt. xiii. 22.
‡ S. Matt. xix. 23.
§ Ps. lxi. 11.

. . . and a fruitless solicitude of the mind.'* And, 'He that loveth riches shall reap no fruit from them.'† And again, 'Riches kept to the hurt of the owner.'‡ An instance of this we have in the Gospel. A rich man, because his harvest was abundant, rejoiced in his expectation of years of comfort: 'But God said to him, Thou fool, this night do they require thy soul of thee; and whose shall those things be which thou hast provided?'§ The Psalmist also teaches us the same truth, saying, 'Be not thou afraid when a man shall be made rich . . . for when he shall die, he shall take nothing away; nor shall his glory descend with him;'‖—that is, we are not to envy our neighbour because he is grown rich, for his riches will not profit him in the life to come; yea, rather let us pity him.

The sum of the matter is this: let no man rejoice in his own or in his brother's wealth, unless it be that it tends to the better service of God. If rejoicing in riches can be made in any way endurable, it is when we spend and employ them for God; for there is no other way of making them profitable. The same principle applies to the temporal goods of title, rank, and office; all rejoicing in which is vanity, unless we feel that these things enable us to serve God better, and that they make the way to Eternal Life more secure. And as we can never be sure that these things enable us to serve God better, it will be vanity to rejoice deliberately in them, because such a joy can never be reasonable. For as our Lord saith: 'For what doth it profit a man if he gain the whole world, and suffer the loss of his own soul?'¶ There cannot be anything worth rejoicing in except that which makes us better servants of our God.

2. Rank, Titles, and Office.

Neither are men to rejoice in their children, because they

* Eccles. i. 14; ii. 26.
† Ib. v. 9.
‡ Ib. v. 12.
§ S. Luke xii. 20.
‖ Ps. xlviii. 17, 18.
¶ S. Matt. xvi. 26.

BOOK III.

3. Domestic relations; (1) Children.

are many, rich, endowed with abilities and natural graces, and prosperous, but only in that they serve God. Neither the beauty, nor the wealth, nor the lineage of Absalom the son of David profited him at all, because he served not God. To rejoice in such a son would have been vanity. It is also vanity to desire children; as some do who disturb the world with their fretting; for they know not if their children will be good and servants of God. They know not whether the pleasure they expect from them may not be turned into pain, tranquillity and consolation into trouble and disquietude, honour into disgrace; and, finally, whether they shall not be to them greater occasions of sinning against God, as is the case with many. Christ has said of these that they compass sea and land to enrich themselves and to make themselves twofold the children of perdition: 'You go round about the sea and the land to make one proselyte; and when he is made, you make him the child of hell twofold more than yourselves.'*

(2) Worldly Prosperity.

If a man's affairs are prosperous, if his undertakings succeed, and all his wishes are gratified, he ought to fear rather than rejoice, for this is a dangerous occasion of forgetting, and offending against, God. It was for this cause that Solomon was cautious, saying: 'Laughter I counted error; and to mirth I said: Why art thou vainly deceived?'† It is as if he said: when all things smiled upon me I counted it error and delusion to rejoice therein; for, beyond all doubt, it is a great error and folly on the part of man if he rejoices in the sunshine of prosperity, when he does not know for certain that it will lead to any durable good. 'The heart of the wise is where there is mourning,' saith Solomon, 'and the heart of fools where there is mirth.'‡ Vain rejoicing blinds the heart, makes it inconsiderate and thoughtless, but

* S. Matt. xxiii. 15. † Eccles. ii. 2. ‡ Ib. vii. 5.

mourning opens our eyes to the vision of our loss and gain. This is the reason why the wise man saith that 'anger is better than laughter;'* and that 'it is better to go to the house of mourning than to the house of feasting; for in that we are put in mind of the end of all, and the living thinketh what is to come.'†

(3) Marriage.

It is also vanity for a wife or a husband to rejoice in marriage, for they know not whether they shall serve God the better in that state. Yea, rather they should feel humbled, because, as the Apostle saith, marriage leads them to set their affections upon each other, and not to give their heart whole unto God. This is why he said: 'Art thou loosed from a wife? seek not a wife.'‡ He that is married ought to live with freedom of heart, as if he had not been married. The Apostle teaches the same doctrine with regard to all temporal goods, saying: 'This, therefore, I say, brethren, the time is short; it remaineth that they also who have wives be as if they had none; and they that weep, as though they wept not; and they that rejoice, as if they rejoiced not; and they that buy, as though they possessed not; and they that use this world, as if they used it not.'§ The Apostle teaches that to rejoice in anything which tendeth not to the service of God is vanity and without profit, for all joy which is not in God brings no good to the soul.

CHAPTER XVIII.

Of the Evils resulting from Joy in Temporal goods.

If I were to describe all the evils that environ the soul when the affections of the Will are set upon Temporal Goods, paper and ink would fail me, and time itself would be too short.

* Eccles. vii. 4.
† Ib. vii. 3.
‡ 1 Cor. vii. 27.
§ 1 Cor. vii. 29, 30.

BOOK III.

Slight beginnings issue in great evils, and in the ruin of great prosperity. A spark, unquenched, kindles a great fire, which may burn up the whole world. All these evils have their root and origin in one principal evil of a negative character involved in this joy, namely, a departure from God.

Joy in creatures ends in loss of God.

For, as the drawing near of the soul unto God with the affection of the will is the source of all good, so the going away from Him, through love of created things, issues in all evils and calamities, in proportion to the joy and affection which unite us to the creature. This is the departure from God. In proportion, therefore, to our departure from God, more or less, will be the evils resulting from it in greater or less extent and gravity; and for the most part they are at once most extensive and most grave.

Four degrees of Departure from God.

There are four degrees, one worse than the other, in this negative evil, from which all the other evils, negative and positive, proceed. And when the fourth degree is reached, all the evils involved in this case will have fallen upon the soul. These four degrees are described in the following words of Moses:—'The beloved grew fat and kicked; he grew fat, and thick, and gross; he forsook God, who made him, and departed from God his Saviour.' *

1. Dimness of Spiritual Perception.

This growing fat of the soul, once beloved, is its absorption in the joy of created things. Hence the first degree of evil, going backwards; it is a certain obtuseness of mind with regard to God, which obscures His blessings, as a cloud darkens the sky, hiding the light of the sun. For the moment the spiritual man rejoices in anything, and gives the reins to his foolish desires, he becomes blind to God, and overshadows with a cloud the pure perceptions of his judgment. 'For the bewitching of vanity,' saith the Holy Ghost, 'obscureth good things, and the wandering of con-

* Deuter. xxxii. 15.

cupiscence overturneth the innocent mind.'* The Holy Spirit teaches here that concupiscence alone, and joy in created things, even when the soul is without previous malice, are sufficient to precipitate it into the first degree of evil; into that obtuseness of mind and obscurity of judgment which destroy the perception of truth and a right judgment in all things. If a man gives way to concupiscence, or rejoices in temporal things, neither his sanctity nor his prudence can prevent his fall.

This explains those words of God: 'Neither shalt thou take bribes, which even blind the wise.'† This is especially addressed unto judges who have need of a clear and vigilant judgment, which cannot coexist with avarice and joy in gifts. Hence God commanded Moses to appoint men for judges who hated avarice: 'Provide out of all the people able men . . . . that hate avarice, who may judge the people at all times,'‡ men who would not blind their judgment by the lust of possession. God does not say men that avoid avarice, but men that hate avarice. For if we would defend ourselves completely against a particular affection we must hold it in abhorrence, and guard ourselves against it by the contrary feeling. The reason why Samuel was always so upright and enlightened a judge was, as he tells us himself, his abstinence from gifts: 'If I have taken a bribe at any man's hand.'§

2. Tædium de Deo.

The second degree grows out of the first, as the text shows: 'he grew fat, and thick, and gross.' Thus the Will becomes gross and distracted, by greater liberty in worldly things. It has no further scruples about the pleasures of sense, and abandons itself to created things. This state grows out of a previous indulgence in joy, for when the soul of man is

* Wisd. iv. 12.
† Exod. xxiii. 8.
‡ Ib. xviii. 21, 22.
§ 1 Kings xii. 3.

BOOK III.

engrossed therein it is the result of yielding to it; and this engrossing of it by joy and desire causes the will to dilate and expand itself on created things. Great evils result from this, because this second degree leads us away from the things of God, and from holy practices, and robs us of all pleasure in them, because we take pleasure in other matters, and abandon ourselves to many follies, to empty joys and pleasures. When the second degree is completely reached, it destroys utterly habitual devotions, and the mind and desire are given up to secularities. Those who have fallen to this second degree, not only have their judgment and understanding blinded as to truth and justice, like those who have fallen into the first; but they are also remiss and tepid in recognising and doing their duty, according to the words of the Prophet: 'They all love bribes, they run after rewards. They judge not for the fatherless; and the widow's cause cometh not unto them.' * This implicates them in sin, especially if such duties are incumbent upon them, for those who have fallen to this depth are not free from malice, like those of the first degree. These, therefore, withdraw more and more from justice and virtue, because they inflame the will more and more by this their affection for created things. The characteristics of those who are in this second state are great tepidity in spiritual things, and a careless observance of them; they perform their highest duties rather as if they were ceremonies, or from compulsion, or from habit, and not from love.

3. Neglect of God's Law.

The third degree of this negative evil is the utter forsaking of God, neglect of His law, because men will not deny themselves in the merest trifle of this world, and, finally, mortal sin committed through concupiscence. This degree is described in the text by the words, 'He forsook God who made him.' This degree includes all those the faculties of whose souls are so immersed in the things of the world—

* Is. i. 23.

in riches and the commerce thereof—that they are utterly regardless of the obligations of the Divine Law. In that which concerns their salvation they are forgetful and dull, but quick and clear in the things of the world, so much so that our Lord calls them 'children of this world,' saying of them, that they 'are wiser in their generation than the children of light;'* that is, more prudent in the management of their own affairs than the children of light in their own. Such persons are nothing in the things of God, but everything in the things of the world. These persons are the truly avaricious; they have so profusely wasted their affections and desires upon created things that they can never be satisfied; their desire and thirst increase the more, the more they depart from the Fountain which alone can satisfy them, namely, God. It is of these that God speaks by the mouth of the Prophet, saying, 'They have forsaken Me, the fountain of living water, and have digged to themselves cisterns, broken cisterns, that can hold no water.'† The covetous man cannot quench his thirst by created things; but he increases it. These persons fall into innumerable sins through temporal goods; of whom the Psalmist hath said, 'They have passed into the affection of the heart.'‡

4. False gods in place of the True One.

The fourth degree of this negative evil is described in the same text thus: 'departed from God his Saviour.' This is the issue of the third degree, of which I have just spoken.

The avaricious man, because he makes light of his want of affection for the Law of God, on account of temporal goods, departs from Him in Memory, Intellect, and Will. He forgets Him as if He existed not, because he has made money and temporal prosperity his god; for avarice is, according to the Apostle, 'the service of idols.'§ This fourth degree extends to forgetfulness of God, to the setting of the heart formally on money which ought to be set formally upon God; as if

* S. Luke xvi. 8.
† Jerem. ii. 13.
‡ Ps. lxxii. 7.
§ Coloss. iii. 5.

BOOK III.

Spiritual Simony.

men had no other god than money. They have fallen into this fourth degree who scruple not to subject Divine and Supernatural things to temporal, as if the latter were God; their duty being to act on the contrary rule, subjecting temporal things to God, as Reason requires. Such was the impious Balaam, who sold for money the gift of God,* and Simon Magus, who 'thought that the gift of God may be purchased with money,'† and attempted to buy it. They thought more of money; they seemed to think that others did so too, and that they would sell the gift of God.

There are many who, in various ways, have fallen into this fourth degree of evil, their Reason is blinded by avarice, and they are the servants of money and not of God; they labour for it and not for Him; they propose to themselves a human and not the Divine reward; making money in divers ways their principal end and god, and preferring it to God, their ultimate end.

Tribute paid by Gold-worshippers.

This class, too, comprises all those miserable men who so love their earthly goods as to esteem them their god; and who therefore shrink not from the sacrifice of their own lives whenever their god suffers the slightest injury; they fall into despair, and for wretched objects inflict death upon themselves; thereby exhibiting, in the work of their own hands, the miserable reward which their god bestows upon them. When their expectations fail them they despair and die, and those who escape this final calamity live in the torments of continual anxiety and misery; no joy enters into their soul, and no temporal happiness attends them; they pay tribute to their god in sorrow of heart, gathering money for the final misery of their just perdition: as it is written, 'Riches kept to the hurt of the owner.'‡

Those also of whom it is said, 'God delivered them up to

* Num. xxii. 7. † Acts viii. 20. ‡ Eccles. v. 12.

a reprobate sense,'* are of this class, for joy, when it makes possessions its end, drags men down to this. Those who do not fall so low are objects of deep commiseration, because they turn back from the way of God. 'Be not thou afraid when a man shall be made rich, and when the glory of his house shall be increased. For when he shall die he shall take nothing away, nor shall his glory descend with him.'† 'Be not afraid when a man shall be made rich;' that is, be not envious of him, thinking him superior to thyself, for when he shall die he shall take nothing away with him, neither shall his glory nor his joy descend with him.

CHAPTER XIX.

The benefits resulting from withdrawing our Joy from Temporal things.

Mortification in little things necessary.

THE spiritual man, then, must be very careful of the beginnings of Joy in Temporal things, lest it should grow from little to be great, and increase from one degree to another. What is small becomes large, out of slight beginnings result great evils, and one spark is enough to set a mountain on fire. However slight his joy may be, let him quench it at once, and not trust that he shall be able to do it later; for if he has not the courage to do so when it is but beginning, how can he presume upon success when it shall have taken root and grown? Remember especially those words of our Lord, 'He that is faithful in that which is least, is faithful also in that which is greater.'‡

He who avoids what is slight will not stumble over what is great. Little things involve great evils, because the fences and wall of the heart are broken down when they enter in. And the proverb says, He who has begun his work has

* Rom. i. 28. † Ps. xlviii. 17, 18. ‡ S. Luke xvi. 10.

BOOK III.

accomplished the half of it. It is for this reason that David admonishes us, saying, 'If riches abound set not your heart upon them.'* If man will not do this for God, and because Christian Perfection requires it, yet because of the temporal advantages, beside the spiritual ones, which such conduct brings with it, he should keep his heart perfectly free from all joy of this kind. In this way he not only delivers himself from those pestilent evils enumerated in the preceding chapter, but also, repressing all joy in temporal goods, acquires the virtue of liberality, one of the chief attributes of God; and which cannot possibly coexist with avarice. Moreover, he attains to liberty of spirit, clearness of judgment, repose, tranquillity, and peaceful confidence in God, together with the true worship and obedience of the Will. He has greater joy and comfort in creatures if he detaches himself from them; and he can have no joy in them if he considers them as his own. He acquires also in this detachment from creatures a clear comprehension of them, so as to understand perfectly the truths that relate to them, both naturally and supernaturally. For this reason his joy in them is widely different from his who is attached to them, and far nobler. The former rejoices in their truth, the latter in their deceptiveness; the former in their best, and the latter in their worst, conditions; the former in their substantial worth, and the latter in their seeming and accidental nature, through his senses only. For sense cannot grasp or comprehend more than the accidents, but the mind, purified from the clouds and species of the accidents, penetrates to the interior truth of things, for that is its proper object.

[Margin: Benefits of self-denial in Temporal goods, for the Love of God: 1. Liberality. 2. Liberty, and Peace. 3. Greater and truer Joy.]

[Margin: 4. Clearness of Spiritual Perception.]

Now Joy as a cloud darkens the judgment, for there can be no rejoicing in created things without the attachment of the Will. The negation and purgation of this joy leaves the

* Ps. lxi. 11.

judgment clear as the sky when the mists are scattered. The former, therefore, has joy in all things, but his joy is not dependent upon them, neither does it arise from their being his own: and the latter, in so far as he regards them as his own, loses in general all joy whatever. The former, while his heart is set upon none of them, possesses them all, as the Apostle saith, with great freedom: 'as having nothing, and possessing all things.'* The latter, while in will attached to them, neither has nor possesses anything, for rather created things have possession of his very heart, for which cause he suffers pain as a prisoner. And, therefore, all the joy he will derive from creatures, will necessarily end in as many disquietudes and pains in the heart which is in their possession.

5. Wider and better possessions.

He who is detached from creatures, is not molested during prayer or otherwise, and so, without losing his time, he gains easily great spiritual treasures. On the other hand, the covetous man runs to and fro, within the limits of the chain by which his heart is bound, and with all his efforts can scarcely set himself free, even for a moment, from the bondage of his thoughts, running incessantly thither where his heart is fixed. The spiritual man, therefore, must suppress the first motions of this joy, remembering, as I said before, that there is nothing in which a man may rejoice except in serving God, in promoting His Honour and Glory, in directing all things to this end, and in avoiding all vanity in them, and in not seeking his own pleasure and comfort.

6. Capacity for God.

The absence of Joy in created good, brings another great and excellent benefit: it sets the heart free for God: which is a disposition meet for all those graces which He will bestow, and without which He will give none. And even in this life, for one joy denied through love of Him and for the

* 2 Cor. vi. 10.

BOOK III.

7. A hundred-fold reward even in this life.

sake of Evangelical Perfection, He will give them a hundred-fold, according to His promise.* But if it were not so, the spiritual Christian ought to suppress all joy in created things because it is offensive in the sight of God. When the rich man, in the gospel, rejoiced, because he had 'much goods laid up for many years,' God was so displeased, that He said unto him: 'Thou fool, this night do they require thy soul of thee.' †

Conclusion. Light Sufferings, and infinite Bliss; or short Pleasure, and eternal Pain.

It is therefore justly to be feared, whenever we rejoice in vanity, that God is looking on and preparing some chastisement for us, the bitter cup of our deservings; for the punishment of such rejoicing is frequently greater than its pleasures. Though the words recorded by S. John concerning Babylon be true: 'As much as she hath glorified herself and lived in delicacies, so much torment and sorrow give ye to her,' ‡ we are not to suppose that the pain will not exceed the joy, because it will be far greater—seeing that for passing pleasures there are infinite and everlasting torments—for the words mean that nothing shall escape its particular punishment, for He who will punish for every idle word, will not pass over our empty joy.

CHAPTER XX.

The Joy of the Will in Natural Goods is Vanity. How to direct the Will to God therein.

Second source of Joy,—Natural Goods.

BY Natural Goods I mean beauty, grace, comeliness, bodily constitution, and all other physical endowments, and also good understanding, discretion, and other rational qualities. Now, for a man to rejoice, because he himself, or those who belong to him, may be thus gifted, and for that reason only,

* S. Matt. xix. 29. † S. Luke xii. 19, 20. ‡ Apoc. xviii. 7.

How created Beauty may lead from God.

without giving thanks to God, who thus endows men in order that they may know Him and love Him the more, is vanity and delusion. 'Favour is deceitful,' saith the Wise Man, 'and beauty is vain: the woman that feareth the Lord, she shall be praised.'* He teaches us that man ought rather to be afraid of his natural endowments, because they may so easily withdraw him from the love of God, and cast him down into error and vanity. This is the reason why physical grace is deceitful: it deceives a man and allures him to that which is unseemly, through empty joy or complacency, either in himself, or in others, so endowed. Beauty is vain; it makes man fall in divers ways, when he values it and rejoices in it, for he ought to rejoice in it only when it enables him to serve God. We ought, therefore, rather to fear, lest perhaps our natural gifts and graces should become occasions of offending against God, through presuming upon them, or excessive estimation of them, arising out of their continued contemplation. He therefore, who is thus endowed, ought to be very cautious, and watchful in his conduct, lest he should furnish another with the opportunity of withdrawing his heart from God even for a moment. For these natural gifts and graces are so prolific in temptations and in occasions of sin, as well to the owner as to the beholder, that scarcely any one can avoid all entanglement of the heart in them. Many spiritual persons, of natural beauty, have, under the influence of this fear, prayed to God for their own disfigurement, that they might not be an occasion of vain affection or joy, either to themselves or to others.

Better gifts, greater responsibility.

The spiritual man, therefore, must purify his Will, and render it insensible to this empty rejoicing, remembering that beauty, and all other natural graces, are earth, from the earth, and soon return to it; that comeliness and grace are

* Prov. xxxi. 30.

BOOK III.

God the Uncreated Beauty.

but smoke and vapour; and if he would escape falling into vanity, he must esteem them as such, and direct his heart upwards unto God beyond them all, rejoicing and delighted that God is all Beauty and all Grace in Himself, supremely, infinitely, above all created things. 'They shall perish, but Thou remainest, and all of them shall grow old like a garment.'* If, therefore, our rejoicing is not in God, it will always be false and delusive. It is to this that those words of Solomon apply which he addressed to that joy which has its sources in created things: 'To mirth, I said, Why art thou vainly deceived?'† that is when the heart suffers itself to be attracted by created things.

CHAPTER XXI.

The evils of the Will's rejoicing in Natural Goods.

Six evils of loving Natural Goods for their own sake.

THOUGH many of these evils and benefits, which I describe under these several divisions of Joy, be common to all kinds of joy, nevertheless, because they flow directly from joy and the rejection of it—though comprised under any one of these divisions—I speak under each head of some evils and benefits, which are also found under another, because connected with that joy which is common to all. But my chief object is to speak of those particular evils and benefits which rejoicing, or not rejoicing, in all things, ministers unto the soul. I call them particular evils, because they flow primarily and immediately from one particular kind of rejoicing, and only secondarily and mediately from another. For instance, the evil of tepidity flows directly from all and every kind of joy, and is therefore common to the six kinds in general;

* Ps. ci. 27. † Eccles. ii. 2.

but that of sensuality is a particular evil, which flows directly only from joy in the natural goods of which I am speaking.

The spiritual and corporal evils, then, which directly and effectually flow from rejoicing in Natural Goods, are, in number, six principal evils.

1. Contempt for others.

The first is vain glory, presumption, pride, and disesteem of our neighbour; for no man can entertain an excessive esteem of one thing without wanting in respect for some other thing. The result is, at least, that we disesteem and despise all else; because naturally, by esteeming one thing we withdraw our heart from all besides, and fix it upon that. It is most easy to glide from this real contempt into an intentional and deliberate despising of others; in particular or in general, not in thoughts only, but in words as well, to the extent of saying that such a person is not like such an one.

2. Sins of the flesh.

The second evil is complacency and sensual delight.

3. Flattery.

The third evil is flattery and empty praise, wherein there is delusion and vanity, as the Prophet saith, 'O my people, they that call thee blessed deceive thee.'* For, even if we speak truly when we praise the grace and beauty of another, it will be strange if some evil be not involved, either in causing him to fall into vain complacency and joy, or in ministering food to his imperfect affections and intentions.

4. Spiritual stupidity.

The fourth evil is a general one: it dulls the reason and the spiritual sense, as the joy of temporal goods does, and in a certain way even more. For, as natural goods are more intimately connected with man than temporal goods are, the joy which they minister makes a quicker and deeper impression upon the senses, and more effectually blunts them. Reason and judgment are no longer free, but overshadowed by the cloud of this joy which is so inherent in us; and hence,

* Is. iii. 12.

BOOK III.

5. Dissipation of mind. 6. Weariness of God.

The fifth evil is the dissipation of the mind by created things. Then the sixth is spiritual sloth and tepidity, which grow into weariness and sadness in Divine things, so that in the end we come to hate them. Pure spirituality is inevitably lost in this joy, at least in principle; for if any spirituality exist, it will be exceedingly sensual and gross, not interior, nor recollected—consisting in sensible delight rather than in the strength of the spirit. If we are in mind so mean and weak as not to destroy the habit of this joy—an imperfect habit of it even is sufficient to sully the purity of our spirituality, without consenting to the acts which this joy suggests—we are living in the weakness of sense rather than in the power of the spirit. This will become manifest in the matter of perfection and fortitude when the occasion shall arise, though I do not deny that many virtues may coexist with great imperfections, but no pure or healthy interior spirituality can coexist with these unchecked rejoicings; for here the flesh almost reigns, which wars against the spirit, and though we may be unconscious of the evil, yet, at least, secret distractions are the result.

Universality and power of the second evil.

I now return to the second evil, which involves innumerable others. No pen can describe, no words can express, the nature and extent of the misery that results from rejoicing in natural grace and beauty. These are daily occasions of murders, of honour lost, of insults, of extravagant dissipation, emulations, contentions, adultery and violence, of the ruin of Saints, comparable in number to the third part of the stars of heaven, swept down to the earth by the tail of the dragon.* 'How is the gold become dim, the finest colour is changed, the stones of the sanctuary are scattered in the top of every street. The noble sons of Sion, and they that were clothed in the best gold, how are they esteemed as

* Apoc. xii. 4.

earthen vessels, the work of the potter's hands!'* Is any condition secure against the poison of this evil? Who has not drunk, be it much or little, of the golden cup of the Babylonian woman, that sitteth on the 'scarlet-coloured beast, full of names of blasphemy, having seven heads and ten horns?'* Neither high nor low, neither saint nor sinner lives, to whom she has not given her cup to drink from, suborning the heart in some thing; for all the kings of the earth have drunk of the wine of her fornication. She seizes upon all conditions of men, the highest and the noblest, the sacred Priesthood itself, and puts the cup of her abominations in the holy place: 'There shall be in the Temple the abomination of desolation.'† Even one spiritually strong scarcely escapes the wine of this cup, which is empty rejoicing. This is the reason why it is said that all the kings of the earth have drunk of it; for there are very few, however holy they may be, who have not drunk and been corrupted, in some measure, by the cups of joy which the pleasure of natural grace and beauty supply. Observe, too, that the word is 'drunk,' for if we drink of the wine of this joy, it seizes on the heart and deadens it, obscuring the Reason, as in men drunk with wine. And if no antidote be taken at once, and the poison expelled, the life of the soul is in danger. Spiritual weakness having grown upon us, this poison will drag us down to such depths of evil that we shall grind in the mill like Samson,‡ deprived of sight, with the hair of our first strength cut off, captives in the hands of our enemies; and afterwards, perhaps, die the second death, as he did the first: the draughts of this joy producing spiritually in us what they did corporally in him, and in many unto this day. In the end our enemies will surround us and say to our great

* Lam. iv. 1, 2.
† Apoc. xvii. 3.
‡ Dan. ix. 27.
§ Judges xvi. 21.

BOOK III.

confusion, Art thou he who broke the cords, tore the lions, killed the Philistines, carried away the gates, and set thyself free from the hands of thine enemies?

Let me now conclude with the requisite instruction for this poison. If you feel your heart moved by the vain joy of Natural Goods, remember how great vanity it is to rejoice in anything but in the service of God, how dangerous it is and ruinous. Remember the punishment of the angels who rejoiced in their beauty and endowments; they fell deformed into the abyss below. And how great are the evils which vanity brings daily upon men! Resolve, therefore, in time to take the remedy, according to the proverb, Resist the evil in its beginnings; remedies are too late, when the disease has grown; for when the evil has grown in the heart, the remedy is too late: 'Look not upon the wine when it is yellow, when the colour thereof shineth in the glass. It goeth in pleasantly; but in the end it will bite like a snake, and will spread abroad poison like a basilisk.'*

Fall of the Angels.

CHAPTER XXII.

The benefits of not rejoicing in Natural Goods.

Benefits of self-denial in Natural Goods;

MANY are the benefits which the soul reaps when it withdraws the heart from this joy. For beside disposing itself for the love of God, and the other virtues, it makes a way for personal humility and universal charity towards our neighbours. When our affections, free from the influence of Natural Goods, which are deceitful, rest upon no one, the soul is free to love all men reasonably and spiritually, as God wills them to be loved. No one deserves to be loved except for his virtues, and when we love in this way, our love is pleasing unto God, and

1. Universal charity.

* Prov. xxiii. 31, 32.

in great liberty, and if there be attachment in it there is greater attachment to God. For then the more this love grows, the more also grows our love of God, and the deeper our love of Him the more we shall love our neighbour: for the principle of both is the same.

CHAP. XXII.

2. Following of Christ.

Another great benefit is the perfect observance of our Saviour's words: 'If any man will come after Me, let him deny himself.'* Now the soul can never do this, if it has any joy in its natural endowments; for he who has, even the slightest self-esteem, neither denies himself nor follows Christ.

3. Tranquillity of mind.

Another great benefit of this self-denial is, that it makes the soul tranquil, empties it of the sources of distractions, controls the senses, and especially the eyes. The spiritual man, seeking no joy, will neither look upon, nor suffer his other senses to be occupied with, these endowments, that he may not be attracted by them, nor be led to waste time or thought upon them, 'according to the likeness of a serpent, like the deaf asp that stoppeth her ears.'† If we set a guard over our senses, which are the doors of the soul, we shall thereby guard and increase its purity and tranquillity also.

4. Purity of heart.

Another benefit, of no less importance, which those who have made progress in the mortification of this joy, obtain, is this: Impure objects and the knowledge of them no longer impress, and sully the soul, as in their case to whom this joy is still somewhat pleasurable. This mortification and self-denial grows into a spiritual pureness of soul and body, of mind and sense, which issues in a certain angelical conformity with God, rendering both soul and body a worthy temple of the Holy Ghost. Man cannot be thus pure if his heart entertains any joy in these natural gifts and graces. It is not necessary to have given consent to any impure act, for this joy is sufficient to sully the soul and senses with the know-

* S. Matt. xvi. 24. † Ps. lvii. 5.

BOOK III.

ledge of evil, as it is written: 'The Holy Spirit of discipline will withdraw Himself from thoughts that are without understanding,'* that is, from thoughts not directed to God by right Reason.

5. Esteem of the good.

Another general benefit is this: Beside our deliverance from the evils already mentioned, we are delivered also from innumerable other follies and evils, spiritual and temporal, especially from that contempt which falls to the lot of all those who value themselves, or rejoice either in their own natural gifts or in those of others. In this way we shall be esteemed as wise and excellent men, as in truth all are who make no account of natural goods, but only of those which are pleasing unto God.

6. Generosity of soul.

These benefits issue in a final one, which is a certain generosity of mind, as necessary in the service of God as liberty of spirit, by which temptations are easily overcome, afflictions endured, and by which virtues grow and thrive.

CHAPTER XXIII.

Of the third kind, Sensible Goods. Their nature and varieties. The regulation of the Will with respect to them.

Third source of Joy,—Sensible Goods.

I HAVE now to speak of Joy in Sensible Goods, wherein the will rejoices. By sensible goods I mean all that is cognisable by the senses, of sight, of hearing, of smell, of taste and of touch, and of the interior working of the imaginative powers; all of which belong to the interior and exterior bodily senses. In order to render the will blind to, and purified from, all joy in sensible objects, directing it to God, we must take this truth for granted. The sense of man's lower nature is not, and cannot be, capable of knowing or comprehending God, as

* Wisd. i. 5.

God not an object of Sensitive Perception.

He is. The eye cannot see Him, or anything that resembles Him; the ear cannot hear His voice, nor any sound that resembles it; the smell cannot perceive any odours so sweet, the palate cannot taste any savour so delicious, nor can the touch feel any contact so exquisite and thrilling, nor any thing like unto Him, and the thoughts and imagination also cannot conceive any form or shape which can possibly be any representation of Him. 'From the beginning of the world they have not heard, nor perceived with the ears: the eye hath not seen, O God, besides Thee; the eye hath not seen, nor ear heard, neither hath it entered into the heart of man.'*

Now, sweetness and delight enter into the senses in two ways: either from the mind through some interior Divine communication, or from outward objects represented to them. But according to the text just quoted, our lower nature cannot know God either in the way of the spirit or in the way of sense; for having no capacity for so great a matter, it comprehends the spiritual and intellectual, sensually only. Therefore to occupy the will with the joy that has its sources in any of these apprehensions, will be at the least but vanity, and an impediment in the way of employing the energy of the will upon God, by rejoicing in Him alone. This is what the soul can never do unless it purifies itself from all joy in sensible things, for if it should rejoice herein at all that will be but vanity. When the soul does not rest here, but instantly, as soon as the will becomes conscious of any joy in any object of sense, elevates itself upwards unto God—that joy supplying motives thereto and power—it is well with it, and then it need not suppress such emotions, but may profit by them, and even ought to do so, so as to accomplish so holy an act: for there are souls whom sensible objects greatly influence in the way of God. Such souls, however, must be very cautious, and

God seen in His works.

* Is. lxiv. 4; 1 Cor. ii. 9.

BOOK III.

watch the issues of this conduct, for very often many spiritual persons indulge themselves in these sensible recreations, under the pretence of giving themselves to prayer and to God. Now what they do should be called recreation, not prayer, and their pleasure in this is their own rather than God's. Though their intention be directed to God, yet the effect is sensible recreation, and the fruit of it is weakness and imperfection, rather than the quickening of the will, and the surrender of it into the hands of God.

Touchstone of sensational pleasures,—Elevation of the soul to God.

I propose here to lay down a rule by which we may know when sensible sweetness is profitable, and when it is not. Whenever, in hearing music, or other agreeable sounds, in smelling sweet odours, in tasting what is delicious, in touching what is soothing, the affections of the will rise consciously in an instant unto God, and that movement gives us more pleasure than the sensible occasion of it, and when we have no pleasure in that cause, but because of its effects, that is a sign of profit, and that the objects of sense minister unto the spirit. In this way we may use them, for now they subserve that end for which God hath made them; namely, that He may be the better known and loved on their account. Observe, too, that he, in whom sensible objects produce this purely spiritual effect, does not for that reason seek them, nor make any account of them, though they excite in him this sense of God; neither is he solicitous about them; and when they are present, the will passes instantly beyond them and abandons them, fixing itself upon God.

The reason why he attaches no importance to these motives, although they keep him in the way of God, is that the mind is so prompt, in and through all, to fly upwards to God, so filled, preoccupied, and satiated with the Spirit of God as to want or desire nothing more: and if it should desire anything for that end, it immediately passes on beyond it, forgets it, and thinks nothing more about it.

On the other hand, he who is not conscious of this liberty of spirit, amid sensible objects and sweetness, but whose will rests and feeds upon them, ought to make no such usage of them, for they will be injurious to him. Though such an one may employ his Reason about them, and in that way labour to make them subserve his spiritual advancement; still, because the appetite delights in them in the way of sense, and because the effect corresponds always with the pleasure which they minister, it is certain that they are a greater hindrance than help, a greater evil than benefit. And when he sees that the spirit of these recreations reigns over him, he ought to mortify it; for the stronger it grows, the greater will be his imperfections and weakness.

Every satisfaction, therefore, whether accidental or designed, which proceeds from the senses, the spiritual man must use only for God, carrying up unto Him that joy of his soul, so that it may be profitable and perfect; remembering that every joy, which is not founded on the denial and annihilation of all joy whatever, however noble it may seem to be, is vanity and without profit, and a hindrance to the Union of the will with God.

CHAPTER XXIV.

The Evils which befall the soul when the will has joy in Sensible Goods.

Evils of loving Sensible Goods for their own sake.

In the first place, if the soul does not quench the Joy which proceeds from Sensible things, by directing it to God, all those evils in general, of which I have spoken, the fruit of every kind of joy, flow also from this joy in sensible things: namely, obscuration of Reason, tepidity, spiritual sloth and the like. But to descend to particulars, there are many evils, spiritual and temporal, into which men fall through this joy in sensible things.

BOOK III.

Inordinate Joy in Sight,

1. Joy in visible things, when we do not deny ourselves therein for the sake of God, produces directly a spirit of vanity, distraction of mind, unruly concupiscence, want of modesty, interior and exterior restlessness, impure thoughts and envyings.

Hearing,

2. The Joy which the hearing of unprofitable things produces, begets directly distraction of the imagination, gossiping, envy, rash judgments, and changing thoughts, from which many and other ruinous evils flow.

Smell,

3. Joy in sweet odours begets a loathing of the poor which is contrary to the doctrine of Christ, a dislike of ministering unto others, an unhearty submission to humble deeds, and spiritual insensibility, at least proportional to the appetite for this joy.

Taste,

4. Joy in meat and drink produces directly gluttony and drunkenness, anger, discord, and uncharitableness towards our neighbour and the poor, and makes us like the Rich Man in his treatment of Lazarus, while he himself 'feasted sumptuously every day.'* From this arise bodily disorders, sickness, and evil impulses, because the provocations of luxury are increased. It is the source of great spiritual torpor also, and it vitiates the desire for spiritual things, so that the soul has no pleasure in them, cannot even endure them, nor in any way occupy itself about them. This joy, too, dissipates all the other senses and the heart, and creates a feeling of general discontent.

Touch.

5. Joy in matters of touch occasions much greater and more pernicious evils, which most rapidly immerse the senses and injure the mind, destroying all energy and vigour. Hence the abominable sin of effeminacy, or the provocations to it, in proportion to this joy. It produces luxuriousness, makes the mind effeminate and timid, the senses delicate

* S. Luke xvi. 19.

and yielding, disposed for sin and wickedness. It fills the heart with empty rejoicing, makes the tongue licentious, and the eyes wanton, and renders the other senses proportionally brutish. It confounds the judgment, and buries it in folly and spiritual stupidity, it begets moral cowardice and inconsistency of purpose, and by reason of the soul's darkness and the heart's weakness, makes men fear even where no fear is. It creates at times a spirit of confusion, insensibility of mind and conscience, because it enfeebles the Reason so that a man can neither take good counsel nor give it, and incapacitates the soul for all moral and spiritual good, rendering it useless as a broken vessel.

All these evils flow from this particular joy. In some people more, in others fewer, more or less intense, according to the intenseness of this joy, and according to the weakness and irresolution of him who indulges himself in it. For there are some people who naturally are more hurt on slight, than others on great, occasions.

Finally, the evils into which men fall through the joy of the touch are as numerous as those occasioned by that of Natural Goods. As I have already described them, I shall not repeat them here, nor the many others also, such as the diminution of spiritual exercises and of corporal penances, tepidity, and indevotion in the use of the Sacraments of Penance, and of the Eucharist.

CHAPTER XXV.

The spiritual and temporal benefits of self-denial in the Joy of Sensible things.

Four benefits of mortified senses.

MARVELLOUS benefits result from self-denial in the joy which sensible goods supply; some are spiritual and some temporal.

1. The soul, by refraining from joy in sensible objects,

BOOK III.

1. Recollection of God.

recovers itself from the distractions into which it falls through the excessive indulgence of the senses, and recollects itself in God. Spirituality and the acquired virtues are preserved and increased.

2. Spirituality of mind.

2. The second spiritual benefit of not rejoicing in Sensible Goods is great; and we may say, of a truth, that the sensual becomes spiritual, the animal rational, that man leads an angelical life, that the temporal and the human become heavenly and Divine. As the man who seeks for pleasure in sensual things, and founds all his joy upon them, ought not, and deserves not, to be called by any other name than this, namely, sensual and animal; so the man whose joy is beyond them, deserves the name of spiritual and heavenly. This is most evidently true, for as the energies of the senses, and the power of sensuality, resist, as the Apostle saith, the energy and power of the spirit, 'the flesh lusteth against the spirit, and the spirit against the flesh;' * so when they diminish and fail, those of the spirit grow and increase; that which impeded their growth having been taken away. Thus the spirit made perfect—the higher portion of the soul, and that to which the communications of God are made—merits those appellations, because it is made perfect by the spiritual and heavenly gifts and graces of God. We have the authority of S. Paul for this; he calls the sensual man—the man who wastes the energy of his will upon objects of sense—the animal man, and the other, whose will is fixed on God, the spiritual man: 'The animal man perceiveth not these things that are of the Spirit of God. But the spiritual man judgeth all things.' † The soul receives in this self-denial an admirable benefit; a disposition meet to receive the gifts and spiritual graces of God.

3. The third benefit is the great increase of the joys and

* Galat. v. 17.

† 1 Cor. ii. 14, 15. Animalis autem homo non percipit.

CHAP. XXV.

pleasures of the Will in this life; for, as our Saviour saith: 'They shall receive an hundredfold.' If thou wilt deny thyself one joy, our Lord will reward thee a hundredfold, spiritually and temporally, in this world; and for one joy indulged in sensible goods thou shalt have a hundred sorrows and afflictions. As to the eye, now purged from all joy in seeing, the soul receives joy, directed to God, in all that is seen, whether human or Divine. As to the ear, purged from all joy in hearing, the soul receives joy a hundredfold, and that most spiritual, directed to God in all that is heard, whether human or Divine. The same observation applies to the other senses. For as all that our first parents said and did in the state of innocence in Paradise furnished them with means of sweeter contemplation, because their sensual nature was subject unto Reason, so he also whose senses are subject to the spirit and purged from all sensible objects, in their first motions, elicits delight of sweet knowledge and Contemplation of God.

3. Increase of Joy in this life; (1) In Sight. (2) Hearing. (3) And the other senses.

To the pure, therefore, high things and low are profitable, and minister to his greater purity; while both the one and the other are occasions of greater evil to the impure, by reason of his impurity. But he who does not repress the satisfaction of his appetites will never enjoy the ordinary tranquillity of rejoicing in God, through the instrumentality of His creatures. All the functions and powers of his senses, who no longer lives after the flesh, are directed to Divine Contemplation. For, as it is a philosophical truth, that the life of every creature is in harmony with its constitution, so also is it beyond all contradiction clear, that he who is spiritually minded—his animal life being mortified—must be wholly tending towards God, for all his actions and affections are those of the spiritual life. Such an one, therefore, pure

To the Pure all things are a pure Joy.

* S. Matt. xix. 29.

BOOK III.

in heart, finds in all things that knowledge of God which is delicious, sweet, chaste, pure, spiritual, joyous, and loving.

From these considerations I come to this conclusion, that, until we shall have so habituated our senses to this purgation from sensible joy, so as to have obtained the benefit of which I have spoken, namely, that instant movement upwards to God, we still need to deny ourselves in all joy, that we may wean our soul from the life of sense. I am afraid, that when not thoroughly spiritualised, we may gratify and invigorate the senses rather than the spirit, under the influence of sensible things; the powers of sense still ruling over us in our conduct, whereby sensuality is increased, maintained, and nourished. The words of our Saviour are: 'That which is born of the flesh is flesh; and that which is born of the Spirit is spirit.'* Lay this to heart, for it is the truth. Let him who has not mortified his senses in sensible things not presume to avail himself of the energy and functions of sense therein, thinking that they will help him to become spiritual; for the strength of the soul will increase the more, if we cast these things aside, rather by the quenching of joy and desire, than by any employment of them that we can make.

4. Joys of Heaven.

It is not necessary for me to speak now of the goods of Glory attainable in the life to come. For beside that the bodily gifts of Mobility and Clarity, in Glory, will be much grander than in those who have not denied themselves in this joy, there will be an increase of essential glory, corresponding to their love of God, for whom they have left all things: because every momentary and fleeting joy, which we now deny, will work in us eternally an infinite weight of glory: 'that which is at present momentary and light of our tribulation, worketh for us above measure exceedingly an eternal weight of glory.'†

No cross; no crown.

I do not refer here to the other benefits, moral, temporal

* S. John iii. 6. † 2 Cor. iv. 17.

and spiritual, the fruits of this Night of Joy, for they are all those already described, and in a higher order, because these joys are more intimately related to our nature, and, therefore, he who denies himself in them acquires a more interior purity.

CHAPTER XXVI.

The fourth kind of goods: Moral Goods. How the will may lawfully rejoice in them.

Fourth source of Joy,—Moral Goods.

The fourth kind of goods in which the Will rejoices are Moral Goods. By these I mean virtues, the moral habits of them, the practice of any virtue whatever, works of mercy, keeping of God's law, politeness, good dispositions and temper. These moral goods, in possession and in practice, deserve, perhaps more than the other three kinds I have mentioned, that the will should rejoice in them. Man may rejoice in these for one of two reasons, or for both together, either because he possesses them, or because of the benefits which they bring with them, of which they are, as it were, instruments or means. Now the possession of the other goods is deserving of no joy whatever, for of themselves they do good to no man, neither is it in them, for they are fleeting and frail, yea, rather they are the occasions of pain and grief and sorrow of heart. Even if they deserved to be rejoiced in for the second reason, namely that man may employ them towards elevating his soul to God, yet this is so uncertain that in general such rejoicing does more harm than good.

Their intrinsic worth, and happy effects.

Moral Goods, however, deserve some Joy on the part of their possessor, for their intrinsic worth. And as they bring with them in their train peace and tranquillity, the right use of Reason, and a consistent conduct, man cannot, humanly

BOOK III.

Virtue to be loved for its own sake.

speaking, possess anything better in this world. And as virtues merit love and esteem, for their own sakes, humanly speaking, men may well rejoice in the possession and practice of them, for what they are in themselves, and for the good, human and temporal, of which they are the channels.

God loves, promotes, and rewards Natural Virtue.

It was in this sense that the Philosophers and wise men and princes of old esteemed and commended virtue, laboured to acquire it and to practise it, though they were heathens, and regarded it only in a worldly light, seeing nothing in it but the temporal, corporal, and natural benefits which resulted from it. They not only obtained those benefits, and the reputation they aimed at, but more than this; God Himself, Who loves all goodness, even in heathens and barbarians, and Who impedes no good, as it is written, 'which nothing hindereth, beneficent,'* increased their substance, honours, dominion, and peace. He thus dealt with the Romans: because they enacted good laws, He made them masters almost of the whole world; He recompensed, for their good customs in a temporal way, those who, because of their unbelief, were incapable of the everlasting reward. God loves moral goods: for when Solomon asked for an understanding heart to judge the people, He was so pleased with this prayer that He said unto him: 'Because thou hast asked this thing, and hast not asked for thyself long life or riches, nor the lives of thy enemies, but hast asked for thyself wisdom to discern judgment, behold I have done for thee according to thy words, ... yea, and the things also which thou didst not ask, I have given thee, to wit, riches and glory, so that no one hath been like thee among the kings in all days heretofore.'†

Two examples; 1. The Ancient Romans.

2. Solomon.

Though a Christian too ought to rejoice in Moral Goods, and in the good works he does, because they minister to his temporal well-being, his joy ought not to stop there where

* Wisd. vii. 22.

† 3 Kings iii. 11-13.

that of the heathens did, who saw nothing beyond this mortal life; but inasmuch as he has the light of Faith, by which he hopes for everlasting life, and without which all things whatever are valueless, his sole and chief rejoicing should be of the second kind, namely, that eternal life is the reward and issue of the good works he does for the love of God. All his care and all his joy ought to be that he serves and honours God by his virtues and good life. For without this intention all our virtues are worthless in the sight of God, as we are taught in the parable of the Ten Virgins. All these had preserved their virginity and had wrought good works, yet five of them, whose joy therein was not of the second kind, directed unto God, but rather of the first, for they rejoiced and gloried in mere possession, were denied admission into heaven, unrecognised and unrewarded by the Bridegroom.*

Merely natural virtue incapable of Supernatural reward.

Parable of the Ten Virgins.

There have been many persons in the world of old times who had some virtue and did good works; and there are many Christians also at this time, who are virtuous men, and who do great things, but their virtue and good works are utterly useless in the matter of eternal life: because they do not, in them, seek the honour and glory and love of God solely, and above all things. A Christian ought to rejoice, not because of his good works and virtuous life, but because his life and acts are such solely for the love of God, and for no other reason whatever. For as works done only for God's honour will have a greater reward of glory, so good works which men do under the influence of other considerations, will end in our greater confusion in the sight of God. The Christian, therefore, if he will direct his rejoicing to God in moral goods, must keep in mind, that the value of his good works, fasting, almsgiving, penances, and prayers, does not

Moral value of good works proportioned to purity of intention.

* S. Matt. xxv.

BOOK III.

Ama, et fac quod vis.

depend on their number, and nature, but on the love which moves him to perform them for God; and that they are then most perfect when they are wrought in the most pure and sincere love of God, and with the least regard to our own present and future interests, to joy and sweetness, consolation and praise. The heart, therefore, must not rest on the joy, comfort, delight, and advantages which holy habits and good works bring with them, but refer all to God, purifying itself from all joy, and hiding itself from it in darkness; and desiring that God only may rejoice in what it does in secret, and all this without respect to any other consideration than God's honour and glory. Thus all the energies of the will, with regard to moral goods, will be all concentrated in God.

CHAPTER XXVII.

Seven Evils to which men are liable if the Will rejoices in Moral Goods.

THE principal evils to which men become exposed through the rejoicing of the Will in good works and a virtuous life are seven in number, and most fatal, because they are spiritual; I shall now give a brief description of them:

1. Self-conceit.

1. The first is vanity, pride, vain glory, and presumption, for no man can rejoice in his own works without attributing a great value to them. From this springs boasting and other faults; an instance of which we have in the Pharisee who in his prayer boasted of his fasts and the other good works he was doing.

2. Rash and contemptuous judgments of others.

2. The second evil is generally connected with the first, and it is this: we come to judge others, and to pronounce them to be comparatively wicked and imperfect, and that their good works are inferior to ours; we despise them in our hearts, and sometimes express ourselves contemptuously about them. The Pharisee had fallen into this also, for in

his prayers, he said, 'O God, I give Thee thanks, that I am not as the rest of men, extortioners, unjust, adulterers, as also is this publican; I fast twice in a week.'* Thus by one act he fell into these two evils, namely, self-esteem and contempt of others, as many Christians do daily, who say, I am not like such an one, neither is my life such as his. Yea, many of them are even worse than the Pharisee; he certainly despised others and pointed out the object of his contempt, saying 'this publican:' they, indeed, are not satisfied with this, but give way to anger and envy when they hear others praised, or that they are doing more, or are more useful men, than themselves.

3. Self-interest and Human respect.

3. The third evil is that, as they look for their own satisfaction in their good works, they will in general do only such as will furnish them with this satisfaction, or obtain the commendation of others. They do all their works, as our Saviour saith, 'for to be seen of men,'† and not for God alone.

4. Loss of Supernatural reward.

4. The fourth evil issues out of the third, and is this: God will not reward them for their good works, because they seek it here in this world in the joy, or the comfort, or the honourable advantages of their good works; of them our Saviour saith, 'Amen. I say to you, they have received their reward.'‡ They will therefore have nothing but their labour, and confusion of face without its reward. The children of men are so miserably involved in this evil that, in my opinion, the greater part of the good works, which are publicly done, are either vicious or worthless, or they are imperfect and defective in God's sight, because men do not detach themselves from self-interest and from human respect. What other opinion can we form of those good works, which men do, or of the monuments which they raise, but which

* S. Luke xviii. 11, 12. † S. Matt. xxiii. 5. ‡ Ib. vi. 2.

BOOK III.

How men seek themselves in their good works.

would have been undone and unbuilt, if their authors had not been influenced by worldly honour, human respect, and the vanity of this life? Is not all this too often done in order to perpetuate a name or a pedigree, or to mark authority and lordship; and that to the extent of setting up armorial bearings in churches, as if they would establish themselves there as Images for the veneration of men? At the sight of these good works of some people, we may well say that men respect themselves more than God.

Subtleties of Self-love.

But passing from these who are the worst, how many are there who in their good works fall into these evils in many ways? Some expect their good works to be extolled, others expect gratitude for them, others enumerate them, and delight in the fact that such and such persons, and even the whole world are aware of them; sometimes they will employ a third person to convey their alms, or to do any other good work, in order to make it the more known; some, too, look both for praise and reward. This is nothing else but to sound a trumpet in the streets, like vain men, but whom God for that reason will never reward.*

Goods works to be hidden from others and from self.

If men wish to avoid this evil they must hide their good works so that God alone shall see them, and they must not wish any one to think much of them. They must hide them not only from others, but from themselves also; that is, they must take no satisfaction in them nor regard them with complacency, as if they thought them of any value. This is the meaning of those words of our Saviour: 'Let not thy left hand know what thy right hand doth.'† That is, do not look with temporal and carnal eyes upon thy spiritual works. When this precept is observed, the strength of the will is concentrated in God, and our good works become fruitful in His sight; but where it is not observed, we shall

* S. Matt. vi. 2. † Ib. vi. 3.

not only lose our labour, but, very frequently, because of our interior boasting and vanity, sin grievously against God. Those words of Job also are to be understood in this sense: 'If . . . my heart in secret hath rejoiced, and I have kissed my hand with my mouth, which is a very great iniquity.'* Here the 'hand' means our good works, and 'mouth' our will which regards them with complacency. This is self-complacency, for the words of Job are, if my 'heart hath in secret rejoiced,' and a 'great iniquity, and a denial against the Most High God.' To attribute our good works to ourselves is to deny them to be God's, from whom all good works proceed, and to follow the example of Lucifer, who rejoiced in himself, denying to God what was His, and arrogating it to himself.

5. No Spiritual Progress.

5. The fifth evil is, that men of this kind make no progress in Perfection; for cleaving to the pleasure and comfort of their good works, when this pleasure and comfort cease — which is usually the case when God seeks their advancement, when He gives them dry bread, which is the bread of the perfect, when He deprives them of the milk of babes, when He tries their strength, and purifies their delicate appetites, so that they may be able to taste the food of the strong — they become generally faint of heart, and fail to persevere, because their good works are no longer sources of pleasure. To this we may apply in a spiritual sense those words of the Wise Man: 'Dying flies spoil the sweetness of the ointment.'† For when mortifications come in their way they die to their good works, abandon them, and lose perseverance, wherein spiritual sweetness and interior comfort consist.

6. False test of value.

6. The sixth evil is a general delusion under the influence of which men mistake the value of their good works,

* Job xxxi. 26–28.

† Eccles. x. i.

BOOK III.

Pain of self-denial better than the joy of sensible pleasure.

considering those wherein they find delight to be of greater importance than those wherein they find none: they praise and esteem the former, but despise and reject the latter; yet those works, generally, in which a man is most mortified — especially when he is not advanced in Perfection — are more pleasing and precious in the eyes of God, by reason of that self-denial involved in their performance, than those good works in which he finds consolation, where self-seeking so easily intrudes. 'The evil of their hand,' saith the Prophet, 'they call good;' * that is, what is evil in their work they say is good. And they come to this because they derive their joy from their good works, and not from pleasing God only. The extent of this evil, among spiritually minded men as well as ordinary Christians, baffles all description, for scarcely any one can be found who doeth good simply for the love of God, without relying on some advantage of joy or comfort, or of some other consideration.

7. Spiritual blindness and weakness.

7. The seventh evil is that man, so far as he does not suppress all joy in moral good works, is the more incapable of listening to reasonable counsel and instruction with reference to his duties. The habitual weakness contracted by doing good works with an eye to this empty joy, so fetters him that he cannot accept the advice given him as the best, or if he does so accept it he cannot act upon it, through lack of resolution. The love of God and of our neighbour is greatly weakened in these persons, for their self-love, which they indulge in with reference to their own good works, makes charity cold.

* Mich. vii. 3.

CHAPTER XXVIII.

The benefits of repressing all Joy in Moral Goods.

CHAP. XXVIII.

1. Victory over Pride.

VERY great benefits result to the soul, provided the Will is restrained from rejoicing in Moral Goods. In the first place, it is delivered from many temptations and illusions of Satan, which rejoicing in our good works secretly involves, as we learn from these words of God to Job: 'He sleepeth under the shadow, in the covert of the reed, and in moist places.'* This applies to the evil spirit, for he deceives the soul in the moisture of joy and in the hollowness of the reed, that is, of good works done through vanity. Nor is it strange that the devil should deceive it secretly in this rejoicing; for, independently of the devil's suggestion, this empty joy is a delusion itself, especially when a feeling of boasting lurks in the heart, as it is written, 'Thy arrogancy hath deceived thee and the pride of thy heart.'† Can there be a greater delusion than that of boasting? The soul is delivered from it by purifying itself from this joy.

2. Greater strength and purity of Will.

2. The second benefit is that our good works are done with greater deliberation and in greater perfection. If the passion of Joy and satisfaction prevails, no deliberation can be had; for then the irascible and concupiscible faculties are so strong that they will not bend to Reason; and, in general, under their influence we change our works and intentions, taking one thing in hand to-day and another to-morrow, beginning everything and bringing nothing to good effect. If Joy be the main-spring of our work, we shall be inconsistent: some are naturally more so than others; and when our joy ceases, we abstain also from our work, and our intentions are abandoned, however important they may be. With

* Job xl. 16. † Jerem. xlix. 16.

Natural Joy a wayward guide.

people of this kind, Joy is the soul and strength of their good works; and when that joy disappears their good works perish; neither do they persevere. These are they of whom Christ saith, that they receive the word with joy, and that the devil takes it away that they may not persevere. 'They by the wayside are they that hear; then the devil cometh and taketh the word out of their heart, lest believing they should be saved.'* Their strength consisted solely in their joy, and therefore to withdraw the will from this joy is an admirable preparation for perseverance and final success. This benefit, then, is as great as is the opposite evil. The wise man regards the substance and benefit of his labour—not the pleasure which it brings: he is not like one beating the air, but he elicits from his good works a durable joy, without demanding the tribute of passing delights.

3. Poverty of spirit.

3. The third benefit is Divine; by quenching this hollow rejoicing we attain to poverty of spirit, which is one of the beatitudes: 'Blessed are the poor in spirit, for theirs is the kingdom of Heaven.'†

4. Prudence and Deliberation.

4. The fourth benefit of suppressing this Joy is, that we become gentle, humble, and prudent in our doings. We shall do nothing in a hurry, carried away by the concupiscible and irascible nature of this joy; neither shall we become presumptuous through overvaluing our good works under the influence of it; nor shall we be unconsciously blinded by it.

5. Union with God

5. The fifth benefit is that we shall become pleasing unto God and man, delivered from the dominion of avarice and gluttony, spiritual sloth and envy, and a thousand other vices.

* S. Luke viii. 12. † S. Matt. v. 3.

CHAPTER XXIX.

The fifth kind of goods, in which the Will has Joy: the Supernatural. Their nature, and the difference between them and Spiritual Goods. How Joy in them is to be directed unto God.

CHAP. XXIX.

Fifth source of Joy.—Supernatural Goods.

I HAVE now to speak of the fifth kind of goods in which the soul rejoices, and which I call Supernatural. By these I mean all those gifts and graces of God, which surpass our natural powers and capacities, called by theologians *gratis datæ*—such as the gifts of 'wisdom and understanding'* given to Solomon, and those mentioned by S. Paul, namely 'faith, the grace of healing, working of miracles, discerning of spirits, the interpretation of speeches, and the gift of tongues.'† Though these are all spiritual gifts, like those of which I am about to speak, still, owing to the great difference between them, I have made a distinction. These gifts have an immediate reference to the edification of others, and are given for that special end, as the Apostle saith: 'The manifestation of the Spirit is given to every man unto profit,'‡ speaking of these gifts. But the spiritual gifts lie simply between the soul and God, in the intercourse of the Intellect and the Will, as I shall explain hereafter. There is, therefore, a difference between them in respect of their object. The spiritual gifts are concerned with God and the soul, but the supernatural gifts, with which I have now to do, are intended for the edification of others; they differ, too, in their nature, and consequently in their functions, and the doctrine concerning them is therefore of necessity different also.

Their object the edification of others.

Their temporal and spiritual benefits.

As to the Supernatural gifts and graces, in this sense, I observe, with reference to self-denial in the matter of Joy, that they involve two grand Temporal and Spiritual benefits.

* 3 Kings iv. 29. † 1 Cor. xii. 9, 10. ‡ 1 Cor. xii. 7.

BOOK III.

The Temporal benefits are the healing of the sick, giving sight to the blind, the raising of the dead to life, the casting out of devils, foretelling of future events, and others of this kind. The Spiritual and Eternal benefits are, that God is known and served through these works by him who doeth them, and by those for whom and before whom they are wrought.

We should rejoice more in loving God than in working miracles.

Now as to the first benefit, namely, the temporal: these supernatural acts and wonders merit little or no rejoicing on the part of the soul, for without the spiritual benefit, they are of little or no profit to men, because of themselves, they are not means of Union with God—that being Charity. Moreover, they may be wrought in persons not in a state of grace and of charity; for they may be either the work of God, as in Balaam the impious prophet, or the work of the devil, as in Simon Magus, or the effects of mere natural but secret causes. These marvellous works, if any of them profit him who works them, are true, and the gifts of God.

S. Paul tells us what the value of these works is, when they are not accompanied by the second benefit, saying: 'If I speak with the tongues of men and of angels, and have not Charity, I am become as sounding brass, or a tinkling cymbal. And if I should have prophecy, and should know all mysteries and all knowledge, and if I should have all faith, so that I could remove mountains, and have not Charity, I am nothing.'* Many men who have thought much of their own good works, when asking to be admitted unto His glory, saying, 'Have not we prophesied in Thy name . . . and done many miracles in Thy name?' will receive for their only answer: 'Depart from Me, you that work iniquity.'†

Man, therefore, ought to rejoice, not in the possession and exercise of these gifts, but in that he elicits from them the

* 1 Cor. xiii. 1, 2. † S. Matt. vii. 22, 23.

second spiritual benefit, namely, serving God in true Charity, wherein consists the fruit of everlasting life. Our Lord rebuked His disciples when they returned to Him with joy because they had power over evil spirits, saying, 'Rejoice not in this, that spirits are subject unto you: but rejoice in this, that your names are written in Heaven.'* The meaning of which, according to sound Theology, is: Rejoice, if your names are written in the Book of Life. Man, therefore, ought not to rejoice, unless he is walking in the right way, doing his good works in Charity. For of what profit is anything in the sight of God which is not His love? Now Love cannot be perfect if it is not strong enough and wise enough to purify itself from all Joy in these things, and to find it only in doing the Will of God. It is in this way that the will is united to God in these supernatural goods.

CHAPTER XXX.

The evils resulting from the Will's rejoicing in this kind of goods.

Three evils of Joy in Supernatural gifts.

HE who rejoices in Supernatural Goods falls, in my opinion, into three principal evils. He deceives and is deceived, loses faith, and becomes vainglorious.

1. Liability to deception.

As to the first, it is very easy to deceive oneself and others, by rejoicing in these supernatural operations. The reason is that, in order to ascertain whether they are true or false, how and when they are to be exerted, it requires great deliberation and great light from God: now our rejoicing in, and esteeming, these operations, are a great impediment to this, partly because the joy in question dulls and obscures the judgment, and partly also because it makes us not only covet these operations extremely, but also inclines us to an unsea-

* S. Luke x. 20.

BOOK III.

Errors in the time or mode of manifesting Supernatural gifts.

sonable manifestation of them. Admitting even that these operations and powers be real, yet these two defects are enough to delude us: either we do not comprehend them as they ought to be comprehended, or we do not profit by them and employ them at the right time and in the right way. For though it be true that God, when He distributes these graces, gives also the light to see them, and the inward movement to manifest them at the right time and in the right way; still those who receive them, because of their self-seeking or some imperfection or other in the matter, may fall into great errors, by not using their gifts with that perfectness which God requires with respect to time and manner. We have an example in Balaam, who, contrary to the Will of God, undertook to curse the people of Israel. God was therefore angry with him, and sought to kill him.* Again, in S. James and S. John, who, carried away by their zeal, would have fire descend from heaven upon the Samaritans, because they refused to receive our Lord. For this He rebuked them.†

It is clear from this that imperfect persons, of whom I am speaking, may be influenced by certain imperfect feelings involved in the joy and esteem of these gifts, to manifest them at an improper time. For when they are free from the like imperfections, they are moved to manifest them only as, and when, God wills; in no other way is the manifestation of them convenient. This is the meaning of that complaint which God makes against certain prophets, saying: 'I did not send prophets, yet they ran; I have not spoken to them, yet they prophesied.' ‡ And again in the same place: 'They cause my people to err by their lying, and by their wonders; when I sent them not, nor commanded them.' § It is said in the same place that they prophesied the delusions of their

* Num. xxii. 22, 23.

† S. Luke ix. 54.

‡ Jerem. xxiii. 21.

§ Ib. 32.

own heart, which they would not have done had they not attached themselves in this abominable way to their gifts, using them as their own.

All this shows us that the evil of such rejoicing not only leads men to make an impious and perverse usage of the gifts of God, like Balaam and those prophets who, by the wonders which they wrought, deceived the people; but even to make use of them without having received them from God, like those who uttered their own fancies for prophecies, and published visions which themselves invented, or which the devil represented to them. For when Satan sees men with such dispositions as these, he opens for them a wide field, and supplies them with abundant materials, intruding himself in diverse ways: whereupon such men spread their sails to the wind, become shamelessly presumptuous, and prodigal in the usage of their great gifts.

How men make a compact with the devil.

The evil does not stop here, for joy in supernatural gifts, and the desire of them, reach so far that, if men have entered into a secret compact with Satan—it is such a compact that enables many to do what they are doing—they venture still further, and enter into an open and avowed compact, making themselves his disciples and allies by an express stipulation. Hence come wizards, enchanters, magicians, soothsayers, and sorcerers. This joy leads men so far, that they seek to purchase with money, not only these gifts and graces, as did Simon Magus, that they may serve the devil, but holy things also, and what I cannot write without trembling, things Divine. May God here show His great mercy! How hurtful to themselves, and ruinous to Christendom are such men, any one may easily perceive. All those magicians and soothsayers among the people of Israel, whom Saul destroyed out of the land,* had fallen into these great abominations and

* 1 Kings xxviii. 3.

BOOK III. delusions, because they would imitate the true Prophets of God.

He who is supernaturally endowed ought, therefore, to cleanse himself from all desire of, and from all Joy in, the exercise of his supernatural gifts; and God, Who gives them supernaturally for the edification of the Church, in general, or of its members, in particular, will also supernaturally direct him in the use of them, in the right way and at the right time. As He commanded His disciples to take no thought beforehand how or what they should speak,* that being a supernatural act of Faith—so also is it His Will, the use of these gifts being of not less importance, that man should bide His time, because the exercise of these gifts is to depend upon His Will. Thus the disciples, in whom the gifts and graces were infused, prayed God to put forth His hand, so that the hearts of the people might bow down before the Faith. 'Grant unto Thy servants, that with all confidence they may speak Thy Word, by stretching forth Thy hand to cures; and that signs and wonders may be done by the name of Thy Holy Son Jesus.'†

2. Loss of Faith. In two ways; 1. As to credibility.

The second evil, loss of Faith, may come from the first, and this in two ways. In the first place, it may concern others; for when a man undertakes to perform a miracle, out of season, and without necessity—over and above that this is to tempt God, which is a great sin—he may not succeed, and so the faith will lose credit and reverence among men. Though sometimes men may succeed in what they thus attempt, because God wills it for some reason or other, as in the case of the Witch of Endor—if it was Samuel himself who then appeared—they shall not always succeed; and when they do succeed, they are not the less in error and blameable, because they use their gifts inopportunely.

2. As to merit.

In the second place, the loss of Faith concerns those who

* S. Mark xiii. 11.

† Acts iv. 29, 30.

are endowed with supernatural gifts; in that they destroy the merits of it. For when men attach so much importance to miracles, they depart from the substantial exercise of faith, which is an obscure habit; and so where signs and miracles abound, there is the less merit in believing. 'Faith has no merit,' saith S. Gregory the Great, 'where human Reason supplies proof.'* God works miracles when they are necessary for the Faith, or for other ends of His glory, and of His Saints. For this reason did God work many signs, before He showed Himself to His disciples; that they might believe without seeing, and so not lose the merit of faith in His resurrection, which they would have done had they seen Him first. He showed to Mary Magdalen first the empty sepulchre, and then the Angels announced His rising again;† for 'Faith cometh by hearing,'‡ so that having heard, she might believe before she saw. And when He showed Himself unto her, it was as the gardener,§ that He might thoroughly edify her in the faith, which in the warmth of His presence melted away. He sent the women to tell His disciples that He had risen; and afterwards they came to see the sepulchre.‖ He set on fire the hearts of the disciples on the road to Emmaus before they knew Him; for He was with them in disguise. And finally, He rebuked them because they did not believe those who told them of His resurrection;¶ and in particular, S. Thomas—because he would have palpable proof of His resurrection—saying 'Blessed are they that have not seen, and have believed.'** Miracles are not pleasing unto God, for He rebuked the Pharisees because they would not believe without them, saying: 'Unless you see signs and wonders, you believe not.'†† Those, therefore, who will rejoice in

'Nec fides habet meritum, cui humana ratio præbet experimentum.'

S. Mary Magdalen.

The two Disciples going to Emmaus.

S. Thomas.

The Pharisees.

* Hom. 26, in Evangel.
† S. John xx. 2; S. Luke xxiv. 6.
‡ Rom. x. 17.
§ S. John xx. 15.
‖ S. Matt. xxviii. 10.; S. John xx. 3.
¶ S. Luke xxiv.15, 26.
** S. John xx. 29.
†† S. John iv. 48.

BOOK III.

these supernatural gifts, inflict upon themselves a grievous loss in the matter of faith.

3. Vain-glory.

The third evil is that men, because of their rejoicing in supernatural gifts, fall into vainglory or some other vanity. The mere act of rejoicing in them, if not purely in and for God, is vanity. This is evident from the fact that our Lord rebuked His disciples, because they rejoiced in that the evil spirits were subject unto them.* If that joy had not been vanity, our Lord would never have rebuked them for it.

CHAPTER XXXI.

The benefits of self-denial in the Joy of Supernatural graces.

First benefit, —God glorified.
1. By being loved more than His gifts.

By denying itself in this joy, the soul gains two great benefits beside its deliverance from those three evils already described. It magnifies and exalts God, and it also exalts itself. God is exalted in two ways. Firstly when the heart and the joy of the will are withheld from all that is not God, and fixed upon Him alone. This is the meaning of David when he said: 'Man shall come to a deep heart, and God shall be exalted;'† for if the heart be exalted above all things, the soul will be exalted also. And because it fixes itself upon God alone, God is exalted and magnified, making known to the soul His own Magnificence and Greatness; for He testifieth of Himself, what He is, in this elevation of the soul above all joy. Now this cannot be done unless the will is emptied of all joy in supernatural gifts, as it is written, 'Be still, and see that I am God,'‡ and again, 'In a desert land, and where there is no way, and no water, so in the sanctuary have I come before Thee, to see Thy power and glory.'§

* S. Luke x. 20.
† Ps. lxiii. 7, 8.
‡ Ps. xlv. 11.
§ Ps. lxii. 3.

As God, therefore, is exalted, when our joy is grounded on our detachment from all things, much more is He exalted when we refrain from joy in His more marvellous works to place it in Him alone; for these graces are of a higher nature by reason of their supernatural character, and therefore to detach ourselves from them to rejoice in God alone, is to give greater honour and glory to God than to them; for the more numerous and important are the things we disregard for the sake of another, the more we esteem and magnify him. Besides, God is exalted in another way when the will refrains from this joy: for the more we believe in God and serve Him without regard to signs and wonders, the more is He exalted in the soul; seeing that our faith in Him is higher than the teaching of signs and wonders. CHAP. XXXI. 2. Even when His gifts are Supernatural.

The second benefit is the exaltation of the soul itself; for by withholding the will from rejoicing in signs and wonders, the soul is exalted in most pure Faith which God infuses into it and increases most abundantly. He increases also at the same time the two other theological virtues, Charity and Hope. Here the soul has the fruition of the highest Divine knowledge through the obscure and detached habit of Faith; of the delights of love through Charity, whereby the will rejoices in nothing but in the living God; and of the satisfaction of the will through Hope. All this is a wonderful benefit which essentially and directly tends to the perfect Union of the soul with God. Second benefit,—the soul ennobled.

CHAPTER XXXII.

The sixth kind of Goods in which the Will rejoices. Their nature. The first division of them.

The chief object of my book being the guiding of the spirit through these Spiritual Goods to the Divine union of the soul with God, it will be necessary for me, and for my Reader, now Sixth and last source of Joy,—

BOOK III.

Spiritual Goods.

1. Their Importance.

that I am speaking of these goods which conduce the most to that end, to bestow particular attention on the matter. For it is quite certain that there are people who, because of their want of knowledge, make use of spiritual things in the order of sense only, leaving the spirit empty; so that there is scarcely any one, the better part of whose spirit is not corrupted by sensible sweetness, the water being drunk up before it reaches to the spirit, which is, therefore, left dry and barren.

2. Their definition.

With reference then to my subject, I say, that by Spiritual Goods I mean all those that move us and help us towards Divine things, in the intercourse of the soul with God, and in the communications of God to the soul.

3. Divided into (1) Sweet. (2) Bitter. Each kind divided into a. Distinct. β. Obscure.

I begin with the generic difference of these goods, namely, Sweet and Bitter. Each of these is again specifically divided. The Sweet Goods are of things clear, distinctly understood, and of things that are not so. The Bitter also are divided into clear and distinct, and confused and obscure.

4. They pertain to the Intellect, Memory, and Will.

These are also distinguished according to the faculties of the soul. Some, being cognitions, pertain to the Intellect; some, being affections, pertain to the Will; and others, being imaginary, pertain to the Memory. For the present I omit to speak of the bitter goods, because they relate to the Passive Night, and I shall have to speak of them hereafter. I omit also the sweet goods of things confused and indistinct that I may treat of them later; they relate to the general confused and loving knowledge wherein consists the Union of the soul with God. I passed it over in the second book, when I was distinguishing between the apprehensions of the intellect, reserving it for more careful consideration in the Book of the Obscure Night. I now proceed to speak of those Sweet Goods, which are of things clear and distinct.

CHAPTER XXXIII.

Of the Spiritual Goods distinctly cognisable by the Intellect and the Memory. The conduct of the Will with respect to Joy in them.

CHAP. XXXIII.

Reformation of the Will analogous to that of the Intellect and Memory.

My labour would be great here if I had now to treat of the manifold apprehensions of the Intellect and the Memory, teaching how to govern the Will with regard to rejoicing in them, if I had not already discussed them at considerable length in the second and in this book. Having there said how these two faculties are to be directed amid these apprehensions to the Divine union, and that the same applies to the will also, it is not necessary to return to the subject here, it being sufficient to repeat that as these two faculties are to be emptied of all such apprehensions, so the will also is to repress all joy whatever in them.

Voluntas prælucet Intellectui.

What I have there said of emptying the Memory and the Intellect of all these apprehensions is applicable to the Will; for seeing that the intellect and the other faculties cannot admit or reject without the intervention of the will, it is clear that the same principle applies to the one as well as to the other. Every explanation, therefore, that the subject requires may be found there, for all the evils and dangers there enumerated will befall the soul if it does not refer unto God all the joy of the will in these apprehensions.

CHAPTER XXXIV.

Of the Sweet Spiritual Goods which distinctly affect the Will. Their diversities.

1. Motive Goods. 2. Provocative. 3. Directive. 4. Perfective.

Everything that furnishes a distinct Joy to the Will may be classed under four heads: Motive, Provocative, Directive, and Perfective. I shall speak of these in order, and first of the

BOOK III.

motive, which are Images, Pictures of Saints, Oratories, and Ceremonies.

First kind of distinct Sweet Spiritual Goods,—Motive; i.e. External means of Devotion.

In that which relates to Images and Pictures of Saints much vanity and empty joy may be found. For while they are of great importance in Divine service, and very necessary to move the will to devotion, as is evident from the sanction and use of them by our Holy Mother the Church—that is a reason why we should profit by them to quicken us in our sloth—there are many people who rejoice more in the painting and decoration of them than in the objects they represent.

Images and pictures are useful, 1. To honour the Saints. 2. To move the Will.

The Church ordains the use of images for two principal ends: that is, for the honour of the Saints, and for the moving of the will and the quickening of our devotion to them. And so far as they minister to this end, they are of great profit, and the use of them is necessary. Those pictures therefore are to be preferred which are most accurately drawn, and which most effectually excite the will to devotion; we ought to regard this more than the value, curious workmanship, and decorations. There are people, as I have said, who look more to the curious nature of the image and its value than they do to the Saint it represents. They so squander that inward devotion, which ought to be spiritually directed to the invisible Saint, in demonstrations of outward affection and curiosity, that the senses are pleased and delighted, and love and the joy of the will rest there. All this is an effectual hindrance to real spirituality, which requires the annihilation of the affections in all particular objects.

They should be of good workmanship, and of a devotional character.

Should not be unbecomingly ornamented.

This is clearly visible in that hateful custom observed nowadays by certain persons who, not holding in abhorrence the vanities of the world, adorn the Sacred Images with those garments which a frivolous race daily invents for the satisfaction of its wanton recreations and diversions. They clothe the images with those garments which in themselves are reprehensible, and which the Saints have always held, and still hold, in detestation. It is thus that they conspire with the devil to procure some sanction for their vanities, involving the Saints therein, but not without offending them most deeply. The consequence is that all modest and sound devotion, which utterly rejects every trace of vanity, is with such people little more than the elaborate and superfluous decoration of images and curious pictures, to which they are attached and on which they base all their joy. You see people who are never satisfied with adding image to image, who reject them if they are not made after a particular pattern, and who must have them arranged in a particular order, so as to please the sense; meanwhile the devotion of the heart is very slight. They hold to their images as Michas to his idols, who when he lost them ran out of his house crying because they had been taken away;* or like Laban, who made a long journey to reclaim them, and in his anger searched for them in the tents of Jacob.†

How bad taste offends Sanctity.

How frivolity takes the place of devotion.

How Images become Idols.

A devout man grounds his devotion chiefly on the invisible; he requires but few images, and uses but few, and such as are more in harmony with Divine than with human taste; fashioning them, and himself upon them, according to the pattern of another world, and the habits of the Saints, and not of this; so that the fashion of this world may not only not excite the desire, but not even recur to the memory, through the sight of anything resembling it or appertaining unto it. Neither are his affections entangled by the images he uses, for if they be taken from him, he is not therefore distressed, because he seeks within himself the Living Image, which is Christ crucified, in Whom he desires rather that all things should be taken from him and that

True devotion requires few Images, and those of a supernatural Beauty;

and seeks in the heart the living image of Christ Crucified.

* Judg. xviii. 23, 24.

† Gen. xxxi. 34.

BOOK III.

True Perfection,—what.

all things should fail him, even those which seemed most to draw him to God; and even when they are taken away from him he is still tranquil. The higher perfection of the soul consists in being tranquil and joyful amid the privation rather than the possession with the desire of, and affection for, these motives. Though it is a good thing to have in our possession these Images and means of greater devotion—for which reason we should choose always those which most promote it—yet it is not Perfection to be so attached to them as to be sorrowful when they are taken from us. Be assured of this, the more you cling to images or sensible motives the less will your devotion and prayers ascend upwards unto God. Though it be true that, because some images are better representations than others and more devotional, we may prefer the former to the latter, still it must be for that reason only, and there must be no kind of attachment lurking in that preference; lest—that which tends to raise our minds to God being forgotten—the means of devotion should become food for sense, immersed in the joy which springs from them: nor should that which has been made use of as a help to devotion through any imperfection become a hindrance, as it sometimes does, even not less so than an attachment to any other object whatever.

Some images may be preferred to others,—why.

Folly in regard to Rosaries.

Granting that some excuse for this may be admitted in the matter of Images, because of our inadequate perception of that detachment and poverty of spirit which perfection requires, at least none can be admitted in the case of that imperfection so generally practised with regard to Rosaries. You will scarcely meet with anyone who has not some weakness in this matter. Men take care that their Rosaries are of a certain workmanship rather than another, of a certain colour or material, and with particular ornaments. One rosary does not contribute more than another towards the hearing of our prayers: he is heard who tells his beads in the simplicity and integrity of his heart, not thinking of anything but how he may please God the most; and not valuing one rosary more than another, except only for the Indulgences attached to it.

Such is our vain concupiscence, that it clings to everything; it is like the dry rot consuming the good and the bad wood. What else is it, when thou pleasest thyself with a curious rosary, seeking one of a particular make rather than of another, but to rejoice in the instrument? Why frequentest thou a particular image, not considering whether it stirs thee up to a greater love of God, but whether it be more curious or valuable than another? Certainly, if thy desire and thy joy were in pleasing God only, thou wouldest not regard anything of this kind. It is very vexatious to see spiritual persons so attached to the fashion and workmanship of devotional objects, to what is merely motive, given up to the curiosity and empty joy which they minister. Such persons are never satisfied, they are perpetually changing one thing for another: spiritual devotion is forgotten amid these sensible means; men attach themselves to them just as they do to any worldly ornaments; and the issue is no slight detriment to their soul.

Worldliness in Prayer.

CHAPTER XXXV.

The subject continued. The ignorance of some people in the matter of Images.

How miraculous Images are to be regarded.

I HAVE much to say of the ignorance of some people with regard to Images: so great is their folly that they have more confidence in one image than in another, influenced therein solely by their preference of the one over the other. This conduct on their part implies great ignorance of the ways of God, of the service and honour due to Him Who chiefly

God sometimes works miracles at particular places,—why.

regards the faith, and interior purity of the suppliant. God sometimes works more miracles at one image than at another of the same kind—though there be a great difference in the workmanship—in order that the devotion of people may be excited there more than elsewhere. The reason why God works miracles and grants graces at one image rather than at another is, that the strangeness of His intervention may stir up the slumbering devotions and affections of the faithful. As the sight of the image serves to kindle our devotion, and perseverance in prayer—both being means to move God to hear and grant our petitions—so before a particular image, because of our prayers and devout affections, God continues to work miracles and to bestow His graces. The faith and devotion with which the image is regarded passing on to the Saint whom it represents.

Worship of Images relative.

As to Images then, let us never dwell upon the curious workmanship they may exhibit, so as to have more confidence in some than in others on that account, for this would be great ignorance; let us esteem those the most by which our devotion is most excited. Thus God, for the greater purification of this formal devotion, when He grants graces, and works miracles, does so, in general, through images not very well made, nor artistically painted or adorned, so that the faithful may attribute nothing to the work of the artist. And very often our Lord grants His graces by means of images in remote and solitary places. In remote places, that the pilgrimage to them may stir up our devotion, and make it the more intense. In solitary places, that we may retire from the noise and concourse of men to pray in solitude, like our Lord himself. He who goes on a pilgrimage, will do well to do so when others do not, even at an unusual time. When many people make a pilgrimage, I would advise staying at home, for in general, men return more dissipated than they were before. And many become pilgrims

Dissipation in pilgrimages.

CHAP. XXXV.

Our Saviour a Living Image.

for recreation more than for devotion. If faith and devotion be wanting, the image will not suffice. What a perfect living image was our Saviour upon earth; and yet those who had no faith, though they were constantly about Him and saw His wonderful works, were not benefited by His presence. This is the reason why He did no miracles in His own country.*

I wish to mention here certain supernatural effects of some images on particular persons. God attaches at times a special influence to certain images, so that the form of them, and the devotion they excite, remain impressed on the mind of the beholder as if they were still present before his eyes. And again, when they are recalled by the memory, the same influence is excited as at the first time they were seen, sometimes more vividly, at others less so; other images even of more perfect workmanship produce no such effects.

Love of art, or sense of the beautiful, not Devotion.

Many persons also have a devotion to images of a certain fashion and not to others. In some, this is nothing more than mere natural fancy or taste, just as we are pleased with one man's looks more than with another's. They will have naturally a liking for them, and their imagination recalls them more vividly, though not so beautiful in themselves as others, because they are naturally attracted to that particular form and fashion. Thus, some persons will suppose that the fancy they have for a certain image is devotion, while in reality it is perhaps nothing more than natural taste and liking.

At other times, it happens that men, while gazing at a particular image will see it move, change colour, make signs, or speak. This, and the supernatural effects just spoken of, are indeed very often real and good effects, the work of God, either to increase devotion, or to support a soul in its weakness, or to prevent frequent distractions, and also very often

* S. Matt. xiii. 58; S. Luke iv. 24.

BOOK III.

false, the work of the evil spirit to deceive and ruin souls. I shall give instruction on the whole of this subject in the next chapter.

CHAPTER XXXVI.

How the Joy of the Will in Sacred Images is to be referred to God, so that there shall be no hindrance in it, or occasions of error.

As Holy Images are very profitable, in that they put us in mind of God and His Saints, and move the will to devotion when we use them in the ordinary way, as we ought; so also are they occasions of great delusions if, when they are the subjects of supernatural effects, we know not how to conduct ourselves as we ought to do in our progress onwards towards God. One of the means by which the devil makes an easy prey of incautious souls, and impedes their progress in true spirituality, is the exhibition of strange and unusual things in connection with images; whether they be those material images which the Church has sanctioned, or those fantastic images represented to the mind, of some particular Saints, or the image of himself transformed into an angel of light,* in order to delude our souls. The devil, in his cunning, hides himself within those very means which are given us as a remedy and support, that he may seize upon us when we are least upon our guard. Holy souls will therefore be ever circumspect in regard to good things, for that which is evil carries its own witness always with it.

Satan's use of Images.

Caution in regard to good things.

I give but one direction, and that is sufficient, for the avoidance of those evils into which souls may fall with regard to images, and for the purgation of the will from joy in them, and for the guidance of the soul to God by means of them,

* 2 Cor. xi. 14.

which is the object of the Church in the use of images. The evils to which the soul is liable are either that it is hindered by them in its flight upwards unto God, or that it uses them in a mean and ignorant way, or that it falls into delusions with reference to them. Now the direction I wish to give is this: we should strive, seeing that images are but motives to invisible things, to move, affect, and gladden the will only in the living spirit which the image figures. Let the faithful soul, therefore, take care that, while contemplating an image, the senses be not absorbed in it, whether that image be material or in the imagination, of beautiful workmanship or of rich adornment, and whether the devotion it excites be spiritual or sensible. Let him not regard these outward accidents, nor dwell upon them, but venerate the image, as the Church commands, and lift up his mind at once from the material image to the living spirit whom it figures, with the sweetness and joy of the will resting on God, or on the Saint invoked, devoutly, in mental prayer; so that what is due to the living and the spiritual may not be wasted on material and sensible objects. He who shall do this will never be deluded, and the mind and senses will not be hindered from advancing onward with great freedom unto God. The image, too, which supernaturally excited devotion, will do so the more abundantly when our affections are thus elevated instantly to God. For whenever He grants us these and other graces, He does so by inclining the affection and joy of the will to that which is invisible. It is His Will also that we should do the same ourselves, by annihilating the powers and satisfaction of our faculties in all visible and sensible things.

Direction how to use Images;—as a means, not as an end.

BOOK III.

CHAPTER XXXVII.

Motive Goods continued. Oratories and places of prayer.

I THINK I have now sufficiently explained how the spiritual man, in the matter of Images, may fall into as great imperfections—perhaps more dangerous ones—as in the matter of temporal and bodily goods. I say perhaps more dangerous, for in considering, and speaking of, these images as holy things, men make too sure of themselves, and cease to be afraid of attachment to them in a mere natural way. Thus they frequently deceive themselves very much, thinking themselves most devout because they delight in holy things; and after all, perhaps, this may be nothing more than natural taste and inclination, which is gratified here as it might have been by anything else.

Vanity in the decoration of Oratories.

The issue is—I am going to speak about Oratories—that some people are never satisfied in adding image to image in their oratories, taking pleasure in the order and neatness of their arrangements, to the end that they may be well furnished and beautiful to the eye. God is not their object in one arrangement more than in another—perhaps less so, for the delight they experience in these decorations is so much stolen from the reality. It is very true that all decorations and all reverence in the matter of images are exceedingly little in comparison with what they represent—and therefore those who treat them with no great decency and reverence are deserving of all blame, as well as those who paint them so clumsily that they rather quench than kindle devotion; and I wish the authorities would prohibit such persons from painting and sculpture because of their gross unskilfulness—but what has that to do with the attachment which you have to these decorations and exterior ornaments when they engross your senses and make heavy your heart, so that you cannot

God should have the best.

draw near unto God, and love Him, and forget all these matters for His sake? If you are deficient in this through carefulness about outward things, not only will He not be pleased with you, but He will punish you also, because you have not sought His pleasure, but your own, in all things.

Christ weeps over Jerusalem,—why.

You may see this truth most clearly in that triumphal procession when our Lord entered into Jerusalem. The people sung hymns of joy and strewed branches in the way, but Christ was weeping,* for their hearts were far from Him while they received Him with outward show of honour. 'This people honoureth Me with their lips, but their heart is far from Me.'† We may say of them, that they formed that procession in honour of themselves rather than of God. It is the same with many at this day, for where great Festivals are being celebrated, men rejoice more in the recreation they furnish—whether in seeing or being seen, in the banquet or other worldly comfort—than in rendering true service unto God.

How men keep the Feasts of God in honour of themselves.

Such inclinations and intentions are not pleasing unto God. Much less do they please Him who, when they are making preparations for a great solemnity, invent ridiculous and undevout actions to create laughter among the spectators, that men may be the more distracted; and who make such arrangements as shall please the multitude instead of such as shall quicken devotion among them. What shall I say of those who celebrate great feasts for ends not belonging to them? of those who make them serve their private interests? of those who are more intent on their personal advantage therein than on the service of God? This they know, and God also Who sees it; and in whichever way the feast is thus observed, let them remember, they keep it for themselves and not for God. What men do to please themselves or others

* S. Matt. xxi. 9; S. Luke xix. 41. † S. Matt. xv. 8.

BOOK III.

God dishonoured in His own Feasts.

God will not account as done for Himself. Yea, many keep His Feasts with solemnity, and yet He is angry with them as He was with the children of Israel, for He slew thousands of them, when they sung and danced before the golden calf, thinking they were observing a feast in honour of God;* or as He was with Nadab and Abiu, the sons of Aaron, whom He slew with the censers in their hands, because they offered strange fire upon His altar;† or as with him who sat among the guests, not having on a wedding garment, and whom He commanded to be cast, bound hand and foot, 'into the exterior darkness.'‡

Satan at Festivals, like a merchant in a Fair.

This shows us how intolerable to God must be these irreverences in those assemblies which are held in His honour. O Lord, my God, how many feasts are kept by the children of men in which the devil is more honoured than Thou? Satan rejoices in these assemblies, for he profits by them like a merchant in a Fair. How often hast Thou to say of them: 'This people honoureth Me with their lips, but their heart is far from Me,' § because they serve Me in vain? The chief ground for the service of God is that He is what He is. Other and lower considerations ought not to enter into the question.

Chief ground for the service of God,—what.

I return to the subject of Oratories. Some people adorn them more for their own pleasure than for God's; some treat them with so little respect, that they think no more of them than of their ordinary rooms; and some do not treat them with so much respect even, for they have more pleasure in what is profane than in what is Divine. But let me now leave this, and speak of those who proceed in a more cunning way—of those people who consider themselves devout. Many of these take such delight in their oratories and in the adorn-

* Exod. xxxii. 19, 28. † Levit. x. 1, 2.
‡ S. Matt. xxii. 11-13. § Ib. xv. 8.

ing of them, that they waste in such occupations all the time which they ought to have spent in prayer and interior recollection. They do not see that by not disposing themselves for interior recollection and tranquillity of mind, they are as much distracted by such occupations as by any other worldly occupation, and that they are every moment troubled by such attachment, especially if it be attempted to separate them from their oratories.

CHAPTER XXXVIII.

The right use of Churches and Oratories. How the soul is to be directed through them unto God.

Sensible Devotion expedient for beginners,—why.

As to the guidance of the soul onwards to God through this kind of goods, I may observe that it is lawful, and even expedient, for beginners to feel a sensible pleasure in Images, Oratories, and other visible objects of devotion, because they are not yet entirely weaned from the world, so as to be able to leave the latter wholly for the former. They are like children to whom, when we want to take anything from them which they hold in one hand, we give something to hold in the other, that they may not cry, having both hands empty. The spiritual man, if he is to advance, must deny himself in all those tastes and desires in which the will has pleasure, for true spirituality has but slight connection with any of these things, inasmuch as it consists solely in interior recollection and mental converse with God. For though the spiritual man makes use of Images and Oratories, yet it is only as it were in passing. The mind dwells in God, forgetting all sensible objects. And though it is better to pray where there is the greatest neatness, nevertheless we should choose that place where the senses are least likely to be entertained, and the mind most likely to ascend upwards unto God. On this

Neatness in churches a reasonable ground of preference.

BOOK III.

Worship of God must be spiritual.

subject we must listen to the answer of our Lord to the woman of Samaria. She asked Him which was the true place of prayer, the mountain or the temple. He replied that true prayer was not tied to the mountain, but that those who prayed in spirit and in truth were they who were pleasing to His Father. 'The hour cometh, and now is, when the true adorers shall adore the Father in spirit and in truth. For the Father also seeketh such to adore Him. God is a spirit, and they that adore Him must adore Him in spirit and in truth.' *

And though Churches and quiet places are set aside and prepared for Prayer—a church ought to be used for no other purpose—nevertheless, in this matter of intimate intercourse with God, that place ought to be chosen which least occupies and allures the senses. It must, therefore, not be a place agreeable and delightful to sense, such as some people search for, lest instead of serving to recollection of mind, it minister to the recreation and satisfactions of sense. For this end, it is well to make choice of a solitary and even wild spot, so that the mind may ascend firmly and directly to God, without hindrance or detention on the part of visible things. Visible things sometimes, it is true, help to elevate the soul, but it is when they are instantly forgotten, and the spirit reposes on God. For this reason our Saviour, in general, chose to pray in solitary places, where there were no attractions for the senses — herein giving us an example — but which tended to lift up the soul to God, such as mountains, which are elevated spots, and generally barren, furnishing no resources for sensible recreation.

Prayer best made in solitary places.

Example of our Saviour.

He, therefore, who is truly spiritual looks only to interior recollection in oblivion of all things, and for that end chooses a place that is most free from all visible sweetness and at-

* S. John iv. 23, 24.

CHAP. XXXVIII.

tractions, withdrawing his thoughts from all that surrounds him, so that in the absence of created things, he may rejoice in God alone. It is wonderful how some spiritual persons are wholly intent on arranging their oratories, and providing places for prayer suited to their tastes and inclinations, and making little or nothing of interior recollection, which is the really important matter. If they attended to this, these arrangements of theirs would have been to them not pleasure but mere weariness.

CHAPTER XXXIX.

Continuation of the same subject.

Inward devotion necessary.

THE reason, then, why some spiritually-minded persons never enter into the true joys of the spirit, is, that they never wholly cease to rejoice in outward and visible things. Let such reflect that if a visible Church and Oratory be a fitting and appropriate place for prayer, and images motives thereunto, they must not so use them as to have all their sweetness and joy in them, and so forget to pray in the living temple, which is the interior recollection of soul. S. Paul, to remind us of this, says: 'Know you not that you are the temple of God, and that the Spirit of God dwelleth in you?'* and our Lord: 'Lo, the kingdom of God is within you;'† to the same effect tend the words already cited: 'They that adore Him must adore Him in spirit and in truth.'‡ God will make no account of your oratories, and the places you have so well prepared, if you attend more to the pleasure which they furnish than you do to interior detachment, which is spiritual poverty, and which consists in denying yourself in all that you may possess.

* 1 Cor. iii. 16. † S. Luke xvii. 21. ‡ S. John iv. 24.

BOOK III.

Directions how to pray.

You must, therefore, if you would purge the will from joy, and the vain desire for it, and direct that joy to God in your prayers, look only to this, that your conscience be pure, your will wholly with God, and your mind earnestly fixed upon Him; and that you choose a place for your prayers, the most solitary and unfrequented possible, and there apply the whole joy and satisfaction of your will to the calling upon God and glorifying His name. As to the trifling joys and satisfactions of outward things, regard them not, but labour to deny yourself in them. For if the soul becomes habituated to the sweetness of sensible devotion, it will never advance to the power of spiritual joy which is to be found in spiritual detachment by means of interior recollection.

CHAPTER XL.

Of some evils to which men are liable who indulge in the sensible sweetness which results from objects and places of devotion.

Evils of attachment to sensible sweetness in Prayer; 1. Interior.

THE spiritual man is subject to many evils in this matter if he will walk therein in the way of sensible sweetness. These evils are Interior as well as Exterior. As to the first: he will never attain to that interior recollection which consists in overlooking and forgetting all sensible sweetness, nor will he acquire substantial self-recollection, and solid virtue.

2. Exterior.

As to the second, he unfits himself for praying in all places alike, and he can only pray in those which are to his taste. Thus he will frequently neglect his prayers, because, as they say, he can pray only out of his own book.

Besides, this affection for particular places is the source of many inconsistencies; for those who indulge it never continue in the same place, nor even in the same state of life; at one time here, at another there; to-day in one cell, to-morrow in another; they make their arrangements in one oratory to-day, and the next in another. Of such people are those whose life is spent in changing their state and manner of living. As these people are influenced solely by that fervour and sensible sweetness which they find in spiritual things, and as they never do violence to themselves so as to become spiritually self-recollected by the denial of their will and by voluntary endurance of inconveniences; so whenever they see a place which seems to them better adapted for devotion, or a state of life better suited to their tastes and inclinations, they run after it at once, and abandon that wherein they were before. Being thus under the dominion of sensible sweetness, they are eager in the search after novelty, for sensible sweetness is uncertain and rapidly passes away.

CHAPTER XLI.

Of the three kinds of devotional places. How the will is to regulate itself in the matter.

Places become devotional, 1. From Natural beauty.

THERE are three kinds or varieties of places by means of which God is wont to move the will to devotion. The first is a certain disposition of the ground—whether on account of the landscape, or of groves, or of its loneliness—which naturally tends to excite devotion. It is profitable to make use of this, provided the will ascends upwards to God, and the circumstances of the place be at once forgotten. For in order to secure the end we must not dwell on the means or the motives longer than necessary. If we set about to refresh our senses, and seek for sensible sweetness, what we shall find will be spiritual dryness and distractions; for true satisfaction and spiritual sweetness are to be found only in interior recollection. Therefore, when we are in such a place, we should forget it, and strive to converse inwardly with God, as if we were not

BOOK III.

there. If we give way to the sweetness of the spot, searching for it in every way, that will be a seeking after sensible refreshment, and instability of purpose rather than spiritual rest. This was the way of the ancient hermits who in the wildest deserts chose a small corner for themselves, sufficient for a most narrow cell, and there they buried themselves. In such an one remained S. Benedict for three years, and another bound himself with a rope that he might not step beyond its length. Many others also, too numerous to mention, have imposed similar restraints upon themselves. Those holy men well knew that if they did not mortify the appetite for spiritual sweetness they never would be able to attain to it, and become spiritual themselves.

2. From Association.

The second kind is something special, for there are some places, no matter whether desert or not, where God is wont to bestow most sweet spiritual favours on some persons in particular. In general the hearts of those who have received such favours are inclined to that place, and they feel at times a great and anxious desire to return; though when they do, they do not find what they found there before; for it is not in their power. God bestows these favours when, how, and where He wills; He is not tied to time or place, neither is He subject to any man's will.

Three reasons for choosing a particular place for Prayer.

Nevertheless it is well to return to such a place, provided all attachment to it be wanting, and to pray there sometimes. There are three reasons in favour of this. First, it appears that God, though not bound to place, wills that He should be glorified there by the object of his favours. The second, by going there the soul is the more reminded of its duty of thanksgiving for the graces there received. The third is, that remembrance of past graces quickens devotion. It is for these reasons that men ought to revisit such places, and not because they think that God has obliged Himself to bestow His favours there in such a way as not to bestow them elsewhere; for in the eyes of God the human soul is a more becoming place than any earthly spot.

Examples of Abraham, Jacob, and Agar.

This principle is found in the Holy Scriptures, for we read that Abraham built an altar in the place where God appeared to him, and there called upon His name, and that he visited the place again on his return from Egypt, and called upon God again at 'the altar which he had made before.'* Jacob also consecrated the place where he saw 'the Lord leaning upon the ladder'; for he 'took the stone which he had laid under his head, and set it up for a title, pouring oil upon the top of it.'† Agar, too, in reverence, gave a name to the place where the Angel appeared to her, saying, 'Verily here have I seen the hinder parts of Him that seeth me.'‡

3. By the Will of God.

The third kind are certain special localities which God has chosen that men may there call upon Him and serve Him. Such a place was Mount Sinai where He gave His law unto Moses.§ Such also was that place which He showed unto Abraham, where the Patriarch was to sacrifice his son.|| And such too was Mount Horeb, whither He commanded our father Elias to go, and where He was to show Himself unto him.¶ Of this kind also is Mount Garganus which S. Michael, appearing there to the Bishop of Siponto, marked out for the service of God, saying: 'I am the guardian of this place, let an oratory be built here in honour of the Angels.'** The most glorious Virgin by a miraculous sign—snow in summer—chose a site in Rome for a Church in her honour, which Joannes Patricius built.†† God knoweth why He chose these places for Himself. All that we need know is that all is for our good, and that He will hear our prayers there, and wherever else we pray in perfect faith. Though there is far greater reason why we

Mt. Sinai. Mt. Horeb. Mt. Garganus. S. Maria Maggiore in Rome. All places fit for the Prayer of Faith.

* Genes. xii. 8; xiii. 4. † Ib. xxviii. 13, 18. ‡ Genes. xvi. 13.
§ Exod. xxiv. 12. || Genes. xxii. 2. ¶ 3 Kings xix. 8.
** Brev. Rom. in Fest. App. S. Mich. lect. 6.
†† Ib. in Fest. S. Mariæ ad Nives.

BOOK III.

should be heard in these places, dedicated to His service, because the Church has consecrated them for that special end.

CHAPTER XLII.

Of other motives to Prayer adopted by many; namely, many Ceremonies.

How external observances become superstitious.

THE useless joys and the imperfection of attachment, in which many persons are involved, in the matter of Prayer, are perhaps in some degree excusable, because they are indulged in somewhat innocently. But the great reliance which some have on a variety of Ceremonies invented by persons of unenlightened minds, deficient in the simplicity of faith, is utterly intolerable. I pass by those ceremonies which comprise certain strange words or phrases signifying nothing, and other matters, not of a sacred character, which an ignorant, rude, and suspicious people intermingle with their prayers. These are clearly evil and involve sin, and many of them imply a secret compact with Satan, whereby men provoke God to anger and not to mercy. I do not mean to speak of these, but only of those ceremonies, which being not of this suspicious class, many persons nowadays adopt in their prayers through an indiscrete devotion. People attribute such efficacy to them, and have such faith in the forms and ceremonies which they throw round their prayers and spiritual exercises, that they imagine their prayers are useless, and unheard by God, if they fail in any one of these singularities, or overstep these arbitrary limitations. They have much more confidence in these forms than they have in real earnest prayer; and this is a great dishonour and insult offered unto God. For instance a Mass must be said with so many candles, neither more nor fewer; by such a priest, at such an hour, neither earlier nor later; on such a day, neither before nor after. Prayers must be offered up, or visits made to a church so often, in such a way, at such a time, with such ceremonies or gestures, neither earlier nor later, nor in any other way. The person who is to undertake this must have such and such qualities. They believe that if any one of these ceremonies be neglected all is to no purpose. There are a thousand other absurdities of the same kind.

What is still worse, and not to be borne, is, that some people will have it that they have felt the effects of this, or that they have obtained what they asked for, or that they know they shall obtain it when all these ceremonious practices have been duly observed. This is nothing less than to tempt God, and grievously to provoke Him to wrath, so much so that occasionally the evil spirit is permitted to deceive such people, and to make them feel or see things utterly at variance with the welfare of their soul. They bring this upon themselves by the self-love which they manifest in their prayers, and by their desire to fulfil their own will rather than the Will of God. Such persons, because they do not place their whole trust in God, will never come to any good.

CHAPTER XLIII.

How the Joy and Strength of the Will is to be directed in these devotions.

Prayer must seek the Will of God.

LET such people then know that the more they rely on their ceremonies the less is their confidence in God, and that they will never obtain their desires. There are some people who labour more for their own ends than for the glory of God. Though they know that God will grant their prayer if it be for His service, and that He will not, if it be not; still, because of their self-love and the hollow joy which they have in it, they will multiply their prayers beyond measure. Now if they

BOOK III.

Order in Prayer.

were to attend to something else of more importance, they would do better: namely, if they set about the purification of their own conscience, and applied themselves to the affair of their own salvation, omitting all prayers which have not this for their immediate object.

If they do this, they will obtain that which concerns them most, and they will obtain beside all else, though they did not pray for it, in a better and readier way than if they had directed all their energies to it. We have for this the promise of our Lord Himself, Who tells us, 'Seek ye,' therefore, first the kingdom of God and His Justice, and all these things shall be added unto you.'* Such seeking is most pleasing unto God, and there is no better way to obtain the desires of our heart than to pray with all our might for that which is most pleasing unto God; for then He will grant us, not only what we pray for, namely, our eternal salvation, but all that He sees to be expedient and profitable for us, though we ask it not, according to the words of the Psalmist, 'The Lord is nigh unto all them that call upon Him, to all that call upon Him in truth.'† They call upon Him in truth who pray for that which is most true, namely, their salvation, as the Psalmist adds, in the same place, 'He will do the will of them that fear Him, and He will hear their prayer and save them. The Lord keepeth all them that love Him.' To be 'nigh' unto men is to satisfy them, and to give them what never entered even into their thoughts to ask for.

The Will of God contains our Temporal and Eternal Happiness.

Examples of Solomon and Abraham.

We have an illustration of this in the history of Solomon. He asked of God wisdom to govern the people—a prayer that was acceptable unto Him—and the answer of God was: 'Because this choice hath pleased thy heart, and thou hast not asked riches and wealth and glory, nor the lives of them that hate thee, nor many days of life; but hast asked wisdom

* S. Matth. vi. 33. † Ps. cxliv. 18, 19, 20.

and knowledge to be able to judge My people, over which I have made thee king: wisdom and knowledge are granted to thee; and I will give thee riches and wealth and glory, so that none of the kings before thee, nor after thee, shall be like thee.'* God kept His promise, and made his enemies live in peace, and pay him tribute. God also, when He promised Abraham to multiply the posterity of his lawful son as the stars of heaven, added: 'I will make the son also of the bondwoman a great nation, because he is thy seed.'†

The Church our Guide in Ceremonies.

The powers of the will, therefore, and the joy it has in prayers, are to be referred to God: without leaning upon ceremonies and private observances which the Catholic Church neither adopts nor sanctions; we must resign to the priest the celebration of Mass, he stands in her place, and has received from her the order of its celebration. Men must not seek out new inventions, as if they knew more than the Holy Ghost and the Church. If they are not heard when they pray in the simplicity of the Church, let them be sure of this—God will not hear them for their own inventions, however numerous they may be.

The Lord's Prayer is enough.

As to vocal prayer and other devotions, let no man rely on ceremonies and forms of prayer other than those which Christ and His Church have taught us. It is quite clear that, when His disciples said unto Him, 'Teach us to pray,'‡ He told them all they were to do in order to be heard of the Eternal Father. He knew His will. He then taught them only the seven petitions of the *Pater Noster*, which include all our wants, spiritual and temporal. He did not teach them many, and other forms of words and ceremonies. He had before told them not to use many words when they prayed, saying, 'When you are praying, speak not much . . . for your Father knoweth what is needful for you.'§ Only

* 2 Paral. i. 11, 12.
† Genes. xxi. 13.
‡ S. Luke xi. 1.
§ S. Matth. vi. 7, 8.

BOOK III.

He charged them with great earnestness to persevere in prayer—that is, the *Pater Noster*—saying, 'that we ought always to pray, and not to faint.'* He did not teach us a variety of prayers, but to repeat often, with care and fervour, these petitions—for they contain the whole Will of God and all our wants also. He Himself, when He fell on His face in the garden and prayed three times to the Eternal Father, thrice repeated the self-same words of the *Pater Noster*, saying, 'My Father, if it be possible, let this chalice pass from Me; nevertheless, not as I will, but as Thou wilt;'†—that is, Father, if I must drink this chalice, Thy Will be done.

The Prayer in the Garden of Gethsemani.

Two places of Retirement.

The rites and ceremonies which He taught us to observe in our prayers are reduced to one of two; either to retire into our chamber, where, away from the tumult and presence of men, we may pray with most pure and perfect heart—'When thou shalt pray, enter into thy chamber, and having shut the door, pray to thy Father in secret;'‡ or to withdraw into the lonely wilderness, as He did, in the better and more tranquil hours of the night.

All hours suitable for devotions.

There is thus no necessity for determined seasons, nor for appointed days, nor for strange methods, nor for words of double meanings, nor for other prayers than those which the Church employs, and in the sense in which she employs them; for all prayers are comprehended in the *Pater Noster*. I am not, by this, condemning, but rather approving, those fixed days which some persons occasionally set apart for their devotions, such as Novenas, and the like: what I condemn is the reliance which men have on the ceremonies and self-devised observances with which they keep them. This is what Judith also did when she rebuked the people of Bethulia, because they had fixed a time within which God was to have mercy upon them. 'Who are ye,' said the

The *Pater Noster* comprehends all prayers.

* S. Luke xviii. 1. † S. Matth. xxvi. 39. ‡ S. Matth. vi. 6.

Prophetess, 'that tempt the Lord? This is not a word that may draw down mercy, but rather that may stir up wrath and enkindle indignation.'*

CHAPTER XLIV.

Of the second kind of Distinct Goods in which the Will vainly rejoices.

Second kind of distinct sweet Spiritual Goods,—Provocative.

THE second kind of Distinct Sweet Goods in which the will vainly rejoices, is that which provokes or persuades us to serve God. This I have called Provocative. In this class of goods are Preachers who may be considered in two points of view: one, concerning themselves, the other, those who hear them. Both in preaching and in hearing, all require to be reminded that the joy of the will must be directed unto God.

Advice to Preachers and Hearers.

As to the preacher, he must bear in mind—if he is to profit his hearers, and not to be puffed up with empty joy and presumption—that his function is more spiritual than vocal: for though it depends on audible words, its power and efficacy is not in the words, but in the spirit which utters them. However high the doctrine he preaches, however adorned his eloquence and sublime his style, the fruits of his sermons will in general be no better than his own spirit. For though it be true that the word of God is effectual in itself, as it is written, 'He will give to His voice the voice of power,'† yet fire, which has the power of burning, will not burn without adequate fuel. Preaching depends for its effects on two conditions: one on the part of the preacher, the other on the part of the hearer: but in general the fruitfulness of preaching is in proportion with the dispositions of the preacher. Hence the proverb, Such the master, such the dis-

Preaching more spiritual than vocal.

* Judith viii. 11, 12.

† Ps. lxvii. 34.

BOOK III.

Fruits of Preaching in proportion to dispositions of Preacher.

ciple. When the seven sons of Sceva, a chief priest of the Jews, attempted to cast out devils like S. Paul, the evil spirit turned upon them in a fury, saying, 'Jesus I know, and Paul I know, but who are you?'* and drove them out of the house naked and wounded. This befell them because of their improper dispositions, and not because Christ would not that they should invoke His name; for when the disciples forbade him to cast out devils in His name, who was not a disciple, He rebuked them, saying, 'Do not forbid him: for there is no man that doth a miracle in My name, and can soon speak ill of Me.'† But He is angry with those who teach His law and keep it not, and who not being spiritual themselves, preach spirituality to others. 'Thou, therefore,' saith the Apostle, 'that teachest another, teachest not thyself; thou that teachest that men should not steal, stealest.'‡ And the Psalmist saith, 'To the sinner God hath said, Why dost thou declare My justice, and take My covenant in thy mouth, seeing thou hast hated discipline and cast My words behind thee?' § Such persons have not that spirit which is fruitful in good.

A good life the best sermon.

It is generally observed, so far as we can judge, that the better the life of the preacher, the greater the fruit, though his style may be homely, his eloquence scanty, and his subject common, for warmth proceeds from the living spirit within. Another kind of preacher will produce scarcely any fruit at all, notwithstanding his fine style and his subject. For though it is true that a good style and action, high doctrines, and correct expression have a greater effect when they accompany true spirituality; still when that is wanting, though the senses be charmed, and the intellect delighted, but little or no substantial warmth reaches to the will. The will remains dull,

* Acts xix. 15.
† S. Mark ix. 38.
‡ Rom. ii. 21.
§ Psalm xlix. 16, 17.

End of preaching not merely to please the ear, taste, or intellect—but to move the will.

and weak as before in good works, though marvellous things have been marvellously told it, but which serve only to please the ear, like a concert of music or the sound of bells. But the spirit does not go beyond its limits, and the voice has no power to raise the dead from the grave. Of what use is it to me to listen to one kind of music which pleases me more than another, if it does not move me to act? Though men may be wonderful preachers, yet their sermons are soon forgotten, when they kindled no fire in the will. This sensible delectation in sermons is not only almost fruitless in itself, but it also keeps back the hearer from true spirituality; for he goes no deeper into the matter than the outward circumstances of the sermon, and praises the preacher for this and that peculiarity, running after him for such reasons rather than for any edification he derives from him. S. Paul sets this before us very clearly, saying: 'And I, brethren, when I came to you, came not in loftiness of speech or of wisdom, declaring unto you the testimony of Christ . . . my speech and my preaching was not in the persuasive words of human wisdom, but in showing of the spirit and of power.'*

Value of a good style.

It was not the intention of the Apostle, neither is it mine, to find fault with a good style, correct diction, and eloquence. These things are valuable to a preacher, as they are in all kinds of affairs; for as a noble expression elevates and restores what is fallen low, so, on the other hand, a mean style ruins even what is noble.

* 1 Cor. ii. 1, 4.

THE

OBSCURE NIGHT OF THE SOUL.

THE

OBSCURE NIGHT OF THE SOUL.

ARGUMENT.

I BEGIN this book with the stanzas which I have undertaken to explain. I shall then explain them line by line. The first and second stanzas describe the effects of the spiritual purgations of our sensitive and spiritual nature. The rest, six in number, describe the various and wonderful effects of spiritual illumination, and union with God in love.

STANZAS.

Song of the soul in the Divine Union of Love.

I

In an Obscure Night,
With anxious love inflamed,
O, happy lot!
Forth unobserved I went,
My house being now at rest.

II

In darkness and obscurity,
By the secret ladder, disguised,
O, happy lot!
In darkness and concealment,
My house being now at rest.

III

In that happy night,
In secret, seen of none,
And seeing nought myself,
Without other light or guide
Save that which in my heart was burning.

STANZAS.

IV

That light guided me
More surely than the noonday sun
To the place where He was waiting for me,
Whom I knew well,
And where none but He appeared.

V

O, guiding night;
O, night more lovely than the dawn;
O, night that hast united
The Lover with His beloved,
And changed her into her Love.

VI

On my flowery bosom,
Kept whole for Him alone,
He reposed and slept;
I cherished Him, and the waving
Of the cedars fanned Him.

VII

Then His hair floated in the breeze
That blew from the turret;
He struck me on the neck
With His gentle hand,
And all sensation left me.

VIII

I continued in oblivion lost,
My head was resting on my Love;
I fainted away, abandoned,
And, amid the lilies forgotten,
Threw all my cares away.

OBJECT OF THE PRECEDING STANZAS.

Before entering on the explanation of these stanzas I must premise that they are the song of the soul in the State of Perfection, in union with God by love; after passing through

After weeping in the night comes joy in the morning.

those deep tribulations and distresses, in the spiritual exercise of the strait way of eternal life. This is the way, as our Saviour saith in the Gospel, by which the soul must ordinarily travel to the high and Divine union with God. 'How narrow is the gate and strait is the way that leadeth to life, and few there are that find it.'* This road being so strait, and they who find it being so few, the soul exults in having traversed it to the perfection of love. This is the substance of the first stanza. The strait way is with great propriety called the Obscure Night, as it appears from the following stanzas. The soul, then, having travelled on this strait road, where so many blessings have come upon it, thus rejoiceth.

* S. Matth. vii. 14.

BOOK I.

OF THE NIGHT OF SENSE.

In an Obscure Night,
With anxious love inflamed,
O, happy lot!
Forth unobserved I went,
My house being now at rest.

EXPLANATION.

BOOK I.

The Obscure Night.

1. Its definition.

2. Means of entering it.

3. Joy in having passed through it.

HERE the soul describes the way and manner of its departure, as to all selfish and other affections, dying thereto and to itself by real mortification, so that it may come to the sweet and pleasing life of love in God. It went forth, from itself and from all things, in an Obscure Night, by which is meant purgative contemplation—as I shall hereafter explain—which leads the soul to deny itself and all besides. This departure of the soul was effected in the strength and fervour of love with which the Bridegroom inspired it in the obscure contemplation for that end. The soul magnifies its own happiness in having journeyed Godwards in that night so successfully as to escape all hindrance on the part of its three enemies — the World, the Devil, and the Flesh — which are always found infesting this road; for the night of purgative contemplation had lulled to sleep and mortified, in the house of sensuality, all passions and desires, in their rebellious motions.

CHAPTER I.

Of the Imperfections of Beginners.

In an Obscure Night.

CHAP. I.

Three states; 1. Of Beginners. 2. Of Proficients. 3. Of the Perfect.

SOULS enter this Obscure Night when God is drawing them out of the state of Beginners, which is that of those who meditate in the spiritual way, and is leading them into that of Proficients, the state of Contemplatives, that, having passed through it, they may arrive at the state of the Perfect, which is that of the Divine union with God. That we may the better understand the nature of this night through which the soul has to pass, and why God leads men into it, it is necessary to touch upon certain characteristics of beginners, that they may perceive the weakness of their state, take courage, and desire to be led of God into this night, where the soul is established in virtue and prepared for the inestimable delights of His love. Though I shall dwell at some length upon this point, I shall do so no longer than suffices for the immediate discussion of the Obscure Night.

Beginners encouraged by sweetness.

We are to keep in mind that a soul, when seriously converted to the service of God, is, in general, spiritually nursed and caressed, as an infant by its loving mother, who warms it in her bosom, nourishes it with her own sweet milk, feeds it with tender and delicate food, carries it in her arms, and fondles it. But as the child grows up the mother withholds her caresses, hides her breasts, and anoints them with the juice of bitter aloes; she carries the infant in her arms no longer, but makes it walk on the ground, so that, losing the habits of an infant, it may apply itself to greater and more substantial pursuits.

The Grace of God,* like a loving mother, as soon as the

* Wisd. xvi. 25.

soul is regenerated in the new fire and fervour of His service, treats it in the same way; for it is then furnished, without labour on its own part, with spiritual milk, sweet and delicious, in the things of God, and in devotional exercises with great delight; God giving to it the breasts of His own tender love, as a mother to her babe. Such souls, therefore, delight to spend many hours, and perhaps whole nights, in prayer; their pleasures are penances, their joy is fasting, and their consolations are the use of the Sacraments and the frequentation of Divine Offices.

Selfish spirituality of Beginners.

Now spiritual men generally, speaking spiritually, are extremely weak and imperfect here, though they apply themselves to devotion, and practise it with great resolution, earnestness, and care. For being drawn to these things and to their spiritual exercises by the comfort and satisfaction they find therein, and not yet being confirmed in virtue by the struggle it demands, they fall into many errors and imperfections in their spiritual life; for every man's work corresponds to the habit of perfection which he has acquired. These souls, therefore, not having had time to acquire those habits of vigour, must, of necessity, perform their acts, like children, weakly.

Work proportioned to habit.

Imperfections in the matter of the seven capital sins.

To make this more evident, and to show how weak are beginners in virtue, in those good works which they perform with so much ease and pleasure, I proceed to explain with reference to the seven capital sins, pointing out some of the imperfections into which beginners fall in the matter of each of them. This will show us plainly how like children they are, and also how great are the blessings of this Obscure Night of which I am about to speak; seeing that it cleanses and purifies the soul from all these imperfections.

CHAPTER II.

Of some imperfections to which beginners are liable in the matter of Pride.

CHAP. II.

First Imperfection,—Spiritual Pride.

WHEN beginners become aware of their own fervour and diligence in their spiritual works and devotional exercises, this prosperity of theirs gives rise to secret Pride — though holy things tend of their own nature to Humility — because of their imperfections; and the issue is that they conceive a certain satisfaction in the contemplation of their works and of themselves. From the same source, too, proceeds that empty eagerness which they display, in speaking before others of the spiritual life, and sometimes to teach it, instead of learning it. They condemn others in their minds when they see that they are not devout in their own way. Sometimes also they give expression in words to that feeling, showing themselves herein to be like the Pharisee, who in the act of prayer boasted of his own good works and despised the Publican.*

This fervour, and the desire to do such and other like acts, is frequently fed by Satan in order that men of this kind may grow in pride and presumption: he knows perfectly well that all the virtuous works of people in this state are not only nothing worth, but rather tending to sin. Some of them go so far as to think none good but themselves, and so both in word and act fall into condemnation and detraction of others. They see the mote in the eye of their brother, but not the beam which is in their own.† They strain out the gnat in another man's cup, and swallow the camel in their own.‡

Sometimes, also, when their spiritual masters, such as

* S. Luke xviii. 11, 12. † S. Matth. vii. 3. ‡ Ib. xxiii. 24.

BOOK I.

Devices of self-love.

confessors and superiors, do not approve of their spirit and conduct — for they wish to be praised and considered for what they do — they decide that they are not understood, and that their superiors are not spiritual men because they do not approve and sanction their proceedings. So they go about in quest of some one else, who will accommodate himself to their fancy; for in general they love to discuss their spirit with those who, they think, will commend and extol their state. They avoid, as they would death, those who depreciate their feelings with the view of leading them into a safe way, and sometimes they even hate them. Presuming greatly on themselves, they make many resolutions, and accomplish little. They are occasionally desirous that others should perceive their spirituality and devotion, and for that end they make many exterior movements, give vent to sighs and practise divers ceremonies; and sometimes, too, they fall into a kind of rapture in public rather than in private—whereunto Satan contributes—and they are pleased when others witness it.

1. Seeking praise.

2. External signs of devotion.

3. Artful Confessions.

Many of them seek to be the favourites of their confessors, and the result is endless envy and disquietude. They are ashamed to confess their sins plainly, lest their confessors should think less of them, so they go about palliating them, that they may not seem so bad: which is excusing rather than accusing themselves. Sometimes they go to a stranger to confess their sin, that their usual confessor may not suppose they are sinners, but good people. And so they always take pleasure in telling him of their goodness, and that in terms suggestive of more than is in them: at the least, they wish all their goodness to be appreciated, when it would be greater humility on their part, as I shall presently show, to undervalue what is their own, and to be anxious that neither their confessor nor anyone else should think them of the least importance.

CHAP. II.

Pride of impatience with self.

Some beginners, too, make very light of their faults occasionally, and at other times indulge in immoderate grief when they commit them. They thought themselves already saints, and so they become angry and impatient with themselves, which is another great imperfection. They also importune God to deliver them from their faults and imperfections, but it is for the comfort of living in peace, and not for God; they do not consider that, were He to deliver them, they would become, perhaps, prouder than ever. They are great enemies of other men's praise, but great lovers of their own, and sometimes they seek it. In this respect they resemble the foolish Virgins, who, with untrimmed lamps, went about in search of oil, saying: 'Give us your oil, for our lamps are gone out.'*

Some, too, fall deeply into these imperfections, and into great evils by reason of them. Some, however, fall into them less than others, and some have to contend with little more than the first motions of them. But scarcely anyone can be found who, in his first fervours, did not fall into some of them.

Conduct of the humble beginner.

But those who at this time are going on to Perfection proceed in a very different way, and in a very different temper of mind: they grow and edify themselves in humility, not only looking on their own works as nothing, but also dissatisfied with themselves: they look upon all others as much better than themselves, they regard them with a holy envy in their anxiety to serve God as well as they do. For the greater their fervour, the more numerous their good works; and the keener the pleasure therein, the more they perceive —for they humble themselves—how much is that which God deserves at their hands, and how little is all they can do for Him: thus the more they do, the less are they satisfied. So great is what they in their love would fain do, that all they

* S. Matt. xxv. 8.

Marks of pure, simple, and true spirituality.

are doing seems nothing. This loving anxiety so importunes and occupies them that they never consider whether others are doing good or not, and if they themselves should ever do good, it is in the conviction that all others are much better than themselves. They think slightingly of themselves, and wish others to do so also, to make no account of them, and to despise what belongs to them; and, moreover, if anyone should praise and respect them they will give them no credit, for they think it strange that anybody should speak well of them.

Persons of this kind, in great tranquillity and humility, are very desirous to learn the things that are profitable to them from anyone, be he who he may—in this respect the very opposite of those of whom I have just spoken, who are willing to teach everybody; and who, when anyone seems about to teach them anything, take the words out of his mouth, as if they knew it already.

But these of whom I am now speaking are very far from wishing to instruct anyone; they are most ready to travel by another road if they be but commanded, for they never imagine that they can be right in anything. When others are praised they rejoice, and their only regret is that they do not serve God themselves as well as they. They are not anxious to speak about their own state, because they think so lightly of it that they are, as it were, ashamed to speak of it to their confessors, for it seems to them unworthy of any mention whatever. But they have a great desire to speak of their shortcomings and sins, or of what they consider not to be virtues: thus they incline to treat of the affairs of their soul with those who have no great opinion of their state and spirit. This is a characteristic of that spirituality which is pure, simple, true, and most pleasing unto God. For as the Spirit of the Divine Wisdom dwells in these humble souls, He moves and inclines them to keep his treasures secretly within, and to cast out the evil. God gives this grace together with other virtues to the humble, and withholds it from the proud.

Persons of this kind will give their hearts' blood for him who serves God, and will aid him to the utmost of their powers. When they commit any imperfection they bear up under it with humility, in gentleness of spirit, in loving fear of God, and hoping in Him. But the souls who in the beginning travel thus towards Perfection are few, yea, very few, and we ought to be content when they do not rush into the opposite evils. This is the reason, as I shall hereafter explain, why God leads into the Obscure Night those souls whom He will purify from all these imperfections in order to their further advancement.

How the humble man bears his own imperfections.

CHAPTER III.

Of the imperfections of Avarice, in the spiritual sense.

Second Imperfection,—Spiritual Avarice.

MANY a beginner also falls at times into great spiritual Avarice. Scarcely anyone is contented with that measure of the Spirit which God gives; they are disconsolate and querulous because they do not find the comfort they expected in spiritual things. Many are never satisfied with listening to spiritual counsels and precepts, with reading books which treat of their state; and they spend more time in this than in doing their duty, having no regard to that mortification, and perfection of interior spiritual poverty, to which they ought to apply themselves. Besides, they load themselves with images, rosaries, and crucifixes, curious and costly; now taking up one, then another, now changing them, and then resuming them again. At one time they will have them of a certain fashion, at another time of another, prizing one more than another because more curious or costly. Some may be seen with an Agnus Dei, and with relics and medals, like children with coral.

BOOK I.

I condemn here that attachment and clinging of the heart to the form, number, and curiosity of these things, because in direct opposition to poverty of spirit, which looks only to the substance of devotion; which makes use indeed of these things, but only sufficiently for the end, and disdains that variety and curiosity in them; for real devotion must spring out of the heart, and consider only the truth and substance which the objects in question represent. All beyond this is attachment and imperfection; and the soul, if it is to go on unto Perfection, must root out that feeling utterly.

Real devotion must spring from the heart.

I knew a person who for more than ten years used continually, without interruption, a cross rudely formed of a piece of blessed palm, and fastened together by a common pin bent backwards, until I took it away. This was a person not deficient in sense and intellect. I knew another who had a rosary made of the backbones of fish, and whose devotion, I am certain, was not on that account of less value in the eyes of God; for it is quite clear that the cost or workmanship of these contributed nothing to it.

Two examples of the spirit of Poverty.

Those beginners, therefore, who go on well, do not rely on visible instruments, neither do they burden themselves with them, neither do they seek to know more than is necessary for them, so that they may act rightly, for their sole object is to be well with God and to please Him; their avarice consists in that. With a noble generosity they give away their possessions; and their delight is to learn how to want all things for the love of God and their neighbour, disposing of everything according to the laws of this virtue; because, as I have said, the sole object they have in view is real Perfection, to please God in all things and themselves in nothing.

The humble man begins with Generosity.

Real Perfection,—what.

The soul, however, cannot be perfectly purified from these imperfections, any more than from the others, until God shall have led it into the passive purgation of this Obscure Night. But it is expedient that the soul, so far as it can, should labour, on its own part, to purify and perfect itself, that it may merit from God to be taken under His Divine care, and be healed from those imperfections which of itself it cannot remedy. For, after all the efforts of the soul, it cannot by any exertions of its own actively purify itself so as to be in the slightest degree qualified for the Divine union of perfection in the love of God, if God Himself does not take it into His own hands and purify it in the obscure fire, as I am going to explain.

God alone can make Saints.

CHAPTER IV.

Of the imperfection of Luxury, spiritually understood.

Third Imperfection,—Spiritual Luxury.

MANY beginners fall into other imperfections, over and above those in connection with the capital sins. I pass them over now, to avoid prolixity, touching on some of the principal ones, which are as it were the source and origin of the rest.

As to the sin of Luxury, passing over what it is to commit it—my object being to speak of those imperfections which have to be purged away in the Obscure Night—beginners fall into many imperfections, which may be called Spiritual Luxury; not that it is so in fact, but because it is felt and experienced sometimes in the flesh, owing to frailty, when the soul is the recipient of spiritual communications. For very often, in the midst of their spiritual exercises, and when they cannot help themselves, the impure motions of sensuality are felt; and sometimes even when they are deeply absorbed in prayer, or engaged in receiving the Sacraments of Penance and the Eucharist. These motions not being in their power, proceed from one of three sources.

First source,—Sensible sweetness.

They proceed occasionally—though but rarely, and in persons of delicate constitutions—from sensible sweetness in spiritual things. For when sense and spirit are both

BOOK I.

Law of the flesh and of the spirit.

delighted together, the whole nature of man is moved in that delectation according to its measure and character. The mind is moved to delight itself in God—that is the higher part of our nature; and sensuality, which is the lower part, is moved towards sensible gratification, because it knows, and admits of, none other. And so it happens that the soul, while in spirit it is praying, is in the senses troubled, to its great disgust, with the rebellious movements of the flesh passively. As these two parts, the higher and the lower, form but one subject, man, they mutually participate in their respective passions, each in its own way; for, as the Philosopher tells us, all that is received is received according to the capacity of the recipient. And so in these beginnings, and even when the soul has made some progress, the sensitive part, being still imperfect, when spiritual delight flows into the soul, mingles occasionally of its own therewith. But when the sensitive is already cleansed in the purgation of the Obscure Night, it is no more subject to these infirmities, because it receives so abundantly of the Spirit of God, that it seems rather to be received into that Spirit itself, as into that which is greater and grander. Thus it possesses everything in the way of the Spirit, in an admirable manner of which it partakes, united with God.

Second Source,—the Devil.

The second source of these rebellious motions is the Evil Spirit, who, in order to disquiet the soul during prayer, or when it is preparing for it, causes these filthy movements of our lower nature, and these, when in any degree admitted, are injury enough. Some persons not only relax in their prayers through fear of these movements, which is the object of Satan when he undertakes to assail them, but even neglect them altogether, for they imagine that they are more liable to these assaults during prayer than at other times. This is certainly true; for he then assails them more than at other times, in order to lead them to intermit their prayers. This is not all;

for he represents to them then, most vividly, the very filthiest images, and occasionally in close relations with certain spiritual things and persons, the thought whereof is profitable to the soul, that he may terrify and crush them. Some are so grievously assailed that they dare not dwell upon anything, for it becomes at once a stumbling-block to them, especially those who are of a melancholy temperament; these are so afflicted as to be objects of the deepest pity. When melancholy is the occasion of these visitations of Satan, men in general cannot be delivered from them till their bodily health is improved, unless they shall have entered on the Obscure Night which purifies them wholly.

Third source Fear.

The third source of these depraved movements which war against the soul is usually the fear of them which men have conceived beforehand. This fear, which a sudden remembrance occasions, in what they see, speak, or think of, makes them suffer these trials without fault on their part.

Sometimes, when spiritual persons are speaking of spiritual things, or doing good works, they become conscious of a certain energy and elasticity arising out of the recollection of persons whom they have seen, and they go on with a certain measure of vain joy. This also proceeds from spiritual luxury in the sense I speak of, and is accompanied at times by a certain complacency of the will.

Test of purely spiritual affection,—what.

Some, too, form spiritual friendships with others, the source of which is this luxury, and not spirituality. We may know it to be so by observing whether the remembrance of that affection increases our recollection and love of God, or remorse of conscience. When this affection is purely spiritual, the love of God increases with it, and the more we think of it the more we think of God, and the greater our longing for Him; for the one grows with the other. The spirit of God has this property, that it increases good by good, because there is a resemblance and harmony between them. But

BOOK I.

when this affection springs out of mere sensuality, its effects are quite opposite; for the more it grows, the more is the love of God diminished, and the remembrance of Him also; for if this earthly love increases, that of God cools down, and men forget Him by reason of that affection of sense, and remorse of conscience is the result.

Difference between huma and Divine Love.

On the other hand, if the love of God increases, the human love decreases, and is forgotten; for as they are contrary the one to the other, not only do they not help each other, but the one which predominates suppresses the other, and strengthens itself as Philosophers explain it. And so our Saviour tells us in the Gospel, saying, 'that which is born of the flesh is flesh, and that which is born of the Spirit is spirit;'* that love which grows out of sensuality ends in the same, and that which is spiritual ends in the Spirit of God, and increases it in the soul. This is the difference between these two affections, whereby we may distinguish between them. When the soul enters into the Obscure Night, these affections are ruled by Reason; that night strengthens and purifies the affection which is according to God, and removes, destroys, or mortifies the other. In the beginning both are lost sight of, as I shall explain hereafter.

In the Obscure Night the affections are ruled by Reason.

CHAPTER V.

Of the imperfections of Anger.

Fourth Imperfection, Anger and Peevishness,—how caused

MANY beginners, because of their inordinate appetite for spiritual sweetness, generally commit many imperfections in the matter of Anger; for when spiritual things minister to them no more sweetness and delight, they naturally become peevish, and in that bitterness of spirit prove a burden to themselves in all they do: trifles make them angry, and

* S. John iii. 6.

they are at times intolerable to all about them. This happens to them generally after great sweetness in prayer; and so, when that sensible sweetness is past and gone, their natural temper is soured and rendered morose. They are like a babe weaned from the breast, which he found so sweet. When this natural feeling of displeasure is not permitted to grow, there is no sin, but only imperfection, which will have to be purged away in the hardship and aridities of the Obscure Night.

Impatience with self or others contrary to humility.

There are spiritual persons, too, who fall into another kind of anger. They are angry with other people's faults, with a sort of unquiet zeal for censure; they are occasionally moved to blame them, and even do so with anger, constituting themselves guardians of virtue. All this is contrary to spiritual meekness.

Saints not made in a day.

Others, again, when they detect their own imperfections, become angry at themselves with an impatience that is not humble. They are so impatient with their shortcomings that they would be saints in a day. Many of these form many and grand resolutions, but, being self-confident and not humble, the more they resolve, the more they fall, and the more angry at themselves they become. They have not patience enough to wait for God's help; this is also opposed to spiritual meekness. There is no perfect remedy for this but in the Obscure Night. There are, however, some people who are so patient, and who advance so slowly in the desire for spiritual progress, that God wishes they were not so patient.

Festina lente.

CHAPTER VI.

Of the imperfections of Spiritual Gluttony.

Fifth Imperfection,—Spiritual Gluttony.

I HAVE much to say of the fourth capital sin, which is Spiritual Gluttony, for there is scarcely one among beginners,

BOOK I.

however well he may go on, who does not fall into many of the imperfections connected with this sin, in his case, owing to that sensible sweetness which is at first to be found in spiritual exercises.

Folly of exterior, without interior, mortification.

Many beginners, delighting in the sweetness and joy of their spiritual occupations, strive after spiritual sweetness rather than after pure and true devotion, which is that which God regards and accepts in the whole course of the spiritual way. For this reason, over and above their imperfection in seeking after sweetness in devotion, that spirit of gluttony, which has taken possession of them, forces them to overstep the limits of moderation, within which virtue is acquired and consists. For allured by the delights they then experience, some of them kill themselves by penances, and others weaken themselves by fasting. They take upon themselves more than they can bear, without rule or advice; they conceal their austerities from those whom they are bound to obey, and some even practise them when they are expressly commanded to abstain. These are full of imperfections—unreasonable people, who undervalue submission and obedience, which is the penance of Reason and judgment, and therefore a more acceptable and sweet sacrifice unto God than all the acts of bodily penance. Bodily penance is full of imperfections when the penance of the will is neglected, for men undertake it merely for the sweetness which attends it.

Penance of Reason, Obedience.

Obedience better than Sacrifice.

Inasmuch then as all extremes are vicious, and as in this course of conduct men follow their own will, the consequences are that they grow in vice and not in virtue; at least they minister to their spiritual gluttony and pride, for they do not walk in the way of obedience. The devil so deceives many of them by exciting their gluttony through this sweetness which he increases, that, since they cannot obey, they either change, or vary, or add to, what is commanded them; so hard and bitter is obedience become. The evil has so grown upon some, that they lose all desire to do their spiritual duties the instant obedience enjoins them; because their sole satisfaction consisted in following their own inclinations, which, in their case, had better, perhaps, have been unattended to.

Folly of self-direction.

Many of these importune their spiritual directors to allow them to do what they have set their minds upon: they extort that permission by force, and if it be refused, they mope like children, and become discontented; they think they are not serving God whenever they are thwarted in their wishes. These persons clinging to sweetness and their own will, the moment they are contradicted, and directed according to the will of God, become fretful, fainthearted, and then fall away. They imagine that to please and gratify themselves, is to serve and please God.

Self-love in unadvised frequent communion.

Others also there are, who, by reason of this spiritual gluttony, are so ignorant of their own meanness and misery, and so insensible to that loving fear and reverence due to the Majesty of God, that they are not afraid to insist on being allowed by their confessors to confess and communicate frequently. And what is much worse, they very often dare to communicate without the leave and approbation of the minister and steward of Christ, purely out of their own head, and conceal the fact from their director. This eagerness for Communion makes them confess themselves carelessly, for they are more anxious to communicate anyhow than to communicate in pureness and perfection. It would be more profitable for them, and a holier course, to entreat their confessors not to enjoin such frequent communions; though the better way between these two extremes is to be humble and resigned. This excessive boldness leads to great evil, and men may well be in fear of some chastisement for their rashness.

These persons, when they communicate, strive with all

their might to find some sensible sweetness in the act, instead of worshipping in humility and praising God within themselves. So much are they given up to this, that they think, when they derive no sensible sweetness from Communion, they have done nothing, so meanly do they think of God; neither do they understand that the least of the blessings of the Most Holy Sacrament is that which touches the senses, and that the invisible grace It confers is far greater; for God frequently withholds these sensible favours from men, that they may fix the eyes of faith upon Himself. But these persons will feel and taste God, as if He were palpable and accessible to them, not only in Communion, but in all their other acts of devotion. All this is a very great imperfection, and directly at variance with the requirements of God, which demand the purest faith.

Invisible grace better than sensible sweetness.

How persons seek, not God, but themselves, even in prayer.

They conduct themselves in the same way when they are praying; for they imagine that the whole business of prayer consists in sensible devotion, and this they strive to obtain with all their might, wearying out their brains and perplexing all the faculties of their souls. When they miss that sensible devotion, they are cast down, thinking they have done nothing. This effort after sweetness destroys true devotion and spirituality, which consist in perseverance in prayer with patience and humility, mistrusting self solely to please God. And therefore, when they once miss their accustomed sweetness in prayer, or in any other act of religion, they feel a sort of repugnance to resume it, and sometimes cease from it altogether. In short, they are like children who are not influenced by Reason, but by their inclinations. They waste themselves in the search after spiritual consolation, and are never satisfied with reading good books, taking up one meditation after another, in the pursuit of sensible sweetness in the things of God. God refuses it to them most justly, wisely, and lovingly, for if He did not, this spiritual gluttony on their part would grow into great evils. For this reason, it is most expedient that they should enter into the Obscure Night, that they may be cleansed from this childishness.

Desire for Spiritual sweetness enfeebles the will.

They who are bent on sensible sweetness, labour under another very great imperfection: weakness and remissness on the rugged road of the Cross, for the soul that is given to sweetness naturally sets its face against the pain of self-denial. They labour under many other imperfections also, which have their origin here, of which our Lord will heal them in due time, through temptations, aridities and trials, elements of the Obscure Night. I will not enlarge upon them here, that I may avoid prolixity: but this will I say, that spiritual soberness and temperance produce a far different temper of mortification, of fear and submission in all things; showing us that the perfection and value of things consist not in the multitude thereof, but in knowing how to deny ourselves in them. Spiritual men must labour after this with all their might, until it shall please God to purify them by leading them into the Obscure Night. And I hasten on with the description of these imperfections, that I may enter on the explanation of it.

Way of Spiritual sobriety,—what.

CHAPTER VII.

Of the imperfections of Envy and Spiritual Sloth.

Sixth and seventh Imperfections,—Envy and Spiritual Sloth.

Beginners are not free from many imperfections in the matter of Envy and Spiritual Sloth. Many of them are wont to experience emotions of displeasure at the contemplation of other men's goodness. They are sensibly afflicted when others outstrip them on the spiritual road; they cannot endure to hear them praised. They are vexed with other men's virtues, and are sometimes unable to restrain themselves from contradiction when they are commended; they

BOOK I.

depreciate them as much as they can, and feel acutely because they are not thought so well of themselves, for they wish to be preferred above all others. All this is at variance with that charity of which the apostle says, it 'rejoiceth with the truth.' * If charity admits of envy at all, it is a holy envy that makes us grieve that we have not the virtues that others have; but still rejoicing that they have them, and glad that others outstrip us in the race that they may serve God, we being so full of imperfection ourselves.

Holy Envy of Charity.

Cause and effects of Spiritual Sloth.

As to Spiritual Sloth, beginners are wont to find their most spiritual occupations irksome, and they avoid them therefore as repugnant to their desire for sensible sweetness, for being addicted to it in spiritual things, they loathe them when this sweetness fails. If they miss but once their accustomed sweetness in prayer—it is expedient that God should deprive them of it at last—they will not resume it; at other times they omit it, or return to it with a bad grace. Thus, under the influence of spiritual sloth they turn aside from the Way of Perfection—which is the denial of their will and pleasure for God—preferring to it the gratification of their own will, which they serve herein rather than the Will of God. Many of these will have it that God should will what they will, and are afflicted when they must will what He wills, and reluctantly submit their own to His Will. The result is that they frequently imagine that what is not according to their will is also not according to the Will of God; and, on the other hand, that what pleases them is also pleasing unto God. They measure Him by themselves, and not themselves by Him, in direct contradiction to the teaching of the Gospel; 'He that shall lose his life for My sake, shall find it.' † That is, he who shall give up his own will for God shall have it, and he who will have it, he shall have it never.

Perfection is to do the Will of God.

They also find it wearisome to obey when they are com-

* 1 Cor. xiii. 6.

† S. Matth. xvi. 25.

manded to do what they like not; and because they walk in the way of consolation and spiritual sweetness, they are too weak for the rough trials of Perfection. They are like persons delicately nurtured who avoid with heavy hearts all that is hard and rugged, and are offended at the Cross wherein the joys of the spirit consist. The more spiritual the work they have to do, the more irksome do they feel it to be. And because they will walk at their ease, gratifying their will along the spiritual road, to enter on the 'strait way that leadeth unto life,'* is repugnant to their feelings and produces heaviness of heart.

Prayer sometimes irksome,—why.

True spiritual joys of the Cross.

Let this account of the many imperfections under which they labour, who are in the first state of beginners, suffice to show them how necessary it is for them that God should bring them to the state of proficients, which He effects when He leads them into the Obscure Night. In that night He weans them from the breasts of sweetness, in pure aridities and interior darkness, cleanses them from all these imperfections and childish ways, and by a way most different from their own, makes them grow in virtue. After all our exertions to mortify ourselves in our actions and passions, our success will not be perfect, or even great, until God Himself shall do it for us in the purgation of the Obscure Night. May God be pleased to give me His light, that I may speak profitably of this; for I have great need of it while treating of a night so obscure, and a subject so difficult.

Good fruits of the Obscure Night.

God alone can purify the soul.

CHAPTER VIII.

Explanation of the first line of the first stanza: 'In an Obscure Night.'

'In an Obscure Night.' This night—I have already said that it is Contemplation—produces in spiritual men two sorts of

* S. Matth. vii. 14.

darkness or purgations conformable to the two divisions of man's nature into sensitive and spiritual. Thus one night or Sensitive Purgation, wherein the soul is purified or detached, will be of the senses, harmonizing them with the spirit. The other is that night or Spiritual Purgation wherein the soul is purified or detached in the spirit, and which harmonizes and disposes the soul for union with God in love. The sensitive night is common, and the lot of many: these are the beginners, of whom I shall first speak. The spiritual night is the portion of very few; and they are those who have made some progress, exercised therein, of whom I shall speak hereafter.

Two Nights,—
1. Of the Senses.
2. Of the Spirit.
First subjects Sense to reason;
Second unites Reason to God.

The first night, or purgation, is bitter and terrible to sense. The second is not to be compared with it, for it is much more awful to the spirit, as I shall soon show. But as the night of sense is the first in order and in fact, I shall discuss it briefly—for being of ordinary occurrence, it is the matter of many treatises—that I may proceed with the discussion of the spiritual night, of which very little has been said, either by word of mouth or in writing, and of which little is known even by experience.

Both painful.

First more common than the second.

As the conduct of beginners in the way of God is mean, in harmony with their tastes and self-love, and as God wills their advancement, and to draw them out of their mean way of loving Him to the heights of the Divine love; to rescue them from the grovelling work of sense and reflections, where they so scantily and unseemlily feel after Him; to elevate them to the practice of spirituality, where they may commune with Him more fully, and in greater freedom from their imperfections—being now experienced in the ways of virtue, persevering in meditation and prayer, through the sweetness of which they have been able to disentangle their affections from the things of this world, and acquired some spiritual strength so as to curb their desires; and being now capable

The Sensitive Night,—how and why God sends it.

of bearing their burdens and enduring aridities, without going back to that more pleasant time when their spiritual exercises abounded in delights, and when the sun of Divine favours shone more clearly upon them as they think, God changes that light into darkness, and seals up the door of the fountain of the sweet waters of the Spirit, which they tasted in God as often and as long as they wished. For when they were weak and tender, this door was then not shut, as it is written, 'Behold, I have given before thee an opened door, which no man can shut; because thou hast a little strength, and hast kept My word, and hast not denied My Name.'*

Now, at last, God leaves them in darkness so deep that they know not whither to betake themselves with their imaginations and reflections. They cannot now advance a single step with their meditation, as they did before, the inward sense being, as it were, suffocated in that night, and abandoned to dryness so great that they have no more any joy or sweetness in their spiritual exercises, as they had before; and in their place they now find nothing but insipidity and bitterness. For now God, looking upon them as somewhat grown in grace, weans them from the breasts that they may become strong, and cast their swaddling-clothes aside: He carries them in His arms no longer, and shows them how to walk alone. All this is strange to them, for all things seem to go against them.

Time and conditions of entering the Sensitive Night.

Recollected persons enter the Obscure Night sooner than others, after they have begun their spiritual course; because they are kept at a greater distance from the occasions of falling away, and because they correct more quickly their worldly desires, which it is requisite to do even at the commencement of the blessed Night of Sense. In general, there elapses no great length of time after they have begun

* Apoc. iii. 8.

before they enter the night of sense, and most of them do enter it, because they generally suffer aridities. The Holy Scriptures throughout, but especially in the Psalms and the prophetical books, furnish many illustrations of the night of sense—it is so common; but, to avoid prolixity, I omit them for the present, though in the course of my treatise I shall have occasion to make use of some of them.

CHAPTER IX.

Of the signs by which it may be known that the spiritual man is walking in the way of this Night or Sensitive Purgation.

Three tests to distinguish the Sensitive Night from sin, tepidity, or bodily weakness.

But as these aridities may frequently proceed, not from this night and purgation of the sensitive appetite, but from sin or imperfections, from weakness or lukewarmness, from some physical derangement or bodily indisposition, I shall here propose certain signs by which we may ascertain whether a particular aridity proceeds from the purgation of sense, or from any one of the sources I have just enumerated. There are three chief signs.

1. No desire of, or sweetness in, creatures.

The first is when men find no comfort in the things of God, and none also in created things. For when God leads the soul into the Obscure Night in order to wean it from sweetness and to purge away its sensitive desires, He does not allow it to find sweetness or comfort anywhere. It is then probable, in such a case, that this aridity is not the result of sin or of imperfections recently committed; for if it were, we should feel some inclination or desire for other things than those of God. Whenever we give the reins to our desires in the way of any imperfection, our desires are instantly attracted to it, be it much or little, in proportion to the affection we regard it with. But still, inasmuch as this absence of pleasure in the things of Heaven and of earth may proceed from bodily indisposition or a melancholy temperament, which frequently cause dissatisfaction with all things, the second sign and condition become necessary.

2. Longing anxiety for God.

The second sign and condition of this purgation are that the memory dwells ordinarily upon God with a painful anxiety and carefulness, the soul thinks it is not serving God, but going backwards, because it is no longer conscious of any sweetness in the things of God. In that case it is clear that this weariness of spirit and aridity are not the results of weakness and tepidity; for the peculiarity of tepidity is the absence of great application to, and of interior solicitude for, the things of God. There is, therefore, a great difference between aridity and lukewarmness, for the latter consists in great remissness of the will and resolution, and in the want of all solicitude about serving God; but the purgative aridity is accompanied in general by a painful anxiety because the soul thinks that it is not serving God. Though this be occasionally increased by constitutional melancholy—so it sometimes happens—yet it is not for that reason without its purgative effects on the desires, because the soul is deprived of all sweetness, and its sole anxieties are referred to God. For when mere bodily indisposition is the case, all that it does is to cause disgust and the ruin of the physical constitution, without those desires of serving God which belong to the purgative aridity. In this aridity, though the sensitive part of man be greatly depressed, weak and sluggish in good works, by reason of the little satisfaction they furnish, the spirit is, nevertheless, ready and strong.

Difference between aridity and lukewarmness.

Influence of melancholy and physical causes.

Purgative aridity,—how and why produced.

The cause of this aridity is that God transfers to the spirit the goods and energies of the senses, which, having no natural fitness for it, become dry, parched up, and empty; for the sensitive nature of man is not naturally adapted for that which belongs to the spirit simply. Thus the spirit having been tasted, the flesh becomes insipid and remiss; but the

BOOK I.

spirit, having received its proper nourishment, becomes strong, more vigilant and careful than before, lest there should be any negligence in serving God. At first it is not conscious of any spiritual sweetness and delight, but rather of aridities and distaste, because of the novelty of the change. The spiritual palate having been accustomed to sensible sweetness, the eyes of the soul are still fixed upon it. And because the spiritual palate is not prepared and purified for so delicious a taste until it shall have been for some time disposed for it in this arid and obscure night, it cannot taste of the spiritual good, but rather of aridity and distaste, because it misses that which it enjoyed with so much facility before.

The sensitive appetite like the Israelites in the Wilderness.

These, whom God begins to lead through the solitudes of the wilderness, resemble the children of Israel, who, though God began to feed them, as soon as they were come into the wilderness, with the manna of heaven, which 'serving every man's will, was turned to what every man liked,'* were more sensible to the loss of the onions and flesh of Egypt—for their taste had been formed to them and had revelled in them—than to the delicious sweetness of the angelical food. So in the midst of the manna they wept and bewailed the flesh-pots of Egypt, saying, 'We remember the fish that we ate in Egypt free-cost; the cucumbers come into our mind, and the melons, and the leeks, and the onions, and the garlic.'† Our appetite becomes so depraved that we long for miserable trifles, and loathe the unchangeable good of Heaven.

The will strengthened by sensible aridity.

But when these aridities arise in the purgative way of the sensitive appetite, though the spirit is at first without any sweetness, for the reasons I have given, yet is it conscious of strength and energy to act because of the substantial nature of its interior food, which is the commencement of Contem-

* Wisd. xvi. 21. † Numb. xi. 5.

plation, obscure and dry to the senses. This contemplation is in general secret, and unknown to him who is admitted into it. Together with this aridity and emptiness the soul feels a longing for solitude and repose, being unable to fix the thoughts on anything distinctly, or even to desire to do so.

Peace found in humble resignation.

Now, if they who are in this state knew how to be quiet, to disregard every interior and exterior work, the accomplishment of which they labour after, and to be without solicitude about everything but the resignation of themselves into the hands of God, and a loving interior obedience to His voice, they would have, in this tranquillity, a most delicious taste of interior refreshing. This refreshing is so delicate that, in general, it eludes our perceptions if we are in any degree anxious to feel it, for it works in the soul when most tranquil and free, and is like the air which vanishes whenever we shut our hands to grasp it.

The words of the Bridegroom which he addressed to the Bride are applicable to this matter: 'Turn away thy eyes from me, for they have made me flee away.' * Such is God's way of bringing the soul into this state; the road by which He leads it is so different from the first, that if it will do anything in its own strength, it will hinder rather than aid His work. The matter was far otherwise once. The reason is this: God works in the soul, in the State of Contemplation, that is, when it advances from meditation to the state of the proficients, in such a way as to seem to have bound up all the interior faculties, leaving no support in the Intellect, no sweetness in the Will, no reflections in the Memory. Therefore, at this time, all that the soul can do of itself ends only in disturbing the interior peace, and hindering the work which God is carrying on in the spirit amid the dryness of sense. This

* Cant. vi. 4.

peace, being spiritual and delicate, effects a work that is quiet and delicate, pacific and utterly alien to the former delights, which were most palpable and sensible. This is that peace of which the Psalmist spoke when he said, 'God will speak in me, for He will speak peace unto His people.'* This brings us to the third sign.

3. Inability to meditate by Imagination and discursive Reflection.

The third sign we have for ascertaining whether this aridity be the purgation of sense, is an inability to meditate and make reflections, and to excite the imagination, as before, notwithstanding all the efforts we may make; for God begins now to communicate Himself, no longer through the channel of sense, as He did formerly, in consecutive reflections, by which we arranged and divided our knowledge, but in pure spirit, which admits not of successive ideas, and in an act of pure Contemplation, to which neither the interior nor the exterior senses of our lower nature can ascend. Hence it is that the fancy and the imagination cannot support or commence any reflections, nor use them ever afterwards.

It is understood here that this embarrassment and aversion of the senses does not arise out of any bodily ailment. When it arises from this, the indisposition, which is always changeable, having ceased, the powers of the soul recover their former energies, and find their previous satisfactions at once. It is otherwise in the purgation of the appetite, for as soon as we enter upon this, the inability to make our meditations continually grows. It is true that this purgation is not continuous in some persons, for they are not altogether without sensible sweetness and comfort—their weakness renders their rapid weaning inexpedient—nevertheless, it grows upon them more and more, and the operations of sense diminish; if it be that they are advancing to perfection. They, however, who are not walking in the Way of Contemplation, meet with a

* Ps. lxxxiv. 9.

very different treatment, for the night of aridities is not continuous with them, they are sometimes in it, and sometimes not; they are at one time unable to meditate, and at another able as before.

God leads these persons into this night only to try them and to humble them, and to correct their desires, that they may not grow up spiritual gluttons, and not for the purpose of leading them into the spiritual way, which is Contemplation. God does not elevate to perfect contemplation everyone that is tried in the spiritual way, and He alone knoweth why. Hence it is that these persons are never wholly weaned from the breasts of meditations and reflections, but only at intervals and at certain seasons.

Not all spiritual persons reach Contemplation.

CHAPTER X.

How they are to conduct themselves who have entered the Obscure Night.

During the aridity of the Night of Sense—when God effects the change of which I have spoken, when He leads the soul out of the way of sense into that of the spirit, from Meditation to Contemplation, where it is helpless so far as its own powers are concerned—spiritual persons have to endure great afflictions, not so much because they are in the state of aridity, but because they are afraid that they have missed the way; thinking that they are spiritually ruined, and that God has forsaken them, only because they find no support or consolation in holy things. Under these circumstances, they weary themselves, and strive, as they were wont, to fix the powers of the soul with some satisfaction upon some object of meditation—they think when they cannot do this, and are not conscious of their labour, that they are doing nothing—but with great dislike and interior unwillingness on the part

Cause of the afflictions of the Sensitive Night,—what.

BOOK I.

of the soul, which enjoys its state of quietness and rest. While they change from one condition they make no progress in the other, because, by exerting their own spirit, they lose that spirit which they had in tranquillity and peace. They are like a man who does his work over again; or who goes out of a city that he may enter it once more; or who lets go what he has caught in hunting that he may hunt it again. Their labours are in vain; for they will find nothing, and that because they are turning back to their former habits.

Necessity of right instruction.

Under these circumstances, if they meet with no one who understands their case, these persons fall away, and abandon the right road; or become weak, or at least put hindrances in the way of their further advancement, because they make efforts to proceed in their former way of Meditation, fatiguing their natural powers beyond measure. They think that their state is the result of negligence or of sin. All their efforts are now in vain, because God is leading them by another and a very different road, that of Contemplation. Their first road was that of discursive reflection, but no imagination or reasoning can reach the second.

Confidence in God.

It behoves those who find themselves in this condition to take courage, and persevere in patience. Let them not afflict themselves, but put their confidence in God, who never forsakes those who seek Him with a pure and upright heart. Neither will He withhold from them all that is necessary for them on this road until He brings them to the clear and pure light of love, which He will show them in that other obscure night of the spirit, if they shall merit an entrance into it.

Conduct to be observed in the Sensitive Night,—Patience and Perseverance.

The conduct to be observed by spiritual men in the night of sense is this: Let them in nowise have recourse to meditations, for the time is now past, and let them leave their soul in quietness and repose, though they may think they are doing nothing, that they are losing time, and that their tepidity

CHAP. X.

is the reason of their unwillingness to employ their thoughts. They will do enough if they keep patience, and persevere in prayer; all they have to do is to keep their soul free, unembarrassed, and at rest from all thoughts and all knowledge, not anxious about what they shall think or meditate, contenting themselves with directing their attention lovingly and calmly towards God; and all this without anxiety or effort, or immoderate desire to feel and taste His presence. For all such efforts disquiet the soul, and distract it from the calm repose and sweet tranquillity of Contemplation belonging to their present state.

The repose of Love.

And though they may have many scruples that they are wasting time, and that it may be better for them to betake themselves to some other occupation, seeing that in prayer and meditation they are become helpless; yet let them be patient with themselves, and remain quiet, for what they are uneasy about is their own satisfaction and liberty of spirit. If they were now to exert their interior faculties, they would only impede and ruin the good which, in that repose, God is working in the soul; for if a man while sitting for his portrait cannot be still, but moves about, the painter will never depict his face, and even what he may have done will be spoiled. So when the soul interiorly reposes, every action and passion, or anxious consideration at that time, will distract and disturb it, and make it feel the dryness and emptiness of sense. The more efforts it makes to acquire support in affection and knowledge, the more will it feel the deficiency which cannot now be supplied in that way. It is therefore expedient for the soul which is in this condition not to be troubled because its faculties have become useless, yea, rather it should desire that they may become so quickly; for by offering no impediment to the operation of infused contemplation, to which God is now admitting it, the soul is refreshed in peaceful abundance, and set on fire with the spirit of love,

God will do His own work in the soul.

BOOK I.

which this obscure and secret contemplation induces and establishes within it.

Meditation on the Life and Passion of Christ an aid to the highest Contemplation.

Still, I do not mean to lay down a general rule for the cessation from meditation; that should occur when meditation is no longer feasible, and only then, when our Lord, either in the way of purgation and affliction, or of the most perfect contemplation, shall make it impossible. At other times, and on other occasions, this support must be had recourse to, namely, meditation on the Life and Passion of Christ, which is the best means of purification and of patience and of security on the road, and an admirable aid to the highest contemplation. Contemplation is nothing else but the secret, pacific, and loving infusion of God, which, if it be admitted, will set the soul on fire with the spirit of love, as I shall show in the explanation of the following verse.

Contemplation an infusion of God.

CHAPTER XI.

STANZA I.

With anxious love inflamed.

Second line of first stanza,—Earnest longing for God.

THE burning fire of love, in general, is not felt at first, for it has not begun to burn, either because of our natural want of purity, or because the soul, not understanding its own state, has not given it a peaceful rest within itself. Sometimes, however, whether that be the case or not, a certain anxiety about God arises; and the more it grows, the more the soul feels itself touched and inflamed with the love of God, without knowing how or whence that feeling arises, except that at times this burning so inflames it that it longs earnestly after God. David in this night said of himself, 'My heart hath been inflamed, and my reins have been changed, and I am brought to nothing, and I knew not.'* That is, 'my heart hath been

* Ps. lxxii. 21, 22.

inflamed' in the love of contemplation; 'my reins,' that is, my tastes and affections also, have been changed from the sensitive to the spiritual way by this holy dryness, and in my cessation from them all, and 'I am brought to nothing, and I knew not.' The soul, as I have just said, not knowing the way it goeth, sees itself brought to nothing as to all things of Heaven and earth, wherein it delighted before, and on fire with love, not knowing how.

Martyrdom of Divine love.

And because occasionally this fire of love grows in the spirit greatly, the longings of the soul for God are so deep that the very bones seem to dry up in that thirst, the bodily health to wither, the natural warmth and energies to perish in the intensity of that thirst of love. The soul feels it to be a living thirst. Such, also, was the feeling of David when he said, 'My soul hath thirsted after the strong living God.'* It is as if he had said, my thirst is a strong living thirst. We may say of this thirst, that being a living thirst, it kills. Though this thirst is not continuously, but only occasionally, violent, nevertheless it is always felt in some degree.

Love not felt at first, but after suffering.

I commenced by observing that this love, in general, is not felt at first, but only the aridity and emptiness of which I am speaking; and then, instead of love, which is afterwards enkindled, what the soul feels amidst its aridities and the emptiness of its faculties is a general painful anxiety about God, and a certain misgiving that it is not serving Him. But a soul anxious and afflicted for His sake, is a sacrifice pleasing unto God. Secret contemplation keeps the soul in this state of anxiety, until, in the course of time, having purged the sensitive nature of man, in some degree, of its natural forces and affections by means of the aridities it occasions, it shall have kindled within it this Divine love. But in the meantime, like a sick man in the hands of his physician, all it has to

* Ps. xli. 3.

BOOK I.

do, in the obscure night and dry purgation of the desire, is to suffer, healing its many imperfections and practising many virtues, that it may become meet for this Divine love, of which I speak while explaining the following line:

Third line,—'O happy lot!'

O happy lot!

When God establishes the soul in the obscure night, that He may purify, prepare, and subdue its inferior nature, and unite it to the spirit, by depriving it of light, and causing it to cease from meditation—as He afterwards establishes it also in the spiritual night, that He may purify the spirit, and prepare it for union with God — the soul acquires such great advantages, though it seems not so, that it looks upon it as great happiness to have escaped from the bondage of the senses in that happy night, and therefore it sings—'O happy lot!'

Fourth line,—The escape from the Sensitive Appetite.

It is necessary now for us to point out the benefits which accrue to the soul in this night, and for the sake of which it pronounces itself happy in having passed through it. All these benefits are comprised in these words:—'Forth unobserved I went.'

This going forth of the soul is to be understood of that subjection to sense under which it laboured when it was seeking after God in weak, limited, and fitful ways, for such are the ways of man's sensitive nature. It then fell at every step into a thousand imperfections and ignorances, as I showed while speaking of the seven capital sins, from all of which the spiritual man is delivered in the obscure night which quenches all desire in all things whatsoever, and deprives him of all his lights in meditation, and brings with it other innumerable blessings towards the acquirement of virtue. It will be a great joy and comfort to him who travels on this road, to observe how that which seemed so rugged and harsh, so contrary to spiritual sweetness, works in him so great a good. This good flows from going forth, as to all affections and operations of the soul, from all created things, in this obscure night, and journeying towards those which are eternal, which is a great happiness and a great good. In the first place, because the desires are extinguished in all things; and in the second place, because they are few who persevere and enter in at the narrow gate, by the strait way that leadeth to life: 'How narrow is the gate and strait is the way that leadeth to life, and few there are that find it!'*

Happiness of leaving the creature for the Creator.

The narrow gate is the night of sense. The soul detaches itself from sense that it may enter into that night, directing itself by faith, which is a stranger to all sense, that it may afterwards travel along the strait road of the other night of the spirit, by which it advances towards God in most pure faith, which is the means of the Divine union. This road, because so strait, dark, and terrible—for there is no comparison between its trials and darkness and those of the night of sense —is travelled by very few, but its blessings are so much the more. I proceed now to speak with the utmost brevity of the blessings of the night of sense, that I may pass on to the other.

CHAPTER XII.

Of the benefits of the Night of Sense.

Joy at the weaning of the soul from the goods of the Sensitive Appetite.

THIS night and purgation of the appetite is full of happiness to the soul, involving grand benefits, though it seems as if all were lost. As Abraham 'made a great feast on the day of Isaac's weaning,' † so there is joy in Heaven when God takes a soul out of its swaddling-clothes; when He takes His arms from under it, and makes it walk alone; when He denies it the milk of the breast and the delicate food of children, and gives it bread with the crust to eat; when He makes it eat the bread of the strong, which is presented, in the aridities and darkness

* S. Matt. vii. 14. † Gen. xxi. 8.

BOOK I.

Benefits of the Night of Sense.

1. Infused Contemplation.

of sense, to the spirit emptied and dried of all sensible sweetness; namely, the bread of infused Contemplation. This is the first and principal benefit, and from which almost all the others flow.

2. Knowledge of our own vileness.

Of these, the first is a knowledge of our own selves and our own vileness. For over and above that this knowledge ordinarily includes those favours which God bestows on the soul, these aridities and the emptiness of the faculties as to their former abounding, and the difficulty which good works present, bring the soul to a knowledge of its own vileness and misery, which in the season of prosperity it saw not. This truth is vividly shadowed forth in the Book of Exodus. There we read that God, willing to humble the people and bring them to a knowledge of themselves, commanded them to lay aside their ornaments and festival attire, which they ordinarily wore in the wilderness, saying, 'Lay aside thy ornaments;' that is, lay aside thy holiday garments, and put on thy common vestments, that thou mayest know what treatment thou hast deserved. It is as if He said to the people: 'Inasmuch as the ornaments you wear, being those of joy and festivity, are the cause why you think not meanly of yourselves—you really are mean—lay them aside; so that henceforth clad in vile garments, you may acknowledge that you deserve nothing better, and also who and what you are.'

Here the soul learns the reality of its own misery, which before it knew not. For in the day of its festivity, when it found great sweetness, comfort, and help in God, it was highly satisfied and pleased, thinking that it rendered some service to God. For though it may not explicitly say so, yet, on account of the satisfaction it feels, some such feeling still clings to it. But when it has put on the garments of heaviness, of aridity and abandonment, when its previous lights have become darkness, it will then possess in reality that excellent and necessary virtue of self-knowledge, counting itself for nothing, and having no satisfaction in itself, because it sees that of itself it does and can do nothing. This diminished satisfaction with self, and the affliction it feels because it thinks that it is not serving God, God esteems more highly than all its former delights and all its good works, however great they may have been. For then many imperfections and ignorances clung to it; but now in the garb of aridity, it derives not only those fruits of which I am speaking, but others also of which I shall presently speak, and much more than I can speak of, as from their proper source and fount of self-knowledge.

3. Reverence for God.

In the next place, the soul learns to commune with God with more reverence and gentleness; and this is always necessary while it converses with the Most High. Now, in its prosperous days of sweetness and consolation, the soul was less observant of reverence, for the favours, of which it was then the object, rendered the appetite somewhat bold with God, and less reverential than it should have been. Thus it was with Moses, when he heard the voice of God; for carried away by the delight he felt, he ventured, without further consideration, to draw near, till God commanded him to stop, saying, 'Come not nigh hither; put off the shoes from thy feet.'* This teaches us how reverently and discreetly in spiritual detachment we are to converse with God. When Moses had become obedient to the voice, he remained so reverent and considerate, that not only did he refrain from advancing, but, in the words of Scripture, 'durst not look at God.'† For having put off the shoes of desire and sweetness, he recognised profoundly his own meanness in the sight of God, for such a state of mind became him when about to listen to the Divine words.

Example of Moses.

The temper of mind to which Job was brought in order

* Exod. iii. 5.

† Ib. 6.

BOOK I.

Example of Job.

that he might converse with God, was not that of delight and grandeur, such as he had before. God left him in misery, naked on a dung-hill, persecuted by his friends, filled with sorrow and grief, covered with worms:* then it was that the Most High, Who lifteth up 'the poor out of the dunghill,'† was pleased to communicate Himself to Job in greater abundance and sweetness, revealing to him 'the deep mysteries of His Wisdom,'‡ as He had never done before in the days of Job's prosperity.

4. Spiritual Illumination.

And now that I am on this subject, I must here point out another great benefit of the Obscure Night and aridity of the sensitive appetite. It is this: God, verifying the words of the Prophet, 'Then My light shall rise up in darkness,'§ enlightens the soul, so that it shall confess, not only its own misery and meanness, but also His Grandeur and Majesty. Not only does the extinction of desires, and the suppression of sensible joy and consolation, purify the intellect for the reception of the truth—for sensible joys and desires even of spiritual things obscure and perplex the mind—but the trials and aridities of sense also enlighten and quicken the intellect; as it is written, 'Vexation alone shall make you understand what you hear.'‖ Vexation shall make us understand how God in His Divine Wisdom proceeds to instruct a soul, emptied and cleansed—for such it must be before it can be the recipient of the Divine influence—in a supernatural way, in the obscure and arid night of contemplation, which He could not do before, when it was given up to its former sweetnesses and joys.

The Prophet sets this truth before us with great clearness, saying, 'Whom shall He teach knowledge? and whom shall He make to understand the hearing? Them that are weaned from the milk, that are drawn away from the breasts.'¶ The

* Job ii. 8; xxx. 17, 18. † Ps. cxii. 7. ‡ Job xxxviii.
§ Is. lviii. 10. ‖ Is. xxviii. 19. ¶ Ib. 9.

temper of mind, then, meet for the Divine influence is not so much the milk of spiritual sweetness, nor the breasts of sweet reflections in the sensitive powers, such as the soul once enjoyed, as the absence of both the one and the other. And therefore, if we would listen to the voice of the great King with due reverence, the soul must stand upright, and not lean on the affections of sense for support. We must be like the Prophet, who said of himself, 'I will stand upon my watch, and fix my foot upon the tower, and I will watch to see what will be said to me.'* To stand upon the watch, is to cast off all desires; to fix the foot, is to cease from all reflections of sense, that we may behold and understand what God will speak to us. Thus out of this obscure night springs first the knowledge of oneself, and on that, as on a foundation, is built up the knowledge of God. 'Let me know myself,' saith S. Augustine, 'and I shall then know Thee, O my God,' for, as Philosophers say, one extreme is known by another.

'Noverim me Domine et cognoscam Te.'

In order to show more fully how effectual is the night of sense, in its aridity and desolation, to enlighten the soul more and more, I produce the words of the Psalmist, which so clearly describe the power of this night in bringing men to the knowledge of God: 'In a desert land, and where there is no way, and no water; so in the sanctuary have I come before Thee, to see Thy power and Thy glory.'† The Psalmist does not say — and it is worthy of observation — that his previous sweetness and delight were any dispositions meet for the knowledge of the glory of God, but rather that aridity and weaning from the sensitive faculties, which are here meant by the 'barren land.' Neither does he say that his reflections and meditations on Divine things, with which he was once familiar, had led him to the knowledge

* Habac. ii. 1.

† Ps. lxii. 3.

BOOK I.

and contemplation of God's power, but, rather, his inability to meditate on God, to form reflections by the help of his imagination, which he describes by a 'land where there is no way.' The means, therefore, of attaining to the knowledge of God, and of ourselves, is the Obscure Night with all its aridities and emptiness; though not in the fulness of the other night of the spirit; for this knowledge is, as it were, the beginning of the other.

5. Humility.

Amid the aridities and emptiness of this night of the desires, the soul acquires also spiritual Humility, which is the virtue opposed to the first capital sin, spiritual pride. The humility acquired by self-knowledge purifies the soul from all the imperfections into which we fell in the day of our prosperity. For now, seeing ourselves so dried up and miserable, it does not enter into our thoughts, even for a moment, to consider ourselves better than others, or that we have outstripped them on the spiritual road, as we did before; on the contrary, we acknowledge that others are better than we are.

6. Love of our neighbours.

Out of this grows the love of our neighbours, for we now esteem them, and no longer judge them as we used to do, when we looked upon ourselves as exceedingly fervent, and upon others as not. Now we see nothing but our own misery, which we keep so constantly before our eyes that we can look upon nothing else. This state is admirably described by David himself in this obscure night, saying, 'I was dumb, and was humbled, and kept silence from good things, and my sorrow was renewed.'* All the good of his soul seemed to him so mean that he could not prevail upon himself to speak of it; and he was silent as to the good of others, because of the pain he felt in the knowledge of his own wretchedness.

7. Docility.

In this state, too, men are submissive and obedient in the

* Ps. xxxviii. 3.

spiritual way, for when they see their own wretchedness they not only listen to instruction, but desire to have it from any one who will guide their steps and tell them what they ought to do. That presumption which sometimes attended them in their prosperity is now gone; and, finally, all those imperfections are swept clean away to which I referred when I was treating of spiritual pride.

CHAPTER XIII.

Of other benefits of the Night of Sense.

8. Liberty of spirit.

THE imperfections of spiritual avarice, under the influence of which the soul coveted all spiritual goods, and was never satisfied in the practices of devotion, because of its eagerness for the sweetness it found therein, become now, in this arid and obscure night, sufficiently corrected. For when the spiritual man finds no more sweetness and delight, as he was wont to do, in spiritual things, but rather bitterness and vexation, he has recourse to them with such moderation that he loses now, perhaps, through defect, what he lost before through excess. Though, in general, to those who are come to this night God gives humility and readiness, but without sweetness, in order that they may obey Him solely through love. Thus they detach themselves from many things, because they find no more sweetness in them.

9. Spiritual Purity.

The soul is purified, also, from those impurities of spiritual luxury of which I have spoken before, in this aridity and loathing of the senses which it now finds in spiritual things; for those impurities proceed, in general, from the sweetness which flowed occasionally from the spirit into the sense.

The imperfections of spiritual gluttony, from which the soul is delivered in the obscure night, have been discussed in

BOOK I.

10. Spiritual Temperance.

a former chapter,* though not all, because they cannot be numbered. I shall not enumerate them here, for I wish to conclude the subject of this night, that I may pass on to the other, with regard to which I have serious things to write. Suffice it, then, to say, that the soul, in addition to the benefits already mentioned, gains, in this night, innumerable others, in its resistance to spiritual gluttony. It is set free from those imperfections there enumerated, and from many other evils greater than those described, into which too many fall, as we learn by experience, because they have not corrected their desires in the matter of spiritual gluttony. For when God, in this arid and obscure night, so curbs the desire and bridles concupiscence that the soul can scarcely feed at all upon the sensible sweetness of heavenly or of earthly things—and this so continuously that the soul corrects, mortifies, and controls its concupiscence and desires, so that the very forces of its passions seem to be broken down—marvellous benefits flow forth from that spiritual temperance, in addition to those I have mentioned; for, through mortifying concupiscence and the desires, the soul dwells in spiritual tranquillity and peace; because, where concupiscence and desire have no sway, there is no trouble, but, rather, the peace and consolations of God.

11. Holy fear of God.

Another benefit is this, a perpetual recollection of God, with fear lest we should be going back on the spiritual way. This is a great benefit, and not the least, of aridity and the purgation of the appetite, for the soul is cleansed thereby from those imperfections which disfigured it through the affections and desires, the effect of which is to obscure and deaden the soul.

12. Patience, Love, and Peace.

Another great benefit of this night is, the practice of many virtues at once; such as patience and longsuffering, which are

* Chap. vi.

well tried in these aridities, when men persevere in their spiritual exercises without sweetness or comfort. The love of God is practised, because men are no longer attracted by sweetness and consolation, but by God only. The virtue of fortitude also is practised, because amid the hardships, and the absence of sweetness, which the soul now endures, it gathers strength from weakness, and so becomes strong: finally, all the virtues, cardinal, theological, and moral, are practised amidst these aridities.

David tells us from his own experience that the soul gains these four benefits in this obscure night, namely, delight of peace, constant recollection of God, pureness of soul, and the practice of all virtues. 'My soul,' saith he, 'refused to be comforted; I remembered God and was delighted, and was exercised, and my spirit swooned away.' He adds also: 'I meditated in the night with my own heart, and I was exercised, and I swept my spirit'* clean of all affections.

13. Gentleness with God, self, and others.

The soul is purified also in this aridity of the desires from the imperfections of envy, anger, and sloth, and acquires the opposite virtues. Softened and humbled by these aridities, by the hardships, temptations, and afflictions which in this night try it, it becomes gentle with God, with itself, and with its neighbours. It is no longer impatiently angry with itself because of its own faults, nor with its neighbours for theirs; neither does it avoid with a kind of dislike the things of God, nor utter unseemly complaints because He does not perfect His work at once.

14. Holy Emulation.

As to envy, the soul is now charitably disposed towards everyone, and if any remain, it is no longer vicious as before, when the soul was afflicted at the preference shown to others, or at their greater progress; for now it yields to everyone considering its own misery, and the envy it feels, if it feels any, is a virtuous envy, a desire to emulate them, which is great virtue.

* Ps. lxxvi. 3, 4, 7.

BOOK I.

15. Fortitude amid aridities.

The sloth and weariness now felt in spiritual things are no longer vicious as they were once. They were once the fruit of spiritual delights which the soul experienced at times, and sought after when it had them not. But this present weariness proceeds not from the failure of sweetness, for God has taken it all away in this purgation of the appetite.

Other innumerable benefits flow from this arid contemplation; for, in the midst of these aridities and hardships, God communicates to the soul, when it least expects it, spiritual sweetness, most pure love, and spiritual knowledge of the most exalted kind, of greater worth and profit than any of which it had previous experience, though at first the soul may not think so, for the spiritual influence now communicated is most delicate, and imperceptible by sense.

16. Twelve Fruits of the Holy Ghost.

Finally, inasmuch as the soul is purified of all affections and sensitive desires, it attains to liberty of spirit, wherein it acquires the twelve fruits of the Holy Ghost. It is also delivered in a most wonderful way from the hands of its three enemies — the devil, the world, and the flesh; for when all sensible delight and sweetness are quenched, the devil, the world, and the flesh have no weapons wherewith to assail it.

These aridities, then, make the soul love God in all pureness, for now its operations depend no longer upon the pleasure and sweetness which it found in its works—as perhaps was the case when that sweetness was present—but only in the desire it has to please God. The soul is not now presumptuous and self-satisfied, as perhaps it may have been in the day of its prosperity, but timid and diffident of self, deriving no satisfaction whatever from self-contemplation. Herein consists that holy fear by which virtues are preserved and grow. This aridity quenches concupiscence, and subdues our natural spirits; for now, when God infuses, from time to time, His own sweetness into the soul, it would be strange if it found by any efforts of its own any comfort or sweetness in any spiritual act or practice.

17. Anxious desire for the service of God.

The fear of God and anxiety for His service increase in this arid night; for as the breasts of sensuality, which nourished and sustained the desires that clung to them, become dry, nothing remains in that aridity and detachment but an anxious desire to serve Him, which is most pleasing unto God, as it is written: 'a sacrifice to God is an afflicted spirit.'*

Last benefit, — Deliverance from the World, the Flesh, and the Devil.

When the soul beholds the many and great benefits which have fallen to its lot in this arid purgation through which it passed, it cries out with truth, 'oh, happy lot, forth unobserved I went.' I escaped from the bondage and thraldom of my sensitive desires and affections, unobserved, so that none of my three enemies were able to hinder me. These enemies of the soul so bind and imprison it, that it cannot go forth out of itself to the liberty of the perfect love of God, by the help of its tastes and desires; without which they can do nothing against it.

And, therefore, when the four passions of the soul, joy and grief, hope and fear, are subdued by persevering mortifications, when the natural sensitive appetite is lulled by continual aridities, when the concert of the senses is silent, and when the interior powers have ceased from discursive reflections—this is the household of man's lower nature—these enemies cannot hinder the spiritual liberty of the soul, and the house thereof remains tranquil and at rest.

CHAPTER XIV.

The last line of the first stanza explained.

'My house being now at rest.' When the house of sensuality was at rest, that is, when the passions were mortified,

* Ps. l. 19.

BOOK I.

concupiscence quenched, the desires subdued and lulled to sleep in the blessed night of sensitive purgation, the soul began to set out on the way of the spirit, the way of proficients, which is also called the Illuminative Way, or the way of infused contemplation, wherein God Himself nourishes and refreshes the soul without the help of any active efforts that itself may make. Such as I have said is this night and purgation of the senses.

Trials of the Night of sense.

But this night, in their case, who are to enter into that other more awful night of the spirit, that they may go forwards to the Divine union of the love of God—it is not everyone, but only a few who do so in general—is attended with heavy trials and temptations of sense of long continuance, but in some longer than in others; for to some is sent the angel of Satan, the spirit of impurity, to buffet them with horrible and violent temptations of the flesh, to afflict their minds with filthy thoughts, and their imaginations with representations of sin most vividly depicted; which, at times, becomes an affliction more grievous than death.

1. The sting of the flesh.

2. The spirit of blasphemy.

This night is also occasionally attended by the spirit of blasphemy; the thoughts and conceptions are overrun with intolerable blasphemies, and, at times, suggested to the imagination with such violence as almost to break forth in words; this, too, is a heavy affliction.

3. The spirit of giddiness.

Again, another spirit, called by the Prophet, 'the spirit of giddiness,'* is sent to torment them. This spirit so obscures their judgment that they are filled with a thousand scruples and perplexities; they can never satisfy themselves about them, nor submit their judgment therein to the counsel and direction of others. This is one of the most grievous stings and horrors of this night, most like to that which passes in the night of the spirit.

* Is. xix. 14.

CHAP. XIV.

The soul purified for the Divine Union by suffering.

God ordinarily sends these violent storms and temptations, in the night of sensitive purgation, upon those whom He is about to lead afterwards into the other night—though all do not enter in—that being thus chastened and buffeted they may prove themselves, dispose and habituate sense and faculties for the union of the Divine wisdom to which they are to be then admitted. For if the soul be not tempted, exercised, and tried, in temptations and afflictions, the senses thereof will never attain to wisdom. 'What doth he know,' asks the Wise Man, 'that hath not been tried? . . . He that hath no experience knoweth little. . . . He that hath not been tried, what manner of things doth he know?'* Jeremias also bears witness to the same truth, saying: 'thou hast chastised me, and I was instructed.'† The most proper form of this chastening, for him who will apply himself unto wisdom, are those interior trials of which I am now speaking. They are the most effectual for purging the sensitive nature from all sweetness and consolations, to which, by reason of our natural infirmities, we are addicted, and most capable of really humbling the soul that it may be prepared for its coming exaltation.

Duration and intensity of trials determined by God;

But how long the soul will continue in this fast and penance of sense no one can with certainty tell. It is not the same in all men, neither are all men subjected to the same temptations. These trials are measured by the Divine will, and are proportioned to the imperfections, many or few, which are to be purged away: and also to the degree of union in love to which God intends to elevate a particular soul; that is the measure of its humiliations, both in their intensity and duration.

And proportioned to strength of the soul.

Those who are endowed with the capacity for suffering, and who have force sufficient to endure, are purified in more intense trials, and in less time. But those who are weak are

* Ecclus. xxxiv. 9, 10, 11.

† Jerem. xxxi. 18.

purified very slowly, with weak temptations, and the night of their purgation is long: their senses are refreshed from time to time lest they should fall away; these, however, come late to the pureness of their perfection in this life, and some of them never. These persons are not clearly in the purgative night, nor clearly out of it; for though they make no onward progress, yet in order that they may be humble and know themselves, God tries them for a season in aridities and temptations, and visits them with His consolations at intervals lest they should become faint-hearted, and seek for comfort in the ways of the world.

From other souls, still weaker, God, as it were, hides Himself, that He may try them in His love, for without this hiding of His face from them they would never learn how to approach Him. But those souls that are to go forwards to so blessed and exalted a state as this of the union of love, however quickly God may lead them, tarry long, in general, amidst aridities, as we see by experience. Having now brought the first book to a close, I proceed to treat of the second night.

O Domine, pati et contemni pro Te!

BOOK II.

OF THE NIGHT OF THE SPIRIT.

CHAPTER I.

The second Night; that of the spirit. When it begins.

CHAP. I.

Description of a soul which has passed through the Sensitive Night.

THE soul, which God is leading onwards, enters not into the union of love at once when it has passed through the aridities and trials of the first purgation and night of sense. It must spend some time, perhaps years, after quitting the state of beginners, in exercising itself in the state of proficients. In this state—like a man released from a rigourous imprisonment—it occupies itself in Divine things with much greater freedom and satisfaction, and its joy is more abundant and interior than it ever experienced in the beginning before it entered the sensitive night; its imagination and faculties being no longer tied down, as hitherto, to spiritual thoughts and reflections, it now rises at once to most tranquil and loving contemplation, and finds spiritual sweetness without the fatigue of meditation. But as the purgation of the soul is still somewhat incomplete — the chief part, the purgation of the spirit, being wanting, without which, by reason of the mutual connection between our higher and lower nature, man being an individual, the purgation of sense, however violent it may have been, is not finished and perfect—it will never be without some aridities, darkness, and trials, sometimes much more severe than in the past, which are, as it were, signs and heralds of the coming night of the

BOOK II.

spirit, though not so lasting as that night; for when the days or the season of this tempestuous night have passed, the soul recovers at once its wonted serenity. It is in this way that God purifies some souls whom He does not raise to so high a degree of love as others. He admits them at intervals into the night of contemplation or spiritual purgation, causing the sun to shine upon them occasionally, and then to hide its face, according to the words of the Psalmist: 'He sendeth His crystal,' that is, contemplation, 'like morsels.'* These morsels of obscure contemplation are, however, never so intense as is that awful night of contemplation of which I am speaking, and into which God purposely leads the soul, that He may elevate it to the Divine union.

That sweetness and interior delight, which the proficients find so easily and so plentifully, come now in greater abundance than before, overflowing into the senses more than they were wont to do previous to the sensitive purgation. And as the senses are now more pure, they can taste of the sweetness of the spirit in their way with greater facility; but since the sensitive part of the soul is weak, without any capacity for the strong things of the spirit, they who are in the state of proficients are liable, by reason of the spiritual communications which reach to the sensitive part, to great infirmities and sufferings, and physical derangements, and consequently weariness of mind, as it is written: 'the corruptible body . . . . presseth down the mind.'† Hence the communications made to these cannot be very strong, intense, or spiritual, such as they are required to be for the Divine union with God, because of the weakness and corruption of the sensitive part which has a share in them.

Cause of ecstasies,—what.

Here is the source of ecstasies, raptures, and dislocation of the bones which always happen whenever these communica-

* Ps. cxlvii. 17.

† Wisd. ix. 15.

tions are not purely spiritual, that is, granted to the mind alone, as in the case of the perfect, already purified in the second night of the spirit. In them these raptures and physical sufferings have no place, for they enjoy liberty of spirit with unclouded and unsuspended senses. To make it clear how necessary it is for proficients to enter into the night of the spirit, I will now proceed to point out certain imperfections and dangers to which they are liable.

CHAPTER II.

Of certain imperfections of Proficients.

PROFICIENTS labour under two kinds of imperfections; one habitual, the other actual. The habitual imperfections are their affections and imperfect habits which still remain, like roots, in the mind, where the purgation of sense could not penetrate. The difference between the purgation of these and of the others, is like the difference between plucking out a root, and tearing off a branch, or like removing a fresh, and an old, stain. For, as I have said, the purgation of sense is merely the gate and entrance of contemplation, and serves rather to harmonise sense and spirit than to unite the latter with God. The stains of the old man still remain in the mind, though not visible, and if they be not removed by the strong soap and lye of the purgation of this night, the mind cannot attain to the pureness of the Divine union.

Habitual imperfections of Proficients. 1. Roots of sin.

They suffer also from a certain dulness of mind, and natural rudeness which every man contracts by sin; a distraction and dissipation of mind, which must be refined, enlightened, and made recollected in the sufferings and hardships of this night. All those who have not advanced beyond the state of proficients are subject to these habitual imperfections, which

2. Dulness of mind.

BOOK. II.

cannot coexist with the perfect State of Union with God in love.

Actual imperfections of Proficients.

But all are not subject to actual imperfections in the same way; some, whose spiritual goods are so much on the surface, and so much under the influence of sense, fall into certain improprieties and dangers, of which I spoke in the beginning. For as they admit into their minds and senses so many communications, so that they have frequent imaginary and spiritual visions—for this happens together with other spiritual impressions to many of them in this state, wherein the devil and their own proper fancy delude the soul—and as Satan is wont with so much sweetness to insinuate, and impress such things upon them, they are easily deluded and influenced by him, because they do not take the precaution to resign themselves into the hands of God, and defend themselves with all their might against these visions and impressions. For now the devil causes them both to believe in vain visions and false prophecies, and to presume that God and His Saints are speaking to them: they also frequently believe in their own fancies.

1. Self-deception.

2. Pride and presumption.

Now, too, Satan fills them with pride and presumption; under the influence of vanity and arrogance they make a show of themselves in the performance of exterior acts which have an appearance of sanctity, such as ecstasies and other phenomena. They become bold with God, losing holy fear, which is the key and guard of all virtue. Many of them become so entangled in manifold delusions, and so inveterate have their falsehoods grown, that their restoration to the pure road of virtue and real spirituality is exceedingly doubtful. They fall into this miserable condition because, too confident in themselves, they gave way to these spiritual apprehensions and impressions when they began to advance on the road of spirituality.

I have much to say of these imperfections, and how much

Necessity of the Spiritual Night for Perfection.

more incurable they are than the others, because they are considered as more spiritual than those which preceded them, but I shall pass on. One thing, however, I must say, to show how necessary for the further advancement of the soul the Spiritual Night is, that there is no one proficient, however great may be his exertions, who can be free from many of these natural affections and imperfect habits, the purification of which must, as I have said, necessarily precede the Divine union. Besides, and I have said it before, inasmuch as the spiritual communications reach also to the lower part of the soul, they cannot be as intense, pure, and strong, as it is necessary they should be for the purpose of the Divine union; and, therefore, if that is to be attained, the soul must enter the second night of the spirit where—perfectly detaching sense and spirit from all sweetness and from all these apprehensions—these communications will guide it on the road of obscure and pure faith, the proper and adequate means of Union, as it is written: 'I will espouse thee to Me in faith,' * that is, I will unite Myself to thee in faith.

CHAPTER III.

Introduction.

True Spiritual sweetness harmonizes sense with spirit, and gives courage to the will.

PROFICIENTS, then, have had experience of these sweet communications, in order that the sensitive part of the soul, allured and attracted by the spiritual sweetness overflowing into the senses, may be harmonised and united with the spiritual part; both parts having to eat of the same spiritual food, each in its own way, off the same dish of their one individuality, that they might be prepared, united and conformed, for the sufferings of the sharp and rough purgation of the spirit which is

* Os. ii. 20.

BOOK II.

before them. In that purgation the two parts of the soul, the spiritual and the sensitive, are to be wholly purified, for neither of them can be perfectly purified without the other, and the purgation of sense is then effectual when that of the spirit commences in earnest. Hence it follows that the night of sense may and should be called a certain re-formation and bridling of the appetite rather than purgation, because all the imperfections and disorders of the sensitive part having their strength and roots in the mind, can never be wholly purged away until the evil habits, rebelliousness and perverseness of the mind are corrected. Therefore, in this night ensuing, both the parts of the soul are purified together: this is the end for which it was necessary to have passed through the re-formation of the first night, and to have attained to that tranquillity which is its fruit, in order that, united together in spirit, they may both be purified and suffer together with the greater courage, most necessary for so violent and sharp a purgation. For if the weakness of the inferior part be not redressed, and if it have acquired no courage in God, in the sweet communions with Him subsequently enjoyed, nature would have given way, unprepared for the trials of this night.

The Sensitive Night a re-formation of the appetite.

The Spiritual Night a purgation of sense and spirit together.

Necessity of Courage.

The intercourse of proficients with God is still most mean, because the gold of the spirit is not purified and refined. They think and speak of Him as children, and their feelings are those of children, as described by the Apostle: 'When I was a child, I spake as a child, I understood as a child, I thought as a child;'* because they have not yet reached Perfection, which is Union with God in love. But in the state of perfection, having grown to manhood, they do great things in spirit — all their actions and all their faculties being now rather Divine than human, as I shall hereafter explain — for God is stripping them of the old man, and

* 1 Cor. xiii. 11.

CHAP. III.

Means of the final purification of the soul.

putting on the new, as it is written: 'Put on the new man, who is created according to God;' * and again, 'Be reformed in the newness of your mind.'† He now denudes the faculties, the affections, and feelings, spiritual and sensitive, interior and exterior, leaving the intellect obscure, the will dry, the memory empty, the affections of the soul in profoundest affliction, bitterness, and distress — withholding from the soul the former sweetness it had in spiritual things, that this privation may be one of the principles, of which the mind has need, in order that the spiritual form of the spirit, which is the union of love, may enter into it and be one with it.

All this our Lord effects in the soul by means of this pure and obscure contemplation, as it is described in the first stanza. True, I have explained that in the beginning of my work, on the night of sense, yet its chief signification belongs to this second night of the spirit, because that is the chief part of the purification of the soul. I shall, therefore, apply it in this sense, and explain it here again.

CHAPTER IV.

The first stanza spiritually explained.

In an Obscure Night,
With anxious love inflamed.
O, happy lot!
Forth unobserved I went,
My house being now at rest.

Paraphrase of the first stanza according to the second Night.

TAKING these words, then, with reference to purgation, contemplation, or detachment, or poverty of spirit — these are, as it were, one and the same thing—they may be thus explained. In poverty, unsupported by any apprehensions, in the obscurity of the intellect, in the conflict of the will, in the affliction and distress of memory, lost in the obscurity in pure faith,

* Ephes. iv. 24. † Rom. xii. 2.

which is the Obscure Night of all the natural faculties, the will alone touched by grief and affliction, by the anxieties of my love of God, I went forth out of myself, out of my low conceptions and lukewarm love, out of my scanty and poor sense of God, without being hindered by the flesh or the devil.

Transformation of Memory, Intellect and Will in the Night of the Spirit.

This was to me a great blessing, a happy lot, for by annihilating and subduing my faculties, passions, and affections—the instruments of my low conceptions of God—I went forth out of the scanty intercourse and operations of my own to those of God; that is, my intellect went forth out of itself, and from human became Divine, for united to God in that purgation, it understands no more within its former limits and narrow bounds, but in the Divine Wisdom to which it is united.

My will went forth out of itself transformed into the Divine will, for now, united with the Divine love, it loves no more with its former scanty powers and circumscribed capacity, but with the energy and pureness of the Divine Spirit. Thus the will acts no more in the things of God in a human way, and the memory also is transformed into the eternal apprehensions of glory. Finally, all the energies and affections of the soul are, in this night and purgation of the old man, renewed into a Divine temper and delight.

CHAPTER V.

Obscure Contemplation is not a night only, but pain and torment also for the soul.

In an Obscure Night,

Night of the Spirit,—its definition.

THIS Obscure Night is a certain inflowing of God into the soul, which cleanses it of its ignorances and imperfections, habitual, natural, and spiritual. Contemplatives call it infused contemplation, or Mystical Theology, whereby God secretly teaches the soul and instructs it in the perfection of love, without efforts on its own part beyond loving attention to God, listening to His voice and admitting the light He sends, without understanding how this is infused contemplation. It is the loving Wisdom of God that produces special effects in the soul, for it prepares it, by enlightening it for union with God in love: that loving Wisdom, which by enlightening purifies the blessed spirits, is that which here purifies and enlightens the soul.

CHAP. V.

The Will passive save to consent and attend.

But it may be said: Why do we call the Divine Light, which enlightens the soul and purges it of its ignorances, the Obscure Night? I reply, that the Divine Wisdom is, for two reasons, not night and darkness only, but pain and torment also to the soul. The first is, the Divine Wisdom is so high that it transcends the capacity of the soul, and therefore is, in that respect, darkness. The second reason is based on the meanness and impurity of the soul, and in that respect the Divine Wisdom is painful to it, afflictive and obscure also.

Why is the Divine Illumination called Night?

To prove the truth of the first reason we assume a principle of Philosophy, namely, the more clear and self-evident Divine things are, the more obscure and hidden they are to the soul naturally. Thus the more clear the light the more does it blind the eyes of the owl, and the stronger the sun's rays the greater the darkness of our visual organs; for the sun, in its own strength shining, overcomes them, by reason of their weakness, and deprives them of the power of seeing. So when the Divine light of contemplation shines into the soul, not yet perfectly enlightened, it causes spiritual darkness, because it not only surpasses its strength, but because it obscures it and deprives it of its natural perceptions.

Answer.

1. It is dark to imperfect faculties from excess of light.

It is for this reason that S. Dionysius and other Mystic Theologians call infused contemplation a ray of darkness, that is, for the unenlightened and unpurified soul, because the great supernatural light of contemplation overcomes the

S. Dionysius.

BOOK II.

forces of the natural intellect and deprives it of its natural way of understanding. David also hath said the same thing: 'Clouds and darkness are round about Him;'* not that this is so in reality, but in reference to our weak understanding, which, in light so great, becomes obscure and blind, unable to ascend so high. And in another place the same truth is declared: 'At the brightness that was before Him the clouds passed'† between Him and our understanding. This is the reason why the illuminating ray of hidden Wisdom, when God sends it from Himself into the soul not yet transformed, produces obscure darkness in the intellect.

2. It is painful from the meeting of contraries.

This obscure contemplation is, in its beginnings, painful also to the soul. For as the infused Divine contemplation contains many excellences in the highest degree, and the soul, which is the recipient, because not yet pure, is involved in many miseries, the result is—as two contraries cannot coexist in the same subject—that the soul must suffer and be in pain, being the subject in which the two contraries meet, and resist each other because of the purgation of the soul from its imperfections, which is being effected by contemplation. I shall show this to be the case by the following induction.

First pain,—Darkness of Self revealed in the Light of God.

In the first place, because the light and wisdom of contemplation is most pure and clear, and because the soul, within which it shines, is impure and dark, that soul which is the recipient must greatly suffer. Eyes afflicted by humours suffer pain when the clear light shines upon them; and the pain of the soul, by reason of its impurity, is immense when the Divine light shines upon it. And when the rays of this pure light strike upon the soul, in order to expel its impurities, the soul perceives itself to be so unclean and miserable that it seems as if God had set Himself against it, and itself

* Ps. xcvi. 2. † Ib. xvii. 13.

Examples of Job and David.

were set against God. So grievous and painful is this feeling —for the soul feels as if God had abandoned it—that it was one of the heaviest afflictions of Job when he was in his trial. 'Why hast Thou set me opposite to Thee, and I am become burdensome to myself?'* The soul sees distinctly in this clear and pure light, though obscurely, its own impurity, and acknowledges its own unworthiness before God and all creatures. And what pains it still more is the fear it has that it will never cease to be unworthy, and that all its goodness is gone. This is the fruit of that profound depression, under which the mind labours, in the knowledge and sense of its own wickedness and misery. For now the Divine and obscure light reveals to it all its wretchedness, and it sees clearly that of itself it can never be otherwise. To the same effect are the following words of the Psalmist: 'For iniquities Thou hast chastised man, and Thou hast made his soul pine away as a spider.'†

Second pain,—Weakness of self felt under the strength of God.

In the second place, the pain of the soul has its sources in its natural and spiritual weakness; for when the Divine contemplation flows within it with a certain vehemence, in order to strengthen it and subdue it, it is then so pained in its weakness as almost to faint away, particularly at those times when the Divine contemplation seizes upon it with a greater degree of vehemence; for sense and spirit, as if bowed down by a heavy and dark burden, suffer and groan in agony so great that death itself would be a relief. This was the experience of Job when he cried, 'I will not that He contend with me with much strength, nor that He oppress me with the weight of His greatness.'‡ The soul bowed down by this burden of oppression feels itself so removed out of God's favour that it thinks—and it is so in truth—that all things which consoled it formerly have utterly failed it, and that no

* Job vii. 20. † Ps. xxxviii. 12. ‡ Job xxiii. 6.

BOOK II.

To the weak soul the gentle hand of God feels heavy.

one is left to pity it. Job, in like circumstances, has said, 'Have pity upon me, have pity upon me, at least you my friends, because the hand of the Lord hath touched me.'* Wonderful and piteous sight! So great are the weakness and impurity of the soul that the hand of God, so soft and so gentle, is felt to be so heavy and oppressive, though neither pressing nor resting on it, but merely touching it, and that, too, in mercy; for He touches the soul not to chastise it, but to load it with His graces.

CHAPTER VI.

Of other sufferings of the soul in this night.

Third pain,—Loss of God felt in conscious unworthiness.

THE third suffering and affliction of the soul is the consequence of the meeting of the two extremes together — the human and the Divine: the latter being the purgative contemplation; the human, being the soul itself. When the Divine touches the soul to renew it and to ripen it, so as to make it Divine, to detach it from its habitual affections and qualities of the old man, to which it clings and adheres most closely, it so breaks and bruises it, swallowing it up in profound darkness, that the soul seems to perish and waste away, at the sight of its own wretchedness, by a cruel spiritual death. It feels as if it were swallowed up and devoured by a wild beast, suffering the pangs of Jonas in the belly of the whale. For it must lie buried in the grave of this obscure death that it may attain to the spiritual resurrection for which it hopes. David describes the nature of this pain and suffering — though it really baffles description — saying, 'The sorrows of death surrounded me . . . the sorrows

Death before the new life.

* Job xix. 21.

CHAP. VI.

of hell encompassed me. . . . In my affliction I called upon the Lord, and I cried to my God.'*

The soul feels abandoned by God and man.

But the greatest affliction of the soul in this state is the thought that God has abandoned it, of which it has no doubt; that He has cast it away into darkness as an abominable thing. This belief in its own abandonment is a most grievous and pitiable affliction. David experienced the same trials when he said, 'Like the slain sleeping in the sepulchres, of whom Thou art mindful no more; and they are cast off from Thy hand. They have laid me in the lower pit, in the dark places, and in the shadow of death. Thy wrath is strong over me; and all Thy waves Thou hast brought in upon me.'† For, in truth, when the soul is in the pangs of purgative contemplation, the shadow of death and the pains of hell are most acutely felt, for these consist in the sense of its being without God, that He has abandoned it in His wrath and has cast it down beneath the burden of His heavy displeasure. All this and even more the soul feels, for a fearful apprehension has come upon it that thus it will be with it for ever. It has also the same sense of abandonment with respect to all creatures, and that it is an object of contempt to all, especially to its friends; and so the Psalmist continues, saying, 'Thou hast put away my acquaintance far from me; they have set me an abomination to themselves.'‡

The prophet Jonas also, as one who had experience of this, both bodily and spiritually, witnesses to the same truth, saying, 'Thou hast cast me forth into the deep, in the heart of the sea, and a flood hath compassed me: all Thy billows and Thy waves have passed over me. And I said, I am cast away out of the sight of Thine eyes: but yet I shall see Thy holy temple again,'—this is the purgation of the soul that it may

* Ps. xvii. 5, 6, 7. † Ib. lxxxvii. 6, 7, 8. ‡ Ib. 9.

see God—'the waters have compassed me about even to the soul, the deep hath enclosed me, the sea hath covered my head. I went down to the lowest parts of the mountains: the bars of the earth have shut me up for ever.'* The bars of the earth are the imperfections of the soul which prevent it from the enjoyment of this sweet contemplation.

Fourth pain,—Emptiness of self felt in the fulness of God.

The fourth kind of pain is caused by another excellence peculiar to this Obscure Contemplation, the sense of God's Majesty and Greatness. This makes the soul conscious of the other extreme, its own poverty and misery; and this is one of the chief sufferings of this purgation. The soul is made conscious of a profound emptiness, and an utter destitution of the three kinds of goods, natural, temporal, and spiritual, which are ordained for its comfort; it sees itself in the midst of the opposite evils, miserable imperfections and aridities, its faculties devoid of all apprehensions, and the spirit abandoned in darkness. And, inasmuch as God is now purifying it in its sensitive and spiritual substance, in its interior and exterior powers, it is necessary for it that it should become empty, poor and abandoned, arid, destitute and obscured. For the sensitive part is purified in aridities, the faculties in the absence of all apprehensions, and the spirit in the obscure darkness.

Now God effects this by means of Obscure Contemplation, wherein the soul not only suffers from the absence and suspension of all natural support and apprehensions, which is a most painful trial—like a person held by the throat and suffocated—but all its affections, and the imperfect habits contracted in the world, are also purged away, annihilated, emptied out of it, or consumed within it, as the rust and mould of metal is burnt away in the fire. But as these things are most deeply rooted in the soul, the sufferings and

* Jon. ii. 4—7.

CHAP. VI.

Illustrations from Holy Scripture.

interior trials which it has to endure are heavy, and in addition to the destitution and emptiness, natural and spiritual, of which I have spoken. The words of the Prophet are now fulfilled:—'Heap together the bones which I will burn with fire: the flesh shall be consumed, and the whole mixture shall be sodden, and the bones shall dry away.'* This describes the pain which the soul suffers in the sensitive and spiritual parts when it is in this state of emptiness and poverty. And so the Prophet proceeds, saying: 'Set it also empty upon hot burning coals, that the brass thereof may wax hot and be melted; and let the filth of it be melted in the midst thereof, and let the rust thereof be consumed.'†

This is the heavy trial of the soul in the purifying fires of Contemplation. The Prophet says that, in order to purge away and consume the filth of the affections which are within the soul, it is necessary for it, in a certain way to be annihilated and undone, because its passions and affections have become natural to it. And therefore the soul, because it is purified in this furnace, like gold in a crucible, according to the words of Wisdom, 'as gold in the furnace He hath proved them,' ‡ feels itself consumed away in its innermost substance in this absolute poverty wherein it is as it were lost. This truth is clearly taught us by the Psalmist, saying: 'Save me, O God, for the waters are come in even unto my soul. I stick fast in the deep mire; and there is no sure standing. I am come into the depth of the sea: and a tempest hath overwhelmed me. I am weary of crying, my jaws are made hoarse, my eyes have failed, whilst I hope in my God.'§

Here God is humbling the soul that He may exalt it hereafter, and if it were not His will that these feelings, when they rise, should be quickly lulled again, the soul would almost immediately depart from the body, but they occur

* Ezech. xxiv. 10.
† Ib. xxiv. 11.
‡ Wisd. iii. 6.
§ Ps. lxviii. 2—4.

BOOK II.

Purgatory in this life.

only at intervals in their greatest violence. They are occasionally so acute, that the soul seems to see hell and perdition open before it. They who are in this state, are those who go down alive into hell, and have their Purgatory in this life; for this is the purgation to be endured there for venial sins. And thus he who passes through this state in the present life, and is purified, either enters not into Purgatory, or is detained there but a moment, for one hour here is more than many there.

CHAPTER VII.

The same subject continued. Other afflictions and trials of the will.

THE afflictions of the will, and its trials here are also immense; they occasionally pierce the soul with a sudden recollection of the evils that environ it, and of the uncertainty of any relief. To this is superadded the memory of past happiness; for souls of this kind, when they enter into this night have, generally, had much sweetness in God, and served Him greatly; but now, to see themselves strangers to so much happiness, and unable to recover it, causes them the greatest affliction. This was the experience of Job also; for he said: 'I sometime that wealthy one, suddenly am broken; He hath held my neck, broken me, and set me to Himself as it were a mark. He hath compassed me with His spears, He hath wounded my loins, He hath not spared, and hath poured out my bowels on the earth. He hath torn me with wound upon wound; He hath rushed in upon me like a giant. I have sewed sackcloth upon my skin, and have covered my flesh with ashes. My face is swollen with weeping, and my eyelids are dim.'* So many and so great

Fifth pain,—the memory of past happiness.

* Job xvi. 13—17.

are the torments of this night, and so many are the illustrations of them furnished by the Holy Writings, that time and strength would fail me were I to attempt to enumerate them. For beyond all doubt, all that can be said of them will fall short, and the illustrations before us will enable us to form some conjecture as to the others.

Lamentation of the Prophet Jeremias.

And now to conclude the subject of the first line of the stanza, and to show what this night is to the soul, I will repeat here what the Prophet Jeremias has said of it: 'I am the man that see my poverty in the rod of His indignation. He hath led and brought me into darkness, and not into light. Only against me He hath turned again and again His hand all the day. He hath made my skin and my flesh old; He hath broken my bones. He hath built round about me, and He hath compassed me with gall and hardship. In dark places He hath placed me as the everlasting dead. He hath built round about against me, that I go not forth. He hath made my fetters heavy. Yea, and when I cry and ask, He shutteth out my prayer. He hath shut up my ways with square stones. He hath made my paths crooked. He is become to me as a bear lying in wait; as a lion in secret places. He hath turned aside my paths, and hath broken me; He hath made me desolate. He hath bent His bow, and set me as a mark for the arrow. He hath shot into my reins the daughters of His quiver. I am made a laughing-stock to all my people, their song all the day. He hath filled me with bitterness, He hath inebriated me with wormwood. And He hath broken my teeth one by one; He hath fed me with ashes. And my soul is repelled from peace; I have forgotten good things. And I said: My end and my hope is perished from the Lord. Remember my poverty and transgression, the wormwood and the gall. I am mindful and remember; and my soul languisheth within me.'*

* Lament. iii. 1—20.

BOOK II.

The suffering soul worthy of compassion.

These lamentations of the Prophet, which so vividly depict the sufferings of the soul, refer to those trials and afflictions which come upon it in this purgation and spiritual night. That soul is worthy of all compassion which God leads into this dreadful and horrible night. For, although it is well with it because of the great blessing in store, and of which this night is the source—since God will raise up good things for it out of this darkness, and bring light over the shadow of death, as it is written: 'He discovereth deep things out of darkness, and bringeth up to light the shadow of death;' * so that His light shall be as extensive as the darkness that is past; 'the darkness thereof and the light thereof are alike,' † —nevertheless, on account of the immense sufferings it endures, and the great uncertainty of any relief—for it imagines that its calamities will never come to an end, God having made it to 'dwell in darkness as those that have been dead of old,' the spirit is in anguish within it, and 'the heart within' it 'is troubled'—its condition is one of deep suffering, and greatly to be pitied.

It derives no relief from spiritual advice.

Besides, the soul derives now no consolation from the advice that may be given it, or from its spiritual director, because of the loneliness and desolation which overwhelm it in this obscure night. Though its confessor may set before it in many ways the grounds of comfort which are to be had in the blessings which these its sufferings imply, yet the soul will not believe him. For being absorbed in the sense of the evils that environ it, and seeing clearly its own misery, it imagines that its spiritual director, not seeing what itself sees and feels, speaks as he does without comprehending its case. It is pained anew instead of being comforted, for it considers that his counsel is no remedy of the evil it suffers from, which is most true; for no relief, no remedy is possible for that pain

* Job xii. 22. † Ps. cxxxviii. 12.

CHAP. VII.

God the only consolation.

—this the more so, inasmuch as the soul is powerless here, like a prisoner in his dark cell bound hand and foot, unable to move or see, and shut out from all help whatever—until our Lord shall have accomplished the purgation of the soul in His own way; until the spirit is softened, humbled, and purified; until it becomes so refined, simple, and pure, as to become one with the Spirit of God in that degree of the union of love which He in His mercy intends for it, and corresponding to which is the greater or less violence, the longer or shorter duration, of this purgation.

Duration and intermission of spiritual sufferings.

But if this purgation is to be real it will last, notwithstanding its vehemence, for some years, but admitting of intermissions and relief, during which, by the dispensation of God, the obscure contemplation divested of its purgative form and character, assumes that of the illuminative and of love. Under this form of it, the soul, like one escaped from the dungeons of its prison into the comfort of space and freedom, enjoys the sweetness of peace, and the loving tenderness of God in the flowing abundance of spiritual communications. This is to the soul a sign of the spiritual health which is being wrought within by this purgation, and a foretaste of the abundance it hopes for. So much so is this at times that it thinks all its trials are over. For such is the nature of spiritual things, when they are most purely spiritual, that when trials return, the soul thinks they will never end, and that all its goodness has perished; and when it prospers in its spiritual course it thinks all its calamities are past, and that it shall always abound in good things. Thus it was with David when he said: 'In my abundance I said; I shall never be moved.' *

The reason of this is that the actual enjoyment of one thing in the mind is inconsistent with the enjoyment of its con-

* Ps. xxix. 7.

BOOK II.

How one intense emotion excludes its contrary.

trary; but this is not the case quite in the sensitive part of the soul, because of the weakness of its apprehensions. But as the spirit is not yet wholly purified and cleansed from the affections of the inferior nature, though more resolute and consistent now, it is still liable to pains, so far as it is under the dominion of these affections. This is evident in the life of David, for when his state changed, he was in affliction though he had said in the day of prosperity, 'I shall never be moved.' Thus the soul, in the actual enjoyment of spiritual blessings, but not observing the radical imperfections and impurity which still remain, thinks that all its trials are over. This thought, however, is of rare occurrence, for until the spiritual purgation is complete, the sweet communications of God are rarely so abundant as to conceal the root that remains behind, in such a way that the soul shall not be profoundly conscious of some deficiency, or that something still is to be done. Nor is the communication such as to allow it to enjoy the relief that is offered it perfectly, for it feels that there is an enemy lurking within, who, though he may be subdued and lulled, will yet return in his strength and assault it as before.

The soul still conscious of imperfections and of danger.

Vicissitudes of joy and sorrow.

And so it comes to pass, for when the soul is most secure it is then plunged at once into another affliction heavier, darker, and sadder than the previous one, and which, perhaps, will be of longer continuance. The soul again is convinced that all goodness is gone from it for ever. Experience cannot teach it: the blessings that flowed out of its former trials, during which it thought that its sufferings would never end, cannot prevent it from believing, in its present trials, that all goodness has perished from it, and that it will never be again with it as it was before. Its present convictions are so strong, grounded on actual feelings, as to destroy within it all the occasions of joy. Thus the soul in this purgation though it seeks to please God, and is ready to die for Him a thousand deaths—for souls thus tried love God with great sincerity—nevertheless finds no relief, but rather an increase of pain herein. For seeking God alone to the exclusion of aught else, and seeing its own miserableness to be so great, it doubts whether God be not angry with it. It cannot then persuade itself that there is anything in it worthy of love, but rather is convinced that there is that in it which should make it hateful not only in the eyes of God, but of all creatures also for ever; it grieves to see within itself sufficient grounds why it should be abandoned of Him whom it so loves and so longs for.

CHAPTER VIII.

Other trials of the soul in this state.

Sixth pain,—Inability to fix the attention on God or Divine things.

ANOTHER source of affliction and distress to the soul in this state is that, as the obscure night impedes the exercise of the faculties and affections, it cannot elevate the mind and affections to God as before, nor pray to Him. It thinks itself to be in that state described by the Prophet when he said, 'Thou hast set a cloud before Thee, that our prayer may not pass through.'* This is the meaning of the words I have quoted before—'He hath shut up my ways with square stones.'† If at any time it prays, it prays with so much aridity, without sweetness, as to think that God neither hears nor regards it; as the Prophet complains, saying, 'Yea, and when I cry, and entreat, He shutteth out my prayer.'‡ And, in truth, this is the time for the soul to put its 'mouth in the dust,'§ suffering in patience this purgation.

It is God Himself Who is now working in the soul, and the soul is therefore powerless. It cannot pray or give great attention to Divine things. Neither can it attend to temporal matters, for it falls into frequent distractions, and the

* Lam. iii. 44. † Ib. iii. 9. ‡ Ib. iii. 8. § Ib. iii. 29.

BOOK II.

Loss of mental power.

memory is so profoundly weakened, that many hours pass by at a time without its knowing what it has done or thought, what it is doing or is about to do; nor can it give the least heed to what it is occupied with, notwithstanding all its efforts.

Inasmuch, then, as the intellect is purified from its imperfect perceptions, the will from its affections, and the memory, also, from all knowledge and reflections, it is necessary that the soul should be annihilated herein, according to the words of the Psalmist, referring to this purgation: 'I am brought to nothing, and I knew not.'* This 'knowing not' extends to these follies and failures of the memory. These wanderings and failures of memory are the result of interior recollection, by which the soul is absorbed in contemplation. In order to prepare the soul, and temper it divinely in all its powers for the Divine union of love, it must, first of all, be absorbed with all its powers in the Divine obscure spiritual light of contemplation, and detached from all affection for, and apprehension of, created things. This continues regularly in proportion to the intensity of its contemplation.

Faculties of the soul absorbed in God.

Thus, then, the more pure and simple the Divine light when it shines on the soul, the more does it obscure it, empty it, and annihilate it, as to all its apprehensions and affections, whether they regard heavenly or earthly things. And also, the less pure and simple the light, the less is the soul obscured and annihilated. It seems strange to say, that the purer and clearer the supernatural light the more is the soul obscured, and that it is less obscured when that light is less pure. But this may be easily explained, if we keep in mind the philosophical axiom that supernatural things are more obscure to the intellect the more clear they are in themselves. Thus the ray of high contemplation, transcend-

* Ps. lxxii. 22.

CHAP. VIII.

ing as it does the natural powers, shining on the soul with its Divine light, makes it dark, and deprives it of all the natural affections and apprehensions which it entertained in its own natural light. Under these circumstances, the soul is not only left in darkness but in emptiness also, as to its powers and desires, both natural and spiritual, and in this emptiness and obscurity is purified and enlightened by the Divine spiritual light, without its ever thinking of its presence, but rather thinking of the darkness that surrounds it.

The light of reason dim in the Light of God.

As a pure ray of light, unreflected by any object, is almost invisible, but becomes visible by being reflected, so the spiritual light which envelopes the soul is, by reason of its pureness, invisible or imperceptible; but when it strikes against any object, that is, when we use it to discern between truth and falsehood, or any particular matter relating to perfection, it then becomes visible at once, and the soul perceives it then much more distinctly than it did before it entered this obscurity. In the same way it perceives the spiritual light which it has for discerning easily the imperfection which is present, as in the case of a ray of light, which of itself is not visible, but which if the hand or any object be passed across its course, the hand becomes instantly visible, and the presence of the sun's light is detected. The soul, therefore, inasmuch as this light is perfectly pure clear and universal, disconnected from all particular objects of the intellect, natural or Divine—its powers are emptied and annihilated with respect to all such apprehensions—most easily and comprehensively understands and penetrates within all things, whether of heaven or of earth, according to the saying of the Apostle: 'The Spirit searcheth all things, yea, the deep things of God.'* It is to this universal and pure knowledge those words refer, which the Wise Man spoke by

An analogy, —Natural light perceptible only when reflected by objects.

* 1 Cor. ii. 10.

BOOK II.

the Holy Ghost, 'Wisdom reacheth everywhere by reason of her purity;'* that is, because not connected with any particular object of the intellect or affections. The characteristic of a mind purified and annihilated as to all particular objects of affection and of the intellect, is to have pleasure in nothing and to have no particular understanding; abiding in emptiness, obscurity, and darkness; embracing all things in its grand comprehensiveness; fulfilling mystically the words of the Apostle, 'having nothing and possessing all things,'† for such poverty of spirit merits such a blessing.

Marks of a purified mind,—what.

CHAPTER IX.

How it is that this Night enlightens the mind while it brings darkness over it.

Light, love and liberty found in the night of the spirit.

It remains for me now to explain that this blessed night, though it obscures the mind, does so only to enlighten it; and though it humbles it and makes it miserable, does so only for the purpose of exalting and setting it free; and though it impoverishes it and empties it of all it holds, it does so only to enable it to reach forward divinely to the possession and fruition of all things, both of heaven and earth, in perfect liberty of spirit. As the primary elements which enter into the composition of all natural substances have no colour, taste, nor smell peculiar to themselves, so that they shall combine with all colours, all tastes, and all smell, so the mind must be pure, simple, and detached from all natural affections, actual and habitual, in order that it may freely participate in the largeness of spirit of the Divine Wisdom, wherein by reason of its pureness it tastes of the sweetness of all things in a certain preeminent way. And without this purgation it is altogether impossible to taste of the abundance

Illustration from the primary elements of matter.

* Wisd. vii. 24. † 2 Cor. vi. 10.

of these spiritual delights. For one single affection remaining in the soul, to which the mind may cling either habitually or actually, is sufficient to prevent all perception and all communication of the interior sweetness of the spirit of love, which contains within itself all sweetness supremely.

One selfish affection or apprehension may make Perfection impossible.

As the children of Israel, merely on account of that single affection, or remembrance which they retained of the fleshpots of Egypt, could not taste the delicious bread of angels, the manna in the desert, which had 'the sweetness of every taste,' and 'turned to what ever man liked,'* so the mind which still clings actually or habitually to any one affection or particular mode of apprehending, cannot taste the sweetness of the spirit of liberty, according to the desire of the will. The reason is this: the affections, feelings, and apprehensions of the perfect spirit, being of so high an order and specially Divine, are of another and different kind than those which are natural, and in order to be actually and habitually enjoyed, require the annihilation of the latter. It is therefore expedient and necessary, if the soul is to advance to these heights, that the obscure night of contemplation should annihilate it first, and destroy it in all its meannesses, changing it into darkness, aridities, loneliness, and emptiness; for the light that is given it is a certain Divine light of the highest nature, surpassing all natural light, and not cognisable by the natural intellect. If the intellect is to be united with that light, and become divinely transformed in the state of perfection, it must first of all be purified and annihilated as to its natural light, which must be brought actually into darkness by means of obscure contemplation.

Because the natural cannot of itself reach the Supernatural.

This obscurity must continue so long as it is necessary to destroy the habit, long ago contracted, of understanding things in a human way, and until the Divine enlightening

* Wisd. xvi. 20, 21.

BOOK II.

shall have taken its place. And inasmuch as the power of understanding, previously exerted, was natural, the darkness now endured is profound, awful, and most afflictive, because it reaches to, and is felt in, the innermost depths of the spirit. And inasmuch as the affection of love, communicated in the Divine union is Divine, and therefore most spiritual, subtile, delicate, and most interior, surpassing all natural sense and affection, the imperfectness of the will and every desire of the same, it is necessary for the fruition, in the union of love, of this Divine affection and most exquisite delight, that the will should be first purified and annihilated, as to all its affections and feelings, left in darkness and distress proportional to the intensity of the habit of natural affections it had acquired, in respect both of human and Divine things. And this must be done, in order that the will, in the fire of obscure contemplation, wasted, withered, and deprived of all selfishness—like the liver of the fish on the burning coals *—may acquire a pure and simple disposition, a purified and sound taste, so as to feel those sublime and wonderful touches of Divine love whenever it shall be divinely transformed, and wherein all its former contrarieties actual and habitual shall be expelled.

Purification of grace equal to habits of nature.

Moreover, in order to attain to the Divine union, for which obscure contemplation disposes it, the soul must be endowed and replenished with a certain glorious magnificence in the Divine communication, which includes innumerable blessings and joys, surpassing all the abundance which the soul can naturally possess—so speak the Prophet Isaias and S. Paul, 'Eye hath not seen, nor ear heard, neither hath it entered into the heart of man what things God hath prepared for them that love Him' †—it is necessary for it that it should be first brought into a state of emptiness and spiritual

The soul prepared by suffering for the Spirit of God.

* Tob. viii. 2.

† Is. lxiv. 4; 1 Cor. ii. 9.

poverty, detached from all help and consolation in all the things of Heaven and earth, that being thus empty it may be really poor in spirit and divested of the old man, and may live that new and blessed life to which it attains in this obscure contemplation which is the state of union with God.

The soul—an exile in the world—at home in God.

And because the soul is to attain to a certain sense, to a certain Divine knowledge, most generous and full of sweetness, of all human and Divine things which do not fall within the common-sense and natural perceptions of the soul—it views them with different eyes now, for the light and grace of the Holy Ghost differ from those of sense, the Divine from the human—it is necessary that the mind should be brought low, and inured to hardships in all that relates to natural and common sense. It must suffer hardships and afflictions in the purgative contemplation, and the memory must become a stranger to all pleasing and peaceful notions, with a most interior sense and feeling of being a stranger and a pilgrim here, so that all things shall seem strange to it, and other than they were wont to seem. For this night is drawing the mind away from its ordinary and common sense of things, and attracts it towards the Divine sense, which is a stranger and an alien to all human ways; so much so that the soul seems to be carried out of itself. At other times it looks upon itself as if under the influence of some spell, and is amazed at all that is around it—all that it hears and sees, which seem to it to be most strange, though in reality always the same. The sources of this feeling are that the soul has become a stranger to the ordinary sense of things, in order that being brought to nothing therein, it might be formed divinely anew. Now this belongs more to the next life than to this.

The soul suffers these afflictive purgations of the spirit that it may be born again to the life of the spirit through the Divine influence, and in these pangs bring forth the spirit of salvation, fulfilling the words of the Prophet: 'So are we become in Thy presence, O Lord. We have conceived, and been as it were in labour, and have brought forth the spirit' * of salvation. Moreover, as the night of contemplation disposes the soul for that tranquillity and interior peace which is so full of delight as, in the words of Scripture, to 'surpass all understanding,' † it is necessary that the former peace of the soul, which, because involved in so many imperfections, was no peace, though it seemed to be a twofold peace, namely, of sense and spirit, should first of all be purified, and the soul disturbed and repelled from that imperfect peace, as Jeremias felt and lamented in the words cited before to express the trials of the night that is now past, namely: 'My soul is repelled off from peace.' ‡

In the spiritual night false peace is lost; true peace is found.

This is a painful unsettling, full of misgivings, imaginations, and interior struggles, in which the soul, at the sight and in the consciousness of its own misery, imagines itself to be lost, and all its goodness to have utterly perished. In this state the mind is pierced by sorrow so profound as to occasion spiritual groans and cries; at times it gives audible vent to them and tears break forth, if there be any strength left, though this relief is but rarely granted. The royal Prophet has well described this state, being one who had experience of it, saying, 'I am afflicted and humbled exceedingly; I roared with the groaning of my heart.' § This proceeds from great sorrow; for sometimes the sudden and sharp recollection of the miseries that environ the soul, produces such pain and suffering that I know not how to describe them otherwise than by the words of Job: 'as overflowing waters so is my roaring.' ‖ For as waters sometimes overflow, drown and fill all places, so this roaring, this

* Is. xxvi. 17, 18.
† Phil. iv. 7.
‡ Lam. iii. 17.
§ Ps. xxxvii. 9.
‖ Job iii. 24.

sense of pain, occasionally so grows as to overflow the soul and drown it, so fills all its affections and energies with spiritual sorrows as to defy all exaggeration.

Such is the work wrought in this night that hideth the hopes of day. It was in reference to it that Job said, 'In the night my mouth is pierced with sorrows, and they that feed upon me do not sleep.' * The mouth is the will, pierced by these sorrows which cease not to tear the soul, neither do they sleep, for the doubts and misgivings which harass it give it no rest.

Great works require great labour.

This warfare and combat are deep, because the peace hoped for is most deep: the spiritual sorrow is most interior, refined, and pure, because the love to be enjoyed is most interior and pure. The more interior and perfect the work, the more interior, perfect, and pure must the labour be that produces it; and the stronger the building, the deeper the foundation. 'My soul fadeth within myself,' saith Job, 'and the days of affliction possess me.' † So, in the same way, because the soul has to attain to the enjoyment and possession, in the state of perfection to which it journeys in this purgative night, of innumerable blessings, gifts, and virtues, both in the substance of the soul and in the powers thereof, it is necessary for it that it should consider and feel itself deprived of them all, and regard them as so far beyond its reach as to be persuaded that it never can attain to them, and that all goodness is perished from it. This is the meaning of those words of the Prophet, 'I have forgotten good things.' ‡

Beginning of Contemplation painful,—why.

Let us see why it is that the light of contemplation, so sweet and lovely to the soul that nothing is more desirable —for it is that whereby the Divine union takes place, and whereby the soul in the state of perfection finds all

* Job. xxx. 17. † Ib. xxx. 16. ‡ Lam. iii. 17.

the good it desires—produces these painful beginnings and awful results? The answer is easy, and is already given in part; this is not the effect of contemplation and the Divine inflowing, from which comes sweetness rather than pain. The cause is in our imperfection and weakness, and in the dispositions of our soul, which is not fit for the reception of that sweetness. And so, when the Divine light shines in upon the soul, it makes it suffer in the way described.

Self the cause of suffering.

CHAPTER X.

Explanation of this purgation by a comparison.

Analogy of the action of fire, to dry, blacken, purify, and ignite fuel.

To make what I have said, and what I have still to say, more clear, I find it necessary here to observe that this purgative and loving knowledge, or Divine light, is to the soul which it is purifying, in order to unite it perfectly to itself, as fire is to fuel which it is transforming into itself. The first action of material fire on fuel is to dry it, to expel from it all water and all moisture. It then blackens it and soils it, and drying it by little and little, makes it light and consumes away its accidental defilements which are contrary to itself. Finally, having eated and set on fire its outward surface, it transforms the whole into itself, and makes it beautiful as itself. Thus fuel subject to the action of fire retains neither active nor passive qualities of its own, except bulk and specific weight, and assumes all the qualities of fire. It becomes dry, then it glows, and glowing, burns; luminous, it gives light, and burns much lighter than before. All this is the effect of fire.

We theorise in this way concerning the Divine fire of contemplative love which, before it unites with, and transforms the soul into itself, purges away all its contrary qualities. It expels its impurities, blackens it and obscures it, and renders its condition apparently worse than it was before. For while the Divine purgation is removing all the evil and vicious humours, which, because so deeply rooted and settled in the soul, were neither seen nor felt, but now, in order to their expulsion and annihilation, are rendered clearly visible in the obscure light of the Divine contemplation, the soul—though not worse in itself, nor in the sight of God—seeing at last what it never saw before, looks upon itself not only as unworthy of the Divine regard, but even as a loathsome object in the eyes of God.

The comparison which I have instituted will enable us to understand what I have said, and what I purpose still to say. *The Analogy of fire shows;*

In the first place, we see how that very light, and that loving knowledge which unites the soul and transforms it into itself, is the same which purifies and prepares it; for the fire that transforms the fuel and incorporates it with itself, is the very same which also at the first prepared it for that end. *1. The same cause purifies and transforms the soul.*

In the second place, the sufferings of the soul here do not proceed from the Divine Wisdom—it being written, 'All good things came to me together with her,' *—but from its own weakness and imperfection, from its being incapable, previous to its purgation, of receiving this Divine light, sweetness, and delight. This is the source of its sufferings. So the fuel, too, is not transformed into fire, at the instant of their contact, if it be not previously prepared for burning. *2. Weakness and imperfection the source of suffering,*

This is the experience of the Wise Man, who thus describes his sufferings before his union with, and possession of, wisdom: 'My entrails were troubled in seeking her; therefore shall I possess a good possession." †

In the third place we learn incidentally how souls suffer in Purgatory. The fire would have no power over them if they were perfectly prepared for the kingdom of God, and union with Him in glory, and if they had no faults to expiate, *3. And cause of Purgatory.*

* Wisd. vii. 11.

† Ecclus. li. 29.

which are the matter on which that fire seizes; for when that matter is consumed there is nothing more to burn. So is it here, when all imperfections are removed, the suffering of the soul ceases, and in its place comes joy as deep as it is possible for it to be in this life.

4. Transformation of love equal to purification by suffering.

In the fourth place, we learn that the soul, the more it is purified and cleansed in the fire of love, the more it glows with it. The more the fuel is prepared for the fire the more it burns; though the soul is not always conscious of this burning of love within it, but only now and then, when the ray of contemplation shines upon it not so strongly. Then the soul is enabled to see, and even to enjoy, the work that is going on; it seems as if the hand of the artificer was withdrawn from the work, and the iron taken out of the furnace, so as to show in some measure the work that is being wrought. Then, too, the soul may see in itself that good which it could not see while the process was going on. Thus, when the flame ceases to envelope the fuel it burns, we see clearly how much of it has been enkindled.

5. Deeper fire, greater sufferings.

In the fifth place we learn how it is that, after alleviations of its pains, the soul suffers again more intensely and sensibly than before. For after the manifestation of the work that has been done, when the outward imperfections have been expelled, the fire of love returns again to purge and consume away that which is interior. Now the suffering of the soul becomes more penetrating, deep, and spiritual, according as it refines away the more profound, subtle, and deeply rooted interior imperfections of the spirit. It is here as with the fuel in the fire, the deeper the fire penetrates the greater is its force and energy in disposing the inmost substance of the fuel for its own possession of it.

6. The soul conscious of remaining imperfections.

In the sixth place, we learn that the soul, though it rejoices intensely in these intervals of peace—so much so that it seems to think its trials over, never to return, even while it is certain that they will soon recur again—cannot but feel, if it observes a single root of imperfection behind—and that is sometimes observed—that its rejoicing is incomplete. It seems as if that root threatened to spring up anew, and when that is the case, it does so quickly. Finally, that which still remains to be purified and enlightened within cannot now be concealed from the soul in the presence of what has been already purified. Thus that portion of the material fuel which is still to be set on fire is very different from that which the flame has purified. And when this purgation commences anew in the inmost soul, it is not strange that it should consider all its goodness to have perished, and that it can never recover its former prosperity; for in these most interior sufferings all exterior goodness becomes invisible.

Keeping this illustration, then, before our eyes, and remembering what I have said, on the first line of this stanza, concerning this obscure night and its fearful characteristics, it may be as well to abandon the subject of these afflictions of the soul, and to enter on the matter of the fruit of its tears and their blessed issues, celebrated by the soul in the following lines.

'O Domine, aut pati, aut mori.'

CHAPTER XI.

A vehement passion of Divine Love the fruit of these sharp afflictions of the soul.

With anxious love inflamed.

Foretaste of God in the night of the spirit.

HERE the soul speaks of the fire of love which, in the night of painful contemplation, seizes upon it as material fire on the fuel it burns. This burning, though to a certain extent resembling that which takes place in the sensitive part of the soul, is still, in one sense, as different from it as the soul is different from the body, the spiritual from the sensitive. For this is a certain fire of love in the spirit whereby the soul, in its dark trials, feels itself wounded to the quick by a certain impression and foretaste of God, though it understands nothing distinctly, because the intellect is in darkness.

Love of God infused into the purified soul.

The mind is now conscious of a deep affection of love, for this spiritual burning produces the passion of it. And inasmuch as this love is infused in a special way, the soul corresponds only passively with it, and thus a strong passion of love is begotten within it. This love has in it something of the most perfect union with God, and thus partakes in some measure of its qualities, which are chiefly actions of God, in the soul rather than of the soul, which is consenting unto them in simplicity and love. It is, however, the love of God only which, uniting itself with the soul, produces this warmth and force and temper and passion, or, as the soul calls it, burning. The more the desires are restrained, subdued, and disabled for the enjoyment of the things of heaven and earth, the more space does this love find for itself in the soul, and better dispositions for its reception, so that it may unite itself with that soul, and wound it. This takes place during the dark purgation in a wonderful way, for God has so weaned the faculties, and they are now so recollected in Him, that they are unable to take pleasure as they like in anything whatever.

All this is the work of God; wrought with a view to withdraw the faculties of the soul from all objects whatever, and to concentrate them upon Himself, so that the soul may acquire greater strength and fitness for the strong union of love which God is communicating in the purgative way; and in which the soul must love Him with all its strength, with all the desires of sense and spirit, which it could never do if the faculties thereof were dissipated by other satisfactions. The Psalmist prepared himself thus for the strong love of the Divine union, for he said, 'I will keep my strength for Thee;'* that is, all my capacity, all the energy of my faculties and my desires, neither will I suffer them to rejoice in anything but Thee.

Concentration of powers of the soul on God.

Here we may perceive, in some degree, how great and how vehement is this burning of love in the spirit when God gathers and collects together all the strength, faculties, and desires of the soul, spiritual and sensitive, so that their harmonious combination may direct all its energies and all its forces towards the real and perfect fulfilment of the first commandment of the law, which comprehends within its scope the whole nature and gifts of man; namely, 'Thou shalt love the Lord thy God with thy whole heart, and with thy whole soul, and with thy whole strength.'†

No satiety in Divine love.

When all the desires and energies of the soul are thus recollected in this burning of love, and the soul itself touched, wounded, and set on fire with love, in them all, what must the movements and affections of these desires and energies be when they are thus wounded and burning with love, when that love does not satiate them, when they are in darkness and doubt about it, and suffering also, beyond all question, a more grievous hunger after it, in proportion to the past experience of it? For the touch of this love and of the Divine fire so dries up the spirit, and enkindles its desires for satisfying its thirst, that it turns upon itself a thousand times, and longs for God in a thousand ways, as David did when he said, 'For Thee my soul hath thirsted, for Thee my flesh, O how many ways;'‡ that is, in desire. Another version reads, 'My soul thirsteth after Thee, my soul is dying for Thee.'

This is the reason why the soul says, 'With anxious love inflamed.' In all its works and thoughts, employments and opportunities, the soul loves in many ways and longs after

* Ps. lviii. 10. † Deut. vi. 5. ‡ Ps. lxii. 2.

BOOK II.

Anxious longing of the soul for God.

God. This longing is so manifold in its forms, always and everywhere abiding, that the soul has no rest, feeling itself to be wounded, inflamed with anxiety; its then state is thus described by holy Job: 'As a servant longeth for the shade, as the hireling looketh for the end of his work, so I also have had empty months, and have numbered to myself wearisome nights. If I lie down to sleep, I shall say, When shall I arise? and again I shall look for the evening, and shall be filled with sorrows even till darkness.'* The soul is in perplexity, it cannot comprehend itself, neither the things of Heaven nor of earth, and is filled with sorrows even till darkness, which—taking the words of Job in their spiritual sense, adapted to the subject before us—is pain and suffering, without the hope of light, or of any spiritual good.

Its two causes,—

1. Spiritual darkness.

2. Infused Love of God.

The anxieties of the soul while on fire with love is very great, because of their twofold origin: the spiritual darkness which envelopes it is one, and that afflicts it with doubts and misgivings. The Love of God itself which burns within it is the other, and that inflames it marvellously, and excites it through the loving wound it has inflicted upon it. These two and simultaneous anxieties are thus referred to by the Prophet: 'My soul hath desired Thee in the night;' that is, in my misery. This is one kind of pain which proceeds from the obscure night, 'Yea, and with my spirit within me in the morning early I will watch to Thee.'† This is the other suffering of desire and anxiety, which proceeds from love, in the bowels of the spirit; that is, the spiritual affections. The soul, however, is conscious, amidst these obscure and loving anxieties, of a certain companionship therein and interior strength, which is so great that, if the burden of this oppressive obscurity were removed, it

* Job vii. 2—4. † Is. xxvi. 9.

would oftentimes feel itself desolate, empty, and weak. The reason is that the force and courage of the soul flow passively from the obscure fire of love; and so, when that fire ceases to envelope it, the darkness, the strength, and fire of love cease at the same time.

CHAPTER XII.

How this awful night is like Purgatory. How the Divine Wisdom illuminates men on earth with that light in which the Angels are purified and enlightened in Heaven.

Two Purgatories.

WHAT I have said enables us to see how the obscure night of loving fire purifies the soul in the darkness, and in the darkness also sets it on fire. We shall also see that, as the dark and material fires in the next life, so the loving, dark, and spiritual fires here, purify and cleanse the predestinate. The difference is that in the next world men are purified by fire, and here, purified and enlightened by love. David prayed for this love when he said, 'Create a clean heart in me O God!'* for cleanness of heart is nothing else but the love and grace of God. 'Blessed are the clean of heart,' saith our Saviour, and it is as if he had said, blessed are those who love, for blessedness can come of nothing less than love.

Difference between them.

Cleanness heart,—what.

The following words of the Prophet also, 'From on high He hath cast a fire in my bones, and hath taught me,'† show plainly that the soul is purified and enlightened in the fire of loving wisdom, for God never grants the mystical wisdom without love; it being love itself that infuses it into the soul. David also saith that the wisdom of God is silver tried in the purifying fire of love: 'The Words of the Lord are pure words, as silver tried by fire.'‡ Obscure contemplation infuses

The infused wisdom of love.

* Ps. l. 12. † Lam. i. 13. ‡ Ps. xi. 7.

BOOK II.

into the soul love and wisdom simultaneously, to every one according to his necessity and capacity, enlightening the soul, and cleansing it of all its ignorances, according to the words of the Wise Man, 'He hath enlightened my ignorances.' *

Infused love and knowledge of the Angels.

Here, also, we learn that the wisdom which purifies the ignorance of the Angels, flowing from God through the highest, down to the lowest, in the order of the heavenly hierarchy, and thence to men, is that very wisdom which purifies and enlightens the human soul. All the works of the Angels, and all the inspirations they suggest, are, in Holy Scripture, truly and properly said to be their work and God's: for, ordinarily, His inspirations flow through the angels who receive them, each choir from the other instantaneously, as the light of the sun penetrates many windows at once, arranged one behind the other. It is quite true that, in one sense, the light of the sun pierces all, yet each window conveys that light to the next, modified according to the nature of the glass which transmits it, and somewhat weaker, according to the distance from the sun. Hence it follows, with respect to the higher and lower Angels, the nearer they are to God the more they are purified and enlightened in the general purgation; the lowest in rank receiving their illumination in a less perfect degree. But man, being lower than the Angels, must, when God raises him to the state of contemplation, receive that enlightenment according to his capacity in a limited degree, and with suffering. For the light of God which illumines an angel enlightens him, and sets him on fire with love, for he is a spirit already prepared for the infusion of that light; but man, being impure and weak, is ordinarily enlightened in obscurity, distressingly and painfully—as the sun's rays are painful to weak eyes—till the fire of love shall have spiritualised and refined him, so

* 'Ignorantias meas illuminavit.' These words have been expunged from Ecclus. li. 26, by the Roman censure.

that being made pure like the Angels he may be able to receive with sweetness the union of God's inflowing love. There are souls who, in this life, are more perfectly enlightened than even Angels. But, in the meantime, this contemplation and loving knowledge come upon the soul through trials and loving anxiety.

Increasing in holiness is advancing in knowledge.

The soul is not always conscious of this burning and anxiety of love; for in the beginning of the spiritual purgation all the Divine fire is employed in drying up and preparing the soul, rather than in setting it on fire. But when the soul has become heated in the fire, it then feels most commonly this burning and warmth of love. And now, as the intellect is being purified in this darkness, it happens occasionally that this mystical and affective theology, while inflaming the will, wounds also by enlightening the other faculty of the intellect with a certain Divine light and knowledge, so sweetly and so divinely, that the will, aided by it, glows in a marvellous manner, the Divine fire of love burning within it with living flames, so that the soul appears to have received a living fire with a living understanding. This is what David referred to when he said, 'My heart waxed hot within me, and in my meditation a fire shall burn,'* so vehemently that I thought it to be already on fire.

Joy of the union of Intellect and Will in God.

This kindling of love, in the union of these two faculties, the intellect and the will, is to the soul a great treasury of delight, because it is certain that the foundations of the perfection of the union of love, for which the soul hoped, are laid in that obscurity. But the soul does not reach this sublime sense and love of God without passing through many tribulations, and accomplishing a great part of its purgation. For other degrees of this union, lower than this, which are of ordinary occurrence, so intense a purgation is not required.

* Ps. xxxviii. 4.

BOOK II.

CHAPTER XIII.

Other sweet effects of the dark Night of Contemplation.

Benefits of the Spiritual Night;

1. Illumination of the Intellect.

2. Pure spiritual affections of the Will.

THIS fire of love throws some light upon the sweet effects wrought in the soul by the obscure Night of Contemplation; for occasionally, amid the obscurity, the soul receives light —'light shineth in darkness'*— the mystical influence flowing directly into the intellect, and the will in some measure partaking of it, with a calmness and pureness so exquisite and so delicious to the soul as to be utterly indescribable: now God is felt to be present in one way, and again in another. Sometimes, too, it wounds the will at the same time, and enkindles love deeply, tenderly, and strongly; for, as I have said, the more the intellect is purified the more perfectly and exquisitely, at times, are the intellect and the will united. But, before the soul attains to this state, it is more common for the touch of the fire of love to be felt in the will than for the touch of the perfect intelligence to be felt in the intellect.

This burning and thirst of love, inasmuch as it now proceeds from the Holy Ghost, is very different from that of which I spoke in the night of sense. For though the senses also have their part in this, because they share in the afflictions of the spirit; yet the root and living force of the thirst of love are felt in the higher portion of the soul, that is, in the spirit — conscious of what the soul feels, and of the absence of what it desires; still all the pains of sense, though incomparably greater than those of the sensitive night, are as nothing, because of the interior conviction that one great good is wanting, for which there is no compensation possible.

Observe here that, although this burning of love is not felt in the beginning of the spiritual night, because the fire of love

* S. John i. 5.

has not yet done its work, God communicates to the soul, instead of it, so great an appreciative love of Himself that its greatest trials and deepest afflictions in this night are involved in the thought which harasses it, namely, that it has lost God, and that He has abandoned it. It may, therefore, be said that from the first beginning of this night the soul is full of anxiety, arising at one time from the appreciation of God, at another from the burning fire of love; and the greatest of its sufferings is this doubt: for if it could be persuaded that all is not lost, and that the trials it undergoes are, as in truth they are, for its greater good, and that God is not offended, it would make no account whatever of its afflictions, but rather rejoice in them, knowing that it is serving God. For the appreciation with which it regards God is so great, though in darkness and unconsciously, that not only would it endure its trials joyfully, but also die a thousand times to please Him. But when the fire of love and the appreciation of God together have seized on the soul, it then gains such strength and energy, and such eager longing after God, the effect of this glowing love, that it boldly disregards all considerations, and sets everything aside, in the inebriating force of love, and, without reflecting on its acts, it conducts itself strangely and extravagantly, that it may meet Him whom it loveth.

Example of S. Mary Magdalen

This is the reason why Mary Magdalen, though noble herself, heeded not the guests, high and low, who were feasting in the house of the Pharisee. She considered not that her presence was inopportune, and that tears were unseemly at the feast, provided she could, without delay, or waiting for another occasion, reach Him for whom her soul was wounded and on fire.* This is that inebriating force and daring of love, which, when she knew that her Love was

* S. Luke vii. 37.

in the sepulchre, guarded by soldiers, and a stone rolled over it and sealed, allowed none of these things to move her; for she went thither before dawn with the ointments to anoint her Beloved. And, finally, it was under the inebriating influence of love that she asked Himself, whom she took for the gardener, and who, she thought, had robbed the sepulchre, where he had laid the Body of her Lord. 'If thou hast carried Him away, tell me where thou hast laid Him, and I will take Him away.'* She did not reflect upon the imprudence of her words; for it is clear that if the gardener had stolen the Body he would not have admitted the fact and the less so, because she intended to take It away herself.

Love inebriates.

Love thinks all things possible.

This conduct of Mary Magdalen proceeded from the vehemence and energy of her love: for love thinks all things possible, and that all men have interests identical with its own; it cannot believe that there is anything to occupy men, or anything to be sought for by them, except that which occupies itself, and which itself is seeking, for it considers that there can be no other occupation or desire beyond its own. Thus, when the Bride went out into the streets and broadways of Jerusalem seeking for her Beloved, she, believing that all were employed, like her, in searching for Him, adjured them, if they found Him, to tell Him that she languished with love.†

Love impatient.

So strong was Mary's love that she intended, if the gardener had told her where he had hidden her Lord, to take Him away, in spite of the prohibition. Of this kind are those anxieties of love which the soul feels when it has made some progress in the spiritual purgation. The soul rises by night, in the purifying darkness, in the affections of the will. As a lioness or a bear, robbed of its whelps, whom it cannot

* S. John xx. 15.

† Cant. iii. 2. v. 8.

find, seeks them anxiously and earnestly, so does the wounded soul seek after God. Being in darkness, it feels His absence, and is dying of love. This is that impatient love which no man can endure long without obtaining his wishes or dying. It is like that of Rachel, when she said, 'Give me children, otherwise I shall die.'*

Conscious unworthiness reconciled with ardent aspiration,—how.

We have now to consider how it is that the soul, conscious of its own misery and unworthiness before God, can be so bold, amid the purifying darkness, as to aspire after union with Him. The reason is, that love gives it strength to love in earnest—it being the nature of love to seek for union, equality, and assimilation with the object beloved, so as to attain to the perfection of itself. And as the soul has not yet attained to the perfection of love, because it has not attained to union with God, the hunger and thirst for that which it has not—namely union, and the strength which love communicates to the impassioned will—render it bold and daring in its wishes, though the intellect, because it is in darkness, tells at the same time that it is an unworthy and miserable object.

Misery of the soul seen in the Divine Light.

I am not disposed here to omit an explanation of the fact why it is that the Divine light, being always light, does not illuminate the soul the moment it surrounds it, as it does at a later time, instead of bringing with it darkness and troubles. This question has been already partially answered, and I now answer it more fully. The darkness and misery of which the soul is conscious proceed not from the Divine light which shines around it, but are in the soul itself, and it is the light which enables it to see them. When the Divine light shines in upon the soul, the soul sees nothing at first but what is immediately before it, or rather what is within it, its own darkness and misery. Now, by the mercy of God, it sees

* Gen. xxx. 1.

what it saw not before, because the supernatural light had not shone round about it. This is the reason why, in the beginning, the soul is conscious of nothing but of its own darkness and misery. But when it has been purified by the knowledge and perception of them, it will have eyes to discern the blessings of the Divine light; and when its darkness and imperfections shall have been removed, it will then behold the great benefits and blessings of this happy night.

Great mercy of God in restoring youth to the soul.

This explains how great is the mercy of God to the soul when He thus purifies it in this strong lye and bitter purgation, as to its sensitive and spiritual parts, from all affections and imperfect habits in all temporal, natural, sensitive, and spiritual respects; by obscuring its interior faculties, and emptying them of all objects, by correcting and drying up all its sensitive and spiritual affections, by weakening and wasting the natural forces—which the soul never could have done of itself—by causing it to die, as it were, to all that is not God, that, being wholly denuded and stripped of its former clothing, it may clothe itself anew in God. Thus the soul's 'youth shall be renewed like the eagle's,'* clothed with 'the new man, which according to God is created in justice.'†

Intellect, Will and Memory born anew to a supernatural life.

Now this is nothing else but the supernatural light shining on the intellect, so that the human intellect becomes one with the Divine. In the same way Divine love so inflames the will that it becomes nothing less than Divine, loving in a Divine way, united and made one with the Divine will and Divine love. The memory also is affected in like manner; all the desires and affections too are changed Divinely according to God. Thus the soul will be of Heaven, heavenly, Divine rather than human.

All this, as is clear from what I have said, is the work of God, who effects it, during this night of the soul, enlighten-

* Ps. cii. 5. † Ephes. iv. 24.

ing it and setting it on fire in a Divine way with an anxious solicitude for God alone, and for nought besides.

It is with great propriety and justice that the soul repeats the third line of the stanza, which, together with those that follow, I repeat again and explain in the following chapter.

CHAPTER XIV.

O happy lot!
Forth unobserved I went,
My house being now at rest.

The soul leaves the house of self-indulgence.

THE happy lot sung in the first of these lines is the result of that which is described in the two lines that follow. The soul describes itself as one who, for the better execution of his purpose, goes out of his house by night, in the dark, the inmates of which being at rest so that none of them could hinder him. The soul having to perform a heroic and rare action, such as that of being united to the Beloved, sallies out, because the Beloved is to be found only without, in solitude. Thus the Bride desired to find him without: 'Who shall give Thee to me for my brother, sucking the breasts of my mother, that I may find Thee without and kiss Thee?'* It is necessary for the enamoured soul, in order to obtain the end desired, to act in the same way; to go out by night when all the inmates of its house repose and sleep; that is, when all its inferior operations, passions, and desires are at rest in this night. These are the inmates of its house which when awake ever hinder its good, hostile when it attempts to set itself free from them. These are they to whom our Lord referred when He said, 'A man's enemies shall be they of his own household.' †

Thus it is necessary that the operations and motions of passion and desire should be lulled to sleep in this night in

* Cant. viii. 1.

† S. Matt. x. 36.

BOOK II.

The passions subdued, the soul goes forth to God.

order that they may not obstruct the supernatural blessings of union with God in love, for while they continue to energise and act those blessings are unattainable. All movement and action on their part, instead of helping, hinder the reception of the spiritual blessing of the union of love, because all natural exertion is defective with regard to those supernatural blessings which God alone secretly and silently infuses into the passive soul. Hence it is necessary that the powers of the soul should be at rest, if it is to receive what God infuses, and should not interfere in the matter with their own inferior actions and base inclinations.

It was a happy thing for the soul that God in this night put those of its household to sleep, that is, all the powers, passions, affections, and desires which belong to the sensitive and spiritual part, so that it might attain to the spiritual union of the perfect love of God 'unobserved,' that is, unhindered by them, because they were all asleep and mortified in that night. O how happy must the soul then be, when it is delivered from the house of its sensitive appetite! None can understand it, I think, except that soul which has experienced it. Such a soul clearly sees how wretched was its former slavery, and how great its misery when it lay at the mercy of its passions and desires; it learns how that the life of the spirit is true liberty and riches, involving innumerable blessings, some of which I shall speak of while explaining the following stanzas, when it will clearly appear, what good reasons the soul has for describing the passage of this awful night as a happy lot.

CHAPTER XV.

Explanation of the second stanza.

In darkness and security,
By the secret ladder, disguised,
O happy lot!
In darkness and concealment,
My house being now at rest.

CHAP. XV. — The second stanza an answer to an objection.

THE soul continues to speak of certain characteristics of the obscurity of this night, again referring to the happiness of which it is the cause. It is replying to an implied objection, and says in substance, let no man suppose that among the tormenting anxieties, doubts, misgivings, and terrors of that night of obscurity, it had run any risk of being lost; yea rather, it had found safety in the darkness, because the obscurity enabled it to escape from its enemies who were ever impeding its departure. In that obscurity it changed its garments, and disguised itself in three colours, of which I shall speak hereafter.* It sallied forth by a most secret ladder, unknown to the whole of its household—which, as I shall show, is a living faith—in such secrecy, for the better execution of its purpose, that it could not possibly be in greater security; and the more particularly so, because in the purgative night, the desires, passions, and affections of the soul are asleep, mortified, and subdued; and these, if awake and active, would never have consented to that departure.

CHAPTER XVI.

How the soul journeys securely when in darkness.

In darkness and security.

THE darkness, of which the soul here speaks, relates, as I have said,† to the desires, and to the interior sensitive and

* In ch. xxi. † Ch. iii.

BOOK II.

Means of the safe journey in the spiritual night.

spiritual powers, which are all to be deprived of their natural light in this night; so that, being purified herein, they may be supernaturally enlightened. The sensitive and spiritual desires are lulled to sleep and mortified, unable to relish anything either human or Divine: the affections are thwarted and brought low, incapable of excitement, and having nothing to rest upon; the imagination is fettered, and unable to make any profitable reflections, the memory is gone, the intellect is obscured, and the will, too, is dry and afflicted, and all the faculties are empty, and, moreover, a dense and heavy cloud overshadows the wearied soul, and alienates it, as it were, from God. This is the obscurity in which the soul says that it travels securely.

Security found in self-mortification,—why.

The cause of this security is evident: for usually the soul never errs, except under the influence of its desires, or tastes, or reflections, or understanding, or affections, wherein it generally is overabundant, or defective, changeable, or inconsistent; hence the inclination to what is not becoming it. It is therefore clear that the soul is secure against error therein, when all these operations and movements have ceased. The soul is then delivered, not only from itself, but also from its other enemies—the world and the devil—who, when the affections and operations of the soul have ceased, cannot assault it by any other way or by any other means.

Man destroys; God saves.

It follows from this, that the greater the darkness and emptiness of its natural operations in which the soul travels, the greater is its security. For as the Prophet saith, 'Perdition is thine own, O Israel; only in Me is thy help.'* The perdition of the soul is exclusively its own work—the result of its own operations, of its unsubdued desires, interior and sensitive—and its good the work of God only. When the soul is hindered from giving way to these evils, the blessings of

* Os. xiii. 9.

the Divine union descend upon it forthwith, in its desires and faculties which that union will render heavenly and Divine. If, therefore, while this obscurity lasts, the soul will look within, it will see how slightly the desires and the faculties have been diverted towards vain and unprofitable matters, and that it is secure against vainglory, pride and presumption, empty rejoicing, and many other evils. It is quite clear, therefore, that the soul which is in this obscurity is not only not lost, but that it gains much, for it acquires virtue.

Why are the natural faculties obscured?

But here a question arises to this effect: Why is it—seeing that the things of God are profitable and beneficial to the soul, and a source of security—that the desires and faculties are so obscured by Him in this night that they cannot enjoy Him or occupy themselves with Him as with other things, but are, in a certain sense, less able to do so? To this I reply, that it is then very necessary for the soul to be clear of its own operations and devoid of all pleasure even in spiritual things, because its faculties and desires are base and impure; and even if they have pleasure in, and are familiar with, Divine and supernatural things, it can be only in a low way.

Because in themselves they are incapable of perfect union with God.

It is a philosophical axiom that all that is received is received according to the condition of the recipient. From this principle it follows that the natural faculties — being without the requisite purity, strength, and capacity for the reception and fruition of Divine things in their way, which is Divine, but only in their own, which is mean and vile — ought to be obscured with regard to the Divine way, so as to secure their perfect purgation. They are to be weaned, purified, and annihilated first, in order that they may lose their own low mode of acting and receiving, and that they may be thus disposed and tempered for the reception and fruition of what is Divine in a lofty and sublime way; but this they can never do if the old man do not die first. Every spiritual gift, if it cometh not down from the Father of

BOOK II.

lights into the human will and desire, however much a man may exercise his taste, desire, and faculties about God, and however much he may seem to succeed, is still not Divinely nor perfectly enjoyed.

Natural taste and facility not spiritual fervour.

As to this I might here show, were this the proper place to do so, that there are many whose tastes and affections, and the operations of whose faculties, are directed to God and to spiritual things; who perhaps imagine all this to be supernatural and spiritual, when in reality it is nothing more, perhaps, than mere natural and human acts and desires. As they regard ordinary matters, so also do they regard good things, with a certain natural facility which they have in directing their faculties and desires to anything, whatever it may be. If I can find an opportunity in the course of this discussion, I propose to enter upon this question, and describe some of the signs by which we may know when the motives and interior acts of the soul in the things of God are natural only, when they are spiritual only, and when they are natural and spiritual together. It is enough for us to know that the interior acts and movements of the soul—if they are to be divinely influenced by God—must be first of all lulled to sleep, obscured and subdued, in their natural state, so far as their capacity and operations are concerned, until they lose all their strength.

The soul delivered from itself and prepared for God.

O spiritual soul, when thou seest thy desire obscured, thy will arid and constrained, and thy faculties incapable of any interior act, be not grieved at this, but look upon it rather as a great good, for God is delivering thee from thyself, taking the matter out of thy hands; for however strenuously thou mayest exert thyself, thou wilt never do anything so faultlessly, perfectly, and securely as now—because of the impurity and torpor of thy faculties—when God takes thee by the hand, guides thee safely in thy blindness, along a road and to an end thou knowest not, and whither thou couldst never travel guided by thine own eyes, and supported by thy own feet.

Four reasons why the dark road is safe; 1. God is the Guide.

The reason why the soul not only travels securely when in obscurity, but also makes greater progress, is this: In general the soul makes greater progress in the spiritual life when it least thinks so, yea, when it rather imagines that it is losing everything. Having never before experienced the present novelty which dazzles it, and disturbs its former habits, it considers itself as losing, rather than as gaining ground, when it sees itself lost in what it once knew, and in which it delighted, travelling by a road it knows not, and in which it has no pleasure. As a traveller into strange countries goes by ways strange and untried, relying on information derived from others, and not upon any knowledge of his own—it is clear that he will never visit a new country but by new ways which he knows not, and by abandoning those he knew, so the soul when it advances in the spiritual life, travels in obscurity, not knowing the way. God Himself, being the guide of the soul in its blindness, it may well exult and say, 'In darkness and security,' as soon as it has penetrated the mystery of its state.

2. Suffering gives strength.

There is another reason also, why the soul has travelled safely in this obscurity; it has suffered: for the way of suffering is safer, and also more profitable, than that of rejoicing and of action. In suffering God gives strength, but in action and enjoyment the soul does nothing but show its own weakness and imperfections. And in suffering, too, the soul practises and acquires virtue, and becomes pure, wiser, and more cautious.

3. The way enlightened by Divine Wisdom.

There is another more particular reason why the soul travels securely when in obscurity. This reason is derived from the consideration of the light itself, or obscure wisdom. The obscure night of contemplation so absorbs the soul, and brings it so near unto God, as to defend it, and deliver it

BOOK II.

God the health of the soul.

from all that is not God. For the soul is now, as it were, under medical treatment for the recovery of its health, which is God: God compels it to observe a particular diet, and to abstain from all noxious things, the very appetite for them being subdued. The soul is treated like a sick man respected by his household, who is carefully tended that the air shall not touch him, nor the light shine upon him, whom the noise of footsteps and the tumult of servants shall not disturb, and to whom the most delicate food is given most cautiously by measure, and that nutritious rather than savoury.

The soul guarded by the obscurity of Divine Contemplation.

Obscure contemplation, which brings the soul so near unto God, is the origin of all these measures, and they are all measures of security to guard the soul. For in truth the nearer the soul is to God, the more obscure the darkness, and the more profound the obscurity, because of the soul's weakness. The nearer a man reaches to the sun the greater the darkness and suffering its light occasions, because of the weakness and impureness of his vision. So great is the spiritual light of God, surpassing all understanding, that the nearer we approach it, the more does it blind us. This is the meaning of those words of the Psalmist: 'He made darkness the covert, the pavilion round about Him, dark waters in the clouds of the air,'* which is obscure contemplation and the Divine wisdom in souls, of which they have experience as of a thing near to the pavilion where He dwells, when God brings them near to Himself. Thus, what in God is light and supreme splendour, is to man obscure darkness, as S. Paul saith,† and as the royal Prophet explains it in the same place: 'At the brightness that was before Him the clouds passed,' ‡ that is, over the human intellect, 'the light of which,' saith the Prophet, 'is darkened with the mist thereof.' §

* Ps. xvii. 12.

† Acts xxii. 11. 'I did not see for the brightness of that light.'

‡ Ps. xvii. 13.

§ Is. v. 30.

CHAP. XVI.

Difficulties in knowing Truth the misery of this life.

O wretched condition of this life wherein the truth is so hardly known! That which is most clear and true, is to us most obscure and doubtful, and we avoid it though it is most necessary for us. That which shines the most, and dazzles our eyes, that we embrace and follow after, though it is most hurtful to us, and makes us stumble at every step. In what fear and danger then must man be living, seeing that the very light of his natural eyes, by which he directs his steps, is the very first to bewilder and deceive him when he would draw near unto God. If he wishes to be sure of the road he travels on, he must close his eyes and walk in the obscurity, if he is to journey in safety from his domestic foes, his own senses and faculties.

God the Tabernacle of protection.

Well hidden and protected then is the soul in the dark waters close to God. For as the dark waters are a pavilion for Him, so they are also to the soul perfect safety and protection, though in darkness, where it is hidden and protected from itself, and from all the injuries that created things may inflict. It is of souls thus protected that the Psalmist spoke when he said: 'Thou shalt hide them in the secret of Thy face, from the disturbance of men. Thou shalt protect them in Thy tabernacle from the contradiction of tongues.'* These words comprehend all kinds of protection; for to be hidden 'in the secret of the face' of God 'from the disturbance of men,' is to be strengthened in the obscure contemplation against all the assaults of men. To be protected in this 'tabernacle from the contradiction of tongues,' is to be engulfed in the dark water. That soul, therefore, whose desires and affections are weaned, and whose faculties are in darkness, is set free from all the imperfections which war against the spirit, whether they proceed from the flesh, or from any other created thing. Such a soul may well say, 'In darkness and security.'

* Ps. xxx. 21.

BOOK II.

4. Courage and vigilance acquired at the outset.

Another reason, not less conclusive, why the soul, though in darkness, proceeds securely, is derived from that courage which it acquires as soon as it enters within the dark, painful, and obscure water of God. Though it be dark, still it is water, and therefore cannot but refresh and invigorate the soul in all that is most necessary for it, though it does so painfully and in obscurity. For the soul immediately discerns in itself a certain courage and resolution to do nothing which it knows to be displeasing unto God, and to leave nothing undone which ministers to His service, because this obscure love is so intensely vigilant and careful of what it is to do, and what it is to leave undone, for His sake, so as to please Him. It looks around and considers in a thousand ways whether it has done anything to offend Him, and all this with much more solicitude and carefulness than it ever did before, as I said when speaking of this anxious love. Here all the desires, all the strength, and all the powers of the soul, recollected from all besides, direct all their efforts and all their energies to the service of God only. Thus the soul goes forth out of itself, away from all created things, to the sweet and delightsome union of the love of God, 'in darkness and in security.'

CHAPTER XVII

Obscure contemplation is secret.

By the secret ladder, disguised.

Three points of explanation; 1. 'Secret.' 2. 'Ladder.' 3. 'Disguised.'

I HAVE three things to explain in reference to the three words of this line. Two of them—'secret' and 'ladder'—belong to the obscure night of contemplation of which I am speaking, and the third—'disguised'—belongs to the way of the soul therein. As to the first, the soul calls the obscure contemplation, by which it goes forth to the union of love, a

CHAP. XVII.

secret ladder, and that because of two characteristics of it. First, this obscure contemplation is called secret, because it is, as I have said before, the mystical theology which Divines call secret wisdom, and which according to S. Thomas is infused into the soul most especially by love, in a secret hidden way in which the natural operations of the intellect and the other faculties have no share. And because the faculties of the soul cannot compass it, it being the Holy Ghost Who infuses it, as the Bride saith in the Canticle,* in an unknown way, we call it secret.

First point. The way secret.

1. Hidden from self,

And, in truth, it is not the soul only that is ignorant here, but everyone else, even the devil; because the Master who now teaches the soul dwells substantially within it. This is not the only reason why it is called secret, for it is secret also in its effects. It is not only secret beyond the powers of the soul to speak of it, during the darkness and sharpness of the purgation, when the secret wisdom purifies the soul, but afterwards also, during the illumination, when that wisdom is most clearly communicated, it is so secret that it cannot be discerned or described. Moreover, the soul has no wish to speak of it, and besides, it can discover no way or similitude to describe it by, so as to make known so profound an intelligence, so delicate an infused spiritual impression. Yea, and if it could have a wish to speak of it, and find terms to describe it, it would always remain secret still. This interior wisdom, so simple, general, and spiritual, enters not into an intellect entangled and covered over by any forms or images subject to sense, as is sometimes the case, and therefore the imagination and the senses—as it has not entered in by them, nor is modified by them—cannot account for it, nor form any conception of it, so as to speak in any degree correctly about it, though the soul be distinctly conscious that it feels and tastes this sweet and

2. And from the devil.

3. Hidden in its effects.

4. Incapable of adequate expression.

* Cant. vi. 11.

BOOK II.

Contemplation beyond language,—why?

strange wisdom. The soul is like a man who sees an object for the first time, the like of which he has never seen before; he handles it and feels it, yet he cannot say what it is, or tell its name, do what he can, though it be at the same time an object cognisable by the senses. How much less then can we describe that which does not enter in by the senses?

Such is the nature of the Divine language, that the more interior, infused, and spiritual it is, the more it transcends all human intelligence; the powers of the senses, interior and exterior, cease, and their harmonies become mute.

Examples of Jeremias and Moses.

The Holy Writings supply both proofs and illustrations of this principle. Jeremias shows the impossibility of revealing and expressing the words of God: for when God had spoken to him, he knew not what to say, except, 'Ah, ah, ah, Lord God.'* Moses, also, is an instance of the interior impossibility, that is, of the interior imaginative sense, and of the exterior also at the same time: for when God spoke to him out of the bush, he was not only more incapable of speaking than before,† but was so 'terrified' that he 'durst not behold;'‡ that is, the imagination itself became weak and silent. The wisdom of contemplation is the language of God addressed to the soul, purely spiritual, and the senses are not spiritual, so they do not perceive it, and so it remains a secret from them, they cannot understand it nor explain it.

Difficulties of Contemplatives with their directors.

This explains why some persons, walking in this way, good and timid souls, who, when they would give an account of their interior state to their directors, know not how to do it, neither have they the power to do it, and so feel a great repugnance to explain themselves, especially when contemplation is the more simple and with difficulty discernible by them. All they can say is that their soul is satisfied, calm,

* Jerem. i. 6. † Exod. iv. 10. ‡ Acts vii. 32.

or contented, that they have a feeling of God, and that all goes well with them, as they think; but they cannot explain their state, except by general expressions like these. But it is a different matter when they have a consciousness of particular things, such as visions, impressions, and the like, these in general are communicated under some species, and the senses participate in them; in that case they are able to describe them. But it is not in the nature of pure contemplation that it can be described; for it can scarcely be spoken of in words, and therefore we call it secret.

5. It hides the soul in the abyss of Wisdom.

This is not the only reason why it is called secret, and why it is so. There is another, namely, the mystical wisdom has the property of hiding the soul within itself. For beyond the usual degree of this hiding, the soul is sometimes so absorbed in this secret abyss that it beholds itself distinctly carried away from all created things to a wild and profound solitude where no human being can reach it, to an interminable desert, which is the more delicious, sweet, and lovely, the more it is profound, vast, and lonely, and the more secret is the soul, the more it is raised up above all created things. The abyss of wisdom so exalts and elevates the soul, bringing it within the course of the science of love, that it makes it not only understand how mean are all created things in relation to the Supreme wisdom and Divine sense, but also, how low, defective, and, in a certain sense, improper, are all the words and phrases by which in this life we discuss Divine things, and how utterly impossible, by any natural means, however profoundly and learnedly we may speak, to understand and see them as they are, were it not for the light of mystical theology. And so the soul in the light thereof, discerning this truth, namely, that it cannot reach it, and still less explain it by the terms of ordinary speech, justly calls it secret.

This property of being secret, and of surpassing all natural

BOOK II.

6. It leads the soul to union with a hidden God.

capacity, belongs to Divine contemplation, not only because it is itself supernatural, but also because it is the guide of the soul to the perfections of union with God, which not being humanly known, we must reach by being divinely ignorant. For, to use the language of mystical theology, these things are neither understood nor known when they are sought, but when they are found and practised. This is the meaning of the following words of the Prophet: 'There is none that is able to know her ways, nor that can search out her paths.'* The royal Prophet also, speaking of this way of the soul, says: 'Thy lightnings enlightened the world, the earth shook and trembled, Thy way is in the sea, and Thy paths in many waters, and Thy footsteps shall not be known.'† All this in its spiritual meaning refers to the subject before us.

Contemplation an infusion of the secret Wisdom of God.

'The lightnings that enlightened the world' is the illumination of the faculties of the soul in the Divine contemplation, the trembling of the earth is the painful purgation of which it is the cause. To say that the way of God, by which the soul draws near unto Him is in the sea, and His paths in many waters, and therefore cannot be known, is to say that this way to God is secret, and as hidden from the senses of the soul, as the way of one who walks over the waters is from the senses of the body, and whose footsteps cannot be known. The footsteps of God in those souls which He is drawing to Himself, making them great in the union of His wisdom, have also this peculiarity, that they are not known. Thus we find these words in the book of Job, impressing upon us this truth, 'Knowest thou the great paths of the clouds, and perfect knowledge?'‡ By this are meant the paths and ways of God, in which He makes souls great and perfect in His wisdom; these are meant by the clouds. Contemplation, therefore, by which God guides the soul, is secret wisdom.

* Baruch iii. 31. † Ps. lxxvi. 19, 20. ‡ Job xxxvii. 16.

CHAPTER XVIII.

How this secret wisdom is also a ladder.

CHAP. XVIII.

Second point. The way a ladder.

1. By it the soul ascends to God by Contemplation,

I NOW proceed to the second part, to show how this secret wisdom is also a ladder. There are many reasons for calling secret contemplation a ladder. In the first place, as men employ ladders to mount up to those strong places where treasures are laid up, so also by secret contemplation, without knowing how, the soul ascends, and mounts upwards, to the knowledge and possession of the treasures of heaven. This is well expressed by the royal Prophet when he says, 'Blessed is the man whose help is from Thee: in his heart he hath disposed to ascend by steps, in the vale of tears, in the place which he hath set. For the Lawgiver shall give a blessing; they shall go from strength to strength: the God of Gods shall be seen in Sion;'* He is the treasure of the citadel of Sion, that is blessedness.

2. And descends in regard to self by humility.

We may call it a ladder, also, because as the steps of one and the same ladder serve to descend as well as to ascend by, so those very communications which the soul receives in secret contemplation raise it up to God and make it humble also. For those communications which really come from God have this property, that they humble and exalt the soul at one and the same time. In the spiritual way, to descend is to ascend, and to ascend is to descend, 'because everyone that exalteth himself shall be humbled, and he that humbleth himself shall be exalted.'† And as the virtue of humility is greatness, for the trial of the soul therein, God is wont also to make it ascend by this ladder that it may descend, and descend that it may ascend; for thus are fulfilled the words of the Wise Man, 'Before

* Ps. lxxxiii. 6, 7, 8. † S. Luke xiv. 11.

BOOK II.

destruction the heart of a man is exalted, and before he be glorified it is humbled.'*

3. It expresses the vicissitudes of the spiritual life.

If the soul will reflect on the nature of a ladder — I omit what is spiritual and not felt — it will see at once the ups and downs of this road; how after prosperity come storms and trials, so that its previous repose seems to have been given it to prepare it and strengthen it for its present sufferings; how, also, after misery and distress come abundance and ease, so that the soul shall seem to have observed a vigil previous to the feast. This is the ordinary course of the state of contemplation, for until the soul attains to repose it never continues in one state; for all is ascending and descending with it. The reason is that the state of perfection, which consists in the perfect love of God and contempt of self, can only subsist on two conditions, the knowledge of God and of oneself. The soul must of necessity be tried in the one and the other — in the first which exalts it, in the second which humbles it — until, perfect habits having been acquired, it ceases to ascend and descend, having arrived at the summit, united with God, Who is at the top of it, and on Whom, too, the ladder rests. The ladder of contemplation, which comes down from God, is shadowed forth by that ladder which Jacob saw in a dream, and the angels of God ascending and descending by it, from God to man and from man to God, Who was Himself leaning upon it.† This took place by night, when Jacob slept, as the Scriptures declare, that we may learn from it how secret is the way of God, and how different from all human conception. This is plain enough, for, in general, that which is to our greater profit — the loss and annihilation of self — we esteem a calamity; and that which is of but little value — comfort and sweetness,

Two conditions of Perfection,— (1) Love of God. (2) Contempt of self.

The ladder of Jacob's dream.

* Prov. xviii. 12.

† Gen. xxviii. 12, 13.

where, in general, we lose instead of gaining — we look upon as the more advantageous for us.

4. It is the science of love.

But, to speak with more accuracy, and to the purpose, of the ladder of secret contemplation, I must observe that the chief reason why it is called a ladder is, that contemplation is the science of love which is an infused loving knowledge of God, and which enlightens the soul and at the same time kindles within it the fire of love till it shall ascend upwards step by step unto God its Creator; for it is love only that unites the soul and God. With a view to the greater clearness of this matter, I shall mark the steps of this Divine ladder, explaining concisely the signs and effects of each, that the soul may be able to form some conjecture on which of them it stands. I shall distinguish between them by their effects with S. Bernard and S. Thomas, and because it is not possible to distinguish them in this life as they are in their own nature, because the ladder of love is so secret that it can be weighed and measured by God only.

Love the unitive virtue.

CHAPTER XIX.

The mystic ladder has ten degrees. Explanation of the first five of them.

First step,— The languishing of love.

THE steps of the ladder of love, by which the soul, ascending from one to another, rises upwards to God, are ten in number. The first degree of love makes the soul languish to its great profit. Here was the Bride when she said, 'I adjure you, O daughters of Jerusalem, if you find my Beloved, that you tell Him that I languish with love.'* This languishing is not unto death, but for the glory of God; for the soul faints away as to sin and all things whatsoever that are not

* Cant. v. 8.

God for God's sake, as the Psalmist testifies: 'My spirit hath fainted away'* from all things after Thy salvation; as it is more fully expressed in another place: 'My soul hath fainted after Thy salvation.'† As a sick man loses all appetite and the taste of his food, and the colour vanishes from his face, so the soul in this degree of love loses all pleasure in earthly things, and all desire of them, and, like one in love, its colour fades away. The soul does not fall into this languishing state except through the vehement heat which descends into it from above, which is the mystic fever, according to the words of the Psalmist, 'Thou didst send thine inheritance a free rain, O God, and it was weakened, but Thou hast made it perfect.'‡ This languishing and fainting away of the soul, which is the first and earliest step to God, I have already explained, when I spoke of that annihilation to which the soul is brought when it begins to stand upon the ladder of contemplative purgation, when it finds no comfort, pleasure, nor support anywhere. In consequence of which it begins immediately to climb the other steps of the ladder.

Second step,—The search for God.

On the second step the soul is unremitting in its search after God. Thus the Bride sought Him in her bed by night; she had fainted away there when on the first step of the ladder, and found Him not. She added, 'I will rise; I will seek Him whom my soul loveth.'§ This is now the unceasing occupation of the soul, 'Seek ye the Lord,—seek His face evermore,'‖ is the counsel of the Psalmist, and never rest until He be found; like the Bride who, when she had questioned the watchmen, passed on in her search,¶ and left them. Mary Magdalen did not remain even with the angels at the sepulchre.** So anxious is the soul now that it

* Ps. cxlii. 7. † Ps. cxviii. 81. ‡ Ps. lxvii. 10.
§ Cant. iii. 1, 2. ‖ Ps. civ. 4. ¶ Cant. iii. 4.
** S. John xx. 14.

CHAP. XIX.

seeks the Beloved in all things; all its thoughts, words, and works are referred to Him; in eating, sleeping, and waking, all its anxieties are about Him, as I have already described it when speaking of the anxieties of love. As love becomes strong regaining health, it commences the ascent to the third step by a new purgation in the night—as I shall hereafter explain—and which issues in the effects that follow.

Third step,—Good works.

On the third step of the loving ladder, the soul worketh, and is fervent, and faints not. Of this step spoke the royal Prophet when he said, 'Blessed is the man that feareth the Lord, he shall delight exceedingly in His commandments.'* If fear, the fruit of love, produces this delight, what will be the effect of love itself? On this step of the ladder the soul looks on great things as little, on many as few, and on length of time as a moment, by reason of the burning fire which consumes it. It is with the soul as it was with Jacob, who 'served seven years for Rachel, and they seemed but a few days, because of the greatness of his love.'† If the love of a created being did so much in Jacob, what will the love of the Creator Himself do, when it shall have taken possession of the soul on the third step of the ladder?

Charity is not puffed up,—why.

Here the soul, because of the great love it has for God, is in great pain and suffering because of the scantiness of its service; if it could die for Him a thousand times it would be comforted. It looks upon itself as unprofitable in all it does, and on its whole life as worthless. Another most wonderful effect is that it looks upon itself as being in truth the very worst of all, for two reasons: first, because its love continues to show it what God deserves at its hands; and secondly, because it acknowledges to itself that even the great things it does for God are imperfect and faulty. Hence confusion of face and affliction when it compares the meanness of its own

* Ps. cxi. 1. † Gen. xxix. 20.

BOOK II.

conduct with the Majesty of God. On this third step the soul is very far from giving way to vainglory or presumption, or from condemning others. These anxious and other effects of the same kind are wrought in the soul when on the third step of the ladder, and so the soul acquires strength and courage to ascend to the fourth.

Fourth step,—Suffering without weariness.

'Amor omnia sæva et immania prorsus facilia et prope nulla efficit.'

When the soul is on the fourth step of the ladder of love, it falls into a state of suffering, but without weariness, on account of the Beloved; for, as S. Augustine saith, love makes all that is grievous and heavy to be light as nothing.* It was on this step that the Bride stood when she expressed her longing for the last, saying: 'Put me as a seal upon Thy heart, as a seal upon Thy arm; for love'—that is, the acts and operations of love—'is strong as death: jealousy is hard as hell.'† The spirit is now so strong, and has so subdued the flesh, that it is as regardless of it as a tree is of one of its leaves. It seeks not for consolation or sweetness either in God or elsewhere, neither does it pray for God's gifts through any motive of self-interest, or its own satisfaction. All it cares for now is how it shall please God, and serve Him in some measure as He deserves to be served, and in some degree corresponding with the graces it has received, and this at any and every cost.

The spirit regardless of the flesh.

Disinterested love.

The spiritual man now is saying in his heart and mind, my God and my Lord, how many there are who seek their own comfort and joy in Thee and who pray for gifts and graces, but those who strive to please Thee, who offer Thee that which costs them something, and who cast their own interests aside, are very few; it is not Thy will to show mercy that fails, O my God! but it is we who fail in using Thy mercies as we ought, so as to bind Thee to show us Thy mercy continually.

* Serm. LXX de Verb. Evan. Matth. Opp. tom. v. p. 383. Ed. Ben.
† Cant. viii. 6.

This degree of love is exceedingly high, for now the soul, earnest in its love, follows after God in the spirit of suffering for His sake, and God therefore frequently and, as it were, continually permits it to rejoice, visiting it sweetly in spirit, for the boundless love of Christ, the Word, cannot look on the sufferings of the souls that love without hastening to their relief. He has promised to do so by the mouth of the Prophet, saying, 'I have remembered thee, pitying thy youth . . . when thou followedst me in the desert,' * which in its spiritual sense is that abandonment which the soul is conscious of with regard to all created things, when it cannot rest upon them or be at ease among them. On this fourth step of the ladder the soul is so inflamed with love, and so set on fire with the desire after God, that it ascends upwards to the fifth.

Fifth step,—The soul panteth after God.

On the fifth step of the ladder the soul longs after God, and desires Him with impatience. Such is now the eagerness of the soul to embrace, and be united to, the Beloved, that every moment of delay, how slight soever, seems to it long, tedious, and oppressive, and it is ever thinking that it has found its love; but when it sees that its desires are disappointed—which is almost continually the case—it faints away through the intenseness of its longing, as it is written: 'My soul longeth and fainteth for the courts of the Lord.' † And now the soul must either obtain its desires or die, like Rachel, who said to Jacob, 'Give me children, otherwise I shall die.' ‡ It is now nourished by love, for as was its hunger so is its abundance, and so it ascends to the sixth step, the effects of which I am about to describe.

* Jerem. ii. 2. † Ps. lxxxiii. 2. ‡ Gen. xxx. 1.

CHAPTER XX.

Of the other five degrees.

BOOK II.

Sixth step,—Running in the way of God's commandments.

WHEN the soul has ascended to the sixth step, it runs lightly to God; and hope too runs without fainting, for love has made it strong so that it flies lightly onwards. It is of this step that the Prophet speaks, saying: 'They that hope in the Lord shall renew their strength, they shall take wings as eagles, they shall run and not be weary, they shall walk and not faint,'* and the Psalmist also: 'As the hart panteth after the fountains of waters, so my soul panteth after Thee, O God.' † The hart when thirsty runs quickly to the water.

Caused by enlargement of heart.

The cause of this quickness which the soul experiences on this step of the ladder is, that charity is enlarged, and the soul is now almost wholly purified, as it is written: 'without iniquity have I run,' ‡ and again, 'I have run the way of Thy commandments, when Thou didst enlarge my heart,' § and thus the soul ascends immediately from the sixth to the seventh degree of love.

Seventh step,—Holy boldness in prayer.

On the seventh step the soul becomes so bold in its intense and loving exaltation, that no prudence can withhold it, no counsel control it, no shame restrain it; for the favour which God hath shown it has made it vehemently bold. This explains to us those words of the Apostle, that charity 'believeth all things, hopeth all things, endureth all things.' ‖ It was in this state that Moses was when he said unto God: 'Either forgive them this trespass, or if Thou do not, strike me out of the book that Thou hast written.' ¶ Men of this spirit obtain from God what they so lovingly pray for, and so the Psalmist says; 'Delight in the Lord, and He will give

* Is. xl. 31. † Ps. xli. 1. ‡ Ib. lviii. 5.
§ Ps. cxviii. 32. ‖ 1 Cor. xiii. 7. ¶ Ex. xxxii. 31, 32.

thee the requests of thy heart.' * Standing on this step, the Bride said boldly: 'Let Him kiss me with the kiss of His mouth.' † But remember it is not lawful to be thus bold, unless the soul feels that the interior favour of the king's sceptre is extended to it, ‡ lest it should fall down the steps already ascended; in all of which humility must ever be preserved. From this boldness and courage of the seventh step, which God grants that it may be bold with Him in the vehemence of its love, the soul ascends to the eighth, where it lays hold of the Beloved and is united to Him.

Humility essential to every step of the ladder.

Eighth step,—The possession of God.

On the eighth step the soul embraces the Beloved and holds Him fast. 'I found Him whom my soul loveth; I held Him; and I will not let Him go.' § Here the desires of the soul are satisfied, but not without interruption. Some souls are thus satisfied; but they quickly fall back, for if they did not, and if that state of satisfaction continued, they would have attained to a state of glory even in this life. For this reason the soul tarries but briefly on this step of the ladder. Daniel, being a man of desires, was bidden, on the part of God, to remain here: 'Daniel, thou man of desires, stand upright.' ‖ The next step is the ninth, the degree of the perfect.

Ninth step,—The sweet fire of Divine love.

On the ninth step the soul is on fire sweetly. This is the degree of the perfect, who burn sweetly in God, for this sweet and delicious ardour is the work of the Holy Ghost in the union of the soul with God. S. Gregory says of the Apostles, that they burned interiorly with love sweetly, when the Holy Ghost descended upon them.¶ The blessings and the riches of God which the soul now enjoys cannot be described. And if we were to write whole books on the subject there would still be more to say. For this reason, and because I intend to speak of it hereafter, I shall now say no

'Dum Deum in ignis visione suscipiunt, per amorem suaviter arserunt.'

* Ps. xxxvi. 4. † Cant. i. 1. ‡ Esth. v. 2; viii. 4.
§ Cant. iii. 4. ‖ Dan. x. 11. ¶ Hom. 30. in Evang.

BOOK II.

more of this step, except that it is immediately followed by the tenth and the last, which does not belong to this life.

Tenth and last step,—The Beatific Vision of God.

On the tenth step of the ladder the soul becomes wholly assimilated unto God in the Beatific Vision which it then enjoys; for having ascended to the ninth, it goeth forth out of the body. Love works in such souls — they are few, and perfectly purified in this life—what Purgatory works in others in the next. For, 'Blessed are the clean in heart, for they shall see God.'* As I have said, this vision is the cause of the soul's perfect likeness unto God. 'We know,' saith S. John, 'that, when He shall appear, we shall be like to Him, because we shall see Him as He is.'† And thus, whatever the soul may be, it will be like unto God, and so is called, and is, by participation, God.

Purity of heart the faculty of seeing God.

Love reveals all secrets.

This is the secret ladder of which the soul speaks, though in the higher steps no longer secret to it, for love reveals itself to it in the great effects it produces. But on the highest step, the Beatific Vision, the last of the ladder, where God leans, nothing remains secret from the soul, by reason of its perfect likeness. And, therefore, our Saviour saith, 'In that day you shall not ask me anything.'‡ Until that day come, notwithstanding the heights to which the soul ascends, something still remains secret from it, and that in proportion to the distance from its perfect likeness to the Divine Essence. In this way, then, by means of mystical theology and secret love, the soul goeth forth from all things and from itself, ascending upwards unto God. For love is like fire, which ever ascends, hastening to be absorbed in the centre of its sphere.

* S. Matt. v. 8. † 1 S. John iii. 2. ‡ S. John xvi. 23.

CHAPTER XXI.

The meaning of 'disguised.' The colours in which the soul disguises itself.

HAVING now explained why contemplation is a secret ladder, I have further to explain what is meant by the word disguised; for the soul says hat it went forth by the secret ladder, disguised.

CHAP. XXI.

Third point; The soul disguised,—why.

For the clear understanding of this it is necessary to keep in mind that to be disguised is nothing else but to hide oneself under another form than our own, either for the purpose of showing, under that concealment, the will and purpose of the heart with a view to gain the goodwill and affection of the person beloved, or for the purpose of hiding oneself from the observation of rivals, and thereby the better effect our object. Such a person assumes the disguise which shall most represent the affection of his heart, and which shall the best conceal him from his rivals.

Its vestments of white, green, and purple, i. e. Faith, Hope, and Charity.

The soul, then, touched with the love of Christ, that it may gain His favour and goodwill, sallies forth in that disguise which shall most vividly represent the affections of the mind and secure it against the assaults of its enemies, the devil, the world, and the flesh. The disguise it assumes is a garment of three principal colours, White, Green, and Purple, emblems of the three theological virtues, Faith, Hope, and Charity; which not only enable the soul to enter into the good graces of the Beloved, but also protect it against its enemies.

1. Faith the breast-plate of defence against the devil.

Faith is a garment of such surpassing whiteness as to dazzle every intellectual vision; for when the soul has put on faith it becomes invisible and inaccessible to the devil, because it is then most securely defended against him, its strongest and most cunning foe.

S. Peter knew of no better defence against the devil than

BOOK II.

Inner garment of Faith:—

faith, for he said, 'Whom resist, stedfast in faith.'* And with a view of entering into favour and union with the Beloved, the soul cannot put on a better garment, as the ground of the other virtues, than the white garment of faith, without which 'it is impossible to please God.'† But with a living faith the soul is pleasing and acceptable unto God, Who says so Himself by the mouth of the Prophet: 'I will espouse thee to Me in faith.'‡ It is as if He said to the soul, If thou wilt be united and betrothed to Me, thou must draw near clad interiorly in faith.

When and how assumed.

The soul assumes the white robe of faith when it goeth forth in the obscure night, walking in darkness and interior trials, receiving no light of consolation from the intellect; not from above, because heaven seems shut and God hidden; not from below, because its spiritual directors can give it no satisfaction. And when it endures patiently and perseveres, amidst its trials, without fainting or falling away from the Beloved, who by these trials and temptations is proving its faith, so that it may be able hereafter to say with the Psalmist, 'For the sake of the words of Thy lips, I have kept hard ways.'§

2. Hope the helmet of protection against the world.

Over the white robe of faith the soul puts on the second colour, green, the emblem of the virtue of Hope, which delivers it and protects from the assaults of its second enemy, the world. The freshness of a living hope in God inspires the soul with such energy and resolution, with such aspirations after the things of eternal life, that all this world seems to it—as indeed it is—in comparison with what it hopes for, dry, withered, dead, and worthless. Here the soul denudes itself of the garments and trappings of the world, by setting the heart upon nothing that is in it, and hoping for nothing that is, or may be, in it, living only in

* 1 S. Pet. v. 9. † Heb. xi. 6.
‡ Os. ii. 20. § Ps. xvi. 4.

the hope of everlasting life. And, therefore, when the heart is thus lifted up above the world, the world cannot touch it or lay hold of it, nor even see it; and the soul, disguised in the vesture of hope, is secure from its second foe, the world. This is the reason why S. Paul calls the hope of salvation a helmet.* Now a helmet is armour which protects and covers the whole head, and has no opening except in one place, where the eyes may look through. Hope is such an helmet, for it covers all the senses of the head of the soul in such a way that they cannot be lost in worldly things, and leaves no part of them exposed to the arrows of the world. It has one loophole only through which the eyes may look upwards; this is the work of hope, to direct the eyes of the soul to God; as it is written, 'My eyes are ever towards the Lord,'† looking for succour nowhere else; as the same Psalmist writes, 'As the eyes of the handmaid are on the hands of her mistress, so are our eyes unto the Lord our God until He have mercy upon us,'‡ hoping in Him.

The soul by hope obtains its desires.

The green vesture of hope—for the soul is then ever looking upwards unto God, disregarding all besides, and delighting only in Him—is so pleasing to the Beloved that the soul obtains from Him all it hopes for. This is why He tells the soul in the Canticle, 'Thou hast wounded My heart with one of thy eyes.'§ It would not have been expedient for the soul, if it had not put on the green robe of hope, to claim such love, for it would not have succeeded, because that which influences the Beloved, and prevails, is persevering hope. It is in the vesture of hope that the soul disguised goes forth securely in the secret and obscure night; seeing that it goes forth so detached from all possession, without any consolations, that it regards nothing, and that its sole anxiety

* 1 Thess. v. 8.
† Ps. xxiv. 15.
‡ Ps. cxxii. 2.
§ Cant. iv. 9.

BOOK II.

is about God, putting its 'mouth in the dust if so be there may be hope.'*

3. The royal robe of Charity shields the soul from the flesh.

Over the white and green robes, as the crown and perfection thereof, the soul puts on the third, the splendid robe of purple. This is the emblem of Charity, which not only enhances the beauty of the others, but which so elevates the soul and renders it so lovely and pleasing in His eyes that it ventures to say to Him, 'I am black but beautiful, O daughters of Jerusalem, therefore hath the king loved me and brought me into His secret chamber.'† This robe of charity — charity is love — not only defends the soul from its third enemy, the flesh — for where the true love of God is there is no room for self-love or for selfishness — but strengthens the other virtues also, and makes them flourish, beautifying the soul and adorning it with grace, so that it shall please the Beloved; for without charity no virtue is pleasing unto God. This is the purple, spoken of in the Canticle, by which the soul ascends to the seat where God reposes: 'the seat of gold, the going up of purple.'‡ It is in this robe of purple that the soul goeth forth in the obscure night out of itself, and from all created things, with anxious love inflamed, by the secret ladder of contemplation to the perfect union of the love of God its beloved Saviour.

Love of God excludes love of self.

The Intellect vested in Faith,

This, then, is that disguise which the soul assumes in the night of faith on the secret ladder; and these are the colours of it, namely, a certain most fitting disposition for its union with God in the three powers, Memory, Intellect, and Will. Faith blinds the intellect, and empties it of all natural intelligence, and thereby disposes it for the union of the Divine Wisdom. Hope empties the memory and withdraws it from all created things which can possess it; for as the Apostle writes, 'Hope that is seen is not hope.'§ Thus the

Memory in Hope,

* Lam. iii. 29. † Cant. i. 4. Off. B. M. V. ant. ad Vesp.
‡ Cant. iii. 10. § Rom. viii. 24.

memory is withdrawn from all things on which it might dwell in this life, and is fixed on what the soul hopes to possess. Hope in God alone, therefore, purely disposes the memory according to the measure of the emptiness it has wrought for union with Him.

and the Will in Charity, leave all things for God alone.

Charity in the same way empties the affections and desires of the will of everything that is not God, and fixes them on Him alone. This virtue of charity, then, disposes the will and unites it with God in love. And because these virtues — it being their special work — withdraw the soul from all that is not God, so also do they serve to unite the soul to Him. It is, therefore, impossible for the soul to attain to the perfection of the love of God unless it journeys, in earnest, in the robes of these three virtues. This disguise, therefore, which the soul assumed when it went forth in order to obtain what it aimed at, the loving union with the Beloved, was most necessary and expedient. And it was also a great happiness to have succeeded in thus disguising itself and persevering until it obtained the desired end, the union of love.

CHAPTER XXII.

O happy lot!

Happiness of the soul in having overcome its enemies.

It is very evident that it was a blessed thing for the soul to have succeeded in such an enterprise as this, by which it was delivered out of the hands of Satan, from the world and from its own sensuality, in which, having gained that liberty of spirit so precious and desirable, it rose from meanness to dignity, from being earthly and human became heavenly and Divine, having its 'conversation in Heaven,' * like those who are in the state of perfection, as I shall proceed to explain.

* Philipp. iii. 20.

I shall, however, be brief, because the most important point—that which chiefly determined me to explain the obscure night to many souls who enter on it without knowing it—has been already in some degree explained, and I have also described, though in inadequate terms, what great blessings descend upon the soul in that night, and what a great happiness it is to be passing through it. This I did that when such souls are alarmed at the trials that have come upon them they may be encouraged by the certain hope of the numerous and great blessings which they will receive in this night. Beside this, it was a blessed lot for the soul on account of what it describes in the following line.

CHAPTER XXIII.

The wonderful hiding place of the soul, which the devil, though he penetrates into other higher places, cannot enter.

In darkness and concealment.

Fourth line of the second stanza explained.

IN concealment, that is, secretly and hidden. So when the soul says that it went forth in darkness and concealment, it explains the more clearly the great security it found in obscure contemplation on the road of the union of the love of God.

The words 'darkness and concealment' mean here that the soul, having gone forth into the obscurity, travelled therefore in secret, unknown to the evil one, beyond the reach of his wiles and stratagems. The reason why the soul is free, concealed from the devil and his wiles in the obscurity of contemplation, is, that infused contemplation, to which it is now admitted, is passively infused into it, in secret, without the cognisance of the senses, and of the interior and exterior powers of the sensitive part. And that, too, is the reason why it escapes from not only the embarrassments which the faculties naturally and through their weakness present before it, but also from the evil one who, were it not for the sensitive faculties, could never know what is passing in the soul. The more spiritual therefore the communication is, and the further it is removed beyond the reach of sense, the less able is the devil to perceive it.

Sense should be ignorant of what is done in the spirit,—why.

This being the case, it becomes a matter of great moment, greatly conducive to the soul's security, that the senses of our lower nature should have no knowledge whatever of the interior conversation of the soul with God, and that for two reasons; first, that the spiritual communication may be the more abundant, which it will be when the weakness of our lower nature does not impede liberty of spirit. The second is, that the soul is more secure because the evil one cannot know what is passing within it. The words of our Lord, 'Let not thy left hand know what thy right hand doth,'* may be, in a spiritual sense, understood of this, and we may understand Him to say: Let not thy left hand, that is man's inferior nature, know what is passing in the higher and spiritual part of the soul. That is, let the Divine communications remain unknown to the lower senses, and a secret between thy spirit and God.

The devil ascertains the state of the spirit by evidences of the sensitive nature.

It is true, when these interior and most hidden communications occur, that the devil, though he knows neither their nature nor their form, ascertains their existence, and that the soul is then receiving some great blessings, merely from observing the silence and repose of the senses, and the powers of our sensitive nature. And then, when he sees that he cannot thwart them in the inmost depth of the soul, he does all he can to disquiet and disturb the sensitive part, which is accessible to him, by fears and horrible dread, intending thereby to trouble the higher and spiritual part

* S. Matt. vi. 3.

BOOK II.

The spiritual assaults of Satan.

of the soul, and to frustrate the blessings it then receives and enjoys. But very often when this contemplation pours its light purely into the mind and offers it violence, the devil, with all his efforts, is not able to disquiet it, for then the soul becomes the recipient of renewed benefits, love, and a more secure peace; in its consciousness of the disturbing presence of the foe, it runs inwardly into itself, without knowing how it comes to pass, and feels assured of a certain refuge where it can hide itself beyond the reach of the evil one; and thus its peace and joy are multiplied, of which the devil attempted to rob it. All those terrors assail it only from without; it sees clearly, and exults, that it can in the meanwhile enjoy in secret the calm peace and sweetness of the Bridegroom, which the world and the devil can neither give nor take away. The soul is now experiencing the truth of what the Bride says in the Canticle, 'Behold, threescore valiant ones . . . surround the bed of Solomon . . . because of fears in the night.'* Strength and peace abound within the soul, though the flesh and the bones are frequently tormented without.

At other times, when the spiritual communications flow over into the senses, the devil succeeds the more easily in disquieting the mind, and in disturbing it with the terrors with which he assails it through the senses. At that time the mental agonies are immense, and occasionally surpassing all description; for when spirit has to do with spirit, the evil one causes an intolerable horror in the good one, that is, in the soul, when it succeeds in disturbing it. This is the meaning of the Bride in her account of what happened to her when she tried to be interiorly recollected, so as to have the fruition of these goods: 'I went down,' she says, 'into the garden of nuts to see the fruits of the valleys, and to look if the vineyard had flourished . . . I knew not; my soul troubled

* Cant. iii. 7, 8.

me for the chariots' and the confused cries 'of Aminadab,' that is, the devil.*

This contradiction of the devil takes place also when God bestows His favours upon a soul by the instrumentality of a good angel. The devil sees this occasionally, because God in general permits it to become known to the enemy, that he may do what he can, according to the measure of justice, against that soul, and that he may be debarred from pleading that he had no opportunity of seizing on that soul as he did in the case of Job. It is, therefore, expedient that God should place these two combatants, the good angel and the devil, on an equality when they contend for a human soul, in order that the victory may be of greater worth, and that the soul, triumphant and faithful in temptation, may be the more abundantly rewarded.

The soul the prize of a contest.

This is the reason why God, in the order of grace, permits Satan to disquiet and tempt the soul which He is guiding therein. When such a soul has real visions, through the instrumentality of an angel, God suffers the evil spirit to represent false visions of the same kind, in such a way that an incautious soul may be very easily deluded, as it has happened to many. We have an instance of this in Exodus, where we read that the magicians of Pharao wrought signs and wonders resembling those wrought by Moses. For when Moses turned water into blood, the magicians of Egypt did the same; and when he brought forth frogs, so did the magicians.†

Moses and the magicians of Egypt.

It is not in bodily visions only that the evil spirit apes God, but in spiritual communications also, which are effected through the instrumentality of an angel, whenever he succeeds in discovering them. For as it is written, 'He beholdeth every high thing,'‡ that is, he apes them, and

* Cant. vi. 10, 11. † Ex. vii. 11, 22; viii. 6, 7. ‡ Job xli. 25.

BOOK II.

Satan cannot imitate spiritual visions.

insinuates himself among them as well as he can. Spiritual visions have neither form nor figure — such is the characteristic of spirit—and, therefore, Satan cannot imitate them, nor occasion others which shall in any way represent them. And so when the good angel communicates spiritual contemplation, the evil spirit, in order to disturb it while the soul is being thus visited, presents himself before it with a certain horror and spiritual confusion, which is occasionally exceedingly painful. Sometimes the soul quickly disembarrasses itself, so that the terror of the evil spirit may have no time to make any impression upon it, and recollects itself, favoured herein by that spiritual grace which the good angel then communicates.

Sometimes, too, God permits this horror and trouble to last a long time, and this is a greater torment to the soul than all the evils of this life can be; the remembrance of which afterwards is sufficient to produce great pain. All this passes in the soul without its doing or undoing anything of itself in regard to these representations or impressions. But we must remember that, when God suffers the evil spirit thus to afflict the soul, it is with a view to purify and prepare it by that spiritual vigil for some great festival and spiritual grace which it is His will to bestow upon it—Who never mortifies but to give life, Who never humbles but to exalt. This speedily ensues; for the soul, according to the measure of the dark purgation past, enters on the fruition of sweet spiritual contemplation, and that so sublime at times that no language can describe it. This is to be understood of those Divine visitations which are the work of an angel, and wherein the soul is not wholly secure, nor hidden in so great obscurity but that the devil succeeds in discovering its state.

God suffers the devil to afflict the soul,—why.

But when God visits the soul Himself, the words of the stanza are then true, for, in perfect obscurity, hidden from the enemy, it receives, at such times, the spiritual graces of

Neither angel nor devil can penetrate the soul directly.

God. The reason of the difference is that God, being the sovereign Lord, dwells substantially in the soul, and that neither angel nor devil can discover what is going on there, nor penetrate the profound and secret communications which take place between Him and the soul. These communications, because the work of our Lord Himself, are wholly Divine and supreme, certain substantial touches of the Divine union between Himself and the soul; in one of these, because the highest possible degree of prayer, the soul receives greater good than in all the rest. These are those touches for which the Bride prayed, saying, 'Let Him kiss me with the kiss of His mouth.'* This being a thing that so intimately relates to God, the soul, anxious to approach Him, values and desires one touch of the Divinity more than all the other graces which He bestows upon it. Hence the Bride in the Canticle, after the many graces there described, is not satisfied, but prays for these Divine touches: 'Who shall give Thee to me for my brother, sucking the breast of my mother, that I may find Thee without, and kiss Thee' with the mouth of my soul, 'and now no man may despise me'† or presume against me. She means that communication which God makes alone, without, and secret from all creatures; and so she says, 'that I may find Thee without, and 'sucking the breast of my mother.' This occurs when the soul in liberty of spirit enjoys these blessings in sweetness and interior peace, and when the sensitive part thereof cannot hinder it, nor the devil by means of that sensitive part interfere with it. Then, indeed, the evil spirit will not venture to assail the soul, because he will not be able to approach it, neither can he know of those Divine touches in the substance of the soul wrought in loving knowledge by the substance of God. No man can arrive at this blessed condition but by

* Cant. i. 1.

† Cant. viii. 1.

interior purgation and detachment, by being spiritually hidden from all created things. It is a work wrought in obscurity, in the hiding place, wherein the soul is confirmed more and more in union with God by love; and, therefore, the soul sings, 'In darkness and concealment.'

The soul conscious of two forces.

When these favours are shown to the soul in secret, that is, in the spirit only, the higher and lower portions of the soul seem to it — it knows not how — to be so far apart that it recognises two divisions in itself, each so distinct from the other, that neither seems to have anything in common with the other, being in appearance so separated and distinct. And, in reality, this is in a certain manner true, for in its present condition, which is wholly spiritual, it has no commerce with the sensitive part.

Thus the soul becomes wholly spiritual, and the spiritual passions and desires are in a great degree extinguished in this hiding place of unitive contemplation. The soul then, speaking of its higher part, sings the last line of this stanza, 'My house being now at rest.'

CHAPTER XXIV.

My house being now at rest.

Explanation of last line of second stanza.

THIS is as much as saying, My higher nature and my lower nature also, each in its desires and powers, being now at rest, I went forth to the Divine union of the love of God.

The two-fold rest,—the flesh at peace with the spirit; the spirit at peace with God.

As the soul is doubly assailed and purified in the warfare of the obscure night; that is, in all the senses, passions, and powers of the sensitive and spiritual parts of it; so, also, in all these senses, passions, and powers of the sensitive and spiritual parts does it attain doubly to peace and rest. The words, 'My house being now at rest,' are repeated at the

CHAP. XXIV.

end of the second stanza, on account of the division of the soul into spiritual and sensitive, which parts, if they are ever to go forth into the Divine union of love, must first of all be changed, corrected, and tranquillised with regard to all the things of sense and spirit, after the likeness of the state of innocence in Adam, notwithstanding that the soul be not wholly delivered from the temptations of our lower nature. These words, therefore, which in the first stanza relate to the tranquillity of our lower and sensitive nature, now, in the second stanza, refer particularly to the higher and spiritual part of the soul; and this is the reason of the repetition.

The soul returned to the likeness of original justice.

The soul obtains this tranquillity and rest of the spiritual house, habitually and perfectly — so far as it is possible in this life — through the substantial touches of the Divine union, which, in secret, hidden from the turmoil of Satan, sense, and passion, it receives from the Divinity, whereby the soul is tranquillised, purified, strengthened, and confirmed, so as to become an effectual partaker of that union which is the Divine espousal of the soul to the Son of God. The instant the two houses of the soul are tranquil and confirmed, with the whole household of powers and desires sunk in sleep and silence, as to all things of heaven and earth, the Divine Wisdom, in the bond of loving possession, unites itself to the soul, and that is fulfilled which is written, 'While all things were in quiet silence, and the night was in the midst of her course, Thy Almighty Word leapt down from heaven from Thy royal throne.'* The same truth is set before us in the Canticle where the Bride, after passing away from those who took her veil away and wounded her, saith, 'When I had a little passed by them, I found Him whom my soul loveth.'†

Divine espousals of the soul with the Word of God.

This union is unattainable without great purity, and purity

* Wisd. xviii. 14. † Cant. iii. 4.

BOOK II.

is attainable only by detachment from all created things and sharp mortifications. This is signified by the robbery of the veil and the wounding of the Bride in the night when she went forth searching after her Beloved; for the new veil of the betrothal cannot be put on till the old veil be taken away. He, therefore, who will not go out in this obscure night to seek the Beloved, who will not deny and mortify his own will, but seek Him at his ease on his bed, as the Bride once did,* will never find Him. The soul says here that it found Him, but only when it went forth into the obscurity anxious with love.

CHAPTER XXV.

In that happy night,
In secret, seen of none,
And seeing nought myself,
Without other light or guide
Save that which in my heart was burning.

The third stanza explained.

THE soul still continues the metaphor of natural night in celebrating and magnifying the blessings of the Night of the Spirit, by means of which it has been able quickly and securely to compass the desired end. Three of these blessings are set before us in this stanza.

Blessings of the spiritual night.

1. In this blessed night of contemplation God guides the soul by a road so solitary and so secret, so remote and alien from sense, that nothing belonging thereto, nor any created thing, can approach to disturb it or detain it on the road to the union of love.

2. The second blessing of the spiritual obscurity of this night is, that all the faculties of the higher nature of the soul are in darkness. Consequently the soul, seeing nothing,

* Cant. iii. 1.

and unable to see, is not detained by anything which is not God from drawing near unto Him, and, therefore, advances freely, unencumbered by the obstacles of forms and figures and natural apprehensions: for these are the things which usually embarrass the soul, and prevent it from being always in union with God.

3. The third blessing is, that while the soul is supported by no particular interior light of the intellect, nor by any exterior guide comforting it on this high road—the obscure darkness has deprived it of all this—love and faith, now burning within it, drawing the heart towards the Beloved, influence and guide it, and make it fly upwards to God along the road of solitude, while it knows neither how nor by what means that is done.

O Domine, non mori, sed pati.

END OF THE OBSCURE NIGHT.